Prais

"Hannah Linder is a master wordsmith with a keen understanding of Regency culture. *The Red Cottage* is a tale of memories lost and rediscovered, where Meg must unravel the past to understand why she fell for Tom and reclaim the bond they once shared. Filled with intelligent writing and emotional nuance, this captivating historical novel offers a richness that lingers far beyond the final page."

—Marcus Brotherton, *New York Times* bestselling author of *The Long March Home*

"Evocative writing and pulse-pounding suspense underscored by deep characterization make *The Red Cottage* the perfect reading experience for lovers of Mimi Matthews and Jaime Jo Wright. Devastatingly romantic in description, Linder's brooding and breathtaking Cornwall setting is as vividly painted as the cottage Tom and Meg hope one day to christen red. Deliciously intriguing and one of the best inspirational romances I have read in an age."

—Rachel McMillan, bestselling author of *The Mozart Code* and *The Liberty Scarf*

"If you enjoy Regency fiction with sweet threads of romance interwoven with mystery and suspense, then you'll want to check out *The Red Cottage*. Hannah Linder is a rising star in this genre."

—T.I. Lowe, Christy Award winning author of *Indigo Isle*

"If you love a passionate Scottish hero who is fiercely protective of the girl he loves, then you'll adore *The Red Cottage*! Hannah Linder weaves a tale of mystery and suspense, along with a swoon-worthy romance and characters that will remain in your heart long after the book is done. A highly enjoyable story!"

—Susan Anne Mason, author of the Courage to Dream, Canadian Crossings, and Redemption's Light series

"Hannah Linder has quickly become one of my favorite authors, and *The Red Cottage* is another poignant, heart-rending romance by her hand. Hannah captures readers from page one, immediately drawing them into the vibrant and playful love between Meg and Tom. Her characters' personalities are vividly written and become like family, to whom you're anxiously waiting to return. Hannah uses Meg and Tom's love to embody our own triune makeup, in that Meg's amnesia couldn't quell the love that her heart and soul couldn't forget. *The Red Cottage* is a page-turner that kept me up way too late and earned me a nice sunburn on the beach because I just had to keep reading one more chapter. A delightful story that stays with you long after you finish the last page."

—Lorri Dudley, Regency author of *The Duke's Refuge*

"I adored this book! Hannah Linder's *The Red Cottage* is an enthralling, beautifully written, powerfully suspenseful romantic mystery that gripped me from the first page. I was so spellbound by every harrowing twist and turn of the tale that I couldn't put it down! Linder's lush, evocative, atmospheric prose draws you in like an ebbing tide, and her complex characters feel so real, they leap off the page. You'll be captivated by and rooting for a feisty yet tender-hearted heroine as she struggles to evade a ruthless killer and uncover a past she cannot recall. You'll fall in love with a strong, troubled, fiercely loyal hero who will stop at nothing to protect the woman he loves. A story about resilience, love, survival, and redemption, this book will make your heart race, leave you breathless, bring you to tears, and ultimately, uplift your soul. Bravo! This was my first Hannah Linder book and now I can't wait to read everything she's ever written."

—Syrie James, bestselling author of *The Mysteries of Pendowar Hall* and *The Secrets of Thorndale Manor*

"*The Red Cottage* is a riveting, masterful blend of intrigue and heart that held me captive from the first page to the last. Hannah Linder weaves a tale so rich in emotion and imagery that I couldn't turn the pages fast enough—and the twist at the end completely shocked me! Highly recommend."

—Darlene L. Turner, *Publishers Weekly* bestselling author

"Linder weaves a masterful tale in this romantic suspense filled with surprising twists, irrepressible faith, and a hero and heroine you cannot help but fall for. Say farewell to sleep until you reach the last page!"

—Jennie Goutet, bestselling historical romance author

"What a delightful read! This story, ripe with historical details, is full of mystery and romance. I was kept guessing to the very end. The writing is lyrical and evocative, drawing the reader into an emotional experience. I highly recommend this book."

—Linda Ford, fan-favorite author of over 100 books, including her a bestselling series, *Love on the Santa Fe Trail*

"How many secrets can one idyllic village hold? You'll want to make certain you've cleared your entire day before reading Hannah Linder's *The Red Cottage*! This tale of love, danger, vengeance, and redemption will keep you guessing and hoping as you race to reach the story's end. *The Red Cottage* simmers with twists, turns, danger, and trouble in this page-turner that makes one wonder if forgotten memories, faith and love are enough to conquer all."

—Donna Mumma, award-winning author of *The Women of Wynton's*

"Hannah Lindner's *The Red Cottage* is enchanting, poignant and haunting. I flipped pages as fast as I could to keep up with rich, textured characters I feel absolutely in love with. If you're looking for a keeper shelf read, this is it!"

—Dani Pettrey, bestselling author of the Jeopardy Falls series

HANNAH LINDER

The RED COTTAGE

YOU are the reason we do what we do here at Barbour Publishing. We promise that we will always use our God-given talents to produce content with you in mind—and that we will remain biblically faithful, no matter what.

Thank you for being the heart of our business.

The Red Cottage ©2025 by Hannah Linder

Print ISBN 978-1-63609-839-5

Adobe Digital Edition (.epub) 978-1-63609-840-1

All rights reserved. No part of this publication may be reproduced or transmitted for commercial purposes, except for brief quotations in printed reviews, without written permission of the publisher. Reproduced text may not be used on the World Wide Web. No Barbour Publishing content may be used as artificial intelligence training data for machine learning, or in any similar software development.

Unless otherwise indicated, all scripture quotations are taken from the King James Version of the Bible.

This book is a work of fiction. Names, characters, places, and incidents are either products of the author's imagination or used fictitiously. Any similarity to actual people, organizations, and/or events is purely coincidental.

Cover design by Hannah Linder
Cover model photography © Rachael Fraser / Trevillion Images

Published by Barbour Publishing, Inc., 1810 Barbour Drive, Uhrichsville, Ohio 44683, www.barbourbooks.com

Our mission is to inspire the world with the life-changing message of the Bible.

Printed in the United States of America.

Dedication

To the one I haven't found. I live in pages until we meet.

Acknowledgment

We have pieces of so many people inside us. Things they've told us, touches they've laid across our hands, laughs, whispers, lessons, prayers, mistakes, songs. As an author, all those "pieces" never settle like dust. They flutter around inside of us and bleed out to paper.

So, thank you.

To everyone, everywhere, whose world has collided with mine. You made me an author. You gave me inspiration.

Murmies, I must thank you first. You always tell me the truth. Whether my hair looks ridiculous, I've tossed myself too dramatically into the depths of despair, or the latest scene of my novel is deplorable, you look me in the eye and tell it to me straight. Your wisdom is something I can never understand, but pray someday to have. God gave you the most wonderful listening ear. I need you—and love you—so much.

Cynthia, every time I reflect on how our paths intertwined, I'm reminded of the Lord's goodness. You are an answered prayer, a dear friend, the best agent, and such a dear encourager. The industry—and myself—are continually blessed by your sweet spirit.

Granddaddy, thanks for sitting on my front porch, letting me climb into your lap, and listening to me ramble about all the silly little nonsenses of my life. We've whiled away many summer afternoons. Watching deer graze in the fields. Listening to the birds. Creaking back and forth in the rocking chair. I cherish the time we spend together. I love you, ol' chap.

Granny, I know you're not here anymore. Sometimes I still dream about you, and even though the moments are hazy and airy, I still get to hug you. I miss your smell. I wish you could have read more of my books, and seen my house, and watched me fill it with all these old treasures. You would have loved what I've done to the place. I hope you can see it from Heaven.

Millie, you're my best friend. Thanks for being game for anything—from dancing in the rain, to taking Sheb to the vet, to eating dripping popsicles on the front porch. I love our adventures.

Wyatt, you make me laugh. Always. You're the funniest person in the world and no one can convince me otherwise. Thanks for being my fellow *Pride and Prejudice* enthusiast, my gym partner, my photoshoot pal, and the one who always runs to my rescue just when I need help.

Daddy, you always make me feel like you're proud of me. Thanks for driving two hours away the moment I need something fixed, telling all your friends about my books, and always watching out for new marketing opportunities. I love you!

Jason (a.k.a. the best stepdaddy ever) you're a staple. The person who holds our family together. Thanks for loading up Carter and riding the four-wheeler down to my house every day in the summer. We have fun playing hide-and-go-seek, don't we? Love you big time.

Adi Mae Wilson, you will probably laugh your way through this, so I'll refrain from being sappy. Thanks for not freezing my peanut-butter-and-jelly sandwich in the freezer *every day*, thanks for not writing me up for popping bubbles at work (even though you threatened to), and thanks for not killing me when we sword fought with brooms between customers. Oh yeah. And thanks for buying every single book I ever write (even though you don't read them...well, except for the bios, which you make fun of me for), and showing up to every book signing wearing your "Hannah Linder's Biggest Fan" shirt. It's kinda overkill, but I love it. P.S. You bribed your way into my acknowledgements, so don't forget our deal.

Friends, I'm so grateful for you.

Leslee and Seth—our shenanigans are the best. Well, besides the time we were almost kicked out of the snow tubing resort for disorderly conduct. *After* we almost died getting there on icy roads. Don't worry, readers. It was a case of mistaken identity, and we blame it on Stover luck and the wrong wardrobe choice.

Laura Conaway, what an adventure we had! Our writing retreat consisted of late evening giggles, a castle photoshoot, lots of brainstorming, and the best life-reflecting talks. I already can't wait to see you again.

Sheb and Mr. Peter McGregor, thanks for watching me drive away every time I leave the house, and perking up with delighted meows and barks every time I come home. My babies.

And Jesus, my wonderful Jesus. You don't just show me love, and you don't just show me kindness. You show me *lovingkindness*. I bask in that sweetness every day. Thank you for knowing me deeper than anyone, seeing my sin, and still blessing me anyway. Tongue cannot tell, nor writer pen, just how awesome You are. I am humbled to be Your servant. You forever are my King.

CHAPTER 1

May 1818
Juleshead Village
North Cornwall, England

"We shall get murdered for this." Frigid water numbed her legs as Meg Foxcroft abandoned the rowboat and plunked knee-deep into moonlit water. She laughed, out of breath from the shocking cold, as she waded for the rocky shore. "Hurry up!"

"Not sure what it matters now."

"It happens to matter a great deal. It is dreadful enough I have lost my shoes, let alone the hour." Before she could scamper up the rocks, his freckled hands snatched her waist. They pulled her back. "Tom—"

"Let him grumble."

"You are not the one who shall be forced to endure scolding an entire fortnight." A wave swayed them back and forth, seeping the water higher up her dress, more evidence that would be impossible to hide from Uncle. "Now let go of me, you terrible fool."

"I wouldnae call terrible the hands that hold yer life, lass." He dragged her deeper and she squealed.

"You would not dare—"

"Recant yer words."

"Tom!"

"Do it or down ye go."

"You are every ounce of absurdity. If I should come dragging home in the middle of the night, drenched without nary a stocking, he shall accuse us to no end and the village shall murmur for weeks."

With a roaring laugh, he dunked her beneath the water, coldness engulfing her the same time her heartbeat thrummed in a mix of delight and fury. She broke the surface with a gasp, swiveled in his arms, raised a hand to slap him.

But he caught her fingers, as he always did, and his lips crashed into hers. Surprise jolted her. He tasted of salt and power and unbearable sweetness, like the confections Uncle was always warning would make her sick. Her chest hammered. Her mind swam—smoothly, softly, like the waves they stood in—until the only thing she understood was the red stubble on his cheeks, the tickle of wet hair on the back of his neck, the familiar firmness of his muscled arms.

"*Ye* are the one who is impossible." He pulled back too soon and did as she'd asked.

As if she truly wanted to go home.

As if she ever did.

Silhouetted vessels bobbed on the water, and the foggy night breeze smelled of fish and sea and distant chimney smoke. She wrung out the skirt of her dress, then her hair, while he yanked off his dripping linen shirt and tossed it over his shoulder.

"Ready?"

She nodded, but she wasn't. His fingers laced with hers. In the shadow of warehouses and decaying buildings and quiet alleys, they slipped through the village with neither lantern nor shoes, the cobblestones gritty against her feet.

In the morning, Uncle would tell her how many shillings a new pair would cost. He would ask how she could be so reckless and where she had lost them, but she wouldn't tell him the sea had stolen them away.

Or that she had slipped into the night again with Tom.

That they had taken out the fishing boat.

That they'd found a quiet shore somewhere, built a sand cottage in the moonlight, laughed so hard her stomach hurt, watched the stars, lost time.

Uncle wouldn't understand.

Neither did anyone else.

But the night held things no one could see in the day. This was theirs, forbidden or not—and though people whispered now, one day she and Tom McGwen would build a cottage not made of sand. She'd plant lilac bushes outside the windows, and he would paint the outside a bright and brilliant red. They wouldn't run about barefoot anymore. No one would call him "Tom boy" nor her an unruly hoyden.

Because she would wear proper dresses, ones that hadn't been patched and sewn from all her adventures. And he would smoke a pipe every evening from his upholstered chair. Together, they'd entertain the most esteemed villagers, including the clergyman, and not even tattling Mrs. Whalley would find blunder in them.

A sigh gathered at her throat when they reached the weathered, green-painted apothecary shop. The bowed windows reflected the orange streetlight.

"I'll be by to see ye in the morning. Save me a bit of bread pudding if ye think of me."

If she thought of him?

She thought of nothing else.

Sadness choked her, an unprepared pierce of longing and too many other things to count. He should not have kissed her tonight. In all the years she'd known him, he had only done so on the rarest occasion.

Always when she was unprepared.

Or when she was angry at him for some trivial thing.

Or when he was leaving.

Like now.

"I want to go with you."

He shook his head and grinned, messing with the wet hair draped across her shoulder. But it was in him too, in his eyes—a reluctance to walk away.

In all these years, he had never departed Juleshead.

Neither had she.

"It will be fine," he whispered, glancing at the window to make certain her uncle did not stir from inside. "I shall be back in a fortnight or sooner."

"Unless they ask you to stay."

"They won't."

"What if they do?"

"Ye worry too much, lass."

"And you not enough."

He pulled her under the arched doorway, finger over his lips, gesturing her to be silent. "Go on before that old goat comes out here waking the world with his uproar."

Tears stung. She was ridiculous for them, she knew. But they flooded over anyway, in testament to her fears, and she closed her eyes when his calloused finger thumbed them away.

"Och, but there is a bit of softness in that ferocious heart of yers."

"Do not tease me."

"What do ye want me to do?"

"I want you to..." She glanced at his face, the splendor of every handsome angle and hard chisel of his jaw. Then his eyes. Blue. Alive. Like the sea, early in the morning, when the ripples twinkled with burning sunlight.

Then...his lips.

Her heart lurched in wild anticipation. Leaning into him for the first time, she swallowed his neck with her arms, kissed him, and pulled back so fast she had to fight for air. "I want you to leave before Uncle catches us. Go."

He laughed but stilled her hand before she grabbed the door. "Meg."

"What?"

"When I come back, I'm going to marry ye."

Blood rushed to her face and her cheeks warmed with the same velocity as her soul. Before she had a chance to answer, he disappeared into the night and fog. *Tom, wait.*

He was a fool, because Uncle would never allow them matrimony.

Not when Tom was still without his own fishing boat and they were both penniless, and still as far away from their red cottage as Juleshead was to the moon.

But as she eased open the door with quiet steps, ecstasy raced in her heart. Her stomach fluttered despite all the reasons it should be sinking.

The RED COTTAGE

Marry ye. His low voice, with its soothing playfulness and Scottish lilt and clumsy gentleness.

He was wonderful.

Whether he married her in a fortnight when he returned or in twenty years when Uncle finally relented and Tom had his boat, she would wait.

Something creaked.

Meg froze halfway across the dark shop, her hand grazing the front counter. Had Uncle heard and awakened?

But the noise had not come from the open doorway on the left side of the room, which led to Uncle's private office, their small parlor, and two bedrooms.

Instead, it had come from the rear counter.

Air trapped in her lungs the same time a shadow darted along the shelves. Bottles crashed. Glass busted. An overwhelming fragrance of herbs and earthy mixtures struck the air in an aromatic warning.

Hunkering, Meg skittered across the room in her dripping bare feet. Thieves had broken inside more than once. Usually, a desperate farmer with a sick wife or child. Or a village street urchin eager to swipe something for trade.

But never in the middle of the night.

Not when someone was home.

Whoosh.

Another shadow lunged in front of her, blocking the doorway. Panic spiked. She stumbled back, screamed, just as the figure lifted something over his head and swung.

Wood and metal cracked her forehead. *Uncle.* Her body smacked the floorboards. The blackness deepened. *Uncle, help—*

"Use the gun."

"Too loud." Slamming, thumping, bottles and vials and bowls busting. "Light it up."

A groan ripped from her throat. She rolled once, pushed up on her elbows, grabbed a cabinet and pulled herself up.

"Rumbold, the girl—"

A second blow struck the back of her skull, battering her with pain. Her mind flashed too many things at once. The crumbling sand cottage.

Saltwater in her face. The boat rocking, rocking, rocking.

Tom.

Blackness sucked her under before she could cry his name.

He was every kind of an idiot.

Blood simmered hot in Tom's veins, racing his heart, as he jogged faster down the blackened street. Too many impulses stampeded him at once. The urge to take off running. Leap and click his heels. Bang on one of the shop windows and whoop until he was hoarse that Meggie Foxcroft would be his wife.

But the sickness crawled through him again. With cold and festering power, it gnawed at all the good things in him, all the energy, until his steps were weighted.

He'd been so close to telling her the truth.

Tonight, as they'd sat cross-legged in the sand, with her hair tickling his face, her words tripping into laughs, their fingers bumping and grazing as they built shapes in the sand...

He had wanted to tell her.

He always wanted to tell her.

Strange, because she knew every other part of him. She knew that he still ate raspberries late in the summer, despite the hives, because they reminded him of Mamm's trifles back home. She knew that he belted Gaelic songs when he took out the boat alone. She knew that he only attended church because she wanted him to, that he fell asleep on any carriage ride, that he sometimes rearranged her uncle's perfectly organized jars just to irritate the old goat.

She knew everything.

All of him.

Except what niggled his heart late at night, when he finally climbed into his pallet in the room above the blacksmith shop. Except how insane her fears tonight truly were.

No one back in North Brumcastle would beg Tom McGwen to stay when he returned tomorrow.

Least of all those in his own house.

The RED COTTAGE

A scream pierced the sleepy night air, raising the hair on Tom's arms. He spun back. The buildings were motionless, the windows black, save for the street lamps glinting off their panes.

A dog yowled in the distance.

A broken shutter clickety-clacked back and forth in the breeze.

Nothing. He yanked the wet shirt back over his head, but instead of taking the alley to the smithy, he backtracked. Meg would despise him for returning.

He would tap on her window, make certain all was well, but she would call him ridiculous and say he fabricated the danger to see her again.

Mayhap he had.

A grin worked at his lips and that same odd sensation sparked through him again. She had kissed him. Why that was significant he was not certain, but it rattled something in his chest. Perhaps because she'd always been timid to his kiss—a little frightened, a little uncertain, her lips always quivering beneath his like a bird ready to take flight.

But tonight was different.

She was different.

Her arms had pulled him closer, deeper, than he'd ever been. Her lips had explored him. She'd still been afraid—he knew that—but in a new way, and it emboldened her affection instead of dimming its power.

Hopping over a puddle, Tom crossed the street to the apothecary and glanced through the white-paned glass. Blackness stared back at him. Should he truly summons her?

His luck, Uncle Owen would stumble out here with his knotty cane and uncouth words. If nighttime excursions riled the old goat now, the prospect of a marriage would send him thundering to kingdom come.

Perhaps it was just as well Tom would be away for a fortnight.

Give Meg time to soften him.

If such a thing were possible.

Smoke. The smell slapped Tom in the face, mingled with the cloying odor of whale oil. *What?* The window fogged. A muffled crash—

Tom darted for the door, heart faltering, as he jerked at the brass handle. Locked. "Meg!" Another bang inside the shop, distant as if it were in the bedchambers. Voices lifted, ones he didn't recognize. "Meg, open up!" Backing up, he grinded his teeth and barreled into the door with his shoulder. The hinges groaned but didn't give. He charged again.

Glass showered over him, pinging to the ground, as he busted through and stumbled inside.

Heat blasted him in the face.

Behind the rear counter, flames licked up the knob-drawered cabinets, flashing light into the darkness, illuminating the room. Broken delftware pottery. Overturned leech jar. Tangled wet hair sprawled on the floor—

Meg. His gut clenched as he drove his knees to the floorboards next to her. He swallowed her up against him. Her head craned back over his arm. Blood on her face, in her eyes, her hair, everywhere. *God, save her.*

The prayer came too quickly. Before he could pull it back.

He was not certain anyone heard or not.

"Meg, ye're fine." He staggered to his feet, started for the door, but a gunshot in the back of the shop splintered him with panic. *Mr. Foxcroft.* Shouts lifted, a guttural scream, one Tom knew by heart.

Coughing, smoke stinging his eyes, he lunged outside and eased Meg onto the smooth flagway. He shook as he palmed back her hair. Then smeared the blood. Then probed her neck.

A weak pulse throbbed his fingertips.

Alive.

Barely.

Meg, Meg, my Meg.

"Tommy?" Mrs. Musgrave was already bustling out of the neighboring millinery shop with her cat, and across the street, Mr. Telfner thrust his head out of the stationer's shop window.

"Lawks, what goes on there?" he yelled, yanking off his nightcap.

"Fire!" Tom stood on knees that jellied. "Get men over here. We need help." He sprang back toward the door, but gray-haired Mrs. Musgrave hustled in his path.

"Dear boy, you cannot think of going back in there—"

"Stay with Miss Foxcroft." He darted past her, into the building, and pulled his damp shirt over his nose. The flames had reached the ceiling. The standing clock in the corner was gone. The rear counter black. The brass scales a discolored silver.

The RED COTTAGE

He ducked his head and hurtled through the flaming doorway, into a sweltering hall, where Mr. Foxcroft's bedchamber door stood ajar. A body lay limp across the threshold, the face and neck blood splattered.

No.

Bent backwards over the bed, Mr. Foxcroft screeched out a curse, struggling against the man atop him. A knife flashed. Then plunged.

Tom leaped on the stranger's back and slung him sideways. They crashed together into a full-length mirror. It toppled over them. Shards everywhere. Puncturing his skin.

Run. He tried to scream the warning, but all that came out was a low grunt as he rolled with the assailant. Pain jabbed in too many places. A fist cracked his jaw. He swung his own.

Blow answered blow like a blinding torrent.

Everything dimmed, black at the corner of his vision—except the shadowed face hovering over him, the smoke constricting his throat, the metallic taste spewing from his mouth and lips.

With raging power, he lunged his forehead into the man's face. A sickening bash of skulls, then the figure fell back.

Tom pounced on him, hands throttling his throat. He squeezed until veins bulged in the neck, until the eyes bugged wide with a gurgling fear. *Meg.* Her face, the wretched wounds. He couldn't let go. He couldn't stop. For what this beast had done to her, to Mr. Foxcroft—

No. Some vague command, in the recesses of his mind, forced his fingers to uncurl.

He rained down his fist instead, until the figure no longer gasped or pleaded or stirred. Tom's heart stammered as he stood. Numbness—confusion—chilled the blood in his veins as he glanced about the room. Hot orange and red light flickered up every wall. The flames roared as loud as his questions. *What is happening?*

He turned to the bed.

Empty.

Except for the bloodstains. *Mr. Foxcroft—*

Sparks landed on Tom's skin, fueling him back into action. He seized the man on the floor, pulled the weight over his shoulders, as something creaked overhead.

A blazing beam crashed to their left, blocking the door.

Tom whirled for the window.

With a heaving cough, he smashed his boot through the closed shutters and hurled the man through.

More creaking behind him. A snap of wood. Then white-hot pain lanced Tom's back as he dove headfirst out the window. He tasted dirt and anguish. Groaning, he writhed against the flames, suffocating the pain, until his clothes and skin no longer burned.

Meg. His mind swam, like a ship bobbing in and out of a turbulent wave. *Got to get Meg—*

"Over here!" Voices anchored him back to the alley. He told himself to move, to crawl to her, but hands touched his face before he had the strength.

"Tommy, dear boy." Mrs. Musgrave's crooning tone. "You have lost the sense God bestowed you."

God had bestowed nothing on Tom McGwen.

Least of all sense.

"Meg—"

"Lie still. You are burnt." Shuffling footsteps, humming voices, the sickening smash of more timber caving. "All is well, dear boy. Do not fret."

But when his vision finally cleared and the light brushed faintly across Mrs. Musgrave's wrinkled face, the lines of her lips were hard and uncertain. As if there were something she had not told him. Something she didn't wish to tell him.

Tom's stomach gutted. "Meg—"

"Dear, I am so sorry." Mrs. Musgrave sniffled. "Most terribly sorry. I turned for but one moment. Poor Lenox, my little cat, was wandering too close to the house, and I hurried over to fetch him, never imagining that—that I would find. . ."

Unbearable fear closed his throat. "Find. . .what?"

"That she would be gone." Mrs. Musgrave dissolved into a sob. "Just gone."

CHAPTER 2

Something scraped across her face. Rough, like callouses moving in circular motions. She smelled too many things at once. The revolting odor of fish. The choking linger of smoke.

Then something softer.

Fainter.

The sour, grassy smell of a wool coat in her face. *Help.* The whimper lifted, but she could not hear her own voice—and it didn't matter anyway, because the jostling didn't stop.

Clomp, clomp. Horse hooves trotting faster.

Reins snapping.

Heavy breathing.

"You won't die." A command—whispered, hoarse, like a lifeline she was meant to grope for. The blackness grew heavy. Her mind screamed, then silenced.

The next time she awoke, the bumping and jarring had ceased. The arms clamped her tighter, until the wool was suffocating and her head split with pain. *Let me be.* Everything hurt, as her weight lifted, as a door groaned into airy coolness. *Please. Let me be.*

She must be asleep, because nothing was real to her.

Sometimes she saw a pink pinafore with white lilacs brimming from the pockets. The tiny petals floated, carried by sunlight and wind, and she swatted her hands to catch them. They melted away before she had the chance.

Other times she climbed onto a window sill. She brushed back a frothy curtain. Someone laughed in her ear. Two yellow-beaked puddle ducks waddled into view, quacking, but they wandered away as quickly as the laughter faded.

No.

Loss churned through her, pushing tears to her closed eyelids as she touched her hand to the glass window. The curtain whipped at her face, harsh and dark.

Stay, please.

"Lie still, Meggie." The voice drew her back from the dream, as he situated her body on cold, dewy grass. "They'll find you here. I promise."

Whimpering, she latched on to the scratchy woolen coat. She strained for a name, for a face to accompany the voice, but the calloused fingers pried her loose before she could remember. She was back with the pink pinafore and blooming lilacs.

Then the white-paned window, and laughter, and ducks.

Then the darkness.

The terrible, enfolding darkness—where she was entirely alone.

He should have gotten there faster. He should have run when he heard the scream.

Another shiver wracked through Tom, despite the warm morning sun cutting through the fog. His steps slowed outside the rubble-stone blacksmith shop with its iron-barred windows and jettied first floor.

He couldn't go in.

He couldn't go anywhere.

What do I do? Meade, the blacksmith, must have already started the fire before his daily walk to Kingfisher's Tavern. Heat poured out of the wide, open entrance doors, pulling at Tom with a force he couldn't resist.

Inside the workroom, he sagged into a chair by the forge. He had to think. He just needed to sit here, breathe, make sense of all the jumbled pieces flailing in his brain.

Meg was gone.

Disappeared.

No.

He shook his head and stood again, wiped his face, choked in the familiar smell of hot steel and soot. All night long, he'd combed the village like a madman. He'd banged on doors. He'd awakened the groom at the livery stable, then the servant boy at the nearby coaching inn.

No one had spotted an injured girl, nineteen years of age with hair the color of nutmeg.

No one had seen anything.

Fury sizzled inside him, like the blue-orange flames in the brick forge. He groped for something. Anything. Metal tongs—and he sent them clattering into the opposite wall.

"Do that again, and I'll be beatin' it o'er your head." Meade filled the workroom threshold. His puffy, red-tinted skin already gleamed with sweat, and corded muscles strained beneath his rolled-up shirt. His eyes hardened. "Looks like someone already did."

Tom dragged his sleeve across his mouth. He tasted blood, ashes, terror.

"I heard." Meade grabbed his cowhide apron from the peg. His movements were stiff, measured, as if he weren't certain what to do or say. "Down at the tavern. Blabber of the fishermen."

"Mr. Foxcroft didn't come out." The words nearly stuck in Tom's throat. "He should have had time."

A nod.

"He was hurt."

Another nod.

"Someone stole Meg."

Meade pumped the bellows. Fire whooshed, sparks snapped, and when he finally glanced up, his features blazed a shade redder. "Turn around."

"I have to go—"

"I said turn, boy." Meade seized Tom by the arm, forced him around. He said nothing about the burnt holes in the linen of Tom's back. Or the endless cuts. Or the oozing, swelling blisters. "Sit down."

"I have to look for her."

"Sit down."

Tom sat back into the chair, grasped the splintery wooden armrests, while Meade ripped the shirt from Tom's back. He hissed in pain.

Neither spoke.

Meade's breath was heavy and ale-scented on Tom's neck as the man rubbed cold alkanet ointment into the burns. His fingers were rough. Careful too. Like the man himself.

When he'd dabbed the last cut with a rag, he gestured toward the door in the back of the workroom. "Go upstairs. Get a new shirt."

"I don't know what to do." Tom clenched his fists when all he wanted was to pound them. He looked at the ceiling. Then the floor. Then the stoic face of Meade—as if the man who had housed Tom for the past seven years could somehow make everything right.

"Only two things I know of." The blacksmith frowned. "Take to the bottle of gin behind that keg over there." He motioned to it without meeting Tom's eyes. "Or pray."

"Miss, can you hear me?" Rustling, then a brush of smooth leather along her hairline. "No, no, such an idea is preposterous. She cannot be so disturbed. Not in this state."

Agony rippled across her temples with breath-stealing power. She grasped the hand on her face, though she wasn't certain if she should thrash it away or hug it closer. *Help.*

"Ride back and return with the barouche."

"With all due respect, my lord, I am uncertain if such a carriage can endure this slope. The gig perhaps—"

"Impossible. She will need room to remain prostrate." A sigh. "I shall examine her myself when we arrive home, and it is my greatest hope this forehead gash is the only injury rendering her unconscious."

A monotone voice answered, then horse hooves pounded—as if she were now alone with whoever cradled her face.

"I am uncertain if you can hear me, miss, but I shall do my best to alleviate your discomfort as quickly as possible. For what it is worth, I have read every volume on modern medicine that could be found in my father's library. I hope the knowledge shall finally meet its use."

Too many words. They swished and sloshed along the painful walls of her mind, like a porridge she spooned through but didn't wish to eat. Of their own will, her eyes slitted open.

Light stabbed her. Branches swayed, budded with green, then a face dipped closer than she was prepared for.

"Your consciousness returns. That is excellent." He shifted her closer. He smelled of horse liniment and cinnamon, a curious scent, and his blond hair gleamed lighter in the sunlight. His cheeks, lips, eyes, possessed little color.

But he seemed confident.

Intelligent.

Someone she could trust.

"You are in a remarkable amount of pain, I presume."

She wasn't certain if it were a question. Or if she should answer. Or if she could.

"I keep an impressively overstocked medicine chest at Penrose Abbey. I am certain we can find something to soothe you while we await Dr. Bagot. He is a mere two-hour journey from here. A manservant is already in route to fetch him."

Water. Her tongue slid over dry, cracked lips.

"You must be parched. I am sorry I have not anything to offer you. Not out here." Darkness doused the sun. Black, then light. Black, then light. She blinked over and over again, and then not at all.

"How you ended up out here alone beneath this elm is quite a curiosity."

Stay.

"I suppose I shall discover it all soon enough. As soon as you are able to speak." He stroked her hair as if she were a child. "I do not suppose you can manage a name, can you?"

She cracked her lips, ready to test her voice, but nothing came to her. Alarm settled in. She scampered about her head, desperate for the answer, but the flood of darkness ebbed again.

"Never mind. Do not think. We shall know all soon enough."

She wanted to believe him, this stranger.

More than that, she wanted to cry the name of someone she loved, someone she knew, someone who would settle her confusion.

She just couldn't remember a name to call.

"I want to see him."

"I am eating breakfast." The justice of the peace, Mr. Willmott, crunched into strawberry-lathered toast, sending a glare to his footman across the drawing room. "Who let this pup inside, anyway? I thought I made it expressively clear yesterday, Mr. McGwen, that even *my* position has limitations."

"The prisoner is no longer in the care of a nursing maid."

"No."

"Nor in the village lockup."

"No again," Mr. Willmott growled as he wiped jam from his multi-layered chin. His unmodish, brown periwig fumed a rancid floral scent. "And before you present me any other facts of which I am already aware, allow me to enlighten you further. I released him this morning."

Tom blinked, brows knitting, as a slow fury wormed through him. "What?"

"He is a ratcatcher from the east side of Juleshead. He had already been summoned by Mr. Telfner to eliminate rodents the following morning, and having arrived early, decided to linger on the street until dawn." Mr. Willmott scooted back his chair. "It was all very simple. He heard the intruder, realized the situation, and rushed in to assist."

"With a knife?"

"Your imagination, I fear, has always been unduly ingenious." Mr. Willmott rose. "Not that I cast any censure upon you. I admit, the situation was dire. You cannot be blamed for misinterpreting their actions—although I daresay, Mr. Foxcroft might have made it out alive had you not."

Pressure swelled in Tom's chest until it was harder to will in air. "He is lying."

"And you are infuriating." Mr. Willmott waddled back to the sideboard and flicked his hand at the footman. "Show McGwen out now, if you please, while I finish my breakfast in peace—"

"And Meg?" Tom shoved aside the servant and circled before the fat, wig-headed fool. He clenched his fists. The steaming scents of eggs, liver, and ginger plummeted his stomach with nausea. "What are we to do about Meg?"

"What I told you yesterday, and the day before that, and the day before that." The man's cheeks mottled. "If you wish to continue this wrathful search of the land, so be it. I shall not prevent you. If it were my wife missing, or one of my daughters, perhaps I would do the same."

"We cannae do nothing."

"Thunder and turf, we have *not* done nothing." Mr. Willmott blew out air. "I have had the constable scouring for witnesses three days straight, a description of Miss Foxcroft is to be printed in the next evening newspaper, and I have sent letters to nearby parishes with requests they notify here if she is discovered." He grabbed the navy lapels of his coat, frustration scraping at his voice. "The rest, I fear, is in the hands of God."

Tom's insides writhed. "I cannae accept that."

"For which I pity you."

"I want the name of the ratcatcher."

"Were you of sounder mind of late, I would give it to you." Mr. Willmott motioned to the door. "Go home, McGwen. I have heard enough accounts to know you have not slept, and I think even you shall agree the best you can do for Miss Foxcroft now is to prevent your own demise."

Tom breathed a laugh. He wasn't certain why. Maybe the exhaustion, the light fever at his brow, the restless jittering of his legs all seeped at his sanity and made Mr. Willmott right.

Perhaps he wasn't of sound mind. Perhaps he never would be again until he found her.

And that was just what he was going to do.

He would not stop or eat or breathe or rest until he did.

She had to run.

The need to rip back the silk, rose-colored bed curtains, shove everyone away, and escape back to the elm tree was overpowering. Sometimes, the wrinkle-faced maid soothed a cool, damp cloth across her forehead.

Other times, a gangly young man—Dr. Bagot, they called him—poured reddish-brown liquid into honey and slipped it to her lips. The taste was bitter. Gagging. She attempted to push his hand away, but every time, someone stronger held her back.

The man from the elm.

Why was he always next to her? Through the fading of gold to blue to black again out the bedchamber window. Through the doctor's probing. The groggy dimness after her medicine, and the newfound terror every time she awoke in this unfamiliar room.

Even now, in her half-witted plan to lunge from the bed and flee toward the door, his warm fingers kept her still. She squeezed. He squeezed back.

"Are you hungry?" For two days, he had been asking her questions. Was she comfortable? Did she require more pillows? A glass of water? The draperies open or closed?

She nodded or shook her head, but never used her voice.

She was not certain why.

Perhaps because she was afraid if she spoke, he would ask more than she could answer. Everything was still too shadowed. A result of the medicine, she was certain—or the pain wracking her skull.

"You may go and rest, Miss Russel. I shall sit with her."

The elderly maid, with her tight gray curls and mobcap, nodded and departed the room. Silence echoed in her wake, save for birds chirping outside the window, and the stranger's chair creaking as he leaned closer over her four-poster bed.

"Now." His eyes smiled. She was struck by the faintness, the lightness, of their color—like a transparent cloud over a clear blue sky. "Shall I order something prepared for you? Broth can only satisfy for so many days before the undeniable need for sustenance begins to cry."

She wanted him here more than she wanted food.

That was insane.

She was as ridiculous and frightened as a child, but she could not even pry her fingers away from his. Why was she here? Why was she injured? Why was no one sitting beside her—except a stranger?

"Perhaps a book then." He nodded, as if that were just the cure she required. "Sometimes, literature is to the spirit what food is to the flesh. I shall be but a moment—"

"No." She clenched his hand tighter when he stood, the single syllable burning her throat. "Please...stay."

If he were astonished or pleased that she spoke, he showed no signs. He returned to his chair and drew it closer still. "Very well, then. If you like, I shall merely sit with you. The doctor says you are much improved, and the fever no longer plagues you. I imagine your strength shall be soon in following."

She should say something. He deserved her gratitude—whoever he was—for bestowing such kindness and ministrations to a stranger.

But she only stared at him. Questions assaulted her, too many to sort.

"I am Benedict Cunningham." As if he heard her thoughts. "Lord Cunningham, in proper address. And you, my dear girl, are a most-welcomed guest at Penrose Abbey."

"How did I. . ." She hesitated. Her heart sped. "How did I come to be here?"

"I was hoping you might tell me." When she didn't answer, he smiled. "I imagine it is a grave tale indeed. One you are likely not recovered enough to endure. Perhaps it would behoove us to discuss more congenial matters for the day. Your name perhaps."

Sweat dampened the bandage about her head. She opened her lips. Nothing.

Except the pink pinafore rippling back and forth, the petals falling, then the window all over again. Laughing in her ear. Strong arms hugging her from behind. *"Look at the ducks."* Swaying bluebells and gooseberry bushes and bright yellow cornflowers. *"See the ducks, Meggie?"*

"Meggie." She echoed the word from her dream. Then, quieter, "Meg."

"Short for Margaret, I presume?"

"I do not know."

He laughed, as if she were teasing him.

She wasn't.

"Very good then, Miss Margaret. . ." He quirked a brow in waiting. "You must supply me a surname, I fear, as it would set gossiping tongues wagging if I were to call you anything less."

The ducks. The pinafore. The window. She scratched through the memory, tearing it apart, rummaging through what little she had. *Meggie.*

Meg. Why could she not remember?

She knew her name.

Her own name.

She must.

Meggie. Meg.

Tears escaped the corners of her eyes, hot and streaming. Everything hurt. Her head. Her heart. She was empty, hollow, like a book ripped of all its pages. *Dear God, please help me.*

But the prayer remained unanswered, and when she finally glanced back into Lord Cunningham's confused eyes, a sob shuddered out of her. "I do not know."

CHAPTER 3

Dusk bled hues of blue and purple across the countryside, dimming the patchwork meadows and rutted road. If Tom rode through the night, he'd make it to Sunderlin Downs, a neighboring village, in nearly three hours.

That is, if he didn't bang on the door of every cottage or hovel he passed. Mayhap he should.

The chance that some work-worn farmer or busy fishwife had been awake the night Meg was stolen seemed preposterous. That they had glanced out the window and could tell him who took her, why, or where was even more of an impossibility.

But he had nothing else.

No traces to follow, save for the ratcatcher. Meade was on it now.

Help me. The words rose up inside him, without direction, as if he spoke to the soul of every man and woman in North Cornwall. Meg would tell him to pray to God.

Meg didn't know he already had.

Once.

Digging his heels deeper into the hide of his mount, he leaned forward and trotted faster. The rent of the mare had dwindled the spare shillings in his sock. What little he'd saved for his bride. For their cottage. As if it mattered now.

Why?

Moisture stung his eyes. The wind in his face, not tears. *Why them?* The Foxcrofts were friends to everyone in Juleshead. They went wassailing the streets at Christmastide. They fed the stray cats out their back door. They visited the sick during lazy afternoons, occupied the same box pew every Sunday at church, and hung caricatures on the shop windows to make passersby laugh.

No one should have ever wanted to hurt them.

Maybe Tom.

But not them.

The twilight faded to night, and only a pale glow of moonlight illuminated the winding country road. His legs twitched. The horse slowed. For miles, hours, he focused on hunting his brain for anything amiss these past weeks.

Had Mr. Foxcroft been more irritable? Had Tom missed an uneasiness in the man he should have detected—something more than his usual grumbling and ill-humored complaining? Had Meg been hiding something? Did she, like Tom, have secrets she was never brave enough to tell?

His shoulders drooped forward. He shook his head, forced himself upright again, but a yawn already stretched his lips. He had not slept in too long. His muscles cramped, his wounds burned with as much pain as the night Papa had dragged him behind their small brick cottage in North Brumcastle.

"Hands on the wall."

Papa's face a splotchy red. Moisture at the edge of his eyes.

The shirt ripped from Tom's back as he faced the house.

Whack.

Birch twigs lashing across his skin. Cutting but not cutting deep enough.

Whack.

Palms grinding brick.

Whack.

Then nothing when there should have been more. The birch rod thrown to the ground. Papa walking away, his shoulders deflated, while the family dog barked in excited confusion at his heels.

He only turned around once. *"I wish ye were not my son."*

Tom flinched back awake, but it was too late. His body slumped from the horse, and he hit the road with a grunt. Instead of remounting, he secured the whinnying mare to a buckthorn tree, then leaned against the mossy stone wall and closed his eyes.

Just a moment.

Then he would shake himself back awake and start again. Mind numbing, he slipped his hand into his trouser pocket and crunched the letter he'd been ignoring ever since Meg disappeared.

The letter calling him home.

Back to a papa Tom was not certain he could face, whether the man was dying or not.

"I wish you to be as candid as possible, doctor. Have you any experience with such a case?"

"In profession? No." On the other side of the door, a bag snapped shut, as if Dr. Bagot were as finished with his doctorial duties as he was with her. "I have witnessed a head injury to cause paralysis. Once, the inability to speak."

The polished, wooden floorboards were cold against Meg's bare feet. She should not have feigned slumber. Nor crept to the door, putting her ear to the crack like a common eavesdropper.

But if anyone needed the truth, it was her.

They had no right to lie to her.

She wanted nothing of their pacifying smiles, their cheerful assurances, as if she were a glass trinket ready to fragment. She wasn't. If she knew nothing else about herself, she knew that.

"But this." The doctor's voice drifted farther down the hall. "This complete inability to remember anything aside from her name is utterly preposterous."

"Preposterous in that it cannot happen—or that it never has before?"

"Both. Neither. I do not know." Their footsteps paused again. "Frankly, my lord, this entire case baffles me. Perhaps the shock of whatever she suffered has muddled her mind. In which event, I imagine her memories shall return as quickly as her strength."

"Or?"

"I have already notified the St. Alban Asylum, in the likelihood she has been admitted there or elsewhere before."

"She is injured, Doctor. Not insane."

"You seem very certain."

"I am."

More footsteps. Then, far enough away she only barely caught their whispers, Lord Cunningham called out, "One more thing, Doctor, before you depart."

"Yes?"

"You seemed, a moment ago at her bedside, as if something occurred to you. Am I in error?"

"You are never in error concerning anything, my lord."

"Do enlighten me."

"I am uncertain my theories would be welcomed." Lord Cunningham must have nodded the doctor on, because he spoke a little louder, "I know more of the body than I do of the mind. But I comprehend enough of human nature to know this."

"Yes?"

"We sometimes forget what we do not wish to remember."

"You think she is in pretense."

"I think I would exercise great caution." A long pause. "If she is not soon recovered, you may be wise to write St. Alban yourself."

She missed someone.

The emptiness caverned through her, ratcheting her heartbeat, as she faced the oval-shaped mirror on the bedchamber wall. A stranger stared back at her.

Brown, copper-streaked hair. Messy and tied in a braid across her shoulder.

A thin face, sharp jaw.

Brown eyes.

The RED COTTAGE

She knew herself, but in an absent way—like a face she'd passed once in a carriage but had long since forgotten. Her chest swelled. Hours ago, a younger maid had entered Meg's chamber with a white muslin dress draped over her arm. "In case you should feel strong enough for dinner," said the girl, with a tentative smile.

Meg had driven her away.

Then she'd scrambled into the dress—not because she intended to venture downstairs or partake of dinner, but because she needed something more than the thin cotton nightdress if she was to escape at dark.

A spasm of panic—then longing, then pain—awoke in the bottom of her stomach. Her hands quivered. They needed someone to still them. The one she missed.

The one who wasn't here.

Mother. Father.

She framed her face. Then traced the four-inch gash across her forehead.

Brother. Sister.

Tears.

Friend. Husband?

She was someone. She had lived among people who cared for her, cherished her, and belonged to her. Hadn't she? Why had they not found her?

Dr. Bagot had said she'd been beaten.

That she'd sustained not only blows to her head but hand-print bruises on her arm, burns on her skin, and a broken nose. Her clothes were ripped, frayed, and singed. Her feet bare. Had she been robbed? Assaulted by a highwayman? Why would anyone injure her this way, then situate her under the elm, alone, as if hoping she'd be found?

Rubbing her arms, she shook the cobweb of questions from her mind. No matter. She did not need answers. Not tonight. She had one thing to think of now: running.

Where, she didn't know.

To what, she had not strength to imagine.

But she could not stay here. Not in this chamber, with the white mantel and pink bed curtains and potted begonias and perfect oil-painted portraits. Not with a wrinkled maid who sneezed too often, or the younger one who smiled too much. Or a doctor who deemed her mad.

Or a gentle-toned lord whose kindness would doubtless wear thin. Perhaps already had.

Squaring her shoulders, she backed away from the mounted looking glass. She was doing the right thing. She would not be locked away for what she could not remember. Too many days had passed already, and the last thing in the world she could bear was an asylum.

She had to go home.

Wherever that was.

She prayed whoever had left her for dead was not waiting when she returned.

Coming here seemed wrong.

He was used to Meg walking next to him, tucking her arm in his, despite the waggling brows. He never entered a church without her. Sometimes it still felt wrong, even when she *was* beside him. Like a slap in the face of God.

If there was a God.

Tom's footsteps echoed in the spacious nave, bigger than the village church back in Juleshead. The vaulted ceiling, decorated with faded gold swirls and panels of the life of Christ, speared him with painted eyes. He walked faster. The air bothered him, that stagnant scent of incense and burning wax and age. "Excuse me."

The rector—an older man, already graying at his side whiskers—glanced up from behind his pulpit. "Oh." His expression fell. "Deed. I thought you were the doctor, come to see about this leg of mine." Shutting a large Bible, he gimped his way down from the three-decker pulpit. "Help you, can I? Just about to head back to the vicarage for the night."

"I will only be a moment. I am looking for someone."

"God is the one who looks for lost sheep." The man grinned. "I stay busy keeping up with sermon notes and tithes, if you know what I mean."

"She is young. Brown hair."

"A runaway?"

"No. Kidnapped."

"Then it is the constable you should be speaking to."

"Already done. He knows nothing. I was hoping ye—"

"I sit in meetings with grumbly church wardens, my fine fellow, and I sort the fruit, barley, and eggs the good people of Sunderlin Downs pay to their Maker. I do not trifle in other affairs. Least of all those involving work or danger." The rector limped past Tom. "Your conundrum sounds as if it involves both."

"I am not asking much." Tom hustled back in front of the rector. "Perhaps an inquiry Sunday. . .if anyone has seen her."

"I imagine the ones who have would not be here."

"It is worth a chance."

"As I said"—the rector rubbed his leg with an irritated sigh—"a matter for the constable. I am only a. . .eh, there you are." He waved to a man who entered, then flicked a dismissing hand to Tom. "Excuse me, fellow. There is nothing more I can do. I am sorry I could not be of help."

Tom bit his lip before something unholy came out.

He had respect, if not faith.

Sometimes.

"Thank ye." *For nothing*. Grinding his teeth, he barreled back the way he'd come, brushing shoulders with the lean newcomer in a gray frock coat and pantaloons.

"Been troubling me all day again. Every time I put weight on it. . .yes, I took the tonic. . .gout, indeed. . .thank you, Dr. Bagot. . ."

Tom slammed his way from the church before he could hear more. Darkness crept across Sunderlin Downs like an inky infection. Like a doom. Like a demon whisper that he would never find Meg at all.

The second her legs dangled over the window ledge, sweat dampened her grip. *Do not look down*. Cool, nighttime air breezed through her, rustling the white dress about her legs. She breathed in the scent of freshly trimmed grass.

I cannot. She pulled her legs back into the bedchamber, but her heart pattered in protest. She had to do this. Slipping back out, she reached for the gnarled tree branch. An oak, she was certain. How, she did not know.

Securing both hands around the branch, she breathed faster. *One, two, three.* On ten she would jump. *Nine, ten.* Perhaps twenty. *Eighteen, nineteen.* Before she could reason out of it, she propelled herself forward. Her body whooshed back and forth in the air.

Help.

She caught her footing in a tree crotch. Then she moved without thought—pulling herself down and over, looping through branches with movements so lithe and familiar she was certain she'd done this before. Had she climbed many trees as a child? Or did she still?

She landed on all fours in soft, damp grass.

Her head spun.

Run. Gathering the muslin dress in her fists, she slipped through what appeared to be a well-kept courtyard. Moonlight illuminated flowered bushes, tall boxwoods, and shadowed cloisters. She hurried to the only side not enclosed by the abbey.

A massive drystone wall. She sprinted the length of it, searching through vines. The door. The gate. Where was the gate?

In the distance, a bark struck the silence.

She flattened against the wall.

Her knees jellied as the sense of entrapment squelched what little courage she had left. She darted for the cloisters. The temperature chilled in the ancient covered passageway.

More howling. Lights glowed across the courtyard.

Hand covering her mouth, she hunkered against the stone plinth. The columns cast black, symmetrical shadows across the walk. She counted them. Lost count. Started again—

"Over here!"

More shouts, then a dog lunged at her from the darkness.

She screamed, covered her face.

Teeth snapped, but someone must have hauled the animal back, because they never sank into her skin. Instead, two hands peeled back her arms.

"Miss Margaret?"

"There is no gate." Tears weakened her voice. She was ashamed of them because she had the sense she was not wont to crying. "I cannot find the gate—"

"The abbey, I fear, has no exit through its courtyard." Lord Cunningham's arms reached beneath her, pulling her against him. "I regret you were so frightened as to search for it at this hour."

She buried her face into his banyan as he stood. Strange, but he still smelled of cinnamon. Stranger still, she didn't want to smell anything else.

"Stevens, go awake Cook and have her prepare a platter of something soothing. Milk and honey and a bit of the laudanum the doctor prescribed."

"Yes, my lord."

"And see to it that another bedchamber is prepared for Miss Margaret. One with windows to the north, so that she might feel less enclosed. This is my fault, in truth. I should have realized such a chamber would be constricting."

Servants scurried away.

The dog yapped once or twice more before the sound of his claws faded in the cloister.

When Lord Cunningham carried her a step, she clenched the silk of his banyan with a racing chest. "My lord, I can walk."

"I fear you are much too exerted. You overestimated your recovery, I fear, in this—"

"I do not remember anything." She pushed at him, until he finally set her down, and backed deeper into the passageway blackness. "I do not understand. Every time I strain to remember, the pain worsens."

"Whatever gave you the idea, my dear girl, I expected you to try at all?"

"I will not be locked away."

"Is that what tonight is about? If so, allow me to return your mind to ease. Dr. Bagot was in error, and even if he were not, I am not in the habit of surrendering anyone to such a torturous establishment, least of all..." The sentence lingered, and she felt, rather than saw, his overwhelming conviction. "Shall we go inside now?"

"One thing more."

"Ask me anything."

She smeared her dripping nose with a shaking hand. "I wish to discover where I am from. I want to go back there."

"It shall be done. I shall send servants out in the morning."

"And if my whereabouts...my identity cannot be discovered...I wish you to know I shall not go on troubling you. The moment you wish it of me, I shall leave."

"You speak absurdity, dear girl." He stepped closer. His fingers reached for hers—soft, without callouses. Why was that so strange to her? "Penrose Abbey is your home for as long as you have need of it. Whether you remember or not, whether you desire a harbor or merely a comrade, it is yours."

She wanted to ask why he would be so benevolent to her. Why he would grace her with such kindly trust—a stranger—when she didn't even know if she could trust herself.

But she was too frightened that if she did question him, her one foothold in a rocking world would shatter. She allowed him to guide her back inside Penrose Abbey, hand in his.

She was penniless.

Homeless.

Nameless.

But he seemed determined to convey, with every new squeeze of her hand, that she was not as friendless as she felt.

He was fevered, but he wasn't sick.

Just like before.

That night seven years ago, when the brick cottage of nine children became soundless. When they all crowded around the bed, looking at each other, not saying anything. Mamm had dried her eyes with a raspberry-stained apron. Papa was stone. He was always stone—but as he leaned against the wall with a baby in one arm and little Joanie in the other, some of his steadiness seemed to crack.

Tom slipped off the chestnut mare, the lights from the whitewashed livery stable aching his eyes. Twilight had already settled over Juleshead. Crickets sang in the distance, that same chorus that had always lured him and Meg into their nighttime mischief.

His stomach protested the memory. He had forgotten what this felt like.

Losing everything all in a moment.

"Day late, yaw are." Young Brownie, the six-foot stable hand, crossed his arms with amusement. "Yaw paid for four but was gone five."

"I need another five."

"When?"

"Morning. First thing." Tom handed over the reins. "Give him plenty of oats. Brush him down good too. He rode hard."

"I don't think yaw have enough."

"I'll pay."

"With what? Hankies and shoe buckles?" Nonetheless, Brownie led the mare back into the stables, asked no more questions, and said that the mare would be saddled and waiting come sunrise.

Tom nodded and crossed the street toward the blacksmith shop. Wind cut through him, smelling of salt and horse sweat.

His mind combatted too many thoughts at once.

Meg hurting. Meg frightened. Meg alone. Meg waiting for him, but he wasn't coming. And then just the sound of her—her laugh washing over him with its breathy sweetness. That had been his salvation the past seven years. The only thing that kept him smiling.

He needed Meg Foxcroft.

She needed him.

Reaching the blacksmith shop, he tried both doors. Locked? Why? Meade should be inside, dousing the fire in the forge and nursing his tankard of gin for the night.

Unless something was wrong.

Unease spiked through Tom's exhaustion as he resisted the urge to climb the side of the shop, pry open the window, and collapse onto his own pallet. He rounded the street instead. As blackness dimmed and quieted the village, the Kingfisher's Tavern was the only establishment not blowing out their candles and closing their shutters for the night.

Don't.

He tried to pull himself back. He was too afraid now, of all times, he would be tempted to gulp down any poison that would numb his pain. He entered anyway, breathing in smoke, and scanned the wood-framed taproom.

A hulking figure, toward the end of the bar, ended Tom's search.

He elbowed and pushed his way through unwashed fishermen and light-skirts. Someone in the room strummed a hurdy-gurdy. Another belted a song in Cornish.

"There be the 'ero." A hand snatched Tom and slung him against the wooden bar. More clapped his back. "I say'ee ought to toast to the man wot runs into a burnin' buildin' to save our own. What do'ee say, gents?"

A clamor of cheers blasted Tom's ears. Fire singed his nerves. "Get off me—"

"Here. Drink this."

Ale sloshed onto Tom's shirt, then a woman's clammy arms slinked around his neck—

"Back to your drinks, fools." Meade. Grunting, shoving, the bar clearing. Then, quieter, "Take to the ale or give it here."

Tom slid over the dull tankard that had been thrust into his hands. He wiped at his shirt. "The shop was locked."

"I locked it."

Tom glanced at the blacksmith's face. His cheeks were too red, eyes too squinted and bloodshot. Something *was* wrong. "The ratcatcher—"

"That all you care about?" Meade downed the ale. "Gone five days. No word. Nothin'. All you want to jabber 'bout is the ratcatcher when I been—"

"Ye knew I was looking for Meg."

"I be many things, but no nursey. You were different. Older. A man almost, but she—"

"What're ye talking about?"

"Blast you, boy, there be a pint of a girl sleepin' in my bed this very minute. I don't be knowin' who she is or what the devil I'm supposed to do with her while you're gallivantin' about, but she—she..."

Tom gripped the edge of the bar in gut-sinking confusion. "She what?"

"Had this sewn into her coat." Meade smacked a letter against Tom's chest. "And says she belongs to you."

CHAPTER 4

No. This wasn't right. This couldn't be right. Papa would never have stood for such a thing, and Mamm would have cried against it.

"Know her?"

Of course he knew her. He had carried her about on his shoulders, pleaded with her to stop following him when he played, and planted her atop Sam, their family spaniel, for rides about the yard.

The same child lay curled in Meade's wrinkled bed linens. Her hair was long, gleaming, a darker blond than it had been at four years old. Her cheeks were pale. Her lips thin. Her brow troubled, even in sleep.

"Been here two days now. I didn't be knowin' what to do with her." Meade shifted closer to the bed, his candlelight twitching her eyelids. "I put her in here. Brought up food."

"Ye kept her in here like a prisoner?"

Meade scowled, but said nothing in his own defense.

Panic drilled at Tom's temples. He reeled back and shook his head. "Must be a mistake."

"If you hain't goin' to be readin' the letter, give it here."

"No." Another step back. Tom clenched the new letter in his pocket—alongside the old one. Why he could not read it, he wasn't certain. Perhaps because he already knew what it said. "I can't take care of her. Not now. Not with Meg. . ." He couldn't finish the sentence.

He didn't have to.

Meade blew out the candle. Darkness swathed them. "Tell you one thing, McGwen, you won't be racin' off again and leavin' me with no child."

"I have to look for Meg."

"You heard me."

"Meade, I—"

"Stay and take care of the girl, or the both of you can be takin' lodgin' somewhere else." He staggered toward the door. "I mean it, boy. This hain't no place for a child. No place for a girl. She don't belong here."

Tom's chest whacked the same time the door yanked shut.

Meade was right.

His sister belonged anywhere other than Juleshead with Tom, the one person who had already ruined their family once. Papa must be desperate to send Joanie here.

That or dead.

This was not her.

Meg eased her hands down the light cotton gown, each dainty embroidered flower notching her discomfort. Pins jabbed her scalp. Her hair smelled burnt, evidence that the maid had left in the papillote iron too long.

A step ahead of her, a wigged footman pulled out a velvet-seated chair. She scooted up to the breakfast room table.

Everything was perfect. The white tablecloth. The porcelain, hand-painted dishware. Gleaming silver teapot. Platters and bowls of fruit, buttered rolls, sliced ham, and lemon cream—all lifting up scents that twinged her stomach.

The footman disappeared.

She was alone—not only in this room, but in the world. She sat entirely still for three minutes. She knew, because she stared at the clock on the mantel across the table. *I'm going back.* She sprung from her chair the same time the breakfast room door hurried open.

"Then it was not a dream at all." Lord Cunningham swept to the table wearing a well-tailored suit, voluminous neckcloth, and glowing expression. He took a seat across from her. "Betwixt here and the library,

I had almost convinced myself the maid was in error with her declaration you had decided to join me."

"I am sorry." The only thing she could think to say. "You must think me terribly ungrateful."

"I think you many things, dear girl, but all of them good."

Was he in earnest? He didn't know her. She didn't know herself.

They were both pretending.

That she should be wearing this dress. That she was good. That they were friends—her and a lord who was likely so far above her in station that had the situation been different, he might not have nodded to her on the street.

"I do not think I would wear this." Embarrassment pinched at her. Odd, that. As if what she wore bore any significance when she did not even know her own full name.

"Your memory is returning?"

"No. It is just that. . .the dress is lovely, but it feels. . ."

"Unfamiliar to you?"

She nodded.

He nodded too. "As does everything else, I imagine. This must be gravely overwhelming." He glanced at the breakfast spread with disinterest. "I confess, I am not hungry. Are you?"

"I could not eat."

"Then we must do something to distract you. Something that shall make you more comfortable. The library perhaps. What do you say?"

She told herself to deny him. Somehow the need to resolve this—to heal herself and remember who she was—chiseled at her with painful urgency. She didn't wish to squander time in the library. She wished to find answers.

"I confess to being intelligible concerning many topics. A gift my father passed down to me. But like him, I am not quite as adept at interpreting matters of the heart." He crossed the table and held out a gloved hand. "Tell me what is wrong, tell me what to do to remedy it, and I shall oblige."

"There is nothing you can do."

"Then please." He tugged her up. "Do your best, if possible, to smile. We shall go to the library, and for a little while we may convince ourselves all is right and well in the world. Would you be so kind as to grant me that small favor?"

"Very well."

"I fear you have already failed."

She lifted a brow.

"To smile," he urged.

The last thing in the world she wanted to do. But he had given her so much and asked so little, so she tucked her arm in the one he offered, glanced up at him, and thought of the only thing that made her happy.

A pink pinafore, white puddle ducks, and a loving voice speaking her name.

By all that was holy, she would find such a voice again. If that person was still out there. If they still loved her. If anyone loved her.

Her heart panged, but she smiled.

All night long, Tom had watched her from the rickety wooden chair in the corner of Meade's chamber. Even with the window open, the room smelled of man—unclean bed linens, sweat, and lingering cheroot smoke.

Joanie was used to the tiny cottage bedchambers, always swept clean by Mamm. The house had smelled of fresh bread in the morning. Everything had come alive in such a sleepy haze as nine children laughed and fussed and scampered about to do their sunrise chores.

Tom rolled a kink out of his shoulder. He stretched his arms.

He should have already been gone.

First to find the ratcatcher, if the rat could be found. Then to search more villages—north, south, east, west of here. Tom had the whole world to comb.

He couldn't just sit here.

And he couldn't leave.

Sucking air in his cheeks, then blowing it out, he finally reached for the letter. He flicked it open with dirt-stained fingernails. He needed to bathe. He needed to eat. He needed sleep.

The sight of Mamm's handwriting sucked him into a painful vortex of comfort and angst. He smoothed out the wrinkles.

> *Tommy, I would have posted the letter, but since you never answered my last, I thought it might be wiser to deliver it with Joanie. Your father and I discussed everything two nights ago. He has been sick for many years now, and I am tired. Many of the girls are married now. Your brothers Isaac and Moses are off to sea, and the two youngest remain with me. You may not have known, but your father took another wee one some time after you left. More than anything, I wish to remain here at the farm. It will not be easy to leave Caleb. I visit him often. Joanie planted marigolds on his grave. I suppose, with both her and I gone, they will die now. I am departing soon with the wee ones to Edinburgh, where I shall live with my sister, though she has only room for the three of us. Joanie is eleven now. She will be married soon and it is my wish that you watch over her until she does. She is a good girl.*

Tom turned the page and swallowed.

> *I am sorry you did not get to come home before the house became empty. It would have been good to see you once more. Your father died this morning. Most of what he inherited from his parents has dwindled, especially these last years with his sickness, but enough remains to see the children and I comfortable. Joanie has a bank note in her coat pocket. Your father felt at least this should go to you. Our heart loved all our children, but you and Caleb were our blood. I wish I had not lost you both.*

The bed squeaked.

Tom hesitated, blinked hard, then lifted his eyes.

Joanie sat up in bed, hair pushed behind her big ears and a look of bashful uncertainty pinkening her cheeks. She was pretty. From the first time Papa had brought her home, after discovering her destitute in a pile of newspapers behind the village wheelwright's, she had possessed a plain but pleasant look about her.

The gaunt, two-year-old urchin had blossomed quickly under Mamm's tender touch. As did all the orphans Papa brought home.

They were good, Tom's parents.

Better than he had realized.

Until it was too late.

"You're crying." Joanie still had the voice of a child. Her eyes were older.

Tom stuffed the letter back into his pocket and made for the door. "I'll get yer breakfast," was all he said as he did exactly what he'd scorned Meade for.

Left the girl alone.

Lord Cunningham had not joined her for breakfast in two days. He did not visit her chamber. Nor send a maid with a stack of books or magazines, as he had done other afternoons.

As if he had not thought of her at all.

Pacing back and forth along her bedchamber stained-glass window, Meg shook her head. This was ridiculous. The man had other matters to attend to, likely far more imperative than a pitiful ward. Had she imagined she would be the object of his attention ongoing?

No.

Of course not.

But she'd already thumbed through the last *Le Beau Monde* magazine, and if she had loved reading before, she despised it now. The room was stifling. Too many times, she'd wandered to the window and longed to push it open—but the old lancet design, with its sharp pointed arch, allowed for no escape.

A dull pain clustered along her forehead, where her cut still itched.

She needed to stay here. She must wait. For what, she was not certain—but she had as little right to leave this chamber, to explore the house, as she did to wear the silk and satin gowns hanging in her wardrobe.

If Lord Cunningham wished to see her, he would.

That was that.

But two hours later, after a maid had delivered dinner on a flower-painted tole tray, Meg abandoned her resolutions. She slipped into a hall fading dim with dusk, where newly lit wall sconces guided her way to the stairwell.

Her breathing slowed.

She scolded herself every step down, but a sense of familiarity—perhaps even pleasure—cloaked her. As if she had done this before. As if the nighttime, the darkness, was wont to luring her away and she was addicted to the thrill of untowardness.

What sort of girl was she?

At the bottom of the stairs, she slipped beyond two ionic pillars, moved left into a hall, and passed dark doorways until she reached one with a sliver of light.

His study.

She raised her hand to knock, thought better of it, and was just ready to scuttle back to her room when—

The door threw open. "I think you should look at—" Lord Cunningham stopped short, eyes widening. "Oh. Miss Margaret." Something about him was different. No, not really. His hair was still intact, his tailcoat wrinkleless, his cravat knotted to perfection.

He backed into his study with a smile that seemed strained. "Forgive me. I was expecting someone else."

"I did not mean to disturb."

"On the contrary. You are just the intermission I am in need of." He circled his desk, hurried shut a large leather book, and nodded for the door. "Shall we take a turn about the garden? It is near dark, but I imagine the moon shall suffice if we are brief."

"I do not wish to take you from whatever business—"

"I need fresh air as much as you, my dear."

Something in his voice, the desperation, stirred her pity—and confusion. "Very well, my lord."

"If you will await me outside my study."

"Of course."

She turned to leave, but not before she saw the wrinkled handkerchief he swept from his desk and thrust into a drawer.

Perplexity struck as she stepped into the hall.

It was bloodstained.

Tom slowed his steps to match hers. Strange, because he was used to Meg half clinging to his arm, running barefoot to keep up with him, like they could take off soaring into the air if they wanted to.

Not dogging behind him with raggedy shoes and a hem with a three-inch mud stain.

Sun burned the back of his neck. He'd be red again by late afternoon. Maybe blistered. He welcomed pain he could grit his teeth through.

"My foot hurts."

The first time Joanie had spoken all day. Yesterday, Tom had delivered her meals, brought up one of Meade's ropes and taught her how to tie a knot, then slipped back out at dusk and spent half the night discovering more about the ratcatcher.

All Mr. Telfner remembered was the name Hector. Few in the east side had heard of the man. Or so they said.

Motioning Joanie into a cobblestone alley, into the damp shade, Tom pulled up a crate. "Here."

Without looking at him, Joanie plopped down and unlaced her left half boot.

Tom tugged it off. "Where's it rubbing?"

She pointed to a fresh, round blister on the side of her arch.

"Might as well take them both off. We'll be there soon." As soon as he figured out where *there* was. They'd been roaming the village for three hours. With the banknote Joanie was sent with, there would be enough for proper lodgings—and someone to look after her.

Something Tom could not do.

Even if he wanted to.

Which he didn't.

"Mamm says good ladies don't take off their shoes." The quiet words, with her chin ducked to her chest, followed a timid glance at his face.

He should have smiled at her. He should have reassured her that soon he would buy her more shoes, that she need not worry over where she'd sleep tonight, and that somehow he'd find a place for her, even if that wasn't with him.

But he untied her second boot and motioned her up. "It's not far now." Mrs. Musgrave was just around the next street corner.

If anyone would take in a child—and take pity on Tom's plight—it was her.

The RED COTTAGE

"Two things I require of you, my dear, if you shall be so kind." Lord Cunningham stood outside her bedchamber doorway, wearing a bright green frock coat, white leather breeches, and spurred top boots. "One, that you accept my most express apology for neglecting you these past days."

"You hardly owe me—"

"And two, that you shall accompany me this afternoon for what I boastfully refer to as a ride in my king's chariot."

She should have exclaimed yes. After all, he was offering her the very thing she'd been in need of—a diversion from her own troubled boredom and a chance to spend an outing in his company.

Instead, her eyes searched him.

For a bandage on his finger.

A nick on his fine, smoothly shaven face.

But even that would not explain the doctor arriving in a black carriage at the crack of dawn, marching into the abbey, and leaving an hour later without ever once visiting Meg's chamber.

"I realize I was not myself last night in the garden." As if his subdued conversations were the cause of her hesitancy. "But I do promise I shall be in brighter spirits today—as shall you, I imagine, once I share the news."

News? About her?

"I shall be but a moment." She smiled to soften the sobriety of her voice, then shut herself back into the chamber. As she fumbled through the motions of replacing her morning dress with a blue crepe gown and white spencer jacket, Lord Cunningham's soft whistling echoed outside her door.

As if he hadn't a care in the world.

She knew he had.

Pulling on white kid gloves, she met him again in the hallway and followed him outside the abbey, into the massive, yellow-painted stables with a slate roof. In the adjoining carriage house, he swept his hand to the shiny vehicle.

"My ostentatious indulgence."

The landau, with its lowered roof and cushioned seats, was a brilliant blue. On the sides were delicate hand paintings of *Aesop's Fables*, each scene depicted in gilded oval frames, like something one would view on the ceiling of a church.

"My father found moral lessons from the Bible rather overdone, so he illustrated life lessons through the magic of ancient Greek fables." Lord Cunningham motioned the stable boy to hitch up the matching bays. "This rather eccentric reminder of all he had taught me was given as a…" She was not certain if he deliberately left the sentence unfinished or if he were only distracted by giving another order to the servant.

Either way, five minutes later she was sitting next to him on the cushioned seat, the sun in her eyes, as the carriage took her away from the only place in the world she knew.

With the only man she knew.

Despite his assurances he would be of a more cheery countenance, he said very little as the road wound them deeper into green countryside.

Her hands perspired inside the gloves.

Anxiousness stole through her, bouncing her heart as recklessly as the carriage jostled with the road ruts. She smelled cinnamon. She smelled earth. She smelled the endless scents of blossoms, grass, morning air—the aroma of freedom, even though she was the last thing in the world from free.

"You had news to tell me."

He glanced at her with a reluctant smile. "You are remarkably courageous, dear girl. It was my thought to conceal this as long as I could, but you make that impossible."

She sat straighter. "You discovered something."

"Yes."

"Who I am."

"Yes again, my dear." When he reached for her hand, she did not resist. The squeezing warmth of his fingers injected her with calm. "My steward was handling business in Sunderlin Downs yestereve. He returned last night with this." Lord Cunningham pulled a folded newspaper from his coat.

She laid it in her lap, eyes blurring as she read over the circled print. WANTED. INFORMATION CONCERNING THE CITIZEN MARGARET FOXCROFT OF JULESHEAD, N. CORNWALL. CITIZEN IS NINETEEN YEARS OF AGE, FAIR COMPLEXION, BROWN HAIR. THOSE WHO ARE ABLE TO GIVE CERTAIN INTELLIGENCE OF THE

The RED COTTAGE

WHEREABOUTS OF MISS FOXCROFT, BEING LIVING OR DEAD, ARE REQUESTED TO DELIVER IT TO THE JUSTICE OF THE PEACE, MR. WILLMOTT OF JULESHEAD, IMMEDIATELY.

"I shall send two footmen to the village forthwith. I think it wise to investigate before returning you to unknown and perhaps dangerous circumstances."

She closed the newspaper with a sickened pulse of her heart. "That will not be necessary." Her chest shuddered. "I want to go home."

"But Miss Margaret—"

"I want to go home. Now."

CHAPTER 5

He couldn't look at the place.

The air still smelled like smoke, ashes, and death. Not even Mrs. Musgrave's rout cakes, as she ushered Tom and Joanie into her millinery shop, could banish the stench from his brain.

The lass stood close to him, as if she feared being abandoned in the colorful room of hats and feather plumes. Likely, she feared Tom too. She knew the story.

Unless she remembered it herself.

"You have not been eating enough." Mrs. Musgrave settled into her chair by the window, motioning to a platter of freshly baked desserts. He tried not to stare at the apothecary's burnt remains through the curtains. "Sit down and eat something. Both of you."

He glanced at Joanie and nodded, but she shook her head in bashful protest. "We are not hungry," he said instead.

"Pshaw. Growing children are always hungry." She chuckled. "Perhaps old women too, hmm?"

"This is my sister." The words felt short, even to his own ears. He was not certain how to say it gentler. "Joanie."

"Most wonderful to meet you, my dear."

"She will be staying in Juleshead."

"I see."

The RED COTTAGE

"Meade has not enough room, and I thought perhaps—"

"You are certain you do not wish to try one?" Mrs. Musgrave swooped up her tortoiseshell cat from the floor and smiled at Joanie. "Sit here in my chair and eat as many as you like. I shall get you a cup of tea." Hobbling toward the side door, she waved at Tom. "You will help me, won't you, Tommy?"

No part of him wished to follow her. She'd only say what everyone else already had.

Except it was more than that.

He sensed it in the way she walked as he followed her into a tiny timber-framed kitchen, where a copper kettle boiled in the hearth. She plopped down Lenox. The cat scurried under a cupboard as fast as Tom wanted to.

"Tommy, dear, you know this is not right."

Frustration locked his jaw. "Ye know I cannae be leaving her with Meade."

"You cannot leave her at all."

"I know nothing about lasses."

"You knew about Miss Foxcroft." Mrs. Musgrave's eyes misted, and her hand shook a little as she grabbed a cracked teacup from a peg. She filled it with steaming tea. "Did you go to the grave?"

They had already placed a marker for Mr. Foxcroft? How had Tom not known?

"The churchwardens wanted to do one for Miss Foxcroft too."

"She is not dead."

"I know."

"They had no right to—"

"Now, now, Tommy. We shall have none of that Scottish temper of yours." She edged closer to him and took his hand in her wrinkled ones. She demanded his eyes.

Because she knew.

That he kept stealing glances out the window to the apothecary. That he could not eat. That he could not get rid of the smell, and that he was dying, and that nothing would ever be the same again.

"Take the young child home with you, and if Meade says a word about

51

it, I shall come after him myself with a hat pin."

"Meade willnae listen."

"*You* are the one not listening."

He pulled away, shaking his head, another wave of anger gaining momentum—but she grabbed his elbow before he reached the door.

"Very well, my dear. The child may stay. After all the times you have wandered over here to fetch my poor kitty from the tree or unclog my chimney, I suppose I can do no less for you."

Tom reached into his pocket for a fistful of coins.

"I think not." Mrs. Musgrave folded back his hand. "You may repay me by eating well. Miss Foxcroft would wish you to take care of yourself, would she not?"

Tom nodded, and like a torturous addiction, his eyes roamed back to the window. A breeze stirred the ashes. He almost wept.

What Meg wanted was to be found.

He had strength enough for that and nothing else.

"Tomorrow," Lord Cunningham said over a dinner of fricasseed rabbit and marrow pudding. "I shall accompany you, of course, and we may even take my king's chariot, if that is agreeable."

She nodded, thanked him, but the food remained untouched. Her knees bounced beneath the table.

How could he smile so easily over this?

As if they were planning an outing. One where they would go hunting for ribbons, or browsing the bookstore—not putting back the pieces of her life she had lost.

Pieces she wasn't even certain would fit together.

Or make the picture she hoped.

Excusing herself from the dinner table with murmurs of a headache, she retired to her chamber and draped herself across the bed. She watched the colors in the stained-glass window fade to black. *"Look at the ducks."* The voice from her past. A comfort, somehow, though it seemed fainter and less distinct with each memory.

Like someone she had not heard in years.

Remember. She rolled to her back. Pressed her hands to her head. Squeezed. *Remember, remember.* She could not go tomorrow. She could not face the world—and the past—without some sort of footing to hold her up. Why was everything void? What was wrong with her?

She was empty.

So utterly, utterly empty.

Lord, I'm scared. Her hands fisted in her hair. Pulling, as if the tension would turn the key. But it didn't. Tears leaked from her eyes so fast the dark room became a blur.

Then a knock. A quiet "Miss Margaret?"

Her chest deflated. Lord Cunningham. Why did he have to come now? He had called her courageous this afternoon, and even though she swiped at the tears with her sleeve, he would hear cowardice when she spoke.

"Miss Margaret, may I speak with you one moment? Please, I shall not bother you long."

She sighed. Pushing her hair from her face, she slipped to the door and cracked it open.

He widened the crack. He entered, when it would have been far more appropriate had he stayed without. "I was not being modest when I told you I rarely possess insight on the delicacies of human emotion."

She held back the quiver in her chin by sheer force of will. Her tears were not half so obedient.

Lord Cunningham smiled again. Slower this time, as if he understood her turmoil. "You poor, lost pet." He hesitated, then touched her hand, then pulled her against him in an embrace as warm and sweet as cinnamon. "Whatever we discover tomorrow, I wish you to know that you are not alone. If the situation is unfavorable, or you find by some strange chance that Penrose Abbey possesses greater allure to you, then home you shall come."

Home. Despite the bulwarks she built to conceal her fears, a sob leaked into his linen tailcoat. She wasn't certain what the word meant. Whether home was here or there or if she would ever recall what the word had once meant to her.

But the desperation to remember drained from her as fast as the tears. She could face Juleshead, whether the lady in the pink pinafore or the man with the soft voice awaited her or not.

Because she was not alone.

Nor half so empty as she allowed herself to think.

Of all the blasted insanities.

Tom chewed on the cold slab of venison Meade had left out for him in the kitchen, but he couldn't swallow. The lump had been in his throat since he left Mrs. Musgrave.

Maybe before that.

Blast.

Joanie hadn't said anything when Tom told her. She'd stared at her shoes. The raggedy ones. The ones Tom was supposed to replace.

"We shall get along quite well, Joanie and I and Lenox," Mrs. Musgrave had said, draping an arm around the child.

Joanie stiffened. Shy, the little lass. Even when Papa first brought her home with her tangled hair and dirty dress and fearful head tilts, she had taken days to babble her first words.

He remembered the first time she'd smiled.

How the family had all gathered around her, clapping their hands, pulling her in for hugs and kisses. Even the dog had yapped in excitement.

He wished she'd smiled today instead of looking at him the way she did. Horrified, devastated, as if pleading with Tom not to—

"Figured you'd be up." Meade's shadow appeared in the crooked kitchen doorway. "I see you got rid of the little mouse."

Tom shoved out of his chair a little too hard. It toppled behind him.

Meade shrugged. "Had to be done."

"Anything on Hector?"

"Word is he caught a coach northbound."

"When?"

"After the fire." Another shrug. "Day or two later."

"Which coach?"

"Don't matter. He's gone."

Tom suppressed a growl. He grabbed the dry bread from his plate, the last hunk of venison, and his tankard of milk. "Leave the light in the window."

"Where you going?"

Tom wasn't certain himself until the words were out, "To get my sister."

The village stirred something inside her. The unshakable desire to rip off her satin gloves, pull the flower-trimmed bonnet from her head, and take off running down the mossy cobblestones.

A blush pinched at her cheeks.

Lord Cunningham leaned closer to her in the landau, surveying their surroundings with mildly interested pleasure. He had resumed his demeanor of treating their journey as if it were some trivial outing. As if he were the gentleman and she the fine lady, and they had chosen the sleepy village of Juleshead for a day of courting and adventure.

He had no idea what sort of creature she was.

How uncivilized her thoughts.

"I say we take a small ride about the main streets, in the event anything nudges your memory. Mr. Willmott has waited this long. I do not suppose another half hour shall be of consequence."

Meg murmured agreement.

On both sides of the street, honey-colored shops and houses jutted their steeply pitched gables into the air. Everything smelled different. Cool, fresh, like last night's thunderstorm and morning.

Rain still glistened on the square-trimmed bushes, the brown-and-gray cobbles, and different-colored shingles swaying from shop fronts. Shelves and books and hats and shoes and dresses were displayed behind the endless windows.

She had lived here?

"Look there." Lord Cunningham pointed across her. "Fires are most unfortunate. I daresay, though, it speaks well to the competence of the villagers. That they were nimble enough to stop such a blaze before it spread is remarkable."

Between two squat shops, the black, crumbled shape of a building fumed a heavy scent of smoke. The odor scratched at her throat. Irritating her. Making her sweat.

"Ah, just the thing." Something else must have drawn Lord Cunningham's attention, for he leaned forward, said something to the driver, and then helped Meg alight in front of a red-painted bookstore. "I am always on the hunt for more medical books. Father kept a list of rarer titles, and since he was unable to complete it before his death, it is now upon me to carry the mantle. Do you mind?"

"No. Of course not."

Ring, ring, ring.

A tiny brass bell rang above the door as they entered. Her heart tripped in time to the noise. She followed him down an aisle of books, wiped more sweat from her forehead, then tugged at the too-tight ribbon choking her neck.

Ring, ring, ring. Her head split. *Ring, ring, ring.* Why would it not stop ringing?

"Miss Margaret?" Lord Cunningham, supporting her arm, pressing her against a row of books. "Are you ill?"

Ring, ring.

"Perhaps you should sit."

"No." Breathy. She doubled over, caught her mouth with her hands, and barely kept back the sickness surging from her stomach.

Lord Cunningham pulled her to the floor and barked something to a stranger in the bookstore. Or maybe the woman wasn't a stranger, because she shrieked Meg's name.

"Oh heavens! It is you."

Ring, ring, ring.

"The poor child."

Ring.

"I shall fetch water...smelling salts...oh, I cannot believe you are back when we all thought..."

Everything faded, all the rows of books and musty scents and stifling shelves. The blackness was warm, but too warm. Flames licked at her. Her throat scratched again, but this time, she could not breath—

Water.

The cool liquid splashed down her throat, spilled down her chin, as tender gloves wiped it back away. Lord Cunningham shifted her nearer. "Better?"

She welcomed air into her lungs as his face came back into focus. She couldn't find her voice, so she nodded instead.

His lordship smiled.

So did the woman, peering over Meg with wire-rimmed spectacles.

"Something overwrought you, I think, though I am not certain what." Lord Cunningham grazed a hand along her temple. "Does your head still pain you?"

"No."

"Dizzy?"

"No."

"Have you any idea at all what might have initiated such distress?"

Her mind scrambled for an answer, for the object or sound or face that had struck her ill. But she was as uncertain of that as she was her own name, and all she could think to answer was, "No."

The wooden bench outside *Dowies Cobbler* creaked as Joanie bent over. She tied the red ribbons of her spotless, nankeen half boots, then glanced back up at Tom for the hundredth time since last night.

A smile stretched her lips.

The same one she'd been giving him all day, followed by her blushing cheeks. She looked at him like Meg did. Like Caleb had. Like all the children growing up—as if Tom were some sort of mesmerizing hero.

He wasn't anything more than a fool.

"They're pretty." Joanie leaned back against the brick wall of the cobbler shop, pushing hair behind her big ears. "Lizzy at church had ones just like it. I used to look at them. Papa said I could have a pair when I was older."

Tom looked away.

He wasn't used to this.

Someone mentioning Papa easily, when Tom had spent so many years pushing the man's name from his mind.

"I cried that morning." Joanie folded her hands in her lap. "Me and Emma and Rosina and Mamm. I prayed every night you would come back. I used to sit in the window above the sink and watch for you."

Tom had never planned to leave.

He had stayed for weeks, months, maybe a year—living among them, bearing Papa's silence, sleeping next to the empty bed. One night he slipped beneath his scratchy bed linens and knew he couldn't wake up again in the same house.

He left before daylight.

Never once came back.

Never could. . .now.

"Emma married a farmer. They have four babies. I would have lived with them, except her husband said they had no room for me." Joanie plucked a loose string on her dress. "Rosina ran away with a soldier. I used to write her letters, but she stopped answering them."

Tom's knee moved up and down. He scratched at his itching sunburn. What to say to the lass? That she was welcome here—with *him*—when he could barely take care of himself?

"Maybe I should get married too." The words were so quiet he had to glance down at her to be certain she spoke. Her puckered chin yanked at his chest.

"Nay, lass." It seemed strange to slip his arm around her when he'd only ever plopped her on his back and ridden her about the cottage floor as if he were the horse. He placed his hand on her knee instead. Squeezed. "Ye just worry about breaking in those shiny new shoes of yers."

"We can go show Meade?"

He almost laughed. "If ye want." Though he was doubtful the burly blacksmith would know what to say—if he said anything. He knew as little, if not less, than Tom did about children. Or lassies.

A brassy ring echoed across the street.

Tom glanced up.

Meg.

His stomach dropped the same time he launched from the bench. He froze. Long purple dress, trimmed with ribbon, a spencer jacket, silver buttons. Her hair was different. Curled around the face, under a bonnet like nothing she'd ever worn.

With uncanny indifference, her eyes skimmed past him.

"Oh," cooed Joanie. "Look at the pretty carriage—"

He ran, dodging a ragpicker's cart, blood pounding in his ears so hard he was deaf to everything else. He circled the fancy blue carriage. Charged her before she climbed in and swung her body against him. "Meg—"

With a frantic yelp, she writhed away.

He was aware of everything at once.

The healing red wound across her forehead. The lack of color in her face. The stark panic rounding her eyes as she backed away, as if—

"Away from her this instant." A strong, white-gloved hand clamped on Tom's shoulder, yanking him backward.

His mind reeled, lagging. He stumbled back. "Meg." Breathing hard. Then not at all. "Meg, it's me."

Her lips shook. Her gaze shook. The world shook.

She was afraid of him.

The realization stabbed him as he took one more step closer, arms spread. She looked ready for flight. Like the first time he'd kissed her, behind the apothecary among the elderberries and chamomile and thyme.

She knew he would not hurt her.

She'd known that then.

"Listen to me. I don't know what ye're doing in that dress and with this man, but I want ye to come home with me—"

"An impossibility, I fear, sir." The gentleman stepped in front of Meg. Tall, broad, with blond hair and a too-large jaw. "Our wish is to speak with Mr. Willmott first and foremost. If you would like to request an audience with Miss Margaret, you may do so in a proper manner." His brow hardened. "*This*, I daresay, is in very bad form."

"Ye did this to her." Tom tried to push past him. "What did he do to ye, Meg—"

"Sir, that shall be quite enough."

"Get out of my way!"

"This is preposter—"

Tom's fist connected with the man's mouth, teeth puncturing knuckles. The gentleman crashed beneath the shadow of the bookstore's awning.

"Meg, I'm trying to talk with ye." He reached for her. "Please, talk to me."

Red blazed her face. Instead of grasping his outstretched hand, she swept next to the stranger and grabbed his face like she'd grabbed Tom's a million times. She crooned out a soft note of compassion. She wiped his blood away with the strange and terrible dress.

Then she looked back at Tom.

All the sweet creases in her face hardened, and the beautiful light in her eyes dimmed, and the love he lived and breathed for was absent.

"Whoever you are," she whispered. "Leave me alone."

CHAPTER 6

The corridor was too narrow. The walls were covered with paper hangings of bright green-and-red parrots and apples, and the single vase of wilted flowers put off a sweet, rotting fragrance.

Meg covered her nose. Not because the smell bothered her, so much as everything bothered her—and the last thing she wanted was to cast up her breakfast in Mr. Willmott's corridor.

Beside her, leaning against a dusty longcase clock, Lord Cunningham dabbed his busted lip for the last time. He thrust the handkerchief into his pocket. "It should not be much longer." But his words lacked conviction.

They had already been waiting twenty minutes.

Without chairs, or tea, or explanation.

"And I shall speak on your behalf, of course." Lord Cunningham sent her a coddling look, as if she were some lost child who needed someone to hold her hand.

Maybe she was.

Maybe she did.

But she shook her head anyway, the slight motion bouncing pain back and forth between her temples. "No. I think it best I go in alone."

"Do you think that wise?"

She nodded.

"I respect your determination to face the situation yourself, but I fear now more than ever you shall need support." When she did not answer, he moved away from the clock to stand next to her, hovering close enough she smelled the sweat on his brow, the coppery scent of his blood, and the cinnamon she was becoming so used to.

More nausea churned her stomach.

She almost shrank away or covered her face again—insane impulses, because he was the only man in the world she could trust. Her one ally in a sea of strangers.

Like the stranger who had attacked her today.

Chills raced along her skin, dampening the back of her neck, as images of him flitted across her mind in numbing succession. The loose, ivory-colored shirt rolled up to the elbows, worn under a dull brown waistcoat. The light red beard. The freckles. He appeared rugged, strong, lithe, but there was something about his face—the fine shapes of his eyes and jaw and lips—that was almost striking.

Had she truly seen moisture in his gaze?

No.

Everything happened too fast, like a blur, and anyone who loved her enough for tears would have sparked some form of memory in her own heart. She would have known him, like the lady in the pink pinafore or the man with the tender whispers.

The stranger had stirred nothing in her.

Except panic.

At the end of the corridor, the same butler who had shown them in appeared again. He plastered on an overly bright smile. "Mr. Willmott shall see you now."

It's time.

Her feet wouldn't move.

Even when Lord Cunningham took her elbow in his palm, breathing into her ear "I am right beside you," her body would not respond.

"Ahem." The butler cleared his throat.

Her knees wobbled.

The corridor narrowed tighter, tighter, tighter.

"Do tell Mr. Willmott there has been a change of plans. I shall write to discuss a more convenient meeting and will, of course, pay for his time." Lord Cunningham directed her for the door. "This way, my dear."

"My lord, I..." Explanation died in her throat. She didn't understand it herself. Except that walking down that corridor, unlocking the key to everything, understanding the stranger with the red beard and tear-moistened eyes...

"Do not fret. Today has been most trying for you. What you need now is rest and quiet and"—he swung her back into the painted blue carriage, his touch on her waist lasting several seconds longer than needed—"and home. You need home."

Meade would kill him, but Tom didn't have time for that now.

Crouching back behind the row of bushes, he wiped more sweat from his forehead. Not that it was hot. He'd been positioned between the round-pruned boxwoods and the shading mulberry tree for the past three hours.

Ever since that blasted blue carriage led him through the gates.

The gentleman had grabbed Meg's waist, pulled her down, and escorted her inside a yellow-stoned abbey. She had gone willingly. Eagerly, almost.

Tom wiped both sweaty palms against his trousers. His legs jittered. His mind kept trying to stampede—running to cliff ledges, out of control, tumbling into air with nothing to hold on to.

Except that she was alive.

Gritting his jaw, he honed in on that and nothing else. No matter that she didn't know him. She was injured. Shocked. She would remember, just as soon as he spoke with her alone.

She *had* to remember.

Minutes stretched long and torturous. His stomach growled, more evidence that Mrs. Musgrave was right that he ate too little, and he snuck mulberries to alleviate the pangs.

When dusk deepened, he almost threw them up.

Heart hammering, he peered over the bushes and darted his gaze across the endless candlelit windows. All were still, save for one on the second floor.

A shadow passed back and forth, as if pacing. Then the candle blew out. The world dissolved into blackness—the one thing he awaited.

Tom emerged from behind the bushes, energy shredding his nerves.

Time to get her.

Time to bring her home.

Lord Cunningham was too good to her.

Meg burrowed deeper beneath the downy coverlet, her clean hair dampening the pillow with scents of rosewater. She curled her legs to her chest in the fresh nightgown. Upon their return from Juleshead, she'd scampered to her chamber with dust on her clothes and webs of terror in her mind.

She had expected Lord Cunningham to leave her alone.

By all accounts, he should have. Did he not have other matters to occupy his mind? Why must he always devote himself to her—as if she were something to him? Something more than a lost creature he had discovered beyond his gates?

After two minutes alone in her chamber, he had knocked on the door. "I am sending in a maid, Miss Margaret," he had said. "Do take your time. Rest as much as you please. And if you should grow weary of solitude, know I shall be awaiting you downstairs with something I think you might enjoy."

The maid had bustled in, cooing and fussing over Meg, with her copper tub of warm water and vials of rosewater. Her easy fingers kneaded gently across Meg's scalp. Lathering soap. Dispelling the tension. Washing more than the dust away.

Then, clean and dry and wrapped in a soft blue gown, Meg did what she'd already told herself she would not do.

Found Lord Cunningham.

He awaited her in the library by a glowing silver candlestick, where he patted her next to him on the pillowed, scroll sofa. "I do not know about you, but a dosage of Lord Byron always sets the world to right." He'd spent the long, quiet evening murmuring poetry into her ear.

Soft words like, "*Peace to thy spirit*" and "*The dew I gather from thy lip*" and "*'Tis your friendship alone I request.*"

Now, alone in her bed, the comfort of those words—of this house, this chamber, the man himself—caused her eyes to flutter shut in peace. She could almost blot out today. She could almost forget the shrieking woman in spectacles and the man with the blazing red beard.

Footsteps.

A creak outside her door. Had Lord Cunningham sent yet another maid? Or had he come himself—

Her door whined open and shut so fast she jerked upright.

A shadow whooshed next to her.

Fingers pressed against her mouth, stilling her scream, as a thousand horrors prickled her skin. She bit into flesh—

"Shhh." He was closer to her, one hand in the back of her hair, his nose against hers. "I'm going to let go of ye, Meg, but ye must be quiet. Hear me?"

She bit again, harder, kicking back her head in protest.

"I willnae hurt ye, lass." Something in his stance—the way he did not panic or move too quickly or alter his voice—dampened some of her panic. "I'm going to step back. It's me."

Me. As if that were supposed to mean something to her. It didn't.

Easing backward, still facing her, he found his way to the window and fumbled to light the candle. A frail light glowed a circle around him, illuminating his face, the freckles across his sun-blushed cheeks, the open neck of his shirt, the bleeding palm he wiped across his trouser pants.

She had injured him?

"I want ye to tell me what happened." He set the candle on the mahogany stand beside her bed.

She glanced from it to him to the door. She should scream. Lord Cunningham would have wanted her to scream. But some strange nudge told her the old Meg would not have cowered.

She stood instead, facing him. "Who are you?"

"Tom." When she only blinked, he said again, "Tom McGwen. Ye were hurt. Something happened to ye. Something to make ye forget."

"How?"

"Someone set upon ye and yer uncle. There was a fire."

"How did I get here?"

"I don't know."

"Was there anyone else?" She hated that her voice quivered. She raised her chin to make up for it. "In the house, when the fire started. My mother and father or a—"

"They died when ye were four."

"Brothers or sisters?"

He shook his head.

"My. . .uncle?"

His face tightened. His eyes slanted downward, and when they edged back up, they brimmed in the candlelight. He shook his head again, as if he wanted to speak but couldn't.

Bile crawled through her.

Threads unraveled, all the pink and green and white of the dream she'd fabricated. There was no sweet mother in a pinafore, sending flowers to the wind. No loving father waiting at some cottage window, hoping for her to come home.

No one had loved her, save an uncle? He was dead? She was alone?

"And you?" Her legs threatened to give, so she backed into the edge of the bed without looking at him. "Who are you. . .to me?"

Too many things reared inside him. The dimly lit kitchen back of the apothecary shop, where she'd sewn the rip in his coat while he twisted her hair into outrageous braids. The knitted stockings she always left out to dry on the sill of her bedchamber window. Her indignation when he snatched them. Her burning face when she found them in unlikely places.

Then, just the sand along that quiet moonlit shore, where nothing mattered and everything was still. She had touched him with sandy fingers. She'd splashed. Laughed. Angered at him, then forgiven him, all in the space of a heartbeat.

The girl standing across from him now looked different.

But the same too.

Her stance was rigid, alert, and she wiggled her toe under the hem of her nightgown. She always did that. The reason her stockings ever had holes. Another matter Mr. Foxcroft scolded her for, as if the scuffed boots and lost hair ribbons and torn dresses were not enough.

In a second of unbidden impulse, he leaned forward and touched her lips with his.

Lightly.

His heart stuttered.

Then...

The sweetness of her, the wholeness, sucked him in like a maelstrom. *Meg*. Safe. Alive. Here with him. He shouted at his mind to pull back, to stop his arms from pulling her close, but the weeks without her had severed his control. She was all the things she'd never been before. Cold and unyielding and scented of smells he did not know—

Her palm stung his cheek.

Twice.

Stepping back, he flinched when she wiped her mouth with the sleeve of her nightgown. As if the touch of him had soiled her. As if he were still the stranger she had spotted on North Chapel Street that first afternoon seven years ago.

"Get out of my chamber before I scream."

"If ye were yerself, ye would want to know the truth—"

"I said get out!" With blazing cheeks and wild eyes, she groped for a glass pitcher on her nightstand and flung it at him.

Water sprayed his chest. Glass busted at his feet.

"Get out and stay out. If you ever dare come in here again, Lord Cunningham shall lock you up or worse, and I shall be glad of it." For the second time, she rubbed at her mouth. Some of her composure cracked. Her voice weakened. "Just leave...please."

Parts of him splintered like the glass he crunched over.

He nodded, fled her chamber, as the shocking realization knifed through him.

Meg was not found at all.

What was she doing awake? Tom slipped inside his too-tiny chamber, the open window bathing the room in milky moonlight and warm air.

From a pallet on the floor next to his, Joanie sat upright. She still wore her shoes. "Tom?"

Tossing his boots in the corner, then unbuttoning his vest, he sank down next to her. "Meade kicked ye out of his bed, did he?"

She giggled. "No, he's too nice."

Too nice. *Harrumph.*

"I said I wanted to sleep in here." Joanie slid a glance at him, smiling. "With you."

Tom pulled the shirtsleeves over his head, threw it against the wall, then stretched out flat on his bed. He pulled a woolen blanket over his shoulders. "Ye cold?"

"No."

"Meade fed you?"

"We went to the market and bought apples and mangel wuzels. Then we went fishing. Meade let me hold the pole, but I wasn't good at it." The floor creaked as she rolled to face him. "He said he wanted to call you terrible names, but he couldn't say such things in front of a wee lass."

Tom rolled his eyes. He'd hear all the names himself, come morning. *Morning.* The word reached back out to slap him. Now what?

He hadn't fished in too long. Who knew if Mr. Flemick would welcome him back. What of Joanie? She couldn't sit up here in this sweltering room all day. Nor follow about Meade to hear him curse. Or watch him drink. Or overhear the man throwing horse shoes across the room, in another ill display of temperament.

"Tom?"

"Hmm?"

"Who was the pretty lady? In the painted carriage?"

"Ye best go to sleep."

"She must be very rich." Joanie rustled her blankets. Her voice drifted softer, groggier. "She had such pretty shoes."

Silence swept over the room, save for the night bugs chirping outside the window and a distant dog howling its misery. Tom's eyes weighted. He willed his mind, his lips, not to recall tonight. He thought of the old Meg instead.

Chasing her down a snowy alley last Christmastide.

Swinging her into an arched, limestone doorway, where Mr. and Mrs. Baker hung their rosemary and holly.

The RED COTTAGE

"Tom, let me go this moment or I shall tell Uncle you cannot come for the feast."

"Ye would never."

Pushing at him, laughing, shaking her head. "I would. You can eat your ol' bread and potatoes with Meade, for all I care."

He tickled her for the threat. She hooted and ducked under his arm, then spun on him with a snowball.

The cold snow exploded at his neck, trickling past his scarf, but by the time he formed his own, she had already fled the alley. He ran, ran hard. "Meg—"

Something banged.

Tom jerked awake, one hand already reaching for Joanie.

"Boy, there's something out here wot I think you need to see." Meade's shadow in the doorway, voice slurred.

Tom turned back to Joanie. "Back to sleep with ye." Then he ripped the blankets from himself, fumbled to find his shirt, and hurried it over his head. When he stepped out into the hall, he eased the door shut behind him. "What is it?"

Meade took a long swig from his bottle before answering. "The ratcatcher."

Harsh, orange-glowing lanterns lit the backyard of the galleried coaching inn. Figures clustered together in the small garden: Mr. Willmott, two hostlers, the constable, and young Brownie from the neighboring livery stable.

Tom preceded Meade into the sphere of lantern light. His stomach fell.

Sprawled out beside a shallow hole, a half-decomposed body stared heavenward among cabbage lettuces, gooseberries, and melons. The clothes were clumped with mud. The face indistinguishable. The bones already protruding through the dark sludge of his rotten flesh.

Mr. Willmott handed a handkerchief-wrapped item to Tom. "The hostler here found the fellow. It seems he and the cook had been flogging the poor dog unnecessarily for digging up the garden."

"Ne'er was so persistent 'bout nothing." One of the hostlers reached down to rub the ears of his liver-and-white colored mutt. "Figured I best

69

bring a shovel out 'ere and see for myself."

Tom unwrapped the handkerchief. A dull pocket watch with busted glass. He flicked it open and read the inscription: To my son Hector.

"What happened?" Meade's voice. "Word had it he paid fare for a coach."

"The most unrewarding coins he ever spent, I daresay." Mr. Willmott retrieved the pocket watch. "Some of you men gather his body, if you please, and deliver him to the church. In the morn, I shall talk with the vicar about arranging a hasty burial."

Tom stepped forward. "Sir, whoever did this—"

"McGwen, I am in no temperament for your badgering tonight." He waved dismissively. "I have already been summoned from a very pleasant sleep, dragged out into this infernal mud, and been forced to behold a sight which shall likely unsettle tomorrow's breakfast." As Brownie and the hostlers draped blankets over the body, then loaded him into a cart, the justice of the peace marched away from the garden.

Tom followed. "Someone must have seen something."

"A matter which shall be investigated fully tomorrow."

"How did—"

"He sustained a devastating blow to the head, if his cracked skull is any indication. I do not suppose you had anything to do with this, hmm, McGwen? You were, after all, the only fool I know of who had interest in a lowly ratcatcher."

"Ye know better than that."

"Perhaps I do." Mr. Willmott yanked open the door of his waiting carriage. "But plague me anymore tonight and I shall have the constable throw you in the village lockup on suspicion of murder." Climbing inside, he threw back a wry grin. "Pleasant night, McGwen."

Tom's legs stiffened as the carriage rumbled away into the darkness.

Meade slapped a hand on his shoulder. "Looks to me like your bloodhound nose wasn't far from the scent."

Which mattered very little now.

The scent was dead.

"Our friend Hector must've known a heap more'n someone wanted told."

"I'll find him." Because whoever had killed the ratcatcher was responsible for the fire. For what happened to Meg. For all the reasons she was lost and unsafe and alone—and unable to remember that Tom was someone she loved.

The kiss clung to her, like the echoes of a haunting dream. She lived it over and over and over again, even though she wished she hadn't lived it once.

The uneven breath on her face.

The soft lips, feathering across her own. Then pressing deeper. Tingling her skin, gaining speed like a runaway carriage.

She'd been frightened, but too many seconds passed before she was able to pull back. Before she *wanted* to pull back. That rankled her. Had she ever been kissed before? Had she ever been kissed by him?

"I daresay, we have quite turned you into the proper lady, have we not?"

Meg turned to Lord Cunningham's voice.

He strode into the sunlit morning room, beaming at her, with another poetry book under his arm. He inspected her sloppy needlework with pride. "A boy riding a cart?"

Meg bit her lip against a laugh. "It is the worst rendition of a cupid firing a canon." She pointed to the open pages of *Ackermann's Repository* from which she'd copied the example. "If I ever used a needle before, I must have only darned socks."

"Nonsense. You could never be anything but wonderful at what you do." He pulled the needlework from her lap, closed the magazine, then settled next to her in the plush window seat. "Thus, if it was socks you darned, rest assured you darned them to perfection."

"I fear your confidence is undeserved."

"You deserve the moon."

Instinctively, she glanced away—across the room, to the porcelain urns, the pianoforte, anywhere but at his face.

"Forgive me if I am presumptuous, but when I entered, you seemed rather lost in your own contemplations." He leaned closer. "Indeed, if I do not miss my mark, you were blushing."

Heat soared up her face. A sensation rolled across her lips. Did he know of last night? Should she confess?

"I do not suppose I could be the object of such a fluster."

Before she could answer, the morning room door banged open. A maid rushed in, sweaty wisps of hair poking out from her mobcap, with a hand to her heart. "My lord. I am sorry, but you are being summoned by—"

"Thank you, Mary." Lord Cunningham surrendered his poetry book to Meg. All the pleasure and easiness drained from his face as he nodded her good day, drew in air, and hurried from the room.

Meg pulled the poetry book to her chest. She may have kept last night—and the kiss—from Lord Cunningham just now.

But she was not the only one keeping secrets.

Of that, she was certain.

Meg did not see him again until dinner. All day, the abbey had been quiet. The servants, what little she spotted about, seemed somber and languid in their duties.

When Lord Cunningham scooted into his chair several minutes late, that same despondency echoed in his own face. "I trust you passed the day pleasantly?"

She nodded. "Yes." No. She had done nothing aside from fumble through needlework she hated in a house that did not belong to her. She spooned warm soup santea into her mouth. "And you?"

His smile lifted, then drooped, all without reaching his eyes. "Certainly."

Silence.

She finished her soup, while he took careful bites of the veal, carrots, and celery on his plate. Questions flitted across her mind. Today in the library, she'd discovered an open book on the writings of Hippocrates. The cover had been worn. The open page tear spotted. Why? What obligation, somewhere in the east wing, kept him for hours—sometimes days—and left him haggard upon his return?

"Lord Cunningham—"

"Tomorrow, I thought—"

They spoke in unison.

She took in a breath and smiled, then nodded him on. "Forgive me, my lord. Tomorrow?"

The RED COTTAGE

"An assembly is to be held at the end of the week in Juleshead. It is, of course, a very modest affair and shall be a gathering of unskilled dancers and even worse wardrobes." He took a quick sip of his barsac wine. "But my father always thought it a worthy charity to make local village balls as splendorous as possible, beyond what the mere subscription fares could render. When he passed, I took on the responsibility of donating to events throughout nearby parishes myself."

"That is generous of you."

"Not quite as noble as your tone implies, but thank you." Lord Cunningham finished his wine in one long drink, then nodded to the footman to refill the goblet. "I have not attended one in years. In truth, since boyhood. My father always enjoyed making a brief appearance to witness the grandeur of his efforts." His eyes grew glassy. "It is the only time in my life that I can ever recall truly having...well, *fun*." He shook his head. "Our social station was, of course, very taxing. Our events were plays and we were all actors, instructed to move about and say our lines to perfection, without ever missing a note. The assemblies had no such expectations."

"Did the whole of your family attend?"

"Father *was* the whole of my family."

"You had no siblings?"

"Much to my chagrin, no. My mother died shortly after my birth, and even cousins were so distant I have still yet to meet them." He stood from his chair, seemingly oblivious to the fact that his plate was still half unfinished and his fourth glass of wine had just been filled. "My books were both mother and brother and sister and playmate to me. But enough of my tedious childhood woes. Do you think, my dear Miss Margaret, that an outing to the humble assembly might cheer your otherwise downhearted countenance?"

"If it was a cure to you, perhaps it shall be for me as well."

"My thoughts precisely. Perhaps there shall be acquaintances in attendance who might stir your memory as well." He crossed the table with new energy in his steps. "Now, if you are finished here, what say you to an evening spent in the garden with more of our poems? I fear we were interrupted from the pleasure this morning, and I should very much like to finish our volume."

The warm invitation soothed her. "I shall wait for you at the folly." While he hurried off in search of the book, Meg weaved her way through the corridors that were finally familiar. She exited into the courtyard, walked the length of a sun-streaked cloister, and wandered into the heart of the garden.

The temple-styled folly, with blooming vines crawling up the pillars, sported a stone bench in the center. She sat and smoothed her dress. Then sighed. Then held her breath.

This was comfortable.

She was safe.

With Lord Cunningham, tucked away in this abbey, she could shrink from the frightening unknowns and angst of what she did not know. Her mind could grow lax. While he read poetry to her or smiled at her or encouraged her, she could exist without questioning anything.

But still.

The stranger returned to her, like an infection of the mind. His buttons had been made of wood. One was missing. His cheeks were sunburnt. She knew, not only because they were leathery and pink but because she felt the heat when his face had been in hers—

A blur of motion flashed before her.

Something whipped against her throat.

Course, rough, digging into her skin and cutting off her scream. A body pressed into her back. She groped at her neck, clawing at the rope, mouth open.

No. Help. Black dots scattered across her vision. Pain rushed up and down her in waves of shock. She couldn't breathe. Her head rocked. The rope tightened.

"Stop!" A shout in the distance, then a vicious bark, but the sounds were ringing and the ringing faded. The rope must have fallen, because her body slumped from the bench. Everything was faint, dim, except the sound of her own frantic gasping.

The air hurt.

Everything hurt.

"Margaret. Margaret." Lord Cunningham, lifting her up, rocking her, smelling of the fruity, apricot scent of his wine. "He is gone, and I am here. You are safe, my dear. I promise you are safe."

Her fading consciousness tried to hold on to the lie, even though she knew it wasn't true.

Her one haven in the world had just been shattered.

She was not certain she would be safe anywhere, ever again.

"What I knowed, I already told the justice of the peace, Mr. McGwen." The gangly, sixteen-year-old balanced a tray of foaming tankards on her hip. "Papa told me not to talk to anyone more about it."

"I'll only bother ye a moment."

"More than you've bothered me before, that's certain." Flipping her braid, she paraded toward the wood-framed doorway to the coaching inn taproom—then stopped short. Beer sloshed. Her eyes travelled the length of Tom with a calculating glint. "What do you 'pose you'll be doing now, Mr. McGwen, now that Miss Foxcroft is gone?"

"She is not gone."

"Oh?"

"About Hector—"

"I know you and Miss Foxcroft used to slip out at night." The girl brushed closer to Tom, scented of yeast and mutton and leather. "Papa says every man needs a woman. He's got a fine horse and one of his best silver pieces tucked away for when I get married."

"Miss Creagh." Tom's patience drained like the beer now dripping from her tray. He resisted the urge to thump the wall with his fist. "I'll thank ye to answer my questions."

"And get myself a whippin' with Papa?" She shook her head, grinning. "I don't rightly think so. Now, if we were alone—"

"Betsey!"

The girl jumped, the tray slid forward, and earthenware tankards clattered to the floor in a spray of brown liquid.

Mrs. Creagh, the innkeeper's wife, marched toward them with a glower.

"Clean this up, you little bird-wit. What have I told you about pestering the men like a...like a little..." Biting her tongue, she turned her glare to Tom. "What do you want, McGwen? If you think you're going to go seducing my Betsey just because your—"

"I came to find out about Hector."

"Did you?" Mrs. Creagh harrumphed. "Well, there's nothing to tell except this. He came for a meal that Thursday, after dark, and paid his fare for the morn's coach. We lodged him in one of the chambers upstairs. No, he didn't speak to the likes o' no one, and no, we heard no struggle during the night." She threw up her hands. "We thought he was on the coach with the rest of the passengers until he turns up dead in our garden. If it weren't for all the pigwidgeons about this place, rubbish like this wouldn't happen."

Frustration lined his stomach. He had more questions, too many more, but none they could answer. He thanked them and quit the coaching inn, the sunshine glaring into his eyes.

Joanie sat where he'd left her—leaning against an old barrel, coddling a couple fuzzy orange-and-white kittens. She glanced up with a soft, familiar look. The same one Papa or Mamm had when they'd stumbled upon another lost waif. "I wish I could keep one. The hostler over there said I could."

Meade was on the verge of throwing Tom and Joanie out already. He'd be in a fit of rage over another stray. Although—

"Mr. McGwen." Betsey came tumbling out the door, drenched in beer from her knees down. Her cheek was red, as if she'd just received a slapping for the clumsiness. "There is one thing. Some little nonsense I found in that man's chamber once he was gone." She glanced back, as if to be certain her mother could not hear. "I don't have it with me now, but if you was to meet me out at the wharves come dark, I would bring it for you."

"What is it?"

"Betsey!"

She grimaced at her mother's shrill voice. "I'll bring it tonight" was all she said before she disappeared back inside. The door slammed behind her.

"Come on, Joanie." Tom helped her up, and when she placed the kittens back into the grass, he plucked them up himself. They wiggled and meowed in his grasp. Meade would murder him. "Let's go home."

"I want to see him." The hoarse words came out a whisper. She'd resisted them all night in her sleepless tossing as she clutched the raw, throbbing line across her neck. But then she'd pulled the possibility back over her. Like a teacup of warm milk and honey or a worn chair by the hearthside, the reality of seeing him again soothed her.

Which was nonsense, of course.

She despised the stranger. Did she not?

He had accosted her in the street. He had invaded her chamber. He had been intense and reckless instead of gentle and calm—and then he had done the unthinkable. He had stolen the first kiss she could ever remember giving.

But he knew her.

Or claimed to.

"If I am ever to learn the truth, it is time I cease hiding from it." Meg resituated herself on the pillow-stuffed chaise lounge in the library. She accepted the cup of willow bark tea on its saucer. "Thank you."

"Admittedly, I do not think it a wise course of action." Lord Cunningham knelt before her at the chaise lounge. He readjusted the soft counterpane across her legs. "If anyone should be summoned for answers, Mr. Willmott is certainly the most objective and, I daresay, safest option."

"We may speak with Mr. Willmott another time."

"Miss Margaret—"

"But I feel, somehow, that while Mr. Willmott might offer me facts concerning my life, Tom McGwen might know more."

"You remembered his name."

Meg glanced away. "Not quite, my lord." Did she really wish to tell him of the kiss now? She was not certain that would help her argument. "I know this must be difficult for you to understand, but I just wish to speak with him."

"I do not trust him."

"Nor do I."

"I took the liberty some days ago to find out more concerning this stranger." Lord Cunningham stood and poured himself a cup of tea. He slanted her a look, a hesitant one, as if asking for permission to continue.

"And what did you discover?"

"McGwen arrived in Juleshead seven years ago, yet no one has the slightest indication of where he came from. He is little more than an uncouth vagabond who lives in a room above the blacksmith shop and does nothing better with his time than render trouble." His lips opened, then shut just as quickly with a look of disgust. As if there were more.

"What are you not telling me?" she croaked, a hand on her throat.

Lord Cunningham smiled away the worrisome look. "Suffice it to say, I do not think McGwen was. . .respectful to you, my dear. I am certain, by no fault of your own."

A tunnel of shame burrowed through her. Flashes of the dark bedchamber, his consuming kiss, drew sweat to her hairline. She should have known he was terrible. What in heaven's name had she been embroiled in? What dark and dishonorable secrets haunted her past?

Perhaps Lord Cunningham was right.

Perhaps it was wrong—and dangerous—to invite them all back to light. But did she really have a choice?

"Someone wishes me harm, my lord." She could not bring herself to say the word *dead*. "I assure you, all I wish to do is find out why. Tom McGwen means nothing more to me than that."

"Then it is Tom McGwen you shall have, tomorrow afternoon." Lord Cunningham lowered his teacup back to the library stand. "I shall go ahead and write the letter now. Rest while I am gone, my dear."

"My lord?" She called out to him as he reached the green-paneled doorway. "There is one thing. About last night."

"It is better you do not think of the ordeal."

"When you brought me inside. . .you called for Dr. Bagot. He was already in the house."

Lord Cunningham's expression remained steady, but his eyes seemed unable to meet hers. Was it her imagination, or did they moisten as he lifted his face to the ceiling and sighed? "Dr. Bagot was here because I had requested his stay at Penrose Abbey."

"Why?"

Lord Cunningham finally met her gaze. His words rasped as much as her own, "Because my daughter is dying."

CHAPTER 7

Meg wanted to see him.

Late evening wind rippled through Tom's shirt, his burns no longer irritated by the scratch of fabric. He jogged to the end of the sagging quay.

Gray-blue water sloshed back and forth against the wooden posts, a soothing motion tampering down the tension spiking through him.

He should never have kissed her.

Too many times he'd wanted to clout himself in the head for doing the one thing she always feared. Before, she'd known her fears were ungrounded. That Tom wasn't like the man in the alley.

Now, she didn't.

He paced the edge of the wharf. The sun burned into the horizon, streaking the sky in shades of red and orange and pink. Any minute, the Creagh lass should be here. Whether this was another unfavorable attempt to entrap him or she actually had information, he was not certain.

But he needed something.

Anything.

He was weary of sitting on his hands, doing nothing, while whoever did this walked free. The ratcatcher was already dead. Mr. Foxcroft was already dead.

Tom had no intention of allowing Meg to die too.

"So it be true."

The RED COTTAGE

Tom swiveled at the booming voice. He braced himself as Mr. Creagh stomped forward, rocking the wharf, with tufts of his unkempt hair ruffled by the wind.

"Caught me own daughter tryin' to sneak out here. You might gallivant about at ungodly hours with that Foxcroft chit, but keep your bloody hands off my—"

"I'll thank ye to say nothing more about Meg." Too many emotions, too many furies, had been simmering in the bottom of Tom's gut. His face heated as they flamed higher. "I came because yer daughter said she found something. In the dead man's room."

He scowled, dug into his pocket, and slapped paper against Tom's chest. "Said she spotted it 'neath the bed. The man must have dropped it. We keep e'erything that gets left, in case a gent wants to come back for it. 'Tis a matter of *respect*." He all but growled the last word, like a dog spitting out a bloody tooth. "Stay away from my daughter, McGwen."

Tom managed a nod when his instincts wanted to pummel the man into the ground. He didn't have time for that. Not now.

When Mr. Creagh tramped away, Tom squinted his eyes at the folded, black-edged paper. The writing was tiny, severe, and said only:

You are not doing a wicked deed. Even God would want them dead.

"I do not want to disturb—"

"Come." Lord Cunningham took her hand, the fiber of his gloves itchy against her fingers. He tugged her through the doorway into a chamber that stole her breath.

She did not wish to behold death.

Pathetic.

She knew that as much as she knew the old Meg would have raised her chin, squared her shoulders, and marched toward any unpleasantness. Perhaps the former Meg Foxcroft had been stronger.

With a thud of finality, the door shut behind them.

Pink-globed oil lamps were lit across the room, each flickering with a soft, surreal glow. A dollhouse sat before the hearth. Books lined a floor-to-ceiling shelf. The walls were papered with pink-and-green floral patterns, and the multi-layered draperies were silk and tasseled and lovely.

But it was the bed, in the center of the room, that drew Meg's eyes.

Surrounded by plush cushions and downy coverlets, the child blinked at Meg in dull curiosity. "Who have you brought, Father?"

"Allow me to introduce the charming Miss Margaret, our newest guest." Lord Cunningham skirted around Meg, sank to the edge of the bed, and pressed a kiss to the child's tight, white-blond curls. "How are you, darling?"

"I am very bored."

"What might I do to alleviate such a state?"

"I want a new maid." The girl sent a pouting glare at the older woman, seated across the room. "Jenny is horrid, and I hate her. Make her leave and get me a new one, please."

"Violet."

"But I do hate her."

"We cannot simply replace a maid as easily as we might order a new miniature horse." He sent an apologetic smile at poor Jenny, as if the conversation were amusing despite its absurdity. "Now, tell Miss Margaret how old you are."

"I am seven, but shall likely never be eight." Her serious, pale-blue eyes held Meg's. Her skin was snowy and perfect, like an ivory doll dressed in bows and satin. Perfect ringlets stuck to her head, short and gleaming, with one falling across her temple.

She was beautiful.

Haunting.

The unexplainable need to draw closer to the bed, nurture her, stir medicine, cool fevers, cure the illness. . .well, it was near choking. Had Meg assisted her uncle before the fire? Was tending bedsides second nature to her?

"How old are you?" Violet asked, as if expecting the information returned.

Meg hesitated. How old had the newspaper read? "Nineteen."

"Father is two and thirty."

"Though much younger in heart," he assured.

The child tilted her head at Meg. "How long do you plan to stay?"

"I am not yet certain."

"Father says he shall never marry again, but if I ask him to, he will. Won't you marry him, please?"

"Oh." Unexpected heat scorched the tips of Meg's ears. The very idea. "I do not think—"

"Because I do so wish to have a party. No one gets married without one, do they? We might have cake and ice sculptures and lemon syllabub—"

"If you wish lemon syllabub, I shall have Cook prepare you a dish tomorrow," said his lordship.

"But I want a party."

"I fear the doctor would not be fond of such a scheme."

"He is terrible. He spoils everything. I hate him too." Violet yanked the coverlets over her head, and though Lord Cunningham attempted to coax her out again, she refused to budge. With a reluctant kiss to her blanketed form, he led Meg back into the hall, where he expelled a breath.

"You must forgive her temperament. It is only the illness that makes her so disagreeable."

"Certainly." Meg smiled to assure him, though something nagged at her. "She is rather a brilliant child, I think."

"Yes. As was her mother." He cleared his throat, and a rare flush of embarrassment extended beyond his cravat. "Of course, you are in no wise bound to wed me for the sake of lemon syllabub and ice sculptures."

Meg laughed away the words. "You need not worry. I shall deter her against the nonsense at every opportunity."

She expected him to agree, to make known his own mission to pacify his daughter by other means. But his eyes stayed still on Meg, heavy and focused and portraying a message that dropped her stomach in unease.

As if his daughter's request were not nonsense at all.

The high-pitched meow echoed throughout the anteroom.

"Shh." Tom cradled the clawing kitten back under his coat flap. "Quit yer whining or I'll let Meade feed ye to the dogs yet." He brushed away the orange-and-white hairs from his vest—and frowned. He never paid his clothes much mind. Before, it never mattered when he snagged a hole in his trousers, because he'd always gone that evening to Meg and she had patched it up. He never cared when his shirts bleached duller in the sun or when the sleeves were a little frayed, because Meade was always soot stained and Meg usually had no shoes and no one seemed to notice anyway.

Here was different.

He leaned against the pristine wall, next to a cherub-sculptural column, on floors that were black-and-white squared marble. Discomfort scratched through him. He combed his hands through his beard, then his hair, for the hundredth time.

He should have worn his Sunday waistcoat.

Or polished his boots.

"Mr. McGwen." The squinty-eyed butler returned, sneezed for the third time, and motioned Tom to follow.

Their squeaking footsteps matched the pound of his chest. Sweat dampened his back, as the ornately carved drawing room doors swung open and the butler announced him.

Wiggling the kitten closer, Tom strode inside. The room swallowed him. Grandeur colors, the suffocating scent of roses, gilded mirrors, and intricate wall murals.

Then Meg.

Sitting on the edge of a striped sofa with her hands clasped in her lap, her eyes watched him with disapproving wariness. Her dress was gold embroidered and navy. Her hair pinned back. Her lips tight. "I am grateful you came, Mr. McGwen."

Had she thought he wouldn't?

"I have many questions, and it is my wish that you would enlighten me." Her focus shifted to the moving bulge inside his coat, one brow raised.

"Brought this for ye."

She did not move.

Nor accepted the kitten when he approached.

"Joanie went to calling it Pippins. Ye can call it what ye like." He settled it on her lap. "Ye always wanted one, but yer uncle would have nothing of it."

Her jaw hardened, but she swept the kitten to her chest anyway.

The meows softened. Faint purring filled the room. "Won't you sit, Mr. McGwen?"

He didn't want to sit. He wanted to sweep her from the couch, pull out the hair pins, tug off the slippers peeking out beneath her delicate trim.

He wanted to catch her face and make her look at him.

Rub her cheeks.

Unwind her unnatural curls.

Make her laugh at him, like she'd always laughed before.

"Mr. *McGwen*."

"I'll stand."

"I would rather you did not." When he did not budge, she came to her feet. Some of that old fury, that old fire, eroded at her stiff formalities. "I shall be very frank with you. After our last two encounters, it is necessity alone that drove me to see you again. I wish to do this as quickly as possible, and then you may leave. Is that understood?"

"I suppose yer coddling lord will make sure of it."

"How dare you insult him."

"I'm insulting *ye*." He grinned, but it trembled. "For letting him."

"I do not have to listen to—"

"Ask yer questions, Meg." He pulled her down onto the sofa next to him. Her arm brushed against his coat. Jolts zipped through him. "Ye hate porridge. Ye know how to make potions and medicines like most women know how to bake bread. And ye would never"—he reached up to flick her perfectly round curl—"wear yer hair like that."

"Do not touch me."

"Ye fight a lot."

"With you?"

"And yer uncle."

"Then we were not close." Her lips flattened, and despite her efforts to look unaffected, disappointment moistened her gaze.

"He was an old goat. Always trying to make ye do what ye didn't want. Fussing with ye. One day ye'd be locking yerself in yer chamber and saying ye'd never speak to him again, and the next day ye'd be on his lap and laughing at him for hiding his smiles." Tom's knees bounced. He looked away. "Ye fought with fierceness but loved the same way."

"I am glad." A whisper. "And you? How did we. . .I mean, how is it we first. . .became acquainted?"

"We were twelve."

"And?"

"I was new in Juleshead. On my own." He moved from the sofa a little too fast, thrusting his hands in his pockets. The memories pricked him like a needle in his flesh. He hadn't eaten in two days. He'd been sleeping in an alley doorway at night and scouring the village for work from dawn till dusk.

He hadn't minded the hunger.

His punishment, he guessed.

For Caleb.

"How did we meet?" she pressed.

"A wee gang of village lads thought to rough me up." He turned his back to her. "Ye thought to stop them." With her weaponized basket, which she swung at many a head. With her hair in messy braids. With her rolled-up trousers and her flushed face and her livid eyes.

When the lads scampered away, she'd stood over top of Tom with her hands on her hips. She knew he was hungry when no one else had bothered to notice. "Come to the apothecary shop tonight, and I'll see that Uncle makes another plate."

He had nodded, but he hadn't gone.

She was everywhere after that—spotting him in the meat market, waving at him across the docks, even showing up at the blacksmith shop on an errand for her uncle after Tom found work and a room.

Maybe he hadn't gone because a lass had rescued him. In some blundering way, she'd taken a swing at his pride and kicked him harder than the street lads.

Or maybe because he knew, all along, that Meg Foxcroft would see things about him he didn't want known. That she'd make him happy. That she'd make him forget what he'd done when it was his duty to remember.

"I suppose it does not matter greatly." Her dress ruffled as she stood. "Not now."

As if it were all over.

As if there were no Tom and his Meg.

The RED COTTAGE

He was back to a world where she didn't know him or love him or care if he stayed in the sun too long or ate raspberries or visited home. His chest tightened. He turned to face her.

She met his eyes with full strength. With one finger, she tugged at her fichu. A dark bruise discolored her skin. "I want to know who wants me dead."

His blood chilled in shock.

Someone had hurt her.

Again.

No.

"Please, Mr. McGwen."

Panic shredded his voice, "I dinnae know."

CHAPTER 8

Too many times she had to look away from him. She wasn't certain why. Perhaps because he had kissed her, this handsome stranger. The shame, the angst, the terribleness of his kiss lingered between them—and the sensations plagued her still. Why could she not get it out of her head?

She had no right to think of his lips.

But she glanced at them now, just one reckless glance.

They were full and firm, surrounded by a well-trimmed beard. Wiry against her skin, she remembered. Why did he have a beard?

Lord Cunningham didn't.

He would look ridiculous.

"When did this happen?" Tom McGwen did not move, but she sensed he wanted to.

On an impulse, Meg circled around the sofa, putting it between them to safeguard herself from another one of his outbursts. The last thing she could bear was to be assaulted again. Even if it were by tender hands. "Night before last. Lord Cunningham frightened the man away but could not see his features. He wore something over his face."

"Ye cannae stay here."

"Do not be ridiculous."

"Meg, this is no time for ye to be stubborn." He said the words with gentle pleading. As if he had coaxed her before. As if she had resisted him.

Then yielded—which she had no intention of doing now.

"We were unaware of the danger then. Now we are not." She straightened her shoulders. "Besides, Lord Cunningham is more than capable of protecting me."

"I want to protect ye."

"You presume too much—"

"I *will* protect ye." Stepping closer to the sofa. Leaning forward. Hands on the back of the furniture as his eyes burrowed into hers with furious passion. "And I will find out who did this to ye. And I will stop them. And I will help ye remember. And I will bring ye home. And I will build ye our cottage. And I will paint it red. And I will marry ye, Meg Foxcroft."

Her breath shallowed. Weakness climbed her legs, and despite the fact she shook her head in protest, her tight grip of emotions began to spiral.

Before she could say a word, Tom McGwen departed the room.

She scrubbed dry her cheeks with vehemence.

He was wrong, in every point.

Because she had no intention of ever seeing the man again.

"Tommy!" Joanie scampered up from behind the kitchen table, little Gyb—as she'd named the kitten—dangling from one arm.

The hearth sputtered with flames, crackling beneath a steaming iron cauldron. The heavy scents of woodsmoke and venison stirred Tom's hunger.

"Meade already left. He said he had to visit a friend."

The tavern, more likely.

"But he said we could eat without him." With the same blissful diligence of Mamm, Joanie bustled around the kitchen—clanking earthenware bowls to the table, pouring mugs of coffee, and slicing two thick chunks of bread from an already stale loaf.

When they sat across from each other, she opened up her hand to him. He hesitated.

He had not prayed—nor linked hands, as Papa taught them—in seven long years. The last thing he wanted was to mutter thanksgiving now. Especially to a God who did not exist.

Or had failed Tom, in every way imaginable, even if He did.

He grasped Joanie's fingers anyway. "Ye can say it, lass."

"I did it last time."

"Go on."

Her prayer was quiet, bashful, but possessed the same sweet sincerity as Meg. As if it never occurred to them that God could not be real or good or just or all the lofty things the vicar shouted from his pulpit.

They ate in silence.

The kitten wandered under the table, climbing up Tom's trouser legs, meowing until Joanie slipped him dripping chunks of venison. Heat from the hearth rolled sweat down Tom's temples.

Everything tasted bitter.

Hard to swallow.

The food settled like millstones in his gut.

"You went to see the lady again." With the table cleared, Joanie untied her linen pinafore and allowed Gyb to play with the strings. "The one from the carriage with pictures on it."

"Meade told you?"

She nodded.

"What else did he say that wasnae his business?"

"You don't want me to know?"

He scooted from the table. "Almost dark outside. Time ye get to bed, hmmm?"

"So you can visit a friend too?"

So he could figure out a way to stop what was left of his pathetic life from unraveling. He needed to keep things together. Needed to keep *himself* together.

For Meg.

And his sister.

With a solemn nod of understanding, Joanie tucked Gyb into her arms and slipped away.

The kitchen was too quiet without her.

He opened a window, found one of Meade's old pipes, and breathed in the tobacco-scented smoke. His head buzzed. He needed to get out of this place. He needed to be closer.

After he'd departed the gates of Penrose Abbey on his livery-rented horse, he'd scoured the neighboring tenant houses and nearby cottages for anything empty.

Almost hidden from the road, a thatched roof and brick chimney had caught his eye. He'd ridden closer.

The place was lifeless, save for a small herd of wild geese in the overgrown yard.

The fence was gray and splintered.

The whitewashed walls grimy.

The door face-forward on the ground.

But as he'd leaned inside, brushing back cobwebs, some of the turmoil in his brain stilled. As if the old place, the old boards, the creaking floor—so close to Meg—might give him something tangible he could fix. Something he could control.

"Tom?"

He glanced back at the kitchen doorway. Joanie stood with sagging shoulders, her eyes wider than crown coins.

"What is it, lass?"

"There's a spider." She wrung her hands. "In the rafters."

"A wee spider won't hurt ye."

"Oh." She nodded, as if he were right of course, as if she should have known better. She turned to leave—

"Wait, lass." He dumped the ashes of his pipe into the hearth, then preceded Joanie up the narrow stairwell and into the chamber. He took off his boot and bit back a grin as he utilized his childhood skill of climbing furniture and edging up walls.

Meg might hate him.

The killer was yet unfound.

He had a sister he did not know what to do with, in a shop he couldn't stay in, with a mind too frenzied to resolve anything.

But he could kill a spider in the rafters.

That much he could do.

"I cannot dance." At the confession, both Lord Cunningham and Violet glanced up from the white-knitted picnic blanket.

For the past week, Penrose Abbey had been different. The ancient corridors were less empty and dim. The windows more sunlit. The rooms all a bit cheerier, with their fresh vases of flowers and the joyous floral scents.

Perhaps it was the absence of Lord Cunningham's secret. Why had he kept such a thing in the first place? Did he not think her capable, after he had borne her troubles, for her to bear his?

Only in her bedchamber, at night, did the merriment pass.

Darkness cloaked her, wrapped about her soul, as she blew out the final candle.

Because she thought of him.

Tom.

She knew every line he'd spoken to her by heart, she felt his lips, and she chilled beneath the powerful intensity of his eyes. When she was awake, halfway into the night, she thumped her pillow and tossed and huffed in frustration. When she was asleep, she was dragged unwillingly back into his arms, into haunting memories of him she knew weren't real.

He had loved her.

That much she felt.

Had she loved him?

Doubtful.

No, she had likely been lonely and he a preying companion. Or foolish and him the luring pursuer. Which explained, of course, her fear of him. Why else should he discomfit her so? Why else should she resist the thought of ever seeing him again but, at the same time, think of nothing else?

Lord Cunningham deemed the man a rogue.

Her past, from all accounts, had been lovely. She had lived a pleasant life with her uncle in a pleasant apothecary shop, pleasantly assisting the ill and aching.

Tom McGwen had been the one stain on her lily-white existence.

She could not be blamed for wishing to rub that stain away.

Or for having trouble doing so.

"Even *I* know how to dance, and I am only seven."

"Violet." Lord Cunningham shook his head at his daughter, though he smiled. "You must remember that our darling Miss Margaret has not all of her memories. She may be more proficient at dancing than either of us."

The RED COTTAGE

"She cannot be better than you."

Lord Cunningham took another quick drink of his ginger beer, as if to keep from a laugh. "My daughter, as you can see, does like to flatter me. What is it you want, my dear child?"

"I wish to go punting on the lake."

"You forget we made our good doctor a promise. An hour of fresh air and that is all. No exertion whatsoever."

Violet crossed her arms over her chest with a pitiful glance at the rippling, sky-reflecting lake. Beyond it in the distance, Penrose Abbey sat crested among trees and bushes, a tranquil backdrop to their picnic.

"Very well." Violet scooped up a handful of nuts and crunched on them a little too loudly. "I am used to being disappointed."

"My dear—"

"Won't you teach Miss Margaret how to dance? I want to watch. Please say yes. You never, ever allow me any amusements."

His eyes hurried to Meg—a bit too eagerly, though he cleared his throat as if this were a sacrifice they both must make for the sake of indulging his daughter.

Meg placed her empty plate back into the wicker basket. "I suppose with the assembly ball tomorrow, I should know a little."

"Precisely." Lord Cunningham helped her to her feet. "Though I warn you, I am no caper merchant. And with no music or set, this might all be quite in vain."

The ridiculous urge to wiggle out of her slippers came over Meg. She ignored the notion.

"Perhaps we should begin with simple footwork. The chassé step, perhaps." He took both of her hands, though she sensed that was not entirely necessary. "*Temps levé* and step forward with your right foot. Very good. Now the left foot follows the right and takes weight."

The breeze was warm, too warm, catching scents of roasted lamb and pickled vegetables and strawberries. She fumbled through the steps once. Then twice.

Violet clapped, though without any true enthusiasm, and Lord Cunningham continually whispered in her ear, "You are marvelous. Now again."

By the time he had pulled and tugged her through the fleuret step and the basic formations of a cotillion, her breathing came faster and the curls brushing against her face were damp with sweat. "I think I have learned so much that tomorrow, I shall likely not remember any of it."

His arm snaked around her back, pulling her against him. "I shall be there to remind you of everything." The skin of his cheek brushed her temple. Smooth, clammy with sweat. His body squeezed her closer.

With a faint laugh, she extracted herself from him and did what she had wanted to do all afternoon: kicked off her slippers. "I think Violet is right. A little punting on the lake would be most restful, and I am certain not even Dr. Bagot could object to such a small adventure."

Lord Cunningham shook his head. "The two of you are against me. Very well. I surrender." But when the servants went about to fetch the punting boat, and Violet hurried another cherry turnover into her mouth, and Meg poured herself a glass of punch...

A hair-raising sensation prickled her.

She twisted every direction on the blanket. She glanced from the lake to the hillsides to the abbey and beyond.

Nothing.

No one watching her.

"Are you well, my dear?" Lord Cunningham settled next to her.

She nodded, but the bumps on her arms remained. Because someone was out there. Whether she had imagined it just now or not, that someone would be back. They would find her.

And they would finish what they'd already failed to do twice.

See her dead.

She was here.

The barrel wobbled beneath him as Tom stared through the smudged panes and paint-peeling slats of an assembly room window. Inside, candles glowed everywhere. They reeked of tallow and grease and memories.

Like the first time Tom had coaxed thirteen-year-old Meg into nighttime mischief. Or she had coaxed him. He couldn't remember now which it had been, but either way, they'd planned everything so well.

The RED COTTAGE

Tom arm wrestled young Brownie into claiming he'd been horse kicked. Meg baked the boy apples to make up for it.

When Mr. Foxcroft was called away to help the boy, just as the yellow summer moon came out, Tom was waiting outside her bedchamber window. They snuck here in the twilight. Stood outside the windows on these very barrels and watched those who had enough coinage to pay for tickets to dance the night away.

"I wish I could dance." Meg's hair was down that night. Wavy to her elbows, catching moonlight, smelling of soap and grapeseed. *"And wear one of those dresses, so I could swish-swish around."* She rocked the barrel with the pretend rustling of a gown.

"Why don't ye?"

"Don't I what?"

"Ye know." He shrugged. *"Wear a dress sometimes."*

"I wear one every Sunday. If you'd come, Tom McGwen, you'd see me."

"I've no time for it."

"Then I hope your ol' boat sinks and you never catch a fish again." She leaned closer to the window, closer to him without meaning to. Her hair tickled his cheek. *"And I would not sit with you, even if you did come."*

"Ye never answered me."

"About what?"

"Why ye dinnae wear dresses."

"Uncle doesn't like me to."

"Why?"

Her bottom lip slipped beneath her teeth. He was never certain if it was candlelight or moonlight or tears that made her eyes so glassy, but she didn't answer. *"Don't ask me things like that, Tom."* Then she pointed to some lady with a too-large feather plume, laughed when Mrs. Whalley spilled her negus, and devised plans they would not execute to break inside the assembly ball.

He had not asked her about the dresses again.

She told him her secret two years later.

He never told her his.

"You don't learn nothing, do you, boy?" Meade's voice behind Tom, yanking him from the past with all the cruelty of a punishing matron.

"Some fools wear trouble 'bout their neck like dogs do chains."

Tom hopped from the barrel and squinted into the darkness.

Two forms, not one, stared back at him.

"Joanie?"

"Told you before, boy. I'll not be the one lookin' after your strays." But unlike his words, his giant hand was gentle as he guided Joanie forward.

And when she stepped into the light of the window, she wore her best dress and polished shoes, with a bright new ribbon in her hair. One Meade must have bought her himself.

"Here." The blacksmith smacked Tom in the chest with two wrinkled tickets. "Some buzzard at the taver—I mean, ahem, my *friend* had a few wot he couldn't use. Fellow was down with a toothache. Happens to him sometimes." Then he turned to Joanie and, whether it was the way she gleamed up at him or only the fact he'd had enough ale to make any fool cheery, his lips inched up into a smile. Barely.

But a smile nonetheless.

The lass was getting to him.

"Now make certain you don't be bangin' and wakin' the dead tonight when you come home or I'll be takin' it out of your hide." He nodded, grunted, then disappeared into the darkness.

Joanie's hand slipped in Tom's. "I hope you're not angry," she whispered. "I told Meade you wouldn't want me to come. But I can wait right here on the barrel and you can come for me when you're done; and I can give Meade back his ribbon if you think I should."

"I think Meade would have no use for it, lass."

Joanie smiled but slipped away from him and took her dutiful seat on the barrel. "I'll only peek in the window once or twice. If you think no one would see."

"Ye won't have to." Tom pulled her back off the barrel. "We go in, we go in together."

Eyes wide, Joanie made a breathless sound half fear and half pleasure.

Tom took her hand.

As he led her around the side of the old building, up the stone steps, and to the brass-knobbed door, his stomach spun with the same trepidation. Because the lass inside was not Meg Foxcroft, who trusted Tom with her secrets and looked at him with soft, trusting, eager eyes.

She was a woman with unnatural curls.

In a dress too low at her chest.

On the arm of a man she would have laughed at, with Tom, only weeks before.

"Tickets, sir."

Tom handed them over, and when the entrance door squeaked open, caught his first sight of Meg's glittering silver gown in the crowd. He couldn't move his feet. Or his gaze.

His precious Meg was a stranger.

And all she would see was a man in plain brown clothes with an improper beard—who had nothing in the world worth making her look twice.

CHAPTER 9

Everyone stared at her. She bumped shoulders with too many people. The white-haired woman—Mrs. Whalley, she said—with loud exclamations of sympathy on her negus-scented breath. "Heaven be merciful, but with all the dilemmas you are always getting yourself into, I thought certain you had finally met your demise."

Another woman, thinner, quieter, with spectacles. "I am Alice Grier. From the bookstore—"

"Miss Foxcroft." This time a gentleman. Large, wearing a ridiculous periwig, with wafer crumbs spilled on his tailcoat. "As justice of the peace here in Juleshead, I wish to offer you my sincere condolences. Mr. Foxcroft was a good man, and his benevolence to this parish will not be forgotten…"

Then him, standing in her line of vision.

Tom McGwen.

A surge of too many emotions welled insider her. Anger that he had come. Relief, almost, that he had. *Absurdity.* She clawed the thought away and resisted the pull to chance another glance at him.

He had trimmed his beard shorter to his face, and the hair, usually a little wind tousled, was combed carefully in place. His cheeks were gleaming and clean, if not a little sun kissed. He wore finer clothes than she'd seen hitherto—black breeches and a simple brown frock coat—and she scolded herself for noticing the strength tightening his sleeves.

The RED COTTAGE

Blood hastened to her face as she tightened her grip on Lord Cunningham's arm. "I—I know none of these people."

"You are doing tremendous." His encouragement was cut off by another gentleman and his wife, who pressed close to Meg and asked her too many questions about fire and injury and a night she had no memory of.

"I fear Miss Foxcroft prefers not to speak of anything so somber." Lord Cunningham guided the conversation to safer topics—the weather of late and how in need of repair the roads were after so much spring rain.

The conversation droned in her ear.

She squirmed.

For the second time, now farther way, Tom McGwen's gaze collided with hers. He stood on the other side of the ballroom, leaning against the timber-beamed wall with a young girl clinging to his hand.

Couples passed between them.

A few grating fiddle notes struck the air.

The haze in the room thickened, as if more than one gentleman were puffing on his pipe—but every time the space between her and Tom McGwen was clear, his eyes remained on hers.

She excepted him to come barreling toward her, but he didn't.

Why?

"Remind me to cease being so sentimental." Lord Cunningham dropped the words in her ear as the couple finally sashayed away to join the set. "These assembly balls are far more rustic and unbearable than my childhood memory recounts. Are you well?"

She nodded, but she wasn't.

"Are you hungry? I have been once already to the supper room, and I fear there is not much to entice save a few wafers, pistachio prawlongs, and as many bruised fruits as you can imagine." His lips grazed her ear. "But perhaps orgeat lemonade?"

"Yes." Her throat was tight. Her slippers tight. The skin on her face tight. "Lemonade, please."

"I shall be but a moment."

In his absence, more strangers were already closing in on her. She murmured excuses. With her forehead thundering, she squeezed past shoulders and bumped her way toward a green-curtained window.

She turned her back to the room, to the music, to everyone.

Then he was there.

Close enough that his stance, as she turned, blocked out the turmoil of the ballroom.

"How dare you come here and follow me."

"Ye ought to dance, Meg."

"What?"

"I said ye ought to dance." His jaw tightened as he looked away, then back to her face. Candlelight danced on his features. He was a stranger, yes—but here, amidst all these faces she'd never seen—he was a faint anchor to familiarity. "Ye said ye always wanted to, so ye ought to do it."

"I would no sooner dance with you than I would—"

"I didnae ask ye to dance with me."

"Margaret." Behind Tom, Lord Cunningham strode forward with a sloshing goblet of lemonade. He pressed it into her hand with narrow eyes. "Everything is well, I presume?"

She hesitated.

Tom answered instead, "Everything is well." Then he was gone, weaving back through the crowd, disappearing into the muted colors of age-faded dresses and drooping feathers.

"It escaped my notice he was in attendance, else I would not have abandoned you."

She took a shaky sip of the lemonade. The sour, tangy liquid nearly choked her. "I wish to go home."

"Then he *has* distressed you."

"No."

"This must cease." Lord Cunningham started forward, but she grasped the sleeve of his tailcoat and skirted in front of him. Lemonade spilled.

"No. It is not him. It is. . .everything."

"I shall not allow him to torment you with each new encounter."

"He did nothing unkind to me."

"He is dangerous."

"You do not know that."

"Yes, Margaret. I know more of the man than you think." Lord Cunningham breathed a resigned sigh, his shoulders deflating. "Nevertheless,

The RED COTTAGE

I am not so unwise, nor so unkind, as to burden you with that now. If you wish to go home, we shall depart immediately. Now finish your drink, and I shall send the servant to prepare the carriage."

Lost. The word cut through her as she backed against the wall, drained her goblet, and waited for Lord Cunningham to return. She should not have come. Lord Cunningham had encouraged that the event might cheer her. That greeting those she once knew might pour light into the darkness of her mind.

He was wrong.

She was wrong—for coming, for imagining she could step back into her old world and somehow still belong. What was the matter with her? How could this happen?

She curled her fist and resisted the urge to scream, hunt down Tom McGwen again, and demand he tell her who she was. Who she *really* was. Why she felt so lost. Terribly, unbearably lost.

"The carriage awaits." Lord Cunningham returned and took her hand in his gloved one. "This way."

This way. Why did his words bounce back off her? *This way.*

Her legs moved, but the floor shifted. The glass slipped between her fingers. Shattered. *No.* She must have kept moving, led by his hand, dragged through endless waves of people, because the old arch-framed door blurred before her...

Her body careened.

She plummeted forward, knees whacking floorboards. *No, no.* Her muscles spasmed. Colors dotted across her vision. *Lost, lost, lost.*

A scream floated somewhere above her, but it was distant and unreal. Her body melted into the floor.

The wood smelled like mildew and cobwebs and soil and death. *God, help me.* She was not ready to die. She had too much to remember. *Please.*

Arms gathered her up. Her face squashed into a solid, earth-smelling chest—but when she squinted up, there was no perfect black kerseymere tailcoat or white neckcloth or shiny pale skin.

"Out of the way!"

"What are you doing—"

A mild oath. Then fresh, cool air. Then grass beneath her back, hands in her hair, with shouts of wine and laudanum. The sky was too big, too black. The darkness reached down and stole her away.

But not before she felt her face itch with the softest lips and beard. For the faintest second, she was not lost.

She had never been here before.

Not in his chamber, with its cracked plaster walls and messy makeshift bed. His patched clothes—and one of her socks—hung from pegs beside the door. The window bore no curtains. The air smelled of salt and soot and whatever Meade had baked downstairs a few hours before.

Tom tucked his woolen blanket under her chin.

Strange, that she should be here now.

In his bed.

When she didn't even know him.

He had the faint urge to grab her stolen sock from the peg, place it next to her, to return the moment she awoke. She probably had dozens of socks now. Ones that weren't threadbare at the heels and discolored from age.

For the first time in three hours, her head curled sideways on his pillow. The ringlets had long since lost their hold. He'd taken the pins out himself.

Her hair was everything it had always been—messy and smooth and wavy across his pillow, like honey he was starved for but forbidden to touch.

Behind, the door squeaked open again and Lord Cunningham's voice whispered into the chamber, "How does she fair?"

"Still asleep."

"My own esteemed physician should be arriving any moment. As soon as she awakens, I wish to transport her to the nearest inn and secure her a proper bed."

As if the pallet on the floor were not good enough. Maybe it wasn't.

But Tom had carried her here anyway.

With Meg collapsed on the assembly room floor, Lord Cunningham had seemed too unraveled to make any decision. As villagers crowded in, trying to assist, clamoring remedies, Tom had done the only thing he could think to do.

The RED COTTAGE

Get wine down her throat, ten drops of laudanum, and bring her home. Where he could sit as close to her as he could.

Watch the door.

The windows.

Everywhere.

"For all my proficiencies in medicine, I fear in a moment of crisis it all abandoned me." Lord Cunningham's words rang with a true note of care. A realization that both comforted Tom.

And bothered him.

"Shout for me the moment she stirs. I shall go await Dr. Bagot." The door squeaked shut just as the first sunbeams of morning slanted through the window. They brightened a million dust motes.

Tom leaned against the wall, counted them, massaged her hand beneath the blanket.

Until her fingers twitched.

"Meg." He slid to his knees, blood pumping, as her sweaty face thrashed back and forth.

Her lashes fluttered.

"Shhh. Ye're not hurt." That wasn't true, but he'd heard both her and Mr. Foxcroft murmur it to frightened patients, and the lie always seemed to do more good than harm. "Ye're doing a wee bit of resting. That's all."

"My lord." Breathy. She squinted up at him, confused, as if neither his words nor his face held the power to sooth her. "Where is. . .Lord Cunningham?"

"Downstairs."

Her eyes fell shut again. "I feel very. . .sick."

"Dinnae speak."

"What happened?"

"Ye were. . ." *Poisoned? Almost killed again?* His blood boiled. "Ye fell ill at the ball. Lord Cunningham and I brought ye here."

"Where is. . ." As if sensing the answer, her sentence trailed off. She jerked from the pillow too quickly. Ripped from the blanket. Yanked from his hand. "Get me out."

"Meg, ye're in no danger."

"Lord Cunningham!" A scream. Veins protruded in her neck as she strained against his arms easing her down. "My lord! Help!"

"Meg—"

Her hand slapped across his face.

The sting zipped through him, like a lightning bolt, and he relinquished any hold on her. He backed away. The other side of the chamber. The farthest corner, but it wasn't far enough. *Can't.* He could not look at her. Instead, he stared at her sock hanging limply on his peg. *I cannae do this.*

She stumbled for the door, but doubled over and retched before she could grab the knob.

Vomit splattered the floorboards.

Stained her dress.

Her hair.

She sobbed, and for the first time in his life, he could not make her stop.

"Miss Foxcroft." The child was a blur of long brown hair and checkered green cotton.

The stairwell narrowed.

Splinters in the banister prickled her flesh.

"Let me help you." Hurrying up the steps, the child weaved a gentle arm around Meg's waist. She smelled warm, like oatmeal scones. "His lordship just departed for the stables. That way he can see the doctor coming."

"I—I need to sit."

"This way." The girl led Meg into a small kitchen, where she scooted a chair with peeling paint out from the table. The hearth fire crackled. "You can rest here. Move, Gyb." She shooed a kitten from the seat, then hurried to dunk a rag into a bucket of water. She hesitated. "May I?"

Meg nodded.

The cool cloth swished at her chin, her neck, then the splotches on her silver-netted dress. The acrid taste of bile soured her mouth. "You were with. . .him." Her stomach quivered. "At the ball."

"Tom is my brother."

"Oh." Another person Meg should know. But didn't. "Forgive me. I—I do not remember your name."

"He probably didn't speak of me." With a careful stroke, Joanie leaned closer. "I don't think he talked of home. Meade said he didn't."

"Meade?"

"The blacksmith. He's outside with the constable. In case they come back."

"They?"

"Whoever put camphor in your lemon—" She bit her tongue as her eyes lifted to someone behind Meg. Her cheeks pinkened. "My name is Joanie, Miss Foxcroft. You can call me Joan if you like. My sisters did."

The hair on the back of Meg's neck lifted. She sensed him behind her. Tom McGwen. In the doorway. Watching her, no doubt, with his troubling blue eyes.

"I hope you liked Pippins."

God, help me.

"Gyb is his brother."

Please.

"They're very troublesome, Meade says, but I think they're sweet."

She should not have run. Nor struck him. Nor looked at him as if he were the one who had slaughtered her uncle and poisoned her drink and stripped her memory.

But the chamber had been too small.

The sickness had disoriented her.

She was weary—and frightened—of being in places she did not recognize with people she did not know. "Excuse me." She stood faster than she meant to, bumping into Joanie and sending the kitten scampering. "I must f–find Lord Cunningham."

"I will walk beside you, miss."

Meg braced herself to face him, but when she turned to the kitchen doorway—Joanie on her arm—he was already gone.

Her heart faltered with a strange measure of regret.

Whether Tom McGwen was untoward or not, whether he was capable of the sins Lord Cunningham accused or innocent, one thing was certain.

He *had* loved her.

He must have.

Because as she clawed at him upstairs, in frightened delirium, she saw it on his face—in the stricken and shattering gape of his lips.

He was as lost as she was.

Or worse.

They were gone. The doctor had arrived, ministered to Meg, and given solemn instructions that she "rest in a more suitable setting." With Meg still wrapped in Tom's blanket, Lord Cunningham had gathered her into his arms and carried her to the waiting landau.

"You hid from her." Meade tied on his leather cowhide apron as Tom leaned against the workroom window.

Where he had, in truth, been hiding the past hour.

"She does not want to see me." The landau disappeared around a street corner. The insane urge to run after her choked him like an iron fist. "She. . .fears me."

"She doesn't know you."

"She should!" He pummeled the wall with his hand. The window rattled. His chest rattled. "I have to get out of here—"

Meade grabbed his arm. "She needs time."

"She needs protection." Tom willed the fire to douse in his blood. "Something I cannae give her when she looks at me like I'm the blackguard who. . ." The sentence hung. He wasn't certain Meade knew about the night in the alley anyway.

He nodded as if he did. "But you're not. Prove it to her."

Seconds ticked away. Tom shrugged out of Meade's hold, grabbed his coat, and headed for the door. "I have to go."

"You're getting good at that."

"What?"

"Running. Hiding." Meade turned to his forge and lifted a half-filled bottle from the floor. He tossed it to Tom. "Might as well try this sometime too. For all the good it'll do."

Tom wedged the bottle between his vest and shirt. Then buttoned his coat. Then ran. He rented another horse from Brownie and galloped his way from Juleshead like the angels of death were nipping at his heels.

He went to the cottage.

The one he should curse and forget.

The RED COTTAGE

Spiderwebs stuck to his face as he entered the damp, mold-scented room and almost tripped over the wooden cask of paint articles. He opened the bag of red pigment. Rubbed the soft powder staining his fingers. Two days ago, he'd brought Joanie here.

They'd roamed the property together. She'd called it lovely.

Meg would have said that too.

Then, with the banknote in his pocket, Tom had located the owner, a local tea dealer on the main street in Juleshead. The man had ushered Tom into a shop that fumed of minty sweetness and, with a toothy smile and too-eager handshake, had agreed to the purchase.

Tom had less than half of his inheritance left.

But he had this.

Tossing off his coat, he kicked the wooden cask into a corner of the room and started with a broom. He swept bat droppings and old nests and leaves across the threshold. Then ripped moth-eaten curtains from the windows. Then stomped a wayward floorboard back into place.

All with the bottle stuck between his shirt and his vest. Sloshing against him. The glass cold and luring through the linen of his shirt. He itched to bite off the cork and guzzle away the sickness in his throat. Anything to get it out of his mind.

Her crying in his bedchamber.

He'd known her—och, *loved* her—two years before he'd witnessed her first tears. They'd been crushing rhubarb roots at the rear counter late in the evening, with only a flickering candle to light the apothecary shop.

She'd used the mortar and pestle with deftness.

But he saw her tremble.

"It wasnae yer fault, Meg." He dumped the powder into a tiny blue-glassed vial. "Ye did all ye could."

"He should have lived." She crushed with aggression. "He was seven and twenty years old. Strong." Grind. Bash. "He fell six feet from a ladder." Grind. Bash. "He should be lying in there with a crippled leg, not dead." The last word faltered.

Helplessness had pulled at Tom. He hadn't known what to say when she threw her face into her hands, bent over the counter, and stifled a terrible sound.

"I did everything Uncle ever taught me."

"Ye did right, lass."

"It doesn't make sense."

"It doesnae have to." He stepped closer. Touched her braid, then stroked her arm with the back of his fingers. All hesitant. Uncertain. As if he were doing the wrong thing.

But she flung against him anyway. Her arms circled his waist, her face burrowed into his shirt, and she clung so hard he felt every choppy breath as if it were his own. "Squeeze me, Tom."

His arms tightened.

His senses hummed alive—with grief because she grieved, with fervor because she needed him, with rapture. . .for no other reason than that he could smell her hair.

"I wanted to speak with Uncle." She smeared her tears. "We told so many people of his death. The wife. The children. The vicar. And I wanted to tell all of them how sorry I was, how frustrated and confused." Her voice dropped. "I couldn't tell anyone but you."

"Ye've nothing to be sorry for, lass."

"I can always tell you." Pulling back, she took a deep breath. "Make me laugh." She scampered to the other side of the counter. With flustered embarrassment, she wiped her nose and cheeks with her apron. "Please. Do something ridiculous before I become a weeping child."

Now, clenching his broom, Tom bristled at the memory. He could not recall what measure of nonsense he had displayed for her. Something absurd, like setting half her uncle's bottles upside down.

With glassy red eyes, she had laughed at him. Her attention was so eager and glowing that he might as well have been the king of the world.

Tom glanced about the dirty, empty cottage with an even bigger hollowness inside himself. His heart shriveled.

He missed that.

He missed her.

Something about the smell bothered her. Even tucked beneath the downy coverlets provided by the inn, she tugged the warm blue blanket tighter against her neck.

She closed her eyes.

Wool.

Earth.

Another faint scent, one she could not identify but had only noticed in the presence of Tom McGwen. 'Twas a nice smell. Whether she wished to admit it or not.

The chamber door opened and closed, and a lanky young woman swept into the room. "My name is Betsey, Miss Foxcroft." She settled a tray next to Meg's bed. "I thought I ought to tell you, on account of you forgettin' things."

"Thank you."

"Here." Betsey lifted a pottery plate to Meg's lap. "Oat cakes, fish, and peas. His lordship downstairs was right ready to pay an extra shilling for more proper courses, but Mamma didn't have nothin' else to fix."

"I am not very hungry anyway." She expected the girl to nod and depart, but instead, Betsey scooted a chair next to the bed and rested her chin on her hands.

Her sharp brown eyes narrowed. "Are you telling the truth?"

"Pardon?"

"About not knowin' nothing."

Meg frowned. "I have lost my memories. Not my wits."

"I can see that. Do you 'pose you'll be marryin' him, then?"

"What?"

"The rich lord. Downstairs. Are you goin' to marry him?"

"I—well, no." She moved her plate back to the tray. A little too hard, perhaps, because the bedstand wobbled and the girl winced. "I am very tired now. Please, I should like to rest."

"What about Mr. McGwen?"

"I do not wish to talk about it."

"All the girls wished to marry him, you know." Betsey stood, crossing her hands across her chest. "He was rightly a mystery to us all. Me and some other girls used to sneak down to the wharves early in the morn, when he'd first be settin' to sea on his boat. He waited until he was out in the water before he took off his shirt. We could still see though."

Meg turned her face away, his smell enfolding her as heat crawled beneath her face. "Did he. . .pay much mind to other girls?"

"When he first came. 'Till you." Betsey leaned over to straighten Meg's pillow. "It was always rightly a puzzlement, though. Why it should be you, when you scarcely ever wore a dress and ne'er did nothin' to look pretty."

"Why are you telling me this?"

"On account of Mamma and Papa teachin' me to be honest, o' course. I just wanted to know how it was 'twix you and that lordy." Tossing her braid over her shoulder, she glided from the bed to the door, almost with a dance to her step. She glanced back at Meg with a triumphant grin. "Me and the girls was just wantin' to know."

The next morn, Tom brought an all-too-eager Joanie—and Gyb—to the cottage. With her hair covered in a white handkerchief, she set to work scrubbing the windows and dusting the walls, while Tom hooked the rickety old door back on its hinges.

"Are we going to live here?" Joanie asked once as the kitten chased a baby mouse back into a wall hole.

Tom hadn't responded.

He didn't know the answer himself.

By the time the newly cleaned windows turned blue with dusk, Tom's muscles ached and Joanie lay flat on her back before the empty hearth. Gyb curled on her stomach and the soft purring filled the room like a lullaby.

Tom hammered the last floorboard in place. He spread himself next to Joanie, hands behind his head, and sighed. "I could fish a week straight and not be so cursed sore."

"You should have waited for Meade to fix the rafters."

"Meade has better things to do."

"He would help."

"For ye, maybe." Tom laughed, then reached for Gyb. "Here, let me see the wee thing."

The kitten stretched on Tom's chest, licked his paw, then settled down again to resume his nap. "Ye were braw help today, lass."

"I was?"

"Aye. Ye work like Papa."

"I like work. Mamm says it's to the soul what rain is to the garden."

He remembered. While Tom had always disappeared for as many chores as he could, Mamm had still possessed a longsuffering, nurturing look as she hauled him back, made him finish what he started, and reprimanded him with her wisdom.

Papa had not been so patient.

Especially after—

"How come you don't never talk of them?" Joanie rolled her head to look at Tom. Her cheeks were dusty, her eyes tired, but she had the same look of Mamm. "You never say nothing about home."

"It was nae longer home to me, lass."

"You didn't have to leave."

" 'Twas best for everyone."

"Because of Papa?"

Tom swallowed. He almost lied, said something dismissive—but he nodded instead. "Aye."

"It wouldn't have lasted forever. He would have talked to you again. I know it." Joanie leaned closer, a careful hand on his arm. "And you still had all of us. And Mamm."

"It's over now, lass. Best we not—"

A horse neighed outside.

Hooves pounding.

"Here." Tom leaned up and handed the kitten over. "Perhaps Meade after all. When the work is finished." An inch of satisfaction squirmed through him as he stepped outside, hinges squealing into the night. He had a door. The cottage smelled of soap and freshness. Every nail was intact, and soon enough, the outside walls would be a brilliant red.

He squinted at the form of a horse tied to the broken fence. Where was—

Something bashed into his face with blunt force.

He crashed back into the cottage, dazed, spots flickering across his vision. *Joanie.* He whipped back through the door. Slammed it shut and slid the latch. "Hide." He staggered. Fire trailed along his cheekbone, stinging, and he was dimly aware that his face and neck were wet. "Hurry!"

"Oh Tom—"

He snatched her by the elbow, dragged her to the empty bedchamber. He slammed her inside. Her whimpers stoked his panic. *Hammer.* He spun around. He needed something. Anything. He spotted the tool across the room—

The door smashed open.

Shadows raced in.

Lunged.

Tom buckled under the weight of two men, their blows thrashing his head back and forth. They yanked him up. Slung him into a window.

Glass shattered around his head, but he barreled forward and rammed one of them in the groin. Down again. Rolling. Busting his fist into a prickly jaw, while someone else pummeled his back.

With a raging growl, Tom surged his fist into the man beneath him.

The figure stilled.

Darkened.

No. Tom breathed faster, harder, spittle spraying from his mouth. A boot knocked him off the body. Then kicked his stomach. Then his ribs.

Tom caught the muddy boot and yanked.

The man fell, but instead of turning on Tom, he dove for the bedchamber. He crashed his way inside before Tom could stop him.

Then a sickening sound battered the air.

Joanie's scream.

CHAPTER 10

"If I had known our stay would be so extended, I would have brought a volume of poems." Lord Cunningham leaned back in his squeaky chair, his white gloved hands a perfect contrast to the scratched and dented table.

Pewter wall scones cast the taproom in a juxtaposition of light and shadow. Figures hunkered at tables, drinking, mostly clothed in articles as drab as the inn itself.

One of the fishermen slanted a look at her.

Another barked her name in a hoarse whisper.

Be calm. Hair stood on her neck, and the wild impulse to bolt back to her chamber nearly sprang her from the chair.

"Margaret, you must not think me so insensible to your turmoil." With a careful finger, he nudged her white porcelain plate closer—filled to the brim with pigeon breast, sweet corn, grapes, nectarines, and pudding. Where had he acquired all this? Did he not think her capable of common dishware and courses?

"Do not excite yourself, my dear." He followed her gaze to the shadowed men in the taproom. "I daresay, if those villagers were about to injure you, they would have already done it. Besides, I have three servants posted out of doors. One hail from me and they shall be upon us."

"Thank you." He was right, of course. Then why were her muscles coiled so tight? Why did she flinch, in her bed, every time footsteps passed by her chamber doorway?

"I assure you, I shall make certain nothing so atrocious occurs again." Lord Cunningham leaned forward. "We shall get you back to Penrose; we shall fortify the abbey; and you may set your heart to rest."

"Am I to hide away the length of my life?"

"Until this fiend is entrapped."

"And if he is not?"

"You are too somber." His light blue eyes smiled, catching sconce light—though they were somehow less fervent than his voice portrayed. "Would it truly be so unfavorable to spend the length of your days in Penrose Abbey, my dear?"

Betsey's words rushed back to Meg in a torrent. Then Violet's. "My lord, you have been so kind to me." The sudden need to clarify their attachment rose. "But certainly, we—"

The *boom* of a door jarred Meg.

Her heart pitter-pattered in her chest, and she twisted in her seat just as a giant man charged into the taproom. Meade, was it? His shirt sleeves were ripped at the shoulders, a black-smeared apron was tied across his waist, and something disturbing discolored his hands.

Blood.

"Miss Foxcroft, I be needin' your help."

She stood on legs already turning to jelly. "What has happened?"

"That doctor o' yours. Where is he?"

"I believe he has retired to his chamber." Lord Cunningham rose too. "But certainly, another local physician might administer to your needs without encumbering Mr. Bag—"

Meade was gone before Lord Cunningham had finished his speech.

"Preposterous." He ripped his napkin from his neckcloth. "We travel home in the morning, and the last thing I wish to do is entangle us further with—where are you going?" Lord Cunningham grabbed her shoulder as she turned.

"With them."

"Impossible."

"The doctor may need assistance, and I have aided my uncle enough to be of some use."

"Before, granted. Certainly not now."

"Perhaps my hands shall remember what my mind does not." She hurried from the taproom, Meade and Dr. Bagot already descending the stairs.

Meg turned to the girl behind the long, wooden counter. "Betsey, have you a cloak?"

"Yes, miss." She nodded and flounced away.

"Margaret, I must insist," said Lord Cunningham. "This is not only unreasonable, it is unsafe."

"Tom still not awake…cold rag on his head…" Snatches of Meade's words hit Meg like a new onslaught of poison. As the two reached the bottom floor, Betsey returned and draped a moth-scented cloak about Meg's shoulders.

"Has someone tried to murder Mr. McGwen?" the girl croaked.

Meade ripped open the door and shoved the doctor through. "Got to hurry."

"Margaret." Lord Cunningham maneuvered in front of Meg, blocking the doorway before she could follow. "That man, whoever he was to you before, is not your concern now."

"I know."

"Then in the name of faith, listen to reason. He is not worth your trouble. Indeed, he is not worth anything."

"I did not say he was." A light tremble fanned through her. Why, she was uncertain. Not for care of Tom McGwen. He was a blackguard who had assaulted Lord Cunningham, invaded her bedroom, kissed her…saved her life, only days before.

She pushed the memory of his arms, the smell of his blanket, out of her mind. She would do no less for anyone. She was the niece of an apothecary. It was in her blood to nurse the injured, and it was no more complicated than that.

"My lord, get out of my way."

With her legs stronger and her stomach less like the tossing sea, the blacksmith shop appeared less ominous. She shuffled inside behind Dr. Bagot and Meade, curiosity—not concern—drumming impatience at her chest. Was the doctor always so lethargic in his gait? Was he untroubled when someone needed his help?

"This way," grunted Meade.

Dripping tallow candles perched in wooden window seals set the rooms in a dim yellow haze as they made their way to the stairs. The steps creaked as they ascended.

Tom's door slammed open before they reached the top. "Joanie." He gripped the doorway to keep from falling. "Where is—"

"She be in my bed."

"I want to see her."

"After the doctor gets you—"

"He looks at Joanie first." Tom rushed into the narrow hallway, but Meade shouldered under him before he stumbled. "I'm fine." Tom yanked free. He burst into the second bedroom like thunder reverberating through clouds.

Dr. Bagot's beaver hat blocked her view.

Then Meade's shoulders.

But as Meg finally squeezed into the too-tiny chamber and skirted along the back wall, her breath snagged.

He leaned over the child in the bed, his hands frenzied as he turned her face from one side to another, searching for injury. "Ye hurt?"

Joanie cried and shook her head.

"Ye tell me the truth, lass, hear?"

"He didn't hurt me." She hiccupped, reaching beneath her dress collar to tug something free. A tiny green string securing a folded note. "He said to read you this. I was afraid to."

Tom eased it from her. He stuffed it away in his trouser pocket. "Ye dinnae have to. Ye need but rest, lass."

"Please, stay with me."

"I will." Meade stepped next to the bed, his giant presence emitting a sense of control. "Bagot, get this fool back to his chamber—"

"He looks at Joanie first." Tom pulled back the thin coverlet. His shoulders deflated, as if he'd already known the child would be cradling her elbow.

Dr. Bagot was already clicking open his bag. "Show me, Miss McGwen, exactly where it is you experience pain."

Shrinking back, without so much as glancing at Meg, Tom left the room.

Tightness pulled at her shoulders. She leaned harder against the wall, clasped her hands, because she had no intention of following him.

Until Meade lifted his gaze to her with pleading eyes.

But a moment. Gathering her dress, she swept back into the hall and approached his already closed door. Her hand was unsteady as she touched the knob. What could she do? What did she know?

Nothing.

Not of his injuries, nor the note in his trouser pocket, nor of him.

But she pushed the knob anyway. Too many candles were lit inside, and although she had expected to find him on the pallet on the floor, he leaned with his arm over his head at the window. The smell of night and chimney smoke wafted in.

"May I see the letter?"

He did not react to her voice. His voice was pain-laced. "Another time, lass."

"This is not because of. . ." The words failed her when he turned.

In the candlelight, he was no more shadow and memory. Every detail of his features was visible—the lacerations across his smooth forehead, the white cheekbone peeking through a swollen and jagged cut.

In the strangest way, he appeared stronger.

Taller.

His gaze steadier, more mesmerizing, even blood-matted. "What are ye doing here?"

"Meade came to the coaching inn. He inquired after the doctor."

"He shouldnae have asked ye to come."

"He didn't."

Disbelief raised his brow, but he did not question her. Instead, he moved to the other side of the room. With a surprisingly steady hand, he poured water from a chipped pitcher into a mismatched bowl.

"Let me help you."

"Not afraid I'll hurt ye?"

"I deserved that, I suppose." She pulled a linen rag from a peg on the wall, then slid next to him and dipped the cloth. The warm water calmed her uncertain hands. She had done this before, had she not?

"I can do it." Tom stopped her before she touched him.

A jolt passed from his fingers to her wrist.

This close, he was taller than she had realized. He smelled like his blanket.

"Look toward the window." When he did not obey, she used one finger to angle his chin, then pressed the rag to his cheek. The white soaked red. Her heart flipped every time he did not wince but she knew he should have.

"Dr. Bagot shall sew this. You may be scarred."

"I dinnae spend much time with the mirror anyway."

The village girls would be disappointed, perhaps. "Are you injured elsewhere?"

"No."

"You are lying, sir."

"Ye've not called me that before."

She dipped the rag back into the water, wrung it, then swept it at his split lip. Unbidden thoughts heated her cheeks. These same lips pouring over hers. Tasting strange and confusing and frantic. He'd been as out of control, as reckless, as the Tom who had just barged into Joanie's room and rubbed her entire face—but just as loving.

Had he kissed other girls as he'd kissed her? Was that the reason shopkeepers' daughters crept to the docks to watch him? Had she done so herself?

The breadth of his chest struck her. The clearness of his eyes. She felt his breath, warm, measured—and a traitorous tingle soared up her spine.

"That's enough." For the second time, Tom put distance between them. He walked to the door and held it open. "I want ye to go back to the inn. See that Meade takes ye. Ye'll be safe with him."

"Mr. McGwen, answer me one thing."

He nodded her on.

"Is what happened tonight, the letter. . ." Why was it so hard to get out the words? "It is not because of me. . .is it?"

Tom did not answer for so long that she knew the answer. "I am sorry." For more than tonight. For several days ago, when she had lashed out at him in this very room, when he had done nothing but keep her safe.

"Goodnight, lass."

She hurried from the chamber and nearly ran back down the stairs. She gripped the railing at the bottom. Whoever he was, whatever atrocities he had done—or *they* had done together—she was beginning to understand one thing: why the old Meg Foxcroft, and every other girl in the village, had seen more than a mere fisherman in Tom McGwen.

Meade's soft snores drifted through the door, the rhythmic sound finally uncoiling the tension in Tom's muscles.

"Sleep," Meade had barked at both Tom and Joanie when the doctor departed. "I'll guard the door."

Tom had argued it was unnecessary. Whoever had done this would not be so quick to return. But Meade had insisted and, with his new bottle of ale and one of the kitchen stools, had taken his position like a sentry.

Tom straddled his chair backwards.

Joanie still slept, her cotton sling visible between her hair and the coverlets. The doctor said she was no more than bruised. She shouldn't be that. Tom should have stopped this, and by heaven, he should have kept her safe.

He dropped his head. The letter wailed from his pocket, like a sharp wind cutting through wet trees. The edges were black again. The mark of grief.

You save the lives of those who take others. You dip your hands in their blood. Cease now before that blood is yours.

Mr. Foxcroft had killed no one. Meg had killed no one. All they'd ever done, the whole of their existence, was restore health and save lives. They had unstained hands.

Unlike Tom.

Rolling over in bed, Joanie's soft breathing came faster. Tears dripped from under her closed eyelids.

"Shhh, lass." Tom moved to the edge of the bed. "Ye awake?"

"Is it morning?" she whispered, eyes still closed.

"Nay."

"Where is Gyb?"

"Last I looked, the wee thing was sleeping on Meade's lap. But if ye tell him I told ye, I'll be denying every word."

She rumbled with a quiet laugh, smearing the wet streaks from her cheeks. She sighed and finally squinted up at him. Her lashes quivered. "Tom?"

"Hmm?"

"Do you wish Mamm had never sent me here?"

"Why would ye say that?"

"I don't know."

"Lass."

She slipped her fingers over her face.

"Look at me, ye wee little ninny." He pried back her hands. "Wouldn't ye know I was thinking to ask the same of ye?"

"You were?"

"I've done little more than leave ye to yerself in that dashed room of mine or drag ye along for errands."

"You bought me shoes."

"And I've no friends for ye. I've not even taken ye to church."

"Meade is my friend. And Gyb."

"'Tis not so grand as ye're saying, Joanie. Any other brother would have done better for ye."

"No, Tom." She leaned up and with her good arm wrapped herself close to his neck. She kissed his cheek. "Isaac and Moses never rode me on their back when I was little. They wouldn't talk to me like you do, now that I'm grown."

"Ye're not so grown as all that." He laughed, though it sent pain rippling along his bruised ribs. "Enough of this fuss. Lie down with ye and go back to sleep."

"You'll be here?"

"Aye."

"What will we do tomorrow?"

"Rest." And show Meg the letter. Because as much as it would frighten her and make her question everything, she deserved the truth.

𝒯𝘩𝘦 RED COTTAGE

Lord Cunningham spoke very few of his usual pleasantries on the journey home. Every moment or so, he licked his thumb, turned a worn page of *A Guide to Health*, and swayed with every jostle in the road without bumping her elbow.

Which he had done, more than once, on the arriving trip.

"I fear you are terribly angry with me, my lord."

"I am never angry." He turned another page. "As I am wont to telling Violet, only momentarily disappointed."

"If my conscience would allow me to apologize, I would."

"But it does not?"

"No." She sighed, placing her hand on the glossy blue edge of the landau. An afternoon breeze rustled across the countryside, scented of brine and flora. "Not when I am certain I would have made the same decision again."

"Then it is of necessity we discuss the matter no further, my dear. I cannot be persuaded to your opinion, and it is certain you cannot be persuaded to mine. Thus"—he snapped his book shut and finally glanced at her—"what do you say we put last night out of our minds? Indeed, this whole trip entirely?"

"I am agreeable to such terms." Meg smiled and held out her hand. "Friends again, then?"

He pulled her fingers to his lips. "Friends again, my sweet one."

They settled back into silence, albeit a more comfortable one, and Meg took to watching the fishing vessels in the distance. They bobbed up and down in rhythm to the sea, some twenty feet beneath the high road.

The beach below was secluded. Jagged rocks were scattered among the rust-colored sand, and the sloping hill between the road and the shore was dotted with bright yellow flowers. Had she come here with Tom? Had she watched him set sail on his boat each morn, then waited for his return each eve? Had she teased him? Told him her secrets?

Loved him?

She forced her eyes back to the road. No matter if she had. Meg Foxcroft—niece of an apothecary, girl of mystery and mischief—was as far removed from who she was now she could not even reconcile the two.

A *zing* shot past her ear.

"Oh." She shifted. "What was. . ." *No.*

From his perch, the driver slumped forward. His tricorne hat was gone. A black-red hole dented his head.

"Down." Lord Cunningham scrunched himself into the landau floor, hands over his head. His breathing raced faster than the carriage. "Down, Margaret!"

"We need to jump!" Another shot whizzed. A carriage lantern shattered. "Now! The reins—"

The driver toppled over. Gone. The horses bolted faster.

With a numbing surge of adrenaline, she flung herself to the opposite seat and climbed for the driver's empty perch. Her dress tangled about her legs. Bonnet ribbons fluttered in front of her face. *God, help me.* Securing her grip on the perch, she leaned forward and groped—

Another shot.

One of the horses downed, the other reared, and the landau raised on two wheels. Then everything whished and whooshed around her. A scream. Mayhap her own. The sensation of falling dropped her stomach, and the shadow of the hurling carriage sent her mind shrieking.

Earth pounded her face.

She flopped downward.

At first groping, resisting, grabbing fistfuls of grass in attempt to catch her fall. Then just floating, not tethered to anything, as her mind grew feathers and wings. She flew into darkness and felt nothing at all.

CHAPTER 11

A dull pain radiated through Tom as the slobbering mutt jumped up and slapped its paws on his thighs. Mud streaked his trousers. "Down, boy."

"Oley's a girl." From the second story of the coaching inn, Betsey leaned over the outside railing. She wiped loose hair from her smirking eyes. "Don't you know a girl, Mr. McGwen, when you see one?"

He rubbed the animal's head, pushing her down with the other hand. He kept on toward the front door without looking up.

"What you want? Come for your ladylove?" Louder. "She ain't here, Mr. McGwen. They left near an hour ago."

He halted and craned back his head. "Where to?"

"That abbey, reckon."

"Did she leave me any word?" He wasn't certain why she would. Still. He had not thought she would dry the blood off his face either. What had possessed her to accompany the doctor last night? She had shuffled into Tom's chamber unafraid. She had stepped close to him, spoken to him, just softly enough he might have pretended nothing had changed.

That she was still Meg.

His Meg.

"Well." Betsey flapped a white sheet, dust flying. "All she said was things I 'pose you wouldn't want to hear." *Flap.* "Things about that lordy." *Flap.* "I'll not be the one to tell you, to be sure."

"Miss Creagh." He tried to rein his anger as showers of dust landed on his face and the infernal dog once again leapt on his trousers. "Talk sense."

"I am. 'Deed, it makes perfect sense why Miss Foxcroft would want to marry him. Why wouldn't she? I would. He *is* handsome, you know. And rich."

Marry him? Repulsion chilled him. Then burned him, like a fever creeping across his brow. No, she would not marry him.

She'd already promised herself to Tom.

Whether she remembered or not.

Lifting the dog off him, Tom strode into the inn and brought his fists down on the long wooden counter. "Has Dr. Bagot departed yet?"

"Decided to stay a day or two longer to take in the sea air." Mrs. Creagh frowned. "Might be in his room. Might not. I don't have time to keep up with every Jack Adams who stays here."

"Which room?"

"Eleven. Second floor." Mrs. Creagh pruned her lips. "But mind you take care of your business and get. This hain't no visiting parlor, see?"

He took the steps two at a time and found room eleven in the first hall. He knocked once. "Dr. Bagot?"

No answer.

He turned to leave, but a faint creak drew him back. So the man was here after all. Tom pushed at the door—

"Oh!" Mrs. Musgrave gave a little start. "Tommy, dear, it *is* you."

He swung the door wider and glanced about the room in confusion. One neatly made bed. A greasy lantern. A crookedly hung mirror above a washstand, where a black-leather medical bag sat beside the pitcher.

No doctor.

"What are ye doing here?" Tom stepped inside, glancing at the cloth-covered platter in her hand. The smell of chocolate wafted from under the linen. "With those."

"Oh, these." Mrs. Musgrave smiled. She wore one of her flower-studded hats, and a bit of powder was smeared across her wrinkled cheeks. Perhaps it was only that which made her face so pallid. "I just thought how nice it would be to bring Miss Foxcroft some of my chocolate biscuits. You do remember she loved them."

He nodded. "How did you end up here?"

"Oh?" Her eyes shifted. "Oh, oh, yes. When I realized she had already departed, I thought I might as well share these treats with someone who might enjoy them." She touched his stitched cheek. "If I had known you looked like this, I would have brought them to you instead. Whatever happened to you, child?"

"Nothing."

"I think perhaps you should wait for Dr. Bagot. He must take a look at you."

"He already has."

"Oh?"

"Yes."

"Then why were you"—Mrs. Musgrave gave a little chuckle—"you know, my dear, looking for him now?"

"I've not been able to talk with him about Meg. I want to know if she will. . ." Remember Tom? Look at him the same? Keep her promise? "Get better."

"You need not worry. Most troubles have a way of sorting themselves." Mrs. Musgrave patted his chest, then leaned up on her tiptoes and planted a small kiss on his cheek. Was it his imagination, or did her breath seem short?

"I must be running along now, dear. Bring little Joanie to see me soon. I am certain Lenox and her new kitten shall quite enjoy each other's company." After settling her platter beside the medical bag, Mrs. Musgrave offered him a faint little wave and bustled away.

Tom sighed.

When he could think straight, he would question Mrs. Musgrave further. Perhaps she was not so much in health as she seemed. But now, he must find Meg.

Clutching his ribs, he lumbered back into the hall. He had two things to give her.

The note.

And all the reasons she could not marry anyone else.

The grass was wet. With a throbbing head, she pushed herself up on her elbows, muscles quivering. Twilight had already settled, making the distant ocean a foggy haze. The wind moaned. She bit back her own complaints. *Lord Cunningham.*

Standing on wobbly legs, feet slipping in the grass, she made her way toward the black shadow of the carriage. "My lord?" She yanked at the crushed door. It didn't budge. "My lord!"

"Over here." The voice came from the bottom of the slope.

Fisting her dress, she skidded down to him and collapsed her knees into the sand. "Are you injured? Can you move?"

He was leaned against a rock, and even in the growing darkness, blood was visible across his temple. He tugged his cravat from his neck. "I think I have twisted my ankle. My head is madness."

"Do not move. Here." She mopped at the blood. "It is no more than a scratch."

"Which is more than can be said for my carriage." Dry anger pulled at his voice, and he pushed her hand away from his head. "Enough, dear girl. You are patting me to death. I shall hitherto sympathize with Violet for being prodded upon all the time."

She scooted back, trying to compose her breath. Pain pulsated through her skull, and too many thoughts scrambled in her brain. The only one she understood was that someone had tried to kill her.

Again.

Why? What had she done that was so terrible, so despicable, that someone would hunt her this way? Had she known before? Or was the old Meg just as oblivious as she was now?

"There is simply no way I shall be able to move from this spot." Lord Cunningham ripped his tailcoat open. Buttons popped. "If Dr. Bagot had accompanied us as planned, he might have been of service."

"Or dead." Meg stood back to her feet, grabbing the rock for support. She studied herself for injury. Other than sore limbs and a pounding headache, she appeared to be unharmed. "I must look for the driver. Perhaps he is yet alive."

The RED COTTAGE

"He is not." Lord Cunningham pointed.

A few feet away, face down in the sand, the man's body was sprawled. Meg hurried toward him. With tears in her throat, she grabbed his stiff shoulder and overturned him. His eyes were half open. Dry and cloudy and. . .so very, very lifeless.

She sniffled. "He is dead because of me."

"Come here, my dear." When she didn't move, he said again in a more demanding pitch, "Come here, Margaret."

She trudged back to him, lowering herself next to where he patted. His arm came around her, pulling her close.

"The blame for this atrocity is not yours to bear."

"You do not know that."

"Of course I do."

"Perhaps I did something, gave someone cause to—"

"There are very few acts hideous enough to warrant murder. I am confident you could not be guilty of one." He hugged her tighter. "Regardless, we are in a very compromised position. I cannot climb to the road, and you cannot venture the journey alone."

"Perhaps with my arm under you, we could—"

"Impossible, my dear. I have not the strength."

"Then I can wave down a carriage from the road."

"Prey to any highwayman or vagabond? I think not." He reached for her fingers, pulled them up to his cheek.

Had she not been so weary, so afraid, she would have drawn away.

"No, Margaret, I think we have little choice but to remain here until daylight and hope someone stumbles upon our plight." He sighed. "Now lay your head upon my shoulder and rest. This has all the makings of a very long night."

A shiver swept up her spine as she rubbed her arms and blinked into the deepening darkness. Whoever had shot at them might still be out there. Every rustle of the grass, every crash of the waves heightened a sense of fear not even Lord Cunningham's arms dissuaded.

Oddly enough, her harried thoughts strayed to Tom. She almost prayed he'd come. That he'd find her.

For the strangest reason in the world, that made her feel safe.

Blast it. The road stretched out before Tom, choked in blackness and fog. The air was moist. A chill prickled through his body like an infection, giving his heart a light stutter.

Meg was gone.

He had arrived at Penrose Abbey an hour later than it would have taken before. He'd ridden slower, one hand supporting his ribs, endeavoring to hit as few ruts as possible.

He would have raced like the wind had he known.

Now it was too late.

He leaned forward, tightness pulling at his stitches. The pain fired him. He should have showed her the note. She should have been aware. Tom and Meade and the constable and anyone else should have guarded her carriage home.

Not again. A holy name was too close to the words. Words that felt, against his will, like a prayer. *Please.*

Yanking the horse to a stop, he tucked the reins under his knee and cupped his hands to his mouth. "Meg!" His bellow echoed. He shouted louder, trotted forward a mile, then yelled again.

No answer on the wind.

No waving shadow on the road.

Heaven help him, he could not find her body. He knew cold skin too well. He'd touched Caleb's face after it happened, straightening his crooked limbs, wiping the drizzle of blood from the corner of his lip.

"Moses, get Papa!" He'd been crying. He never cried. *"Hurry!"*

All the feet had pattered on the old, leaf-strewn floor—Isaac, Moses, his sisters. Seconds later, they had all squeezed through the crumbled doorway and disappeared.

Tom had glanced up. The ruins of Satchwell Priory stared down at him, with their broken cloisters and lichen-covered stones and narrow six-foot walls. What had possessed him to climb the wall? To leap across the eroded window frame?

He should have known Caleb would follow him.

Caleb *always* followed him.

Everything had been quiet while he waited, the smell of blood nauseating. Dry leaves had skittered with the wind. Forest trees had creaked. The sun had blinded him through a glassless window, harsh and wretched, making the sweat slide down his face.

"Please, God." He'd been afraid to move Caleb from where he'd fallen, so Tom bent over his chest and grabbed his shirt.

The same one Tom had worn last year. Caleb had grown into it with pride. He always wanted what Tom had. Always wanted to do what Tom did. "*Please, God, dinnae let him die. Please, please. I beg of Ye, dinnae let him die.*"

Now, Tom sucked in air and yanked the reins to his chest once again. He would find Meg tonight. She would be safe. *He* would save her.

And he would do it with nary a prayer.

They were unheard anyway.

That much he knew.

"Why do you read these?" Meg reached across his legs to grab the medical book. The spine was cracked, and a few loose pages fell into her lap. "You believe Violet might be cured?"

"I believe anything is possible."

"And Dr. Bagot?"

"He, among other physicians, imagines it to be some form of cancer. There is much we do not know." Lord Cunningham gathered the wayward pages. He tucked them inside the red hardback. "But my obsession with medicine, I fear, cannot all be laid to Violet's charge."

"You studied before?"

"Yes." He hesitated, and she was certain he would say no more when he sighed. "You see, this is not my first experience with a terminal illness. By the time I was eleven years old, my father was confined to his bed or, on occasion, a wheelchair. Thus began his feverish obsession with these." Lord Cunningham raised the book. "He suffered insurmountable pain. Doctors knew nothing. It"—another sigh—"it changed him."

"I am sorry."

"At thirteen, I was sent off to Westminster for schooling. When I returned later for Michaelmas, my father's steward awaited me on the steps. He explained that Father had declined in my absence. He died shortly after my departure. No one told me, I imagine, so as not to affect my studies."

"Then you were never given the chance to say goodbye."

"You must cease being so tender, my dear." Lord Cunningham pulled her head back onto his shoulder. "It was many years ago. Perhaps we do not ever fully recover from our tragedies, but we certainly learn to bury them. I have no wish to unearth mine at present." His yawn whispered into the night. "Close your eyes, darling, and rest. I shall keep watch for anything astir."

He spoke as if she were a child, frightened of shadows beyond her bed curtains. "I shall watch too," she whispered.

But the sound of his breathing slowed, his shoulder slumped beneath her, and the lulling roar of the water stilled the rushed pattern of her heart. Her eyes became heavy. *Stay awake.* She stared at the hillside—the faint yellow flowers in the moonlight, the lifting fog, the carriage.

Then the moon was gone.

Everything was faint and empty, and a cottage appeared in the pink light of sunrise. A woman stood in the garden. She flung something from her pinafore, and the ducks all waddled to her side, quacking. Meg rushed to the woman too. *"Mamma."* The arms swallowed her. Gentle, delicate, then soft lips fell to her cheek.

Just as quickly, the cottage was gone.

The woman gone.

Different lips roved over her. Hot, demanding. Clammy fingers slid across her skin and into her hair—

Meg flinched, opened her eyes.

Lord Cunningham.

She leaned back, startled, wiping the taste of him from her tingling mouth. "My lord."

"We are already compromised, my dear. Look."

She glanced around them, disoriented. How long had she been asleep? The sun burned a line of orange across the water, and the sky had transformed from blackness to a cloudy blue. Her skin was moist with dew.

Soreness ebbed and flowed throughout her muscles in protest of both her position last night and the fall.

Lord Cunningham reached for her face—

She gasped and scooted away from him, wiping tangled hair out of her eyes. "Do not touch me."

"Whoever finds us now shall make no delays, I am certain, in spreading the latest *on dit* among all of the parish. Scandal is always rousing to the ears, I am afraid."

"You had no right." She pushed to her feet, stumbled away from him. She turned for the hill.

"Where are you going?"

Her shoes slipped in the wet grass. She flung them off, climbed with her hands.

"It is not safe, Margaret! Be reasonable." He shouted more, words that she muffled consciously.

All she listened for was the ocean, a steady roar—her own throbbing heart, the tear of her dress, the seagulls in the distance. *How could you?* She wiped her mouth, for the second time, with her shoulder. Panic strengthened her climb. When she finally reached the road, she stood alongside it with limp arms and choppy breaths and perspiration that had nothing to do with the exertion.

She never wished to be kissed again.

Tom drew the reins of his horse as he rounded another curve.

Midway down the straight stretch, a yellow-and-black mail coach had halted its route, and more than one gentleman peered down the edge of the hill.

Then Meg.

She emerged from behind the coach, an oversize coat draped over her shoulders. She wore no shoes. Hair fell around her shoulders as she called something down the slope.

Tom picked up speed, relief unsnagging the hook in his chest. *Thank mercy.*

By the time he neared the coach, three gentlemen were lugging a groaning Lord Cunningham into the already crowded carriage.

"Now, load up! We're six deuced minu'es behind." A short, nubby man—presumably the coachman—waved a hand at Meg. "We're loaded seven already, so's unless yew wants to be waitin' for me to send someone back, yew'll have to climb on someone's lap."

"That won't be necessary." Tom swung down from his horse. "I'll be returning the lass."

The coachman growled. "Yew know this man, miss?"

Meg's eyes flew to Tom. Her cheeks paled, and for a second, he was certain she would shake her head. She said instead, "Yes."

"And yew'll be pleased to ride with him?"

Another long pause. "Yes."

The coachman nodded, mumbled something about eight minutes lost, then jumped back on his perch and whipped at the four mismatched horses.

Tom did not approach her. He stood by his horse, rubbing the animal's face, and watched her glance about.

"I lost my shoes."

He nodded. She always did.

Instead of looking for them, she tucked her hair behind her ear and approached him in the massive chamois coat. She seemed uncertain, a little afraid. Of Tom? Or something else?

"Here." He took her waist and swung her up. "I'll walk if ye want. We're not a far piece from Sunderlin Downs."

"No. We shall be much faster if you ride."

He mounted behind her. He was too conscious of everything—his arms sliding around her, her sleeves brushing his, the smell of her hair in his face. He gave a quiet *cluck, cluck* with his tongue, and the horse trotted forward.

They rode in silence.

Birds tweeted a bonnie morning song, their tune bouncing from treetop to treetop across the countryside. The fog had lifted. The yellow-green grass shimmered with dew, and the chilled air settled in his lungs. He tried not to hold his breath.

Or speak first.

Or ask her all the things he had to clench his jaw to keep back.

"I instructed the coachman to deliver Lord Cunningham to the doctor's office. He will be gone still, of course, but I have heard mention of a most capable nurse."

"Is he injured badly?"

"I believe it is only his ankle."

"And you?"

"I am unharmed."

He knew the tone well enough to know something was amiss, but he would not press. He'd done that enough.

"Lord Cunningham kissed me." She grabbed the horse's mane in a white-knuckled grip. "You kissed me."

Heat fired beneath his cheeks.

"And both times, I was. . ." Her breathing came faster. "I was afraid. Why?"

Dread cropped through him. He had never imagined being the one to...explain what had happened that night in the alley. If she had forgotten, had he any right to remind her?

"Mr. McGwen."

"I think this is not the time to speak of it."

"Now is very much the time." Her back stiffened. "I want to know."

CHAPTER 12

For a long time, he told her nothing. Had it been Lord Cunningham, she would have used a piteous voice and coaxed him into telling her anything.

Tom McGwen was different.

He did things his own way, in his own time—and if they had ever fought in the past, perhaps that was why. He was as headstrong as she. Perhaps more.

The weight of her question ground into her, like bricks being stacked on her already heavily laden shoulders. She should have suspected before. Her discomfort every time Lord Cunningham maneuvered close. The instant flight sensation every time lips swept innocently across her own.

"The carriage was no accident, lass."

"I know." She should have fought against the change in subject, but a small part of her wished to run from it anyway. "There were gunshots. The driver is dead."

"Ye saw nothing?"

"No."

" 'Tis luck ye survived."

"It was God."

No answer. His arms widened around her, a curtesy he'd demonstrated ever since she mentioned the kiss, as if he were unwilling to make her feel trapped. "I wanted to show ye the note."

"Have you no belief in God, Mr. McGwen?"

"I'll say no word against Him."

"That is hardly an answer."

"Here." Behind her, he reached into his pocket and slipped a black-edged letter into her hand. "I plan to speak with Mr. Telfner, the stationer, 'pon my return. Mayhap he'll know the paper."

"Or the handwriting." Meg skittered over the words with a fresh churn of sickness. "What does this mean. . .the lives of those who take others?"

"Ye did naught but help folk, lass."

"This is some sort of. . .vendetta against me. Against my uncle." The letter blurred. "For something we did. Perhaps for someone we lost."

"Ye could not save everyone. Ye did yer best."

"Whoever wrote this would not be so certain nor so righteous in their crusade of justice had there been no fault."

"Meg."

"I must have done something. I must have allowed someone to die."

"I know ye, and I say ye didn't."

His confidence, his utter belief in her, steadied her tattered nerves. 'Twas almost a comfort. When she could not even trust herself, to have someone so assured of her innocence, her goodness, her integrity. . .

More than anything in the world, she wished to believe him.

She was not certain she could.

Not if all the things Lord Cunningham warned were true. How much had the lord not told her? How many secrets about Tom McGwen would she unbury later?

Somehow, she didn't fear them.

She should.

Instead, the tightness twisting and pulling inside her finally loosened. Perhaps it was only the sway of the horse—the constant clacking of hooves, the soothing sun in her face—that made her lean back against his chest.

She meant to apologize, explain how weary she was, but Tom said nothing and his breathing was even, steady, next to her ear. She stared at his hands.

Strong, tapered fingers. Freckles. The faintest protruding veins.

They were nice hands.

Lord Cunningham's were pale, his fingers too long and smooth. His palms a little damp, sometimes, though it was likely from the gloves—and she certainly could not fault him for that.

Meg yawned. She should not think such things. None of this mattered. Nothing mattered except remembering what she'd forgotten, knowing who she was...and extracting herself from the web of whomever wanted her dead.

When the horse finally trotted into Sunderlin Downs, she had to fight to keep her eyes open.

Tom pulled the reins in front of Dr. Bagot's office—a tall, square-bricked building down Plumgate Row. Across the street, a barrow-woman shouted, "Lemons—ripe, ripe lemons!" while a gang of children chased a scraggly dog into an alley.

"Ye awake?"

She nodded and bit back a pinch of protest when he dismounted.

He pulled her down next to him. "I'll walk ye in."

"You need not bother." Lord Cunningham, she imagined, would already be dismayed at Meg's choice of company. 'Twould be in bad form to frustrate him more.

"Stay away from the windows. See that ye keep yer doors locked."

"I will."

"Dinnae leave this office until yer lord has sent for servants."

"Already done, I am certain."

"I'll speak with the constable and see to it the driver's body is—"

"You need not trouble yourself." She raised her chin in false assurance. "Lord Cunningham is most capable, and I've no doubt at all he has already seen to the details. This was our tragedy after all, Mr. McGwen. You must be anxious to return to your sister."

As if he had not heard anything she said, he continued, "And then I'll find yer shoes." The smallest grin worked at his lips, the pull of it somehow disarming. He gave a hard little nod. "Now go lie down somewhere and sleep."

She huffed and spun for the door, rankled that he thought it his right to order her about. Or rankled, perhaps more so, that her lips smiled back.

The RED COTTAGE

"A little higher, my dear." Lord Cunningham sucked air through his teeth as Meg stacked another feather-stuffed pillow beneath his ankle. "Yes, yes. That shall suffice. Elevation seems to alleviate my pain, if nothing else."

"The nurse assured us your ankle is not broken."

"It might well have been for all this agony I am suffering." Lord Cunningham sighed and reached for the glass the nurse had left by his bedside. Meg suspected laudanum, judging by the glassiness of his eyes. "And you, my dear? You appear very drawn. How long have you been sitting here next to me?"

"Less than an hour. The nurse sent an errand boy to fetch a new carriage and servants from Penrose." She tucked the bed linens higher up his neck. "They shall arrive soon."

"I should not have been so heedless to fall asleep."

"You were weary."

"As are you." He glanced about the wide upstairs room—complete with a singular bed, a cluttered desk in the corner, an examining table, and a hanging skeleton body in the corner. "Here. As we are quite alone and propriety has already been breached, you may sit next to me. I daresay that chair must be most disagreeable after such an ordeal."

She stood. "I am not tired, my lord." The lie bolstered her with a new wave of energy. She moved to the window, knees jittering as she peeled back the curtain.

Below, the street bustled with wagons and dog carts and basket-laden hawkers. The cadence of their noises drifted to Meg like a raspy whisper that everything was still well. She was still alive. Was he down there? Had he—or *they*—already discovered where she hid?

"Margaret, please sit next to me."

She did not wish to look at him, let alone settle next to his side. Nevertheless, she returned to her chair. The air lodged in her throat.

"I assured myself, for your sake, I would remain silent and cumber you not with any unpleasantness. Remorsefully, I seem to possess no such powers of restraint."

"Go on."

"It was in a most unorganized and improper manner that I was thrust upon the passengers in the mail coach."

"Yes."

"I was in grave pain, I was uncommonly ill of temper, and I was as angry at myself, as I was at you, that your passage home was with the dreaded Mr. McGwen." Lord Cunningham took the last sip of the reddish-brown medicine, scrunching his face. "So you must forgive me for the lack of wisdom and discretion in such an hour."

"Pray, my lord, what are you saying?"

"They know, my dear." His pale eyes drilled into her. "They are all quite aware of our compromised situation. That we were. . .alone. . .the length of the night."

"Which could not be helped." She stood again, nearly knocking over the chair. "We were victims of a cruel attack and cannot be blamed for—"

"I fear wagging tongues are never so kind." Lord Cunningham frowned. "This terrible incident, along with any mysteries of your past, may prove to be our ruining."

"My reputation is of no consequence."

"I fear I cannot be so yielding."

Eyes widening, she glanced at his face. The same overwhelming sense of being lost—and alone—hollowed through her. "I understand." Her shoulders slumped as she turned. "I fear you are right. It was only a matter of time, and now that the danger has escalated, it would be wrong of me to stay."

"Dear—"

"You have been very kind to me."

"Margaret, you are not listening to me." He groaned and the bed linens rustled as if he'd swung his legs over the edge. "I am not asking you to depart Penrose Abbey nor to abandon my company." He limped behind her, hands falling on her shoulders, and whispered, "I am asking you to marry me."

The corridor was long, the stained-glass windows casting colorful hues onto the gleaming hemlock floor boards. Lord Cunningham's footsteps matched hers. He had spoken without abate on their journey back to Penrose, as if nothing had changed.

As if her world had not altered.

Again.

"...Consequently, there are many features of the home you have yet to explore. Perhaps when you are rested again, I shall give you the tour myself."

She would have been kind to say anything.

Nod, at the least.

But all she could think was to keep moving—to make it to her chamber, where she would slam the door, turn the lock, and breathe.

"I have been equally negligent in delighting you with the abbey's history. I assure you, even for one who would rather study casebooks, it is a matter of interest."

Marry her? Had that been his intention all along?

"The monastery was founded in 1147..."

His reason for helping her?

"...but was surrendered for dissolution in 1539. After a house fire nearly two centuries later, the abbey was gutted and reconstructed to more modish architecture."

Had she been wrong to accept his charity, the comfort of his support, though she suspected his heart was involved? Had she trampled his grace?

"Thus, our Penrose Abbey."

The word *our* stuck in the air, sucking the wind from her lungs, as they halted before her bedchamber door.

For the hundredth time, he touched a light finger to the bandage on his head. No blood dotted the linen, but he winced just the same. "I can see I have bored you with my lessons, however, so you must allow me to finish when we are both in better health and spirit."

"You have not bored me, my lord." She stared at the doorknob. "I am only uncertain—"

"Do not say anything yet. We have both endured much, and to make any decision on so irrational a mind would be criminal."

"I fear I have encouraged you when I—"

"Indeed. You have." He slipped a finger under her chin, lifted her face to him. "But only because, whether you wish to admit it or not, you have thought of this too."

Was he right?

Days flashed across her memory. Sitting next to Lord Cunningham, smelling cinnamon, lulled by the rhythm of his deep-voiced poetry readings. The picnic. Dancing with him. Laughing with him—her one friend in a world of strangers.

Yes, she had thought of it too.

The realization soured through her like curdling milk.

"A maid is already on her way. You must promise to do nothing but sleep."

The one thing she felt certain she could not do. Not now. She nodded anyway. "As must you."

"We shall speak again after breakfast."

"Very well."

"All shall be resolved."

"Yes."

"Good evening, my dear." With a firm kiss to her forehead, he departed down the corridor, his footsteps echoing in a discordant beat.

Meg shut herself inside. When the maid knocked several minutes later, she did not answer. Instead, she dropped to her hands and knees, coaxing out the white-and-orange kitten hidden beneath the bed skirt. What had Tom called the thing?

Pippins.

Ridiculous name. She'd taken to calling it Marigold instead, something sensible and pretty—but now, she found herself murmuring, "Come here, Pippins. I shan't hurt you."

The kitty poked out its head, eyes wide, ears flat. With a meow, it darted out from the bed and zoomed across the room. Then under the *escritoire*. Then slowly, toward Meg's outstretched hand.

After several sniffs, the furry creature allowed Meg to hold it against her body. She had touched the thing so little. She had even been so negligent as to allow her maid the duty of feeding and watering—because accepting the creature had seemed somehow like accepting Tom.

More guilt swamped her. She stroked the kitten harder, until the bedchamber window turned dark and the kitten purred in sleepy contentment.

Breakfast. Tomorrow. Her mind hurt. Her body hurt. *Marriage.* She tried to imagine what she would say to him—what dress she would wear downstairs, if her fork would tremble, or if she would drink of her morning cocoa without the faintest flinch. *"You have thought of this too..."*

A noise in the distance. A faraway rider.

Dr. Bagot?

No. He had never arrived in anything but a carriage.

Taking Pippins with her, Meg rushed out into the corridor and found a window not colored with the isolating stained-glass pattern. She brushed back the curtains, but had no view of the entrance drive.

Tom. The thought drove her to the stairs. She padded down them without a light, nearly stumbled, and winced when the kitten's claws pricked her chest in fear.

In the anteroom, the shadow of the butler was just pulling shut the door, his light flickering from the gust of night air. "Miss Foxcroft."

"Who arrived?"

"Why, no one, miss." He smiled, candlelight glimmering off his walrus-ivory dentures. He swept something behind his back. "In truth, I was just ready to depart for bed. May I assist you back to your chamber?"

"Tom McGwen was here." She stepped closer. "Wasn't he?"

"Miss Foxcroft—"

"He brought my shoes. Give them here."

He hesitated, then sighed. "Very well. Anything you wish, of course, Miss Foxcroft." He surrendered a pair of muddy half boots. "But I have been instructed not to allow—"

Meg brushed past him and out the door, ready to shout the name of Tom McGwen.

But the steps were empty, there was no movement on the pea-gravel drive, and the distant thud of pounding horse hooves faded into silence.

Meg clutched Pippins with a ragged breath. She should not have wished to see him. Not tonight, of all nights.

But he had answers she needed. If she was to make any decision regarding her future, she must first understand her past.

"Are ye ready then?" Tom glanced down the black chimney hole, a foot on each slope of the thatched cottage roof. He hoped the groaning and creaking was no omen the boards were about to cave.

When Joanie's answer rose up the chimney, Tom dropped the rope with a furze bush tied in the middle. Seconds later, she tugged the bush down.

Scratch.

Scrape.

Thunk.

"A bird nest!" Joanie laughed below, coughed, then shouted, "Up again!"

They repeated the process, pulling the bush up and down, until his hands were covered with soot—and the chimney, hopefully, was not. He pulled the bush out for the last time, the branches and crushed yellow flowers stained black and gray. A flurry of ashes swirled around him as he turned—

"Mr. McGwen."

He straightened, stilled, heartbeat grinding into his chest with a burst of speed.

Below, hand shading her eyes, Meg stared up at him. She wore something elaborate—a sort of green-velvet riding habit, with yellow gloves and the same boots he had rescued the night before. Her expression was hard. Her shoulders tight. As if she wished him to think her calloused, unaffected, and determined.

Which he might have believed if not for her eyes.

"Yer lord allows ye to go roaming by yerself, does he?" Frustration nipped him. He slung the bush off the roof. "Ye should know better."

"He does not allow nor disallow me to do anything. I am not imprisoned, sir."

"No." He tied the rope about his waist, secured it around the brick chimney, and lowered himself back to the ladder. "Just stupid."

"I did not come here to be insulted."

"Then ye shouldnae have come." Rung by rickety rung, he climbed down. When he reached the ground, he turned on her. "Someone wants to do ye harm, and until that man is found, ye'll be staying out of the open and going nowhere alone. Ye understand?"

"You are not my husband nor my guardian."

"Meg."

"Miss Foxcroft to you."

"Fine. Miss Foxcroft." He brushed at his shirt sleeves. Hard. "Since it's apparent ye need no one to tell ye anything, I suggest ye start looking to yerself and using yer own wits."

"I fully intend to."

"Good."

"Which is why, in fact, I am here." Her chin raised a notch. She wore no bonnet, and the loose wisps of her brown-red hair gleamed in the morning sunlight. Pink stole across her cheeks. "I wish to finish our discussion."

"It *is* finished."

"You have no right." She stepped toward him, arms tight at her sides—and he had a faint memory of a younger Meg with wild hair and patched trousers, raising a kitchen ladle over her head.

She had swatted at him twice and missed.

He couldn't remember why, unless it was the time he scooted the candle too close by accident and she lost part of her braid in flames. Or the day Maryanna Hopkins landed a surprise kiss on his cheek on the church steps after Sunday service.

"If you were any measure of a man at all, you would tell me."

"So ye think ye can persecute me into it, do ye, Meg Foxcroft?" He'd been grieved so long, missed her so, that he'd forgotten how blasted infuriating she could be. How impossible. How quickly she could get his blood heated. "Fine." He motioned to the cottage door.

As she nodded and marched inside, he tried not to think. Everything would have been so different. She would have begged him to paint the walls red before he ever cleaned the chimney. She would have flounced about the yard. Pointing at things. Gathering stones to frame her garden. Peeking in the windows and squealing. And running up to him, every few minutes, to throw her arms about his neck and tell him it was wonderful.

The ashes burned his throat as he followed her inside.

His steps were heavy.

If God was of the mind to take memories, He should have taken them from them both.

Lord Cunningham had likely arrived to the empty breakfast table. The realization should trouble her. She was wicked to forsake him and disappear when, at this very moment, she was supposed to accept the offer of becoming his wife.

His wife. For him to touch, possess, keep forever. Her skin crawled. *Our Penrose Abbey. Ours.*

"Joanie." Tom must have motioned the girl outside, for she gave a shy smile to Meg, curtsied, then slipped from the cottage. The door groaned shut.

All of Meg's nerves sharpened. She had a sense of being trapped—like she'd been with Lord Cunningham after the accident when he'd kissed her.

But Tom did not so much as look Meg's way. He grabbed Joanie's broom and went to work, sweeping hard at an old bird's nest, dirt, and flurrying ashes on the floor.

Meg took a step back, covering her nose and mouth with a handkerchief. She waited.

He swept.

Silence.

"Are you so contrary as to make me ask again?"

He gave her a quick side glance. He wore a soot-stained white shirt, the sleeves rolled up past his elbows, the sweaty cotton sticking to his back. The outline of his muscles, the strength and veins of his neck, gave her heart a tiny plunge.

She stared out the window—to the sloping green hills, the crab apple tree—anywhere but at Tom McGwen. "Well?"

"It happened to ye the spring before I came." *Swish.* "Ye were twelve." *Swish.* "Sent on an errand to deliver valerian to Mrs. Whalley, who was suffering another of her headaches."

Discomfort zipped up Meg's spine. Her mouth dried. "And?"

"It was dark on yer way home. Ye cut through the alley between the cobbler and the wine merchant." The swishing halted. His lips pressed, his face angled farther away from her, as if he were as afraid to look at her as she was him.

No. Do not tell me. She took a step back—

"A lad named Tobias Graham followed ye."

No.

"He hurt ye. Someone heard ye screaming, and he ran before…" Tom cleared his throat. "He ran before he took all of yer innocence."

"Does everyone..." A knot wedged in her throat. "Do they all know this of me? In the village?"

"Nay. The man who found ye was a sexton at the church. He carried ye to yer uncle, swore himself to secrecy, and even helped yer uncle in paying Graham to board the next ship out of Juleshead. He never came back."

She nodded. "I see."

Silence again.

She faced the window, holding her arms as a cold sensation of filthiness slinked through her. She was damaged. Irrevocably damaged. The incontrollable need to bury the truth, hide this secret, brought a blur of moisture to her eyes.

Then her heart pumped faster.

If she and her uncle had guarded this secret so well, kept it for so many years, why had she ever told Tom McGwen? She turned back around, looked at him.

He stood straight and rigid, eyes trained on hers, with an expression she could not decipher. Something about his face pulled at her, softened her. The pleasing shape of his eyes, with their dark red lashes and gleaming assuredness. The lines in his forehead. The sun-blush of his cheeks. The full, easy smoothness of his unmoving lips.

The lips she had given herself to in a different life.

Despite her fears.

Despite the alley.

The words rushed out of her before she could stop them, "I must have trusted you very much." To tell him such things about herself. To believe he would not alter the way he looked at her. Or leak the truth. Or find another village lass—one who had not been soiled and robbed of her precious purity.

Tom's nod was slow, a little sad, when he whispered back, "Ye did."

She did not return to Penrose Abbey. The reins were loose in her hands. She was aimless, listless, as her distance from both the cottage and abbey stretched wider.

She was not certain she would ever go back.

To either.

Sunlight—and shame—warmed her face as the horse discovered a small cart path in the field. She followed the trail. When it met with a grassy arched bridge, she dismounted and wandered to the middle. *I cannot do it.* She sat, legs dangling over the stone edge as the brown creek water rushed and splashed beneath her. *I cannot.*

She was not strong enough to marry Lord Cunningham.

And she was not strong enough to tell him she couldn't. Was she?

Tom's story colored again in her mind. She imagined it so well. As if she'd opened a book, read over the pages, and watched through words as someone else endured agony. Lord Cunningham had a right to know. If she were to be his bride, he must be privy to her secrets as surely as Tom was.

That bothered her.

That she had told Tom so much.

That whoever she was before had. . .

She tried to slam shut the imaginary book, but scenes rushed through her with flashing vividness. Her kissing him and laughing at the same time. Her holding his face. Feeling his jaw, his soft beard, while her nose brushed his. Then her doing the one thing she wanted to do now—crying, but not alone. Pressed close to him, swallowed in the arms that looked so strong, certain that nothing in the world could penetrate his strength and hurt her. Had it really been such a way? Had he truly made her safe? And happy?

In anger, she grabbed a fistful of grass. She slung it into the creek. *Kerplunk.*

The memories weren't real.

Mere fragments of her imagination.

In many ways, she was grateful she was no longer the girl who remembered the alley. The one who had nightmares haunting her soul. But another part—the smallest part of her—envied the Meg Foxcroft who had Tom McGwen to love.

Brushing at her clothes, Meg stood and remounted her horse. She turned back to Penrose Abbey, her heart alternating between each mile, not certain if she would reject Lord Cunningham when she returned or accept him.

By the time she made it through the gates, she was determined.

This had nothing to do with Tom.

The decision was for herself, because she could not entrap herself in marriage when so many questions still prowled through her. She would tell him tonight. At the dinner table. After his third glass of wine and only when he prodded—

"Miss Foxcroft." One of the maids, Tillie, met Meg as she entered the anteroom. Sweat lined her forehead. Her clothes were rumpled, damp, and her eyes had a stricken panic.

Meg dropped the riding crop, lungs squeezing. "What is it?"

"Miss Violet. She. . ." Tillie hiccupped on a sob. "She be dying and Lord Cunningham be gone."

CHAPTER 13

Blood dotted the white pillows and left a wretched smear of pink beneath Violet's nose. Her curls were damp. Her breathing loud, labored in the silent room.

"No." With a weak hand, she swatted something away from her face, eyes shut. "Get them off me. Hate them. Papa, please."

"She has been doing this an hour." Jenny settled a ceramic leech jar next to the bed, her jerky movements rattling the lid. "I have sent a manservant for the doctor, but who knows where he is. And Lord Cunningham departed early, as soon as. . ." Jenny's sentence faltered and she glanced at Meg through accusing side eyes.

Guilt fissured like an earthquake ripping through ground. "He departed to look for me."

"The servants cannot find him anywhere."

"He shall return." She swept to the bed. "Soon." Ripped back the coverlets. Peeled off the leech in the crook of Violet's thin, white-colored arm. "I need linens to staunch this blood flow and Cinchona bark powder. Hurry."

"But the leeches—"

"Do more harm than good." She wasn't certain where the words came from. Something her uncle had believed, despite common practice? "Jenny, hurry!"

The maid whimpered but rushed from the chamber, the door crashing shut behind her.

Meg wiped at the blood with a damp rag. Her heartbeat galloped as she placed a finger beneath Violet's earlobe and counted the dim pulse. The fever was too high. Some sort of infection. If they could diminish the fever, perhaps she would not...

Die? Meg nearly choked. She swept her hands along the girl's soft, burning cheeks. "You shall be well, dear Violet."

"Papa." The girl squinted her eyes open, tears leaking down her face. "I want Papa."

"He is coming."

"I want him now." Violet coughed and a fresh stream of blood trickled from her nose to her lips. She wept.

Mouth dry, chest tightening, Meg pulled back the coverlets and slipped in bed beside the child. She pulled Violet into her arms. *Do not let her die.* She kissed the scorched forehead and shuddered. *Please, God. Please.*

The corridor was silent, black, save for the dull light under Violet's door.

Lord Cunningham had returned an hour after dark.

Mary had told him first. Then Tillie had brought him upstairs. Then Jenny had cried and asked if she ought not to have listened to Miss Foxcroft and taken away the jar of leeches.

Meg had still been in bed with Violet when Lord Cunningham burst in.

His hair had been wild, wet with the evening rain, and his eyes were strange and unreadable when they collided hers. "Please, leave us." Not unkindly. Just tentatively, as if his voice were close to giving out and his composure near to demise.

Meg had departed the chamber and found the nearest hall chair. One by the window where a steady *pitter-patter* of rain tortured the panes. *My fault.* Lord Cunningham should have been here when his daughter awoke sick.

He would have been had Meg not disappeared.

She was thoughtless.

Rash.

Terrible.

Pulling her legs beneath her, she leaned her head against the hard wooden chair. Hours passed. She closed her eyes but did not sleep.

Sometime during the night, a soaked Dr. Bagot hurried down the hall, wet boots squeaking, breathing hard. He hurried into the chamber and did not come back out.

Meg covered her face with both hands. She wanted to be inside. She wanted to help.

But she was not certain Lord Cunningham would let her even if she could.

"Well?" Tom stared at the crinkled letters that Mr. Telfner spread out across his ink-stained counter.

Another grunt.

A closer glance through his quizzing glass.

Then Mr. Telfner straightened, nodding his head as if he had determined something significant. "It is most certainly wove paper."

"I need more than that. What about the black edges?"

"Yes, indeed. The edges." Mr. Telfner scratched his oiled black hair, and turned his attention back to a package of uncut quills. He spread five on the counter before he went to work with his penknife. "Mourning, to be sure. I have heard of the sentiment, but have yet to see it practiced." He glanced up at Tom with a smile. "Until today, of course."

"Then you did not line the pages?"

"I should think not." Mr. Telfner pointed at the letters with his knife. "You must examine the edges, my good boy. They are uneven, and too much ink has been applied so as to make the paper overly saturated. Work of someone inept, and certainly no job I would lay claim to, even if I had done it."

Exasperation rippled across Tom's shoulders. He should have known this would lead him nowhere. Everything else did. "And the handwriting?"

"The most fascinating of all." Mr. Telfner glowed as if the puzzle—the mystery—was a playful challenge to his intelligence. "It is very strained and deliberate. Notice how many places the pen stilled, as if mind and hand did not work in effortless rhythm."

"Which means?"

"Either the writer used a hand they are not wont to using."

"Or?"

"They are mimicking the writing of someone else." Mr. Telfner shrugged. "Either way, of course, the author of such letters wishes to remain unidentified."

Tom gathered the letters, stuffed them back into his pockets. He took a deep breath that smelled of papery vanilla and Mr. Telfner's too-strong hair oil. "Thank you, sir."

"Come by more often. The street is not the same without you and..." He seemed to think better of speaking her name, so he coughed and said instead, "Mrs. Musgrave will wish to see you, to be sure. You will call on her?"

"Yes." Tom started for the door—

"And boy?"

"Yes?"

"It is not much, but as most periods of mourning are less than two years, perhaps that shall aid in your search." When Tom didn't respond, Mr. Telfner shrugged. "Our unknown author, it would seem, has lost someone they very much loved."

Which was exactly what would happen to Tom if he could not discover who that person was.

"Dr. Bagot." Meg fell in step beside the man, aware that blood ringed his fingernails. Earlier that morning, she'd witnessed Jenny hurrying back into the chamber with the leech jar. "How is she?"

"She would be better if you had allowed her nurse to follow my instructions."

"With all due respect, sir, I did not think it wise."

"You have enough knowledge of medicine to gainsay common practice then." His steps quickened. "Remarkable, Miss Foxcroft. Especially for one who cannot remember her own name."

She accepted the injury without so much as a blink. "You do not answer me."

"The child will live."

"For how long?"

At the end of the hall, the doctor narrowed his eyes on her. Then he gripped the banister and started down the stairs, tautness in his shoulders. "The fever has broken. Your ministering of bark powder was serviceable. That much I can praise you for."

"I do not seek your praise, sir."

"Good."

"You shall remain at Penrose Abbey?"

"Unlike you, yes." At the bottom of the stairs, he looked at her again. Something about his eyes, the searching expression, troubled her. "A word of advice, Miss Foxcroft, if you permit it."

Her limbs tensed. She nodded him on.

"You say you have forgotten your past." The faintest embers of disgust burst into flame. "Do not think everyone else will too."

"Sit here. Let me look at you." Mrs. Musgrave placed a steaming cup of honey tea into Tom's hands, then gave a slight tug to his beard. "You should dispose of this, you know. I miss that impish face of yours."

"It keeps me warm."

"Humph. Like as not, you fear showing the boy beneath it." She settled into a wingback chair, sunlight from the curtained millinery window streaking across her face. Her skin seemed papery, pallid, as if she'd ceased the afternoon strolls she used to love. "Your sister is well?"

"Aye."

"You must bring her to see me. We should get along very well, I think, and perhaps I shall send her home with a bit of lace or ribbon." Had she not done as much for Meg a hundred times?

His old life—not so many days ago—heaved through him. Kneeling here in this same parlor, winding the longcase clock because Mrs. Musgrave forgot how. Meg on the floor, feeding bits of muffin to Lenox. The smell of spices and springtime through the open window. Days that were lazy, quiet, slow.

Days he missed.

"I wish you would bring Miss Foxcroft to see me too." Mrs. Musgrave blinked at him, her expression shifting. "You shall, will you not?"

"Meg is not the same."

"She must not lose all her friends, even if she has lost her memories."

"It is not that easy." Tom gulped down the tea in one scalding swallow. He leaned forward and placed the rose-painted cup back on its saucer. "She wants very little to do with the likes of us." He paused. "With me."

"You must have patience, Tommy."

Something he did not have. Along with responsibility, sense, and a hundred other things Papa never allowed him to forget. Tom stood, restless. "I must leave. Joanie and I will be moving to the cottage tonight. For good."

"Heavens. However shall Meade manage without you?" Mrs. Musgrave rose to grab his hand. She smiled, but the corners of her lips quivered a little and a twinkle of moisture filled her gaze. "Indeed, how shall any of us?"

"Ye know I'll be back to see my favorite lass."

She nodded but couldn't speak. Her cheeks whitened.

"Mrs. Musgrave?"

"I. . ." A breath escaped. She reached back for her chair, grasped it, sank into it with a little whimper. "I am sorry. . .I just. . ."

Tom knelt beside her. "Ye're sick."

"No, my dear."

"I'll go for a doctor—"

"You are not listening." Mrs. Musgrave clucked, though a tear escaped the corner of her eye. "You never listen. You are always off and running and doing whatever it is you do."

He wasn't certain what to say, nor what she meant, so he only stared at her.

She kissed his forehead. "If Mr. Foxcroft were alive, he would have nothing at all in his shop to heal what ails me. I am just an old woman who has no one to talk to save her dead husband and her little cat." Her chuckle was tear-clogged. "Elias would think me senseless, would he not? If he knew I still talked to him?"

Tom remembered very little of Mr. Musgrave—a wiry little man, quiet-tempered, who never did more than nod his greeting to Tom in those early days. He had passed four months after Tom arrived in Juleshead.

"But never mind me, dear boy. You must forgive an old woman for a bit of melancholy now and then." She pushed back to her feet, bustled into the kitchen with promises of a treat, and returned with a basket of freshly baked apple puffs. "For your first night at the cottage," she crooned.

Tom laughed and said he could not promise the puffs would make it to the cottage. Then he bid her goodbye, headed out into the street, and resisted the strange niggling that all was not as well as Mrs. Musgrave promised.

He intended to find out why.

"Violet is feasting on raspberry rose flummery, and you have yet to eat anything." Lord Cunningham spoke the words from her open bedchamber doorway.

Meg yanked the tortoiseshell comb through her hair, not glancing at him through the mirror of her dressing table. She couldn't.

"I wish to speak with you, darling."

"Do not call me that." She combed harder, ripping through knots, then settled the comb back with forced calm. She lowered her face. "Please. I am undeserving." For more than today. For whatever terrors in her past Dr. Bagot had spoken of. How much did the man know of Meg Foxcroft? Did he speak of the alley? The vengeful black-edged notes? Or something else?

She would have run after him, begged him to explain, had she been courageous.

She wasn't.

"It is true, I left because of you." Lord Cunningham took one step into her chamber. "But not to scour the countryside. I already knew you heard me discussing Mr. McGwen's new cottage, and I was certain, in your turmoil and uncertainty, it was him you would seek out."

Heat collected at her cheeks. "You speak as if he means something to me."

"He does."

"Did."

"Regardless, I was convinced that despite your temporary reluctance, after a day or so you would rejoice in the prospect of a life here at Penrose Abbey. You must know that even though you did not appear for breakfast, I finished my meal with vigor, not the least daunted by such a

The RED COTTAGE

discouragement." He stepped closer. "I left for Sunderlin Downs forthwith. If I was to wed you, I wished to do it properly and without any hindrance to either of our reputations. It is not yet whispered abroad of your situation. Very few, I daresay, know of your stay at the abbey."

"I do not understand."

"It is very simple." Another step. He stood behind her now, hands hovering over her shoulders, hesitating for several heart ticks before he finally grasped them. "I invited a guest to Penrose Abbey. Your own companion—who, after our long tête-à-tête, has agreed to instruct you in all manners of becoming the most accomplished lady." Lord Cunningham's gaze found hers through the mirror. Weariness hung in his expression, darkness sagged beneath his eyes, evidence of the three sleepless nights in Violet's chamber. "I realize now my blunder." A weak smile. "My hopes were quite in vain."

Pity constricted her throat. She was torn betwixt the niggling desire to squirm out of his touch and the throbbing need to soothe his internal wounds. "My lord."

"I shall make any arrangements you deem necessary. You can ask nothing too much. If you wish your own townhouse in London or your own trip abroad with friends, you shall have it."

She bit her lip. Thoughts, decisions, flitted through her in a troubling mass of bewilderment. She had determined to reject him. The words lodged in her, along with Tom's story of Tobias Graham, Dr. Bagot's distrust, and a thousand other things she had no bravery to pour out before him. "Perhaps I am not the lady you think me."

"Nor I the gentleman you think me."

With a weak touch, heart sinking, she laid her fingers across his. This was right. For her sake and even more for his. "I have no friend save you, and every other place in the world is strange to me."

"I shall give you a new life, anywhere you wish."

"I already have one." She stood on legs that were unsteady. "With you."

The cottage room was different this time of night. The dying flames licked and sparked from the hearth, putting out the scent of smoke and Joanie's hare soup. Everything was soft and shadowed. The nighttime breeze tickled coolness along the back of his neck.

"Gyb, no." Joanie extracted the kitten's claws from her nightgown, but other than a protesting meow, the room was quiet.

Melancholy.

Empty.

Like him.

From his position on the floor, arms draped over his knees, he tightened his lips around the pipe. He puffed. The bitter tobacco filled his senses like salt to open wounds, because Meg had always known he'd do this.

"You'll sit in a chair. One of those big soft ones, with damask cushions and everything." She had drawn the shape of one with her hands. *"And then we shall invite over Mrs. Whalley. I'll serve her tea, and you'll smoke your pipe and say things like 'yes, indeed' and 'fine weather, is it not?'"* She had laughed as if such a picture were the funniest thing in the world.

At the time, it was.

He pulled the pipe from his lips. He almost tossed it into the fire, but instead, jumped to his feet and glanced at Joanie.

She did not look up. Cross-legged by the window, she entertained Gyb with a ratty blue ribbon, but her lips curved downward.

Chagrin swarmed him. What kind of brother was he?

Joanie should be laughing, playing, and feasting over the apple puffs in delirious celebration. He should be cheering. They should be happy—right now—because the cottage was theirs and tomorrow they'd paint it red and maybe soon he'd build enough furniture to make it a home.

If Joanie needed anything, it was that.

He would give it to her.

Whether Meg was here or not.

"A thing or two we'll be needing to settle, lass." Tom grabbed his hat from the peg and whipped it against his thigh to remove the dust.

Joanie squinted up in confusion. "Where are ye going?"

"Stay here." He darted out of the cottage, jogged to the slightly withered crab apple tree, and plucked four or five unripened fruits. When he burst back inside, Joanie had her arms crossed in confusion.

"We can't eat those."

"They're not for eating, lass. They're for determining."

"Determining what?"

He emptied his hat, then tossed it across the room. "Who does the dishes."

"Tom." She laughed, likely because she already knew he would not do them even if she did triumph in his little game. But when he backed to the farthest wall and chucked a green-yellow crab apple across the room, she joined him.

"You missed."

"Hush with ye." His second apple landed squarely in the hole of his hat. The third rolled out. The fourth smacked the wall.

Joanie snickered as she gathered them and took her own turn. "Do not look at me." She missed a second time. "Tom, please. You must not watch or I shall do terrible."

"Ye already do terrible." He did a fast spin and threw one with his back turned. He roared when it landed. " 'Tis a bonnie life of dishes ye'll be having. Accept yer defeat."

"I would not be a McGwen if I did." She rolled up her sleeves, rubbed the apple between her palms, then beamed up at him with an adoring blush of pleasure. Just like she'd done years ago. Like all the children had done.

Something unexpected pinched his throat. Everything in his whole world was wrong right now.

But this was one thing right.

The next morning, one of the maid's awoke Meg with a gleaming, cerulean-blue gown draped across her arms. "She said you should wear this, miss."

Meg resisted the urge to crawl back beneath the coverlets. "She?"

"You best hurry."

Yawning, Meg allowed the maid to assist her into a soft linen chemise, then the stays. "Not so tight," she gasped. "It is constricting."

"Her ladyship said everything must be done to precision." The maid motioned to the dressing table once Meg was fully adorned in the silk, flower-netted gown. "The papillote iron is already hot."

Meg seated herself and stared in the oval mirror—watched as the limp copper hair transformed into tight, dramatic curls and a braided coil atop her head. She rubbed her eyes. Would Lord Cunningham notice they were swollen? She had not slept half the night. Even when she did, her slumber was restless.

Until the dream.

Somewhere between tossing and flipping her pillow upside down and glancing at the window to make certain no one lurked, sleep had conquered. She'd been somewhere strange. The edge of a cliff, early in the morning, with sea gulls gliding below sun-crested clouds.

She'd stared out across the sea and nearly stumbled.

Pebbles shifted under her feet.

Her body careened—

And then him. Tom McGwen, yanking her from the ledge, crushing her between his powerful arms and heart-racing chest. She told herself to push away. She should. She wanted to.

But at the same time. . .she did not want to.

She allowed him to kiss the top of her head, then her cheek, then her neck, then her lips. He was warm and soft. Sensations ruffled through her like the wind, staggering them closer to the cliff.

"Miss?"

Meg jerked. She glanced at her face in the mirror, touched her cheeks to will back the heat. Such a dream meant nothing. *Tom* meant nothing.

She knew enough of his character to be certain of that. Didn't she? Then why was she still so affected by him?

The maid finished with her ministrations, and Meg hurried downstairs to the drawing room, where her new companion was said to be waiting. She took in a breath. There was no reason to be unsettled. Was there?

Inside the room, a slender woman turned from the window. Her hair was whitish blond, her wrinkles softened with powder, her sharp chin lifted in a posture of scrutiny. "You must be Miss Foxcroft."

"Yes." Meg took another step forward. She tripped on the rug. "I fear I have not yet the pleasure of knowing your n–name. Lord Cunningham has told me little."

The woman smiled—regally, coolly—and approached Meg with her shoulders straight. Her dress was simple, white with delicate embroidery and a revealing neckline. She smelled of lemon and musk. "You bite your fingernails."

Meg glanced at her hands with a burn of surprise. She had never noticed.

"Your back is not straight. You maneuver your steps with the ease and heedlessness of a brutish farmer."

The insult left a slash of pain through Meg's midsection. She stood straighter, eyes wide, but could not seem to tear her gaze from the woman.

"Your speech lacks practice, and your confidence is waning." The woman leaned closer still and took a delicate sniff. "And you smell of the woods and stables. The worst of your failings yet."

"Miss—"

"My lady, to you." The woman's jaw protruded. "Whenever you enter an occupied room, you must bow. Then you must sit. But you must never, *never* stand here beyond the threshold, your poise forgotten, as if you had no sense at all."

"I assure you, I have sense." She bit the inside of her cheek, but it didn't stop the zing of anger. "Where is Lord Cunningham?"

"He has departed on business for the day. In truth, I requested it. I cannot instruct you properly with members of the opposite sex observing us, as if this were all a game." She smiled again. "It is not."

"I fear you misunderstand."

"No, I fear you do."

"I have no intention of—"

"Under my hand, you will learn decorum, needlework, musical concepts, language, fashion—and most of all, the ability to conceal this preposterous show of emotion." The woman nodded back to the door. "First, go upstairs and bathe. You will even your fingernails and you will powder your face against this ridiculous darkening complexation. It is clear no one has taught you anything."

"I like the sun."

"It is modish to be pale."

"Then I shall not be modish."

"Miss Foxcroft." The woman let out a small sigh. "You quite misjudge me. I am not unkind nor severe, only candid. And it is that forthrightness which has polished many a young lady in my years at the female seminary.

Lord Cunningham approached me and requested I guest here at Penrose Abbey to assist you in every way that I can. If this is not agreeable to you, I shall not waste either of our time." She waited only a second before marching to the door—

"Wait." Meg ground down her pride with her molars. "Lord Cunningham is to be my husband. If he wishes I learn from you, I shall."

"Very well. You may call me Lady Walpoole, and we may begin with our lessons in the library." She motioned Meg through the door. "After your bath, of course."

She had waited all day for Lady Walpoole to dismiss her. Then two more hours for Lord Cunningham's carriage to roll back through the wrought-iron gates.

Now she stood outside his study door.

The crack allowed her a glimpse of his face as he stripped off his burgundy tailcoat, poured himself a glass of brandy, and creaked back into his chair. Sweat glistened off his white skin. His expression was everything she knew, everything familiar, everything she should love.

She *would* love.

A weak throb of disappointment eddied through her. She resisted such an impulse. Lord Cunningham was kind. He had rescued her when so many would have thrown her away. For the first time, she could do something for him—something that would make him forget, if only for a moment, that his daughter lay dying in the upstairs bedchamber.

Tom would not understand.

That didn't matter.

Not in the least.

"Dr. Bagot?" Lord Cunningham must have heard her, for he twisted in his seat.

"No." She guided the door open with a cautious hand. "It is me. Am I disturbing you?"

"You?" He drained the brandy in his glass. "The weather disturbs me. These correspondences disturb me. I even disturb myself." His eyelids half fell. "But never you."

"I wished to speak with you concerning Lady Walpoole."

"She is not so very disagreeable already, pray?"

"She..." Meg arched her back straighter as the woman's reprimands surfaced. "She is dedicated, and I am certain I shall gain worlds of knowledge from such a teacher."

"You are perfect as you are. It is only for your sake I have arranged for the lessons at all. I wish my wife to be just as confident, just as superior, as any other lady of the *ton*."

Meg smiled, discomfort spinning through her as he walked around the desk. He caught her hands. Fondled them. Then scraped them against his damp cheeks—while the only thing she could think about was last night. The cliff.

Tom.

No, not Tom.

"My lord, there is one thing I must ask." She removed her hands to pat some imaginary stray curl back in place. "You have brought Lady Walpoole here to reconcile me with my future."

"In essence, yes."

She braced herself for his disapproval. "I wish to reconcile with my past."

CHAPTER 14

Weakness drilled Meg's knees as the manservant lifted her down from the carriage. No, this could not be. Her mind deceived her. This was too ridiculous, too preposterous, to be true.

"Mr. McGwen shall return me." She spoke the words without looking at either of the two footmen who had been sent to escort her.

They must have known her discomfiture, because one of them coughed away a smile and the other glanced again at the cottage. "Very good, miss." After a look passed between them, they climbed into the carriage and whipped the reins.

Meg drew in a breath she couldn't release. Who knew if they would report such a thing back to Lord Cunningham. No matter. The situation would last no longer than it took for Mr. McGwen to acknowledge her presence.

Which he did not do.

Even when she approached.

Humiliation sizzled beneath her skin as she stared from the dripping red cottage to the swishing paint brush to the red-pawed kitten playing in the grass. Anywhere but at...him.

She cleared her throat.

He cleared his.

"Mr. McGwen, you cannot be serious."

"The color?" He slabbed more red onto the wall. "A wee bit gaudy, is it?"

"No. I mean"—she flustered, angered, then flustered again—"not the color. You."

Sunlight glistened off the sweat on his back as he turned. Despite every plea within herself, her eyes skittered over him. Muscles shaped his arms, his shoulders, his red-haired chest.

He was solid and agile, with a readiness that made her certain he could outrun the wind or fight the wild. But it was his eyes that made her shiver.

Their softness.

The faint, sunlit twinkle.

She ignored the pull and crossed her arms. "McGwen, will you please put on a shirt?"

"Only got two. They'd not be worth a farthing after this." He dunked his brush back into the copper bucket of paint. "Besides—"

"This is most compromising and—"

"Ye've already seen me without one before." Before she had a chance to rage over the words, he angled his back to her again and pointed across his shoulder. "Fish hook. Ye dug it out yerself."

She stepped closer and her breath dropped. Tiny scars pinkened his flesh, as if he'd been slashed in too many places to count. "You were injured."

"Ye pulled it out."

"No, not the fishing hook. Something else. The cuts."

"What are ye doing here, Miss Foxcroft?" The way he spoke her name, the edge of distance in his voice, was altering. "I don't think yer lordy would be pleased ye've come."

"He is quite aware that I have. I assure you."

"What do ye want?"

She had been prepared to tell him of the forthcoming matrimony, but the only thing that came out was, "I have spoken with Lord Cunningham, and despite his qualms, have decided it is imperative I discover all I can of my past."

He stared, the sun in his eyes. "What are ye saying?"

"That I wish to know everything about myself." Her heartbeat hastened. "And I wish you to teach me."

"I'm not a good teacher." He'd been teaching her things for the past seven years. How to maneuver cod traps. How to swim. How to put squid bait on a long iron hook.

This was different.

Wariness lanced him, and he ripped another vine of ivy from the cottage wall. "I've told ye everything, lass."

"I want to *see* everything." She moved closer to him, fervor glittering her eyes. "I know I am the niece of an apothecary. I know my name. I know where I attended church, and now I know my own secret." Her hands clasped. "I want to know more. I want to know what I did in the evenings, what books I read, who I laughed with. My weaknesses and my strengths."

"Ye didn't read." He slapped more paint on the wattle-and-daub wall. "And ye laughed at me."

"I see."

Slap.

"You do not wish to help me."

Stroke.

"Why?"

His mind pulled in too many different directions. Eating roasted hazelnuts in front of the hearth last Allantide. Belting sea shanties to Brownie's wheel fiddle one afternoon by the rocky shore. Grumbling as he worked and tugged the knots from her hair with that old bone-carved comb.

She always had tangles.

He always worked them out.

"I thank you for your time, sir, and apologize I have misused it so tiresomely." He almost laughed as that old temper fired her voice and she spun to leave.

How she planned to do so, he was not certain.

The carriage was gone.

"Fine." Tom threw the brush to the ground, fighting an irksome grin. "Go inside. There's a shirt and trousers on the floor in the bedchamber. Joanie will show ye. Put them on."

The RED COTTAGE

"What?"

"Ye heard me."

"You cannot be earnest." She glanced from her dress to the bucket of paint, understanding softening—but not diminishing—the concern between her brows. "I most certainly shall not wear your trousers."

"Aye, but ye would." He grunted. "What ye wouldnae do is let me paint the cottage alone."

Several seconds fled in silence.

A breeze fanned through them, rustling the leaves of the crab apple tree, touching her curls, cooling the sweat on his skin.

Then she huffed in resignation and marched inside.

His reluctance swelled. He wiped his forehead. All this time, he'd had his memories—the old Meg, fresh in his mind, as far removed from the woman of Penrose Abbey as night was to noon.

He was not certain he was ready to reckon the two.

He could not lose them both.

The netted silk and spotless white linen piled at her feet, strange against the tarnished floorboards. She adjusted the gusset ties back of the waist. The woolen trousers were airy and itchy against her legs, and her elegant leather walking boots seemed ridiculous against the frayed hems.

Joanie pulled the soft white shirt over Meg's head. The girl had been washing and salting a calf's head in the main room, with a stewpot of sweet herbs, onion, mace, and pearly barley prepped by the hearth.

"You'll need help," she'd offered, then followed Meg into the tiny bedchamber.

Meg should have declined.

All of this.

But she popped her head through the shirt hole, annoyed that she still recognized Tom McGwen's smell in the fabric—and that it was so pleasant a scent.

"Thank you." She had expected herself to experience discomfort. To look at herself in this outlandish garb and feel as if she were stepping out of her own skin. Instead, a sense of freedom brushed across her consciousness.

She could move without restraint. No harsh stays pinched her ribs or tight neckline suffocated her bosom.

"Your hair was so perfect." Joanie tiptoed and eased a hair needle back in place. "If we had undone the buttons, we might not have mussed it."

"It is no matter." Meg was half tempted to throw her head in a bucket of water and shake everything free anyway. "A maid shall remedy whatever disarray I have made of myself before dinner."

"Would you like me to hang up these clothes?" Joanie lifted the dress and undergarments. "I shouldn't wish them to wrinkle."

"You are kind."

"It is no trouble." The girl blushed, eyes falling, everything about her features and manner in contrast to Tom McGwen. He was rash, his face sharp, his hair blazing like the sun come close of the day. Joanie was quiet. Her features were soft and fresh, her ways unassuming, and she had a thoughtfulness about her that made every movement seem deliberate and full of care.

"You look nothing like him." Meg had not meant to say the words aloud, but Joanie only smiled and smoothed the dress.

"None of us did. Well, except C–Caleb."

"There are more McGwens?"

"Nine of us now." Joanie lifted the chemise from the floor. "We don't share blood. We all come from different places but ended up in the same home. That's how it was meant to be. Mamm says, anyway."

"I never visited." Meg tilted her head. "I never visited with Tom, else I would have met you before, would I not?"

"We were very far away." Joanie hung all Meg's garments on little knobby pegs, then pulled open the bedchamber door. She glanced back as if she wished to say more, but then only smiled. "Tom is waiting for you."

She could not complain when she had asked for this. If it took laboring in trousers and a patched shirt to attain answers, she would. Meg started through the cottage—

"And Miss Foxcroft?"

Meg turned, a little startled by Joanie's serious eyes. "Yes?"

"He is still my brother." A pause. "He was a brother to all of us."

"Yes. Of course." Meg was not certain why the girl felt the need to defend him, nor why she tripped over the name Caleb, nor why Tom McGwen never once visited home.

She did not ask.

She came for answers about herself.

Not him.

"This was not what I expected when I agreed upon your little venture." Lord Cunningham waited for her inside the anteroom dressed in immaculate black tailcoat and pantaloons, bright white socks, and buckled slippers. He raised a brow at the smudges of red she'd left behind. "I would hail the doctor and deem it blood did you not appear so collected."

"Paint." She had scrubbed as much from her hands and arms as possible but had been too afraid to soil the dress to change. "I have not missed dinner?"

"No." He lifted his watch fob with an amused smirk. "Though I daresay, I am not at all convinced you have ample time to make amends of yourself. Lady Walpoole prizes first punctuality and second formality, both of which you could not manage." He placed her arm in his and patted her hand as they walked. "Do not worry. I shall escort you to your chamber, where you may bathe and change. A servant shall send up a tray."

"Thank you. I'm ravenous."

"Without doubt. Should I be angry?"

"Angry?"

"That instead of presenting my betrothed a seat and cup of tea, securing a proper chaperone, and answering her questions, he has instead turned her into a boy-clothed hoyden. Did he harness you to his plow once you finished his painting?"

Meg was not certain whether to laugh or be furious herself. "There are no chairs."

"Pardon?"

"In his cottage. He has no chairs with which to offer me a seat, his only furniture being a small table and two makeshift pallets. Thus, I do not think it fair to accuse him on that account." She shrugged. "As to your second concern, we had a chaperone."

"His sister."

"Yes."

"I specified *proper*, you must remember."

"Which she is, to the utmost." Meg sighed, liveliness coursing through her body as strongly as the hunger—and the aches. Had her muscles truly grown this lax in so few months?

"What manner of excuse do you have for his mastery over you?"

"It was my choice."

"Oh?"

"I petitioned him to teach me everything he knows of Meg Foxcroft. His methods, it seems, include *showing* rather than telling."

At her bedchamber door, Lord Cunningham cupped her shoulder. His eyes sobered. "I cannot tell if I am wise or foolish for allowing you these liberties."

Allowing her? Meg frowned but forgave him, all in the same heartbeat. He was afraid. As was she. "I cannot marry you until I do this."

"I hope you shall still marry me when you do."

"You doubt me."

"I doubt him." Lord Cunningham guided her back into the wall, face dipping to hers. "I doubt his scruples, his involvement in your danger, and even this." He flicked paint off her cheekbone with a gloved finger. "You must not allow him to beguile you, my dear. I cannot bear for him to ruin you twice."

"You assume much." She pulled his hand back down, just as his fingers ascended into her hair. "About Tom and. . .who we were before."

"It is not my wish to distress you."

"How much do you know?"

"Dear."

"Please."

His sigh spread over her face, warm but oddly disagreeable, like a fruit left unattended a day too long. "It is no secret among residences of Juleshead that your courtship with McGwen was anything but respectable. He enticed you into the night, as if you were a common trollop, and for all his years of courtship—could you call it that—he failed in his one chance to make it right. He did not marry you."

The RED COTTAGE

Disappointment throttled her, but the words felt unreal. She had many offenses against Tom. He had acted untoward so many times and made her livid more than that.

But beneath the beard and brashness, she had a recurring sense she could...well...trust him.

Maybe it was the way he had rushed into Joanie's chamber and rubbed the girl's face the night his sister had been injured. Or maybe it was just the way Joanie looked at him. As if he were the sun and moon. As if he could do anything.

Meg didn't know. She didn't know him *well* enough to know.

"I am sorry." She lifted her head. "You only mean to protect me, for which my gratitude knows no bounds. But tales grow larger sometimes in the hands of little people."

"You do not believe me."

"I believe you do not know the truth any more than I do." Meg ducked under his arm and pulled open her chamber door. "Goodnight, my lord. Tomorrow, I promise I shall give myself fully to Lady Walpoole and her lessons."

He nodded, bowed, and forced a smile she detected was not sincere. How long would he stand by and permit her to hunt down the truth? What would she do when he stopped?

She was restless.

Meg had imagined the warm bath and the japanned tray of food would have induced sleep after so long a day. It didn't. She lifted her eyes to the mirror across the room, almost proud that her cheeks glowed a soft, sun-burnt pink.

She did not wish to examine today.

If she was invigorated, it was only the result of physical labor and the sweet countryside air. Which was quite ordinary. After all, had she not been injured and bedridden endless days in a row? Then kept inside, like a fragile figurine, lest anyone attack?

Finding her wrapper, she shrugged it on and left her bedchamber. She navigated to Violet's door and gave a light tap.

"Who is it?" Jenny's sleepy voice.

"Miss Foxcroft."

Seconds later, the door opened to Jenny's tousled hair and watery eyes. "Oh, miss, you quite frightened me." From slumber, it seemed. "Come in."

"You may retire. I shall stay with the child."

"But his lordship—"

"Shall not mind, I assure you."

Jenny looked as if she might argue further, but the thought of rest must have been too overpowering. She nodded and ambled from the room.

"She snores, and I hate it." Violet sat cross-legged on top of her coverlets, a doll on each side of her and a book in her lap. She appeared stronger, and though her cheeks lacked much color, her little bow-shaped lips were more pink than blue. "Did Father send you to read to me?"

"No." Meg sat on the edge of the bed. "In truth, I was quite forbidden to attend dinner, so I thought I might seek out company with you."

Violet grinned at this. "What did you do?"

"It is too terrible to tell."

"Tell me!"

Meg laughed and scooted closer. She whispered her naughtiness of boy's trousers and red paint into Violet's ear, and the girl threw back her head with a cackle.

"I bet Father glowered."

Glowered? Meg almost laughed. "That is a big word for such a small child."

"I read a lot." Violet nodded to her book. "I have already read this one fourteen times. *The History of Little Goody Two-Shoes*." She flipped to the next page. "I love Margery."

"Shall I read to you?"

Violet nodded, and after they'd situated themselves against pillows and Violet had pulled both dolls into her arms, Meg began. She read in tones that were hushed and animated. Though she found little delight in the story itself, Violet's swift corrections to Meg's mispronunciations had both of them giggling.

When the book was finished, Violet sighed and yawned. "Miss Foxcroft?"

The RED COTTAGE

"Hmm?"

"Will you read a little longer?"

"You must sleep now."

"I hate sleeping."

"Come now. It shan't be as terrible as all that." Meg slid off the bed, tugged loose the coverlets, and helped Violet under them. "Do you wish to sleep with your dolls?"

"No. I am not a baby."

"Oh. But of course." Meg removed the toys to their own doll-sized beds on the floor. "Better?"

"Will you stay?"

"I fear all this reading has made me tired too."

"Just a little longer. Please." The last word—spoken without that usual demanding pitch—softened Meg's resolve. The child was unruly. She was pampered.

But she was as destitute as little Margery Meanwell in the children's book. Not of shoes, care, food, and shelter—but of company, affection, and hope.

Meg nestled next to the girl under the coverlets, a little surprised when Violet cuddled into Meg's chest. For a long time, she prayed. *Help Violet to be well.* Her hair was damp and cool against the pillow, and Violet's skin was warm against hers. *Do not let Lord Cunningham suffer greatly. Make him happy. God, make me love him.*

Violet's breathing turned heavier, slower, a little wheezy.

Keep me safe. Meg's eyes slid shut. *Make me a better woman than I was.* Sleep drifted, like a fog settling over her, then lifting again. *Help Joanie. Help. . .* She pulled back the name Tom, because she was afraid to think of him.

All evening long, he'd crowded on the outskirts of her mind, and if she lowered her bulwarks once, he would barge in. *Help him, God.* The prayer came anyway. She must have been too tired to keep up the walls.

How quiet he'd been today as she stood two feet away and stroked paint onto his cottage. "Ye're doing it wrong," he told her once. He'd walked over, grabbed her wrist, and swept the brush up and down in a smooth and vertical motion. "See?"

She had nodded. "You must forgive me if I am inept. I have never painted before."

"Yes, ye have."

Her pulse had sprinted, and her skin tingled a little where his work-roughened fingers had touched her bare wrist. She should have worn gloves. But how could she have known he would touch her?

He spoke next to nothing over the next two hours. He never did put on his shirt.

But when Joanie finally emerged from the cottage, declaring dinner would be finished soon, Tom took Meg to the water pump, watched her clean the paint, then did the same himself. He rode her back to Penrose Abbey on the back of his horse.

"If it is agreeable to you, I shall come again in a day or two. I do hope our second lesson shall be a trifle more enlightening."

He had swung her off his animal without dismounting himself. "Ye willnae come alone."

"No, I will not come alone. Good day, Mr. McGwen."

He looked at her a second longer than he should have. Slow, careful—not angry or exasperated as she had first suspected. Almost. . . wary? Of her? He rode away without saying anything.

That silence haunted her into sleep.

CHAPTER 15

"You were not kind to her." Joanie slipped onto her knees next to Tom, where he'd already spread out across his pallet for the night. She twisted backwards. "Will you button me, please?"

He leaned up and fumbled with her button. "There."

"Thank you."

"Now go to sleep with ye."

She felt her way to the other side of the room, blankets rustling as she settled into her own pallet. She sighed. "Tom?"

"Lass," he growled.

"Just one thing more, and then I won't talk."

"What?"

"Why were you so unkind to her?"

"I wasnae unkind."

"You didn't talk."

He searched for words to defend himself. He didn't have any. "Och, go to sleep." His final command spiraled the tiny, dark bedchamber into silence. He stared at the rafters. He rubbed a hand down his face. Then, low, "I dinnae know what to say to her. I dinnae know how to talk to her anymore."

Joanie's shadowed form raised her head.

"And I've a fear she'll not love anything about her old life." His face tightened. "Not now."

"Maybe you should do something nice for her. I didn't remember you much when I came. I was afraid you would wish me gone. But when you gave me my new shoes, I thought you were. . ."

A noise outside the cottage, altering his focus.

He whipped up. "Hush."

"Was that a horse?"

"Stay here. Dinnae move." He crept from the bedchamber, pulling the door shut behind him. His nerves snapped to attention. In the darkness, he ducked below window view and stood only long enough to grab the double-barrel rifle above the mantel.

He swung around just as the door crashed open.

"Move and I'll kill ye."

The bulky shadow took a staggering step inside. "If you can."

Meade? Tom lowered the gun, although he was tempted to fire a bullet next to the man's head. "Blast, what are ye doing? I could have shot ye."

"Brownie said you bought a horse." Meade stumbled inside and tried to hang his hat on the peg. He missed. "Gun too. You gonna spend every last nicker on this place?"

Tom decided not to answer. "It's eleven o' clock at night."

"Came home. Found this." Meade tried one pocket, grunted, then searched another. He finally found what he was looking for tucked in his left boot.

Tom snatched it and looked for a candle. He lit it and read over the familiar script.

> *They are blind who close their eyes. If you wish the truth, perhaps you should call again upon your friend. Mrs. Musgrave knows more than she tells.*

Mrs. Musgrave? What did she know or have to do with any of this?

"You sleep. I'll guard." Meade reached for the rifle as if he expected trouble, but Tom shook his head.

"It is nae threat, but ye best not ride home like this."

"I can sit saddle."

"Take my bed."

"I'll be takin' the barn." With nothing more and forgetting his hat, Meade swaggered from the cottage and slammed the door behind him.

Tom stared at the black-edged note in his hands. The words made him cold. This better lead him to answers—and fast.

Meg's time was running out.

"You have an artless hand, Miss Foxcroft." Lady Walpoole handed Meg another cutout paper. This one appeared to be a bugle. "See there, an empty space. You may situate it between the manor and the tree."

Or your forehead. Meg resisted the urge to smack the paper into the woman's face. With a careful hand, she swished on the glue and secured the bugle to the folding screen.

After a morning of letter writing and table etiquette, Lady Walpoole had ordered a manservant to carry this lumbering screen into the courtyard. For the past three hours, they had been laboring to paste on decorative pictures, and when the glue had ample time to dry, they would come back to paint on the varnish.

"Decoupage," Lady Walpoole explained. "All ladies of breeding are well accomplished in the skill, and if you are incompetent, you shall have nothing at all to talk of with your peers."

What sort of conversation would this make, even if she were master at it?

"You are sagging again."

Meg straightened.

"Keep your elbow inward."

Fine.

"Chin up."

"I cannot look down if my chin is up." Meg blew out air in frustration and applied another cutout with a little too much force.

Lady Walpoole frowned. "Very well, Miss Foxcroft. I see I have quite exhausted your patience."

Had she been so obvious?

"You may go indoors and spend the next hour reviving your enthusiasm. I shall finish here."

"Thank you." Meg gave the woman her first real smile of the day. She started away, remembered to curtsy, and turned back to do so.

Lady Walpoole did not appear impressed. "Do not forget, the dancing master shall arrive in precisely an hour. You shall meet us then in the ballroom, wearing something other than your morning dress. Understood?"

"Yes, my lady." Before the woman could devise another form of torture, Meg hurried to the cloisters, found the door, and rushed indoors. As much as she enjoyed the fresh air—the rose bushes in bloom, the floral garden scents, the dog at play in the folly—she'd rather lock herself in the dankest room of the abbey than endure any more of her ladyship.

She undid her bib-fronted apron.

Then pulled out her hair needles and shook the locks free as she hurried through a corridor toward the stairs—

Movement.

In the window.

Meg froze and jerked back, a flight instinct urging her to run. Tasseled draperies covered part of the window, but a quaint view of the courtyard boxwoods was still visible through the pristine panes.

Her mind scurried as she took a tentative step closer. She peeled back the brocade fabric, looked everywhere.

Nothing.

No one was here. No one had watched her.

But as she hurried away down the corridor, stuffing the hair needles in her pocket and folding her apron, gooseflesh dotted her skin.

She could have sworn she'd seen a face.

Mrs. Whalley was in the millinery shop when Tom arrived, trying on a tall bonnet with too many flowers and bows. "It does rather improve upon the shape of my face, to be sure. Although I shall have to speak with Charles, as I have not quite enough pin money." She barked out a laugh, but the sound came to a grating halt when her eyes met Tom's in the mirror. "Oh. Dear me. I had not at all imagined myself to be observed."

"Mrs. Whalley." Tom nodded a stiff greeting.

Hers was equally stiff. "I must say, I am quite surprised to see you here, as I heard it mentioned only last evening that you took residence outside of our little village. I daresay your father's inheritance must have been ample indeed, have you the funds to purchase a cottage and cease fishing altogether."

Tom bristled at the infernal woman's tone. Ignoring her, he moved to the counter, where Mrs. Musgrave was busy thrusting ostrich feathers into the ribbon of a new straw hat. "May I speak with ye a moment?" he asked.

Mrs. Whalley sashayed beside Tom. "Dear Mrs. Musgrave, do not think of bothering over me. Left alone, I shall probably try on every bonnet—and likely buy three of them." She flicked a hand at Tom. "You have *company*. Good society is just what our own dear Tom needs, I think."

Mrs. Musgrave scooted over a tiny brass bell. "Do ring if you need something, please. I shall only be a moment." She motioned to Tom. "Come along, dear."

In the kitchen, she set a pewter kettle to boil, then pointed to one of her yellow-and-flower-painted chairs. "Sit down. Are you hungry?"

"I could eat a wee bit of whatever's in that jar over there."

She beamed in delight. "I just baked them this morning. Millefruit biscuits."

Once she'd fetched two glasses of milk and biscuits enough for ten of them, Tom reached into his pocket. He slid the note across the table.

"What is this?" She plucked it up. Some of her color drained.

Silence.

Tom cupped his hands around the cool milk, eyes steady on her face, as an erratic pulse beat at his throat. "Well?"

"I cannot imagine why this. . .I mean, whatever could I have to do with it?" She dropped the note, as if the touch of it burned her. Her eyes pooled tears. "I must go and see to Mrs. Whalley. She would never ring the bell, but I am certain she shall need my—"

"Ye're upset." Tom bounded to his feet and stopped her before she reached the doorway. A touch to her arms confirmed what he already suspected: She trembled.

"Look what you have made me do. Now I am crying again like a silly old fool." She waved an anxious hand. "I do not want anything to do with this, Tommy. Not anything at all."

"Ye know something."

"No."

"Meg needs you." He tried to bite back the passion heating his voice. "I need you. If ye have any idea who wrote such a letter, then maybe ye can—"

"I do not know who wrote the letter." Her voice gave out on the last word, and she turned back to the kitchen. She went to the cupboard, where Lenox napped on the top shelf, and pulled out a pottery bowl without disturbing him. She lifted a folded piece of paper. "I only know I received one too."

Candlelight wavered across Tillie's face, accenting deep shadows beneath her eyes. She crept closer to the bed. "Very sorry, miss, to disturb you. Are you certain you be awake?"

Meg laid a hand across her thrashing heartbeat, willing the fear to settle. She'd awoken the same time the door whined open. She'd fought with the coverlets. Then battled the scream in her throat—half wondering if it would make any difference.

If she was going to die, she might as well keep her dignity.

But it was only Tillie—dressed in an age-yellowed nightgown and matching night cap—holding out a dripping candle and looking for all the world as if she had just received a fright herself. "At first I thought we would be robbed. I was ever so terrified and would have woken his lordship, but then I recognized the horse."

"What horse?"

"The one what brought you home the other night." Tillie slipped closer to Meg's side, her whisper quickening, "So's I went to the door, on account of him knocking so loud it might near rise the dead. And he said that I should fetch you. And I said that Miss Foxcroft be sleeping, but he said it didn't matter 'cause you would have to leave now if you was to make it to church."

Church? Tom McGwen wished to take her to church?

"What time is it?"

"Several hours before dawn."

"I thought so." Arguments slid to the tip of her tongue, all the reasons she could not possibly go with him. The hour was too early; Lady Walpoole would likely faint; Lord Cunningham would scowl his disapproval.

The words never came out.

Instead, she threw back the coverlets and took Tillie's candle. "Help me dress. Hurry."

"You mean you be—"

"Any gown will do. I expect I had not an impressive wardrobe at my uncle's apothecary shop, and no one ever minded then." She had to admit there must have been a little freedom in that. Wearing whatever you wished. Slouching, if you chose. Leaning in and gulping down your tea instead of raising it to your lips and sipping like a pretty little painted puppet.

Five minutes later, she was dressed in a simple yellow gown with a light blue spence jacket, her hair twisted back in a loose chignon. "Gloves?"

"These are soiled, but—"

"Never mind. They shall do." Meg hurried for the door but turned back with a sharp breath. "Tillie? You shall tell Lord Cunningham where I've gone?"

"Yes." Uncertainty crimsoned her cheeks. "I hope he shan't be angry."

"He never is."

"With you."

Meg gave the girl a reassuring smile, then hurried through the dark abbey corridors, down the stairs, and to the anteroom. Her heart pounded again. Not from fear. Something else.

She stopped before bursting out the door, shaking her head. What was she doing? This was unseemly. Absurd. Even if her old nature had been so reckless, she knew better now.

Go back. A dull warning, but she reached for the door anyway. She stepped outside, the blackness enveloping her, the night fragranced and chilly against her skin. "Mr. McGwen?"

Night bugs chirped in answer.

Had he gone already? She snuck down the steps, dragging her stained glove along the stone railing. His horse waited at the bottom. No Tom. She turned—

Hands swung her up in one effortless motion. She let out a small yelp, swatting, but she was planted atop the saddle before her fighting rendered any good.

Then he was behind her, arms caging her in. "Sit tight with ye," he grumbled in her ear. "And for once in yer life, keep yer mouth shut."

She wanted to be angry. She wanted to insist they take a carriage and, even more, that he never grab her again without proper consent. Which he would not receive. Not again.

But as the horse took off at a wild gallop and the air beat at her face, none of that mattered. She lost her fury to the wind, her heart to the night. And she couldn't help thinking—no matter how wrong this was—that she could not remember feeling more exhilarated in her life.

He had braced himself for her confounded fury. She had asked him to teach her, raising her lofty chin and standing there in her fancy clothes as if Tom were a servant she was bidding to polish her shoes.

He knew her well enough to know one thing.

She would fight him on everything.

She always did.

Blast. He thrust his heels harder into the horse's sides, their speed gaining through the fog-moistened night. Mud splattered behind them. What would she think of Juleshead upon closer inspection?

He had a million places he wanted to show her.

None that would impress. Or mean anything.

That was the root, perhaps, of his foul temperament. Not that Meg would fuss at him. Not that she wore her perfect, tailored clothes. Not even that she demanded Tom teach her, after all these terrible weeks of despising the sight of him.

No.

He widened his arms again, but her wind-loosened hair still tickled his face. 'Twas only that the life she'd forgotten was small. The stockings he wanted to return were threadbare and worthless. The wharves a little grimy. The shore where they'd played without luster.

Painters would never go there.

She probably wouldn't either after she saw it through new eyes.

He hardened his gaze on the road ahead, keeping the sigh trapped inside him. He would not think of such things. This was what Meg wanted. To know the truth.

The RED COTTAGE

He would give it to her.

What she did with it was out of his hands.

He would focus his attention, instead, on keeping her safe. Mrs. Musgrave had not shown him the letter. Mrs. Whalley had bustled into the kitchen, peppering questions about a certain ugly looking turban, and Mrs. Musgrave had no choice but to smile back her tears and slip the note away in her pocket.

She had reached for Tom's hand just before she left. "Come back tomorrow after church. The shop will be closed, and we may talk then."

He was afraid to find out what had spurred such a tormented look on her face.

He was more afraid not to.

Tom McGwen spoke very little to her the length of the ride, and Meg did not bother trying to penetrate his silence. If he wished to brood, so be it.

Besides, he had made it very clear he did not wish to hear her voice. Fine.

She did not wish to hear his either.

By the time they reached Juleshead, most of the village lights were still unlit, and only a faint hue of yellow softened the sky. Their horse hooves clip-clopped on the cobblestones. The air smelled like primrose bushes and brisk freshness as they passed gold-colored storefronts and row houses.

A mother goose and her ducklings wandered into the street. Tom waited until they passed before urging his horse forward again.

When they reached a round-tower church, Tom tied his horse to a beech tree and swung Meg from the saddle. He led her inside.

The nave was empty and narrow, with an old stone altar and white plastered walls. A massive window with fifteenth-century tracery filtered dusty sunlight into the room.

"Here." Tom motioned her into a box pew. "We're early."

She situated herself, pulled off her gloves, and resisted the urge to scoot farther away when Tom sat next to her.

The fabric of his brown coat touched her jacket. Odd that it stirred a faint rustling in her chest. She fidgeted. Sighed. Then finally gave in to her discomfort and slid an inch away from him. "Now what?"

"We're early."

"You said that already."

He glanced at her, neither with amusement nor annoyance, and leaned back in his seat. He propped his boots on the opposite bench.

"In truth, sir, I did not imagine you attended services."

"I wish ye wouldnae call me that."

"Sir?"

"Aye."

"What did I call you before?"

"Same thing as everyone else." He stroked his beard. "My name."

"Very well. Tom." Turning toward him, leaning an elbow on the box pew wall, she studied his face. "You did not answer me. I seem to recall your reluctance during a previous conversation to acknowledge the handiworks of God."

"I come to church."

"Begrudgingly?"

Tom sent her a quick side look before turning his eyes back to the front of the nave. A wry grin quirked his lips. "Listening to the vicar is like hearing yer uncle rattle off tincture recipes."

"But you do believe." When his lips flattened, she prodded, "Do you not?"

Pain bothered his face—a look she knew only because she'd felt the cold prongs of despair herself. Surprise flicked through her. Tom McGwen knew grief. And it had nothing to do with her or now or anything that had happened as consequence to the black-edged notes.

He had told Meg her own secret. Had he ever told her his?

As the cloud vanished, he pointed across the church with a smirk. "See that pew?"

"Yes."

"One time old Mr. Hickinbottom, the sheepherder, had another of his falling sicknesses. He toppled over in the middle of the vicar's sermon, and while everyone else was whispering and doing nary a thing, ye climbed over the box pew, pulled him out into the aisle, and set to cradling his head until it passed."

Warmth flushed over her at the admiration in his voice. "It must have been a spectacle."

"The vicar gave you a lecture. Mr. Hickinbottom gave you a sheep."

"He did?"

"Aye."

"What happened to it?"

"Mutton stew." He laughed. "Ye hated to eat anything ye'd named, but yer uncle wanted it gone soon as ye carried it into the shop. It bleated a whole night before he lost his patience."

How very much she wanted to take in his words, live and breathe them, until they colored all the emptiness of her mind. "Tell me more." A strange homesickness wafted through her. "Anything about me. Or my uncle. What we were like."

"Ye laughed a lot." Tom shook his head, tender crinkles at his eyes. "Come evening, especially. When ye were tired. When it was the three of us."

"We spent a great deal of time together."

"Aye."

"Did you..." She regretted the question that almost slipped out. When Tom raised a brow, she plunged forward anyway. "You spent time with other village girls too, I presume?"

He seemed a little surprised by her curiosity. A little pleased too—annoyingly so.

"Not that it matters to me." Meg shrugged. "I just supposed you did."

"Why?"

"I—well, because—"

"Ye think me a wee bit handsome?" The daring grin that widened his lips made her glare.

"Certainly not. *Sir*." The last she added with no small amount of defiance as she tightened even closer to her end of the box pew.

Tom did not seem bothered. He leaned closer, his intentions unclear, when—

Voices and footsteps echoed behind them. An elderly couple bustled down the aisle, paused in cheerful greeting, and found their seats at the front of the church.

"Later," Tom whispered. What had he been ready to say? Or do?

As a clock on the wall ticked by at an irritating rate, others wandered in. A mother with five towheaded children, a trio of three young maids, more husbands with their wives.

When the bell struck its first booming note, Joanie and Meade slipped into the box pew behind them. He clapped Tom on the shoulder. "Nod off and I'll be hammering the back of your head."

"Might need to do the same to ye, after last night," said Tom.

Meg glanced back at the blacksmith. She had never seen his hair slicked back and his skin scrubbed clean of the usual soot. Despite the tidiness of his appearance, however, his eyes were red rimmed.

Joanie brightened. "I brought this for you." She handed over two light-pink hollyhocks. "I made Meade stop along the road so I could pick them."

"Oh, they are lovely." A little drooping, a little hand crushed, but sweeter than all the perfect blooms in the Penrose garden. The innocent token of friendship startled Meg with gratitude—and comfort.

The bell ceased.

The vicar climbed his pulpit, wearing a white surplice and bands, and read in a scratchy voice from the *Book of Common Prayer*. Sunlight glowed behind him. Everything hummed around her, tiny noises—one of the tots whimpering, a pew creaking, Meade hiccupping behind them.

And Tom.

She detected his breathing and was far too aware of every twitch he made. She was not certain if she had shifted or he had, but the inches between them had lessened.

Only once during the whole service did she glance at his profile.

He was relaxed, sleepy, and his eyes had a steady kindness. For a fleeting second, she had the wildest impulse to lean against him, slip her arm through his, and make herself at home in a world she had once lived in.

She ripped the thought from her heart with a set jaw. She was here to learn about the old Meg Foxcroft. Not become her.

Of all the places Tom could take her next, a millinery shop was the last she would have expected. What was he going to do, buy her a hat?

An old woman greeted them at the door, and judging by her enthused embrace and the startling kisses she planted on Meg's cheek, the milliner was a friend. Or used to be.

A light quiver weakened Meg's knees as the wrinkly hand clasped her own.

"Come in, come in." The woman led them into a quaint parlor decorated with mismatched trinkets, a tall old clock, and sagging damask furniture. "I am Mrs. Musgrave, dear. Tommy tells me you do not remember."

Meg glanced at him.

He sat on the edge of his chair, elbows on his knees, and smiled. Somehow she gained courage from his unaffected look. She relaxed.

They sat, the three of them, for over an hour.

They talked of Lenox—a fat old cat who slinked from one lap to another, kneading the rug and yawning between each of his naps. Then they spoke of desserts, trifling village gossip—and Mr. Foxcroft.

Mrs. Musgrave said he was a good man. That she put flowers on his grave every week or so.

But her voice was a little stilted, a little hoarse, and she glanced at Meg with a puzzling look. One that belied her smiles. Her kisses. Her sweetness.

Meg's discomfort reared all over again.

Tom must have noticed. He stood. "Ye forgot something."

"Oh?"

"Ye've two hungry beggars on yer hands."

"Oh, you." Mrs. Musgrave chuckled, waved at him, and said that Meg should wait right here and rest. Tom she needed in the kitchen.

They disappeared, leaving Meg alone, confused. The same sickness soured her stomach as she rose to the window and stared out at the black-timbered remains of her uncle's shop. Why had the old woman looked at Meg that way?

Mrs. Musgrave had been all kindness, all coos and gentle laughs.

Then, in one instant, accusations and distrust had engulfed her eyes, leaving Meg singed. What had she done to warrant such doubt? And was such a crime so terrible she deserved to die?

"I want to see the note."

"I do not think you do, my dear."

Tom went to the cupboard himself, pulled out the bowl, and found it just where she'd stashed it before. He read over the words with a gut-stitching pain:

> Mr. M did not die of apoplexy. I do not have proof, but if you search your heart, you will know it to be true. He was slaughtered by the ones he sought to save him. There are wolves in our sheep.

"I cannot sleep and I cannot eat." Mrs. Musgrave stared at him, white lashes wet, her face blotched red. "Elias had been ill for months. It all happened so sudden. He was bent over the hearth, putting embers in our bed warmer. . .and he just dropped it on the floor and said he couldn't feel himself." Mrs. Musgrave hugged her arms. "He was strange after that. Tripping over his words. Falling over when there was nothing to make him stumble. Finally, he said he could not live this way. He went to see Mr. Foxcroft." She palmed her face dry. "He did not come home."

"Ye believe this." His hands ached to shred the paper. "A letter from someone who cannot even show his face."

"Sit down, dear."

"I'll stand."

"I've corn and haddock, and if you wish buttered bread, I can—"

"Ye looked at Meg like ye dinnae even know her."

Mrs. Musgrave went into the larder and came back with a bowl of pears. She rearranged them in the bowl, and when she finally looked up, her wrinkled lips formed a devastated line. "Perhaps I do not know Meg. Perhaps you do not either."

"Ye cannae mean that." War raged in his chest. He stepped closer. "Meg wouldnae do such a thing. If I have to prove that to you and whoever wrote this note, I will."

"I do not wish it to be true."

"It isn't."

"All these years, I had this prick. Right here." She clutched her heart with white-boned knuckles. "I knew something was not right. I felt it. And for the first time, I think I know why." She reached for the note, cradled it against her as if it held the keys to the world. "You are a good boy, Tommy. I do not wish to see you suffer more than you already have."

A muscle jerked in his jaw.

"But like you, I have realized I must find whoever wrote this note. I must discover the truth." Her entire body trembled. "Whether you believe it or not."

CHAPTER 16

They should go back. If Lord Cunningham had not already sent an army after her, he would if she was not returned before dark.

For the second time today, Tom grabbed her hand. She thought to protest, but the gesture seemed more practical than affectionate. From the millinery shop, he'd dragged her to the smithy, where they'd eaten warm pasties with Meade and Joanie. Then on to the graveyard, where he'd shown her Mr. Foxcroft's tombstone. Then the curiosity shop, where they'd piddled about and purused the old and scruffy treasures.

His fingers were strong, almost too strong.

The alley narrowed, then opened up to weathered quays and a translucent green sea. He jogged to the end of a wharf, freed her hand, sat, and dropped his legs over the edge.

She remained standing. "I think it time we depart."

He patted beside him.

"I am in earnest."

"Sit down with ye before I throw ye in." Ever since their departure from the millinery shop, he had been distracted, his brow a little heavy, as if his mind were solving problems elsewhere.

Now, his eyes lifted to hers in full attention.

A faint pricking sensation breezed the back of her neck, and she threatened her lips not to return his grin.

He raised a brow, as if giving her one last chance to comply. Had he always been so demanding? Or she only more indulging?

"Oh, fine." She plopped down next to him, sighing away her frustration. "You realize, of course, I shall never hear the end of this from Lord Cunningham."

"Yer uncle always survived. I think yer lordy will too."

"Were we so imprudent?"

"Depends on who ye ask."

"What if I ask you?"

He took off his coat, tossed it beside him, and rolled up the sleeves of his shirt. "I think ye worry about it all too much. Ye were happy. 'Tis all ye need to know."

"Surely, you cannot blame me for my inquiries." She stared out across the water—the blue-orange evening sky melting into the horizon, the seagulls mewing above them, the anchored fishing vessels bobbing in the waves. "It is not enough to know I was happy. I must know *why* I was happy in order that I might be so again."

"I'll tell ye how."

"How?"

"Find out what makes ye get out of bed in the morning." He shrugged, smiled. "My Mamm used to write things. I had nae time for words when I was wee, but she'd sing them to me at night or say them in my ear when she was scrubbing me clean."

"That is lovely."

"'Whatever it is, keep it,' she said. 'Then ye'll be happy.'"

"What made her happy?"

"Her wee ones. Papa, I guess." He rolled his shoulders again. "I never asked."

"And you?"

He looked at her, then away, the wind stirring his hair the same time it tousled hers. He jumped up too quickly, grabbing her hand. "Come on."

"Where?"

"To see the boat." Energy radiated from him like a lightning bolt from his fingers to hers as they took off running back down the wharf. She almost laughed. She grumbled instead, murmuring how they should go home, that they had not time.

At the rocky slope, he hesitated, staring at her with a roguish twinkle.

The RED COTTAGE

Then he swooped her into his arms.

"Tom!" She had not meant to cry his name. *Sir* would have been far more effective—and he deserved no more, especially after this.

Climbing over the rocks, he splashed knee-deep into the water and waded toward a small, two-masted boat. The canvas sails were rolled tight, and a fiery orange sun cast the vessel in an unearthly glow.

"Here." Up to his waist in water, Tom swung her into the boat. "Careful of the mess. Mr. Flemick takes little care."

"Mr. Flemick?"

Tom climbed in next to her and rubbed a wooden plank clean so she could sit. "He owns it. Used to catch for him."

"You stopped."

"Aye."

"Because of me?"

"Because I had nae time." Dripping, he scooted in next to her and clapped his knees in pride. "Well, what do ye think?"

She curled her nose. The boat was despicable. Empty wine glasses littered the floor, along with a slush of fish entrails and seaweed. The stench was repugnant. "It is..." Why was she compelled to say something gracious? To *feel* something gracious?

Maybe because the boat mast had her initials carved in the wood.

Or because the sun bathed them in such a warm light and the waves rocked the boat in such a soothing motion. Or maybe it was only that he smiled at her.

The boat was dear, not for anything it had to boast of but for the memories it still possessed for him. Memories she had lost. Memories she couldn't get back, even if he took her everywhere and showed her everything.

"It is a very good boat." She resisted the sudden sting of emotion. "To be certain, I cannot remember ever boarding any better."

"Careful, lass."

"Pardon?"

"Ye're being kind. His lordship willnae approve."

"I wish you would not tease me about him." Meg stood, wobbled, and frowned at him when he steadied her arm. "I can manage myself, thank you. Now, if you are quite finished showing me your boat, I think it would be wise to consider our departure—"

A gunshot rang in her ear.

Terror drenched her like water so cold she lost feeling. *Duck.* She didn't have time.

Tom tackled her down, shoving her body between two wooden boat slats. He covered every inch of her. Hid her face with his hands. "Ye're fine. Ye're fine."

She was not fine.

Something slimy and cold squished into her ear. The rotten scent of fish and blood made her stomach heave, and had it not been for him—the familiar scent of his wet shirt—she would have retched.

Hours fled.

No.

Seconds.

He shifted, his breathing fast. "Stay down."

"Tom, no—"

"Stay. Down." He lifted himself off her, the boat creaking, the waves lapping and slurping beneath the rough wood.

She counted the seconds. He would go down first. Then her. She hoped they threw her overboard. She'd rather fade into the sea, loose and cold and drifting, than to burn like her uncle. She didn't want to be ashes. *Please, God.*

A mild oath carried with the breeze, then Tom pulled her up. "Look."

She followed his finger to shore, where a ratty-bearded man plucked a gray pigeon from the quayside. "He did not. . .I mean, I was not. . ."

"Old Jabez. Local poulterer." Tom rolled down the sleeve of his shirt and swiped it across her cheek, the linen fabric soft and calming.

She almost leaned into his touch. Just long enough for her legs to gain their strength and the bile to slip back down her throat.

"Ye're all right." He said it again, slower, as if determined to make her believe him. She was not certain she did.

Hoisting her back into his arms, he lowered into the water and carried her to shore. The cool, salty liquid splashed her clothes, reminders she was still alive, still breathing.

For now.

Back on the quayside, he ran for his coat and came back to drape it around her shoulders. "I dinnae want to take ye back. I want ye to stay here with Meade, where I can guard ye."

"I cannot hide from my danger when it follows me everywhere."

"I can keep ye safe."

"Ye didn't before."

His eyes flinched, but it only made his jaw stronger and his stance broader. "I'll promise ye this. I willnae let it happen again."

She had no way of knowing if Tom McGwen kept his promises. A pull inside her whispered he did.

The days stretched longer than before. Too many times, amid all her dancing lessons and reading and netting purses, Meg stole glances at the clock.

Never had the hours chimed with such lethargy.

Or the hands moved so slowly.

Why?

She should be grateful. She should be eager to fulfil her role as lady and wife—not bored. But the listlessness droned in her brain, weighting her limbs, and drawing her back to places she didn't wish to go.

The graveyard.

Tom had knelt next to Mr. Foxcroft's grave, and his smooth voice—with its musical Scottish lilt—had been fond as he told her stories.

Then the curiosity shop. The building had been old, the shelves a little bowed, and the dull collection of useless trinkets had been anything but interesting. Tom had made it so anyway. Perhaps she should not admit that.

But it was true.

He had slipped on a glove puppet of Punch, mimicking the same rasping, swazzle-sounding voice that might be heard from a street show. She had shaken her head at him, tickled with mirth.

Side by side, they'd weaved through the clutter. He had plucked things off the shelves, made jesting remarks, laughed now and again.

All of it, everything they said, had been pointless and little.

Nothing like Lord Cunningham's poems.

Or his medicinal knowledge.

Even so. She jabbed a pianoforte key with too much gusto. Tom was...well, fun.

"Is that what you think?"

Meg nearly fell from her seat as Lord Cunningham strode into the music room. Embarrassment warmed her cheeks, as if he'd comprehended her thoughts. Which he hadn't, of course. Had he?

"Lady Walpoole, she plays the pianoforte with grave unhappiness." Lord Cunningham moved behind her to inspect the sheet music. "Perhaps this is too difficult a piece for one who has never played anything."

"I shall ask Tom." Meg did not mean for the words to slip. "After all, we cannot be certain I was entirely without musical skill."

"It is no mystery to me." Lady Walpoole rose from her armchair, her grimace patronizing. "Good afternoon, my lord. I hope you have the afternoon free and might join me in encouraging Miss Foxcroft to exercise more patience."

"She has every virtue. You cannot convince me otherwise."

"Virtue without accomplishment is imbalanced."

"But still beautiful." Lord Cunningham swept Meg's hand from the ivory keys. He kissed her knuckles. "In fact, I do indeed have the afternoon free and was hoping it would not be too troublesome for me to steal your pupil away."

Lady Walpoole feigned a smile. "You are quite at your leisure, my lord. I have letters to finish in my chamber if my presence is no longer needed." She curtsied. "Until dinner."

When she had departed the room, all grace and easy movements, Lord Cunningham turned to Meg. He sank down to his knees, gathering her hands. "Violet tells me you have spent every night with her. I came here to scold you for being too kind, but now I want nothing more than to devour you."

An odd vibration worked through her. Like a note she'd played wrong in an otherwise beautiful song. "Violet is lonely."

"We are all lonely, my dear."

"You should endeavor to spend more time with her."

"My hours are devoted to her in other ways. She is not old enough to understand. You, of course, must see the need—"

"She is less in need of your study and more in need of your company, I think." Meg gave his hands an encouraging squeeze. "I say this not to injure you, my lord. Only that you might not regret a moment passed when. . ." A dam constructed in her throat.

The same emotion mirrored in Lord Cunningham's eyes. He lowered his head. Nodded. "You are right. Of course. You are all wisdom, and I am all fool."

"Do not say such a thing."

"Who was I until you came to me?"

"My lord—"

"I was betrothed at fourteen to the daughter of my father's most substantial business acquaintance. We had known each other our whole lives, and she was as interested in science as I was in medicine." He gazed over her face—from her chin, to her nose, to her eyes, to her lips, where he lingered too long. "We were compatible. We matched each other in both intelligence and sensibility, and though our hearts were not united with romantic fervor, we were both quite content without it."

"You did not love her?"

"No." He swallowed. "Yes. I do not know. I wept when she died, but more from loss of companionship than any true bereavement." He released her hands. "You must think me terrible."

"I think you honest."

"What I feel for you is—"

"I must be no less honest with you." Meg squirmed away from the bench, ridding herself of his bothersome touch as thoughts flitted back through her mind. The places her mind had lingered these past days. The laugh she heard in her sleep. "You speak of romantic fervor as if it were the missing link to your happiness."

He followed her to the window. "*You* are the missing link to my happiness."

"I know so little of myself. Least of all my own heart."

"I am many things, my dear, but naive is not among them." He turned her around. "I know, of course, the complications of your involvement with Tom McGwen. Even a stranger, he possesses power over you."

"That is not true." Was it? Why else did every encounter with the infuriating man make her uncomfortable...and warm?

Too warm.

As if she were holding frigid hands too close to the flames.

"I am not blind to the realization that even in anger, he has the tantalizing ability to make you flush. To make these pretty eyes of yours..." He stroked her temples, then said in a sultry voice, "Burn like fire."

"You wish me to end my time with him."

"On the contrary. I wish you to see him as much as you wish." Lord Cunningham smiled. "If I am ever to win your affections, I must first be certain it has not already been done."

Before she could answer, the double music room doors parted. The butler stepped in with a dubious bow. "A visitor has arrived."

"I shall come presently."

"Very good, my lord, only..."

"Only what?"

"It is not you the man requests, my lord." The butler turned his gaze to Meg. "It is her."

"An odd request, Mr. McGwen, even for you." A faint puff of smoke departed the vicar's nostrils as he tossed his cigar into one of the scraggly church bushes. "Follow me inside if you please."

This marked the second time Tom had entered a church without Meg next to him. He rubbed the back of his neck and almost grunted. She would have been proud.

Mr. Sprigg led the way inside the nave, where two skinny girls washed the windows and a young boy polished the box pews with a rag and tung oil. The scent of soap perfumed the air.

"Two years, you say?" The vicar found his parish registry in the shelf of his three-decker pulpit. He carried it to a stool and sat. "Here it is. The column of burials. Seven and twenty names."

"May I see?"

Mr. Sprigg raised a cynical brow but surrendered the book. "Far be it from me to deny you anything. This is the most concern you have displayed in holy affairs for a long time."

"'Tis nae spiritual matter, sir."

"Hmmm."

"Do ye remember the causes of death?" Tom dragged his finger along the column of names. "Enoch Rowe?"

"Consumption."

"Jane Pearce."

"Whooping cough."

Tom read the list aloud. Some he remembered, like little Grace Phipp. The child had borne tiny red blisters across her face, her arms, then everywhere. Meg had been quiet weeks after the child passed of smallpox. "Elisabeth." No surname.

Mr. Sprigg cleared his throat, his breath reeking of cheroot. "Apoplexy."

Awareness pebbled the flesh on the back of Tom's neck. The same demise as Mr. Musgrave. "Elisabeth who?"

"The woman had no name." The vicar took back the book, scanning through the last few entries. He rattled off the causes of death—more consumption, a fall from a ladder, measles. He snapped shut the registry. "I hope this has been enlightening. At the very least, I pray the reality of our susceptible nature will have you listening more intently during Sunday prayer."

Tom grinned, a little sheepish at the reprimand, but shoved back the creeping darkness of man's mortality. "One more thing. The woman named Elisabeth. Do ye know anything about her?"

"The entire ordeal was one of delicacy." The vicar slid off his stool. "She had no name because, like many others of her nature, she did not wish to be remembered."

"Where can I find her family?"

"She had none."

"Lodgings? Employment?"

"I think it best you end your search in the church and not—"

"Please, sir." Tom grabbed the man's arm, stopping him, then withdrew with a hurried look of apology. "Forgive me. I didnae expect ye to understand what I'm asking, but I swear to ye I'm only trying to do good."

"Swear neither by the heaven nor the earth, Mr. McGwen."

"Och, aye. But the girl—"

"You listen as little to my private instruction as you do to my sermons." The vicar scowled and shook his head, incredulous. "Very well. There is an establishment on the east side of Juleshead. It is a house of sin, whose end shall be bitter as the wormwood if they do not repent. Elisabeth, God have pity on her soul, did not." He skewered Tom with a look of warning. "I advise you to stay away. You have enough of the devil pulling at your soul without handing him the reins."

The words sounded too much like the hatred in Papa's eyes.

Tom nodded, grumbled his thanks, and fled from the church. The same need to tell Meg the truth, what he had done, cramped inside him again. Just as it'd done all these years.

But he was too much a coward to face Meg.

And he was too much a coward to face God.

"I thought ye'd forgotten me." Tom sat at his rustic wooden table, his beard trimmed tight and his hair a little damp and ruffled, as if he'd just scrubbed his face with soap and water. He finished off the last of his porridge.

Meg shut the cottage door behind her. Already, his nearness set her heart to scampering. "You have chairs," she observed.

"Built them yesterday." He scooted out from the table and turned the chair for inspection. The craftsmanship was lacking, the design primitive compared to Lord Cunningham's lustrous armorial chairs. But the carpentry seemed solid, like something that would last for centuries.

"Look at this." He moved to the hearth, where a large, brown-and-green braided rug now spread across the floorboards. "Mrs. Dickey learned how to make them in America. She brought it over. Said it was for dragging Mr. Dickey home all those nights."

"Mr. Dickey?"

"He dips a wee bit too deep sometimes." When she raised a brow at him in question, he said "Ye know" and guzzled an imaginary bottle.

"Oh." Meg nodded her understanding. "I see."

"Hungry?"

"I've eaten."

"Ye dinnae like porridge anyway." He rubbed his fingers through his hair, eyes bright, and some of his vivaciousness tried to penetrate her own disposition.

She attempted a smile. And failed.

"I've work to do in the garden." He moved for the peg, shrugged on his familiar brown coat, and grabbed a linen seed bag. "If ye've a mind to help, I can fetch ye my trousers again."

"I can assist you perfectly well in this."

He smirked as if he'd expected as much. Outside, they hiked to the left of the cottage, where he'd already tilled several long rows beneath the crab apple tree. The morning sun was high, the warmth rippling on the back of her neck as she knelt in the dirt beside him.

They planted seeds together.

She with the bag, dumping them into his palm.

He digging into the soil, dropping seeds into holes, covering them up with dirt-ringed fingernails. Their shoulders brushed. Fingers touched. She smelled him along with earthy moisture as the back of her dress dampened with sweat.

Lady Walpoole would have a conniption when she saw Meg's stained knees. Perhaps Lord Cunningham too.

She didn't care.

She should.

"What's bothering ye, lass?" They'd spoken back and forth—little things about the weather, the vegetable seeds, the garden. How Joanie was helping Mrs. Musgrave with new hats. How the cottage windows still needed curtains.

This question ripped through her, dragging down the barrier always between them. The one she had built. The one she scrambled to resurrect.

"Nothing, I assure you."

"Ye're a liar."

"And you are insolent." She grabbed a fistful of dirt and daubed it on his arm, smearing it down his sleeve, lips quirking with a smile.

"Ye're a sure sailor for one with nae sea legs."

"What is that supposed to mean?"

"That ye should take care." He glanced at his sleeve, then back to her face, eyes daring, alive, willful. "I'm a wee bit stronger and faster than ye."

"Am I supposed to be afraid?"

"If ye had sense."

"Which you are implying I do not."

Shaking his head, he went back to work with his hands, then moved to another row. She thought she heard him mumble something under his breath.

Rubbing soil from her dress, she followed him. They fell back into the same rhythm, the silence filled with distant bird songs, her lip between her teeth.

So he was not going to ask again.

That rankled her.

Which was nonsense, because she hadn't wanted to tell him in the first place.

"Yesterday, I had a visitor."

Sun pinkened the back of his neck, highlighted the red in his hair, as he remained fixed on his task.

"When the butler showed me into the drawing room, he was gone. No one saw him leave, and no one knew his name."

"Ye think he was there to do ye harm."

"No. This was different." Anxiety pin-pricked her chest. "But I thought...well, I thought he might have..."

"Might have what?"

"I do not know. It is ridiculous. *I* am ridiculous." She exhaled and pushed to her feet, dropping the bag of seeds, turning—

"Lass, wait."

"I told you. I do not wish to speak of it. Not when I have nothing to prove any of this is true, and what little mind I do have left is confused more than it is sane."

He blocked her on the outskirts of the garden, hands in his pockets, eyes drilling into her. "Prove what?"

"It has only been the past days. Perhaps a sennight. I cannot rid myself of the feeling." Her shoulders slumped in confusion. "I think I am being watched."

CHAPTER 17

Meg arrived the very next morning, this time with her hair uncurled and whipped back in one of the braided buns he'd seen her wear before. She wore a blue-and-white-striped dress and worn apron, as if she'd borrowed clothes from one of the Penrose scullery maids.

The first thing she did was bustle to the cottage windows. She measured their length with a notched paper tape.

"What are ye doing?"

"If Lady Walpoole is going to torture me with accomplishments, I might at least use them for something practical." She spun. "Yellow, I think. Do you not?"

"Dinnae matter to me."

"I suppose you would leave them bare if you had not someone to sew them for you."

He shrugged, grinned.

Her lips widened, but she whirled back around before he caught the full sunbeams of her smile. Something inside him shook. Seeing her here, measuring his windows, talking to him, her hair bonnie.

He had not slept last night.

The words had pierced him, like a fish hook catching in his flesh. *"I am being watched."* Her imagination likely. Or the men who wanted her dead. The men Tom was supposed to have found, stopped, and locked away by now. *"This was different."*

Urgency branded him, a hot iron to his soul. He needed to do something. What? Hunt down the brothel where Elisabeth with the forgotten name was said to have died? Read Mrs. Musgrave's letter again?

The dead had no tongue.

And the dead were the only ones, right now, who had any hope of snuffing down the lies concerning Mr. Foxcroft. Och, and they *were* lies. Were they not?

The old man's face shaped in Tom's memory. The receding white hair, wiry eyebrows, jerky movements, and inability to look anyone quite in the face. He was strange, the old goat. He'd always been strange.

But Meg had loved him.

In some ways, Tom had too.

"Where is Joanie?"

"Still making hats." Tom grabbed his rusty shears from the mantel. "Ever trimmed bushes before?"

"I think you would know the answer to that better than I would."

"I dinnae know everything about ye, lass." Tom nodded her outside. The four bushes planted outside the cottage were faded, drooping, and lopsided. Only a few wilted flowers bloomed among the branches.

"Go to clipping as ye see fit." He placed the shears in her hands. "Like this."

Snip.

Her hands were soft in his, jarring his senses.

Snip, whack.

"Your instructions are far less precise than those of Lady Walpoole." Meg removed herself from his grip, her cheeks pinkening. She'd blushed at him so seldom before. Little he'd done had ever taken her by surprise.

She'd known him too well. What he thought before he spoke. What mischief drove him to nonsense. Anyone else would have discouraged him or scolded him, but she had matched his folly and been a culprit in all his impish trouble.

"You may finish your work in the garden," she said. "I can manage here."

"I've a better idea."

"Oh?"

"It is hot, ye love to swim"—he swooped the gardening tool away from her—"and there's a stream half a mile away just waiting for the likes of us."

"The likes of us, indeed." She resumed trimming the bush, this time snapping them with her fingers. "I hardly think so."

"Why?"

"The fact you need ask such a question speaks detrimentally to your character."

"Ye know nothing of my character."

"I know enough."

He would have dismissed the comment as more of her cursed defiance, but something about her voice stilled him. The brittle rasp. The downward pull at her lips.

He frowned. "Ye are serious."

"I think you should work on your garden."

"Whatever ye've heard, ye're wrong." Was that her opinion of him? Ire wetted his palms. If he knew who had whispered lies in her ears, he'd cuff the sense out of them. Tom seized her hand. "And we're going swimming, lass. If I have to drag ye there and dunk ye in myself."

If she had realized one thing about Tom McGwen, it was only how impossible he was. That, and how impossible it was to remain angry with him.

The stream was flanked on both sides by ancient, gnarly trees. Bracken, gorse, and tiny wildflowers mingled with the grass, and the water caught blue reflections from the sky. Tom had kicked down the growth and now sat pulling cotton stockings from his feet.

She wasn't certain what about him disarmed her.

How he could enrage her, then amuse her, then endanger her, then comfort her, all in the span of one heartbeat. He was complicated.

Lord Cunningham she understood. She knew enough of his past to forgive his failings; she comprehended his tragedies enough to condone his obsessions; and despite everything, she still found him pleasing. She wished to marry him.

Except she did not.

"Dinnae tell me ye need help with that."

The niggling twitch in her chest gave way to distraction. "What?"

He nodded to her feet. "Yer shoes."

"What about them?"

"Ye forgot how to take them off, did ye?"

"No, I did not forget." She loosened her shoelaces deftly. "Look away." He laughed.

"I am quite serious, sir. Look away or I shall not get in at all."

"I've seen yer ankles before, lass."

"Well, you shall not see them now." She waited until he'd tossed both shoes over his shoulder—who knew if he'd ever be able to find them again in all this grass—and rolled up the legs of his trousers. He started to pull the shirt over his head.

Her blood flow spiked. "You will leave it on or I shall never see you again."

"Och, Meg, yer temper."

"It is not my temper. It is my sense. Now keep it on."

"Fine." He pushed up the loose sleeves of his white shirt, slid closer to the water, and splashed in.

Only then, with his back turned, did she remove her shoes and stockings. She followed his lead by tossing them over her shoulder. What was she doing?

She should never have come today.

Not twice in a row.

She'd awakened early, and in the predawn light, the empty halls of Penrose Abbey had seemed so excruciating. The crossed swords on the walls, the stagnant smell of old syringas in a vase, those solemn ancestral paintings in their golden frames.

With numbing boredom, she'd crept to Lady Walpoole's chamber. Soft snores had drifted out into the hall. Much like rumbles of thunder, promising another rainy day.

On impulse, she'd raided a maid's wardrobe, badgered a footman into escorting her, and ran to the one person she should be running from. Yet. . .was not discovering her past more important than studying the Latin alphabet?

Up to his waist in the current, Tom shook water from his hair. "Ye coming, or do I have to run up and catch ye?"

She scooted closer to the edge, dipped in a toe. "It is cold."

"Come on, ye ninny."

"Do you always resort to insults?"

A clapping sound, then water splashed over her in an icy shower. She squealed and shivered, just as his hand grabbed her foot. He tugged. She slid.

The stream swallowed her and a shocking burn stung her nose as water rushed up her nostrils. She flailed and broke the surface, gasping, retaliating...laughing, despite every fiber of her body demanding she not. "You wretched, wretched fool." She hurried more water into his face. "You have no right to sling and toss me whenever you please."

He wiped his eyes. His lashes stuck together—like the shirt clinging to his carved chest.

"Ahem." She cleared her throat. To get the water out of her lungs of course. "If you are finished, I am ready to leave."

"Nay." He grinned. "I'm not."

She glanced about them—the babbling water, the silent trees, the overwhelming vastness of isolated countryside. How many times had she been alone with him in her life? Had it been this way before?

The world feeling so small.

Him so big.

Them so...close.

"Ye have questions." He lowered into the water, pushing it away from him with muscled arms, his gaze trained on her face. "Ask them."

"I liked flowers, did I not?"

"Thistles and daisies."

"Did I bake?"

"Aye." A chuckle. "Not well, but aye."

"Did I do anything of great significance?" She curled her toes in the cool mud. "I mean, I must have sung or played something or been fair at some form of accomplishment."

He lifted his shoulder in a shrug.

"Surely I was good at something."

"Ye weaved baskets. Sometimes."

"Was I proficient at it?"

His narrowed eyes dashed her anticipation. She sank deeper into the current, the water lapping against her chin and rushing through her dress in cold waves. "What of my character?"

"Ye've been listening to wagging tongues."

"You evade the question."

"Nay."

"Then tell me."

"There is nothing to tell." She expected his face to color, for signs of remorse or guilt to contort his face. But his eyes still smiled, firm and certain, with that glow which seemed so brimming with animation. "Ye were blameless. Ye were good. To people. To yer uncle." The nub in his throat moved. "To me."

"There was talk of nighttime excursions."

"They were innocent."

"One who has no shame does his deeds in the light."

Tom blew air from his cheeks. "It was yer uncle. He fussed about..."

"About what?"

"Our getting married."

"So you stole me into the night."

"I dinnae expect ye to understand." Lines of frustration formed on his forehead and he waded closer. He sank face to face with her. "Maybe it wasnae right. Ye'd know better about that than me. But there wasnae shame in it, lass. If ye believe nothing else I've told ye, believe that."

Emotion whirlpooled inside her. She was surprised to find she did.

They stayed too long.

Meg forgot her demands that Tom return her, and she wasn't certain he would have listened anyway. The stream had carried them downward as steadily as Meg asked her questions.

Every answer fascinated her. She inserted colors, places, names into the empty chambers of her mind, until the space felt furnished and lived in.

'Twas a strange feeling.

A good one.

When the water shallowed, Tom held her hand and they stumbled over smooth, slime-covered rocks. The stream wound them farther into the countryside. Once, they trekked up the bank, climbed over a fieldstone wall, and hurried across a meadow of sheep.

"It's over here." Tom ran her to a hedgerow. "Ye love these."

When he handed over a plump blackberry, she popped it into her mouth. Flavor burst across her tongue, sweet enough to make her smile, tart enough she wrinkled her nose.

"Yer uncle used to send us out for blackberry leaves every summer."

"He must not have opposed us greatly."

"He liked me being with ye. Thought I would keep ye safe. But only for running errands or staying close to the shop, where he could keep an eye on the likes of us."

The sun glittered as she shaded her eyes and ate another berry. "He was not fond of you?"

"Och, he was."

"Then why was he so against..."

"Me marrying ye?"

"Yes." Why did the words have such difficulty coming out? A fresh wave of heat spread across her cheeks. "If he had no reservations concerning you, he must have had them concerning me."

"Och, nay, lass." Tom stuffed his pockets with berries, then started back through the tall meadow grass. " 'Twas only that he didnae want to lose ye. Ye were all he had."

"Surely a marriage would not have taken me from him. How terribly stubborn."

His beard parted with a grin. "Like ye."

She gainsaid him—of course—but the words sang in her mind as they walked back for the cottage. Why did everything he said of her, whether unfavorable or not, sound so soft?

As if he were praising her, even though he called her stubborn.

As if she amused him.

Pleased him.

By the time they reached the cottage, the moon already hung in the pink evening sky, and her legs felt raw from the chafing of wet layers. "Our shoes." She glanced down at their bare feet, frowning. So much for concealing her ankles. How had she forgotten?

Tom swung open the cottage door. He said something dismissive—that he'd fetch them tomorrow—then ushered her into the tiny bedchamber. "Betwixt my clothes and Joanie's, ye should be able to find something."

"That is unnecessary, as we shall be starting for the abbey now."

"When ye're dry."

"Tom."

He shut the door before she could say more. Sighing, rankled that she was about to do as he wished, she rummaged through patched shirts, wrinkled pinafores, and paint-stained trousers. She settled on one of Joanie's loose cotton dresses, though the short sleeves fit a bit too snuggly for comfort.

Her hair was the true tragedy.

The braid had come unraveled hours ago, and her fingers caught in too many tangles to remedy without her maid. Must she always return to Penrose Abbey looking like an unsightly beggar?

"Done in there?"

"Coming." She gave up, threw her hair behind her shoulders, and joined Tom in the main room.

He was hunched by the hearth, stoking kindling into flames, his cheeks glowing pink from a day spent in the sun. He had not changed, but the white shirt seemed dry and loose. "Sit here. I'll get ye something to eat."

"I am not hungry."

He ignored her and went to cutting a loaf of bread and slapping cold fish meat onto an earthenware plate. He settled it into her lap. "Eat."

"Where is yours?"

Scooting next to her by the hearth, he snatched a piece of bread from her plate.

"Tom McGwen, you are uncouth."

A shrug. "Saves on dishes."

"I am especially not hungry now." She shoved it over to his lap, proud she had at least taken a small stand on propriety. Even if she were sitting here—alone with a stranger in his cottage—with no stockings and not even her own apparel.

The flames crackled into the silence. The windows dimmed a deep blue, the room was swallowed in shadows, and the rug beneath them was soft to her bare feet. Her shoulders relaxed. She slouched again, shoulder bumping his, as he polished off another slice of bread.

The sweet, buttery smell rumbled her belly.

No.

Ridiculous girl, she could be feasting at Penrose Abbey right now with an illustrious spread before her, in a dining room three times the size of this cottage.

With a furtive look, she reached for a slab of fish.

Well.

Just one bite wouldn't hurt.

The food soothed her, coaxed her deeper into comfort she had no right to entertain. She ate more. Tom told her stories. He spoke in a hushed voice, one that banished all her defenses and made her smile at him.

He set the empty plate on the other side of him. "Turn around."

"What?"

"Ye cannae have yer hair drying like that. Ye'll be pulling and yanking it out for days." He twisted her to face away from him. "I'll be right back." He jogged into the bedchamber, then returned with something metal flashing in his hand. He plopped down behind her. "Now sit still with ye."

"What are you doing?"

"Dinnae worry. I never liked this anymore than ye did." His hands scraped the hair away from her face, behind her ears, down her back.

She was unprepared. Tingles burned where he touched. "You need not do this."

"I am used to it."

The metal comb eased through her tresses. Careful. Gentle. His breath touched the back of her ears and sent odd vibrations across her chest. Sweet vibrations. Vibrations that made her want to lean back into him and close her eyes.

"Tom?"

"Hmm?"

"Why did you love me?"

He worked another tangle from her hair. Sparks fluttered in the hearth.

"Tom?"

"I dinnae know what to say, lass. I'm nae good at words."

"There must have been something. Betsey says all the village girls were fond of you. Why should it have been me you chose?"

Another long silence. The sound of the comb gliding. Then his sigh. "I guess because ye were the thing."

"What thing?"

"That made me want to wake up in the morning."

"I made you happy."

"Aye."

"And you made me happy?"

"Aye."

"I am sorry." Tears filmed her vision. She trampled the urge inside her that wanted to reach back and catch his hand in some sort of gesture of contrition. "For being so. . ."

"Pigheaded?"

"You have not been exactly congenial either."

"I dinnae know how much more congenial I can be than kissing ye." He draped smooth, damp hair back across her shoulder, then whispered in her ear, "Dinnae fash yerself, lass. All is well—"

The door banged open, letting in a whipping breeze.

Meg jumped, swiveled. Her heart sank with guilt the same time Lord Cunningham stepped through the threshold.

"Margaret." A black carrick coat whipped about his shoulders. "I am rejoiced to find you just where I thought I might."

The man was a milksop.

Tom reached for another soft strand of hair and would have continued combing, but Meg flurried out of his touch and stood to her feet.

"My lord," Meg squeaked. "What are you doing? Violet. Is she—"

"She is well." He entered the cottage as if it were his domain, a couple livery-dressed servants following him inside. One of them shut the door. "In truth, I was ill at ease tonight. The gardener spotted fresh boot prints in the courtyard, and the dog has not ceased barking the evening long."

Hair raised to attention on the back of Tom's neck. He stood. "Ye checked the grounds?"

The RED COTTAGE

"Thank you for your insight, Mr. McGwen. Most certainly, the entire estate has been combed for predators." His eyes smoldered like blue fire. "At the abbey, I can guarantee her safety. Elsewhere, she is not so secure."

"You are mistaken," said Meg. "I am equally secure here."

"With one guard as opposed to four and twenty? I think not, my dear."

"Mr. McGwen has kept me very safe, I assure you." Meg skirted around the table—likely to hide her bare ankles, he guessed—and leveled her shoulders. "I appreciate your concern, my lord, but this was an inconvenience you need not have bothered with."

"You are never a bother."

His tone punched like sour vinegar down Tom's throat.

"A word with you, Margaret." The man cut a glance at Tom. "Alone, if Mr. McGwen has no objection."

Tom started for the door, but Meg said instead, "Never mind, Tom." Did she realize she'd spoken his Christian name? "Lord Cunningham and I shall speak outside." Face stoic, she marched out, the lordy on her heels.

Tom was tempted to move to the window, where their shadows hovered close to one another. The fool inside him panged to listen. *Needed* to listen.

Instead, he moved back to the hearth. He lugged a log into the fire and embers danced. Then wandered. Then faded into nothing.

Like the last of his patience seeping away.

"She is right."

"You are not being sensible, dear."

"No, I am not. Neither are you." Meg moved deeper into the darkness, closer to the paint-peeling barn. Bats fluttered from holes in the thatched roof, soaring over their heads. "I presume she has departed?"

"No. Lady Walpoole, though very perturbed to discover your mysterious outings have been with an unchaperoned gentleman, remains to purify your tainted social conduct." His steps matched hers. "Her words, not mine."

"That is not why you came."

"No."

"Nor why you followed me in the name of danger."

"You require patience, Margaret, and I have embodied it. You require time, it is yours. You require your past, handed back to you on a silver platter, and I have given it to you." He guided her back into the barn wall, one hand over her head. "But I am as red-blooded as any man, so you must forgive me if small traces of envy arise to flaw my character."

Meg flattened her back against the rough wood of the barn. The air held a chill, made sharper by the dampness of her hair and the harsh realities on the brink of her consciousness. "You were right, and I have been wrong." Another rush of tears. "And in too many ways, Tom was right too."

"I do not understand."

"I did love him."

"You remember?"

"No."

"Darling—"

"Listen, my lord. Please." She slipped under his arm, too aware of the feeling of Tom's fingers in her hair, on her neck, just moments before. "I thought I could discover my past without suffering any injury from it. I thought I could face the future with you if I were unfettered by all of these questions." She hugged her arms. "But the truth is, as much as I wish to imagine my life began the day you rescued me under the elm tree, we both know it did not."

"What are you saying?"

"That I cannot have both. I cannot have this." She swept her hand to the cottage, ashamed that the tears finally lost control and rolled free. "Whatever I felt for Tom is...still there, somewhere inside me, whether I wish to admit it or not."

"This is not your fault."

"Nor is it yours, which is why I cannot allow you to suffer for it." She smeared the tears with the back of her sleeve. "If things were different...in another life, I may have explored this new sentiment for Tom. I may, eventually, have loved him back."

Lord Cunningham handed her a silk handkerchief.

She dabbed her eyes dry, and a mantel of duty fell over her shoulders, heavy and stifling. But she would grow stronger. This would be easier to carry. If she owed anything to anyone, it was to Lord Cunningham.

The one who had saved her life.

The RED COTTAGE

Protected her.

Now loved her—the Meg of today, not yesterday. "I gave you a promise, my lord, in the hopes I might please you. I gave that promise in haste. I need time to think. To choose how much of the old Meg Foxcroft I wish to carry into the future."

"You wish to withdraw your consent to our matrimony?"

"I wish to postpone my answer, if you are not averse to it. And in the meantime, you must know I shall not be so unkind to you. If there are any more lessons with Mr. McGwen, they will be conducted at Penrose Abbey, with you present or any chaperone of your choice."

"You are fair, you are forthright, and you are perfect." He dipped his head up and down in acquiescence. "It shall be as you have deemed it."

"Thank you, my lord."

The back of his hand dragged down her cheek, smearing away the last of her tears. "No, my darling. Thank *you*. For making me realize, all over again, how much I love you."

She was struck with the impression it would be right to return his sentiment. But the words gathered on her tongue, then dissolved, and she said nothing back.

The up-down rhythm of the horse stormed the uneasy waves in her stomach. *Forget it.* She had done what needed to be done. Hadn't she known that from the start of her lessons? That this was only temporary?

She had not said anything to Tom. Likely because she was a coward.

She'd only returned to the cottage long enough to slip back into her still-damp clothes and bid Tom a murmured goodnight.

He had not spoken back.

Only looked at her, as if he knew. Did he understand her so well?

In the distance, several low-pitched hoots echoed across the night. One footman rode ahead, Lord Cunningham beside her, and another footman behind. The field sloped into a grove of trees, and beyond the wooded path, Penrose Abbey would be waiting.

Home.

She swallowed. Why was she doing this? Pretending to grieve the loss of adventures she'd only ever resisted? She'd spent all of her time with Tom McGwen accusing him. Then quarreling with him. His offenses were to blame, of course. What were they again?

Violence.

His potent, unexpected kiss.

Always doing what she did not expect.

Somehow, in light of him sitting on the floor untangling her hair or grinning beside her in church or showing her his absurd fishing boat with boyhood pride, none of the offenses seemed so reproachful.

Never mind.

This was better.

As she'd told him today, one who had no shame did his deeds in the light. What was wrong with restricting their visits to the proper course of conduct? Why couldn't they sit and take tea together like anyone else?

A twig snapped in the grove.

"Whoa." The footman paused ahead, lifting a hand in warning. He twisted in his saddle and surveyed the woods around them.

"What is it, Snell?"

"Heard something, my lord."

Meg's chest thumped, then settled as a hare-sized shadow leapt from a shrub. The creature darted across the path and disappeared.

She dismissed a pent-up breath. "It was nothing." When would she no longer require guards for her every outing? Or cease feeling eyes on her back?

The horses moved forward again, hooves crunching pine needles and leaves—

A blinding flash of light, heat on her face, a *boom* exploding her eardrums.

The horse reared beneath her. Screaming, she groped for the animal's mane, but her body was already midair.

No. She slammed into prickly earth. Craned her head up.

The ground shook beneath her as a second explosion engulfed the footman ahead. White flames ate him. Smoke mushroomed. She smelled gunpowder and charred flesh in one revolting, gagging breath.

My lord?

Pushing herself up, she squinted through the orange-lit haze of smoke. The second footman limped toward her, gun drawn, holding on to his knee. The horses were gone. Where was Lord Cunningham?

There.

She caught a faint flash of him, his billowing carrick coat, as he galloped his horse through the trees. She blinked hard. *Out of control.* Yes, his horse was out of control. Or he could not rule the reins. Not with the blast.

She was too dazed to think of any other reason he might be running away.

The footman's garlic breath puffed heavily in her face. His weight bore into her, causing a dull ache in her neck, as she lumbered him through the tangling undergrowth. "Keep going," she panted. "We are nearly through the trees."

She was not certain where else the man was injured. Had he been thrown? Was that blood dripping beneath his livery sleeve?

"Down." His trill voice made her drop.

They hit the ground just as a rock whizzed into the air above them.

Then footsteps, plowing closer...more than one.

"They're h–h–here." Someone she did not recognize. Another rock, bouncing off a tree trunk. "Give me th–that lantern."

Terror trickled through her. Slow at first. Then gushing as light spilled into the darkness. *No. Help. Tom.*

"Run." The footman elbowed her in the ribs, and the pain sprang her off the ground.

She hoisted his arm. "Come."

"Go without me!"

"No. Please." Awareness sharpened everything. The light swimming in the corner of her eye, the dark figures racing toward her, the cold stickiness of the footman's blood on her hands.

Then a rock struck her shoulder. She ducked overtop the servant, whimpering, as a second belted her spine. *Tom, please.* He was not coming. She knew that.

Two bony hands grabbed her shoulders and reeled her into a tree.

Her hair snagged in the bark as she sank to the ground.

They peered over her, both of them, and the swinging lantern light ousted the shadows.

One was tall. Deathly thin. Dark-circled eyes and ragged layers of mismatched clothes.

The other was young. Fifteen, maybe sixteen, with dented cheeks and a turkey-feathered hat. "Kill her," he spat. "Hurry up."

The other grabbed another rock from his pouch. "W–w–wants her alive n–now, 'member?" With a growling noise, he cocked back his fist—

A gunshot blasted behind them, and her hands moved over her face. She moaned as the boy's sharp fingers snatched her arm and dragged her from the tree.

"Someone's here," he gasped.

Curses.

Fire catching the treetops.

"Get the girl and let's get—"

"N–no time. Run." He said something else, something muffled about not going to Bodmin Jail for the likes of thirty guineas, before the boy released his hold. They darted through the trees, disappearing before she'd made it to her wobbly feet.

"Sir." She didn't even know the footman's name. She stumbled to him, dropped down to her knees, and unfastened the brass row of buttons. Her fingers shook. "Are you well?"

"My gun," he rasped.

She glanced at his bloody hand. He still held the weapon. Why had he not fired?

He grimaced in shame, lips losing color. "Never had to kill anyone before, Miss Foxcroft."

"They are gone now. This may hurt." She extracted his injured arm from the sleeve of his coat, then ripped fabric away from the wound. The white of a snapped bone protruded through the flesh of his lower arm. "I need to get this wrapped until we get to Penrose and Dr. Bagot can—"

"Move over."

Meg whirled, muscles coiling for action, but the man emerging from the bushes didn't point his gun. Indeed, he did not even look at her.

"Stay away from him," Meg spat.

He knelt next to the footman anyway, and with deft and wrinkled fingers, straightened the broken arm and pressed the bone back in alignment. "Rip off a portion of your petticoat. I'll need it to secure this break."

Meg hesitated.

The footman's eyes rolled back and his head fell sideways in unconsciousness.

"Hurry up, girl. Now."

She did as he said, knees shaking, and watched the white-haired man wind the bandage with as much efficiency as Dr. Bagot.

"Who are you?"

Still, he did not glance up at her. He moved to the footman's leg and probed. Several seconds passed before he grumbled under his breath, "I'm your uncle."

CHAPTER 18

Exhaustion ached her bones, and the harsh drawing room lights stitched pain across her forehead. She accepted the cup of green tea. The steam was moist and warm against her face as she stared down into the rippling yellow liquid.

Anywhere but at them.

Either of them.

"Margaret, I think it time we discuss what you said when you first arrived home." Lord Cunningham took a seat next to her, the settee creaking. "I believe everyone in this room is fully aware that this gentleman cannot be your uncle."

The older man leaned forward in his wingback. From the light of a wall sconce, she had a chance to examine him better. His clothes were plain—brown coat and breeches, green waistcoat, and black-velvet watch fob. He had brooding eyes. Deep wrinkles in his face. Slightly disheveled tufts of thinning white hair.

The teacup shook in her hands. He was alive? Was it possible?

"Heard about your mind." His gaze remained on some unknown object across the room. "Other things I can fix. Mix something up for. Ailments of the mind are for God."

"If you are indeed her uncle, why have you not come sooner?"

"Did. Been moseying around for the past week or two."

The RED COTTAGE

Lord Cunningham stood. "You are the gentleman who called, then had the unfavorable indecency to disappear."

A terse nod.

"You have allowed your niece—and everyone else—to assume you were dead."

"Safer that way."

"For whom, pray?"

The man snorted, yanking up his waistcoat and shirt. A dark pink scar twisted into his abdomen. "Almost died. Didn't know who was after me. Had to do something with Meggie and leave her somewhere safe."

Meggie? The childhood dream returned to her. The pink pinafore and white duck and petals. This man spoke the truth. He *was* her uncle, wasn't he?

"Why here, of all places?" asked Lord Cunningham.

"I knew your father."

"How?"

"Doesn't matter now. Long time ago." Her uncle scratched his chin. "He owed me a favor. Thought this might settle the debt."

Lord Cunningham finally looked down at her. His look was pensive, strange. From irritation at the unexpected guest? Or shame in himself? He cleared his throat before she could decide. "The hour is very late, Mr. Foxcroft—if that is indeed your name." He flicked his hand at a servant. "My footman will escort you to your chamber. We shall discuss this more fully tomorrow, at which time I shall require proof of your identity."

The stranger turned to Meg, face reddening. Moisture sprang to his eyes then was gone. "Go sleep, Meggie." As he moved past her, he landed a small, awkward pat to her cheek. "I'll fix this for you. Just like I always do."

She was too weary, too confused to allow the words to penetrate her emotions. When he was gone, she took a trembling sip of tea and left the cup on the stand. "I am going to bed."

Lord Cunningham reached for her. "Margaret, we must talk."

"Not tonight." She nearly ran for the door. She had not strength for his excuses. Nor, at present, the will to believe them.

Violet's sweet coverlets folded around Meg like a cocoon. The child was already asleep. Little Pippins was curled at the foot of the bed, and the steady creak of Jenny's rocking chair soothed Meg's nerves.

Burrowing deeper, Meg hugged the child's back. Touching someone filled her emptiness. Holding another person kept back the tears. *I am all right.* If Tom were here, he would tell her that.

Not that she needed Mr. McGwen.

She shivered. Everything repeated in her mind like flashes of lightning. The gunpowder kegs exploding. Lord Cunningham running. The two men's faces, haggard and dirty. She should have grimaced at their memory, but something about them had seemed, well, less heinous than she had imagined.

More desperate.

Lost.

I am your uncle. The last of her family resurrected from the dead, flesh and bone. Why had she refused to speak with him downstairs?

She didn't know what to say.

More than that, she didn't know what to think of him. He was coarse, direct, and grumbly—all the things Tom had described. But there was a peculiarity in his manner no one had warned her about. Something about the twitch of his eyes. The lack of light.

The rocking chair ceased groaning.

Jenny left.

Meg left too, dragged away by the black sea of sleep. She dreamed of pinning floral wool fabric to a wingback chair in Tom's cottage. She hummed. The braided rug was littered with playful kittens, the boots she thought she lost, and the metal comb Tom used to brush her hair.

A hand feathered down her cheek.

She blinked, sleep fading, and wondered if it had only been a figment of her dream. "Tom?"

His silhouette dropped closer. His fingers brushed her lips.

"What are you doing?" She tried to sit up, but he guided her back down. "How did you know?"

"Och, but ye've nae sense to hold yer tongue." He palmed her cheeks. Just as gently as he'd done to Joanie the night she'd been injured. "Close yer eyes and rest."

"My uncle—"

"We'll talk on the morrow."

"Everything is wrong."

"Nay."

"I am so confused."

"We'll set it all to right together."

She allowed her eyes to drift shut again, but she caught his hand before he withdrew. "Tom?"

"Hmm?"

"Promise you shall return in the morning?"

"I'll do better than that." He squeezed. "I willnae leave this room."

She was faintly aware that he crossed the chamber in the darkness, grabbed a chair, and pushed it back against the door. He sank into it with his arms crossed. Like a wall, strong and solid and impenetrable.

Comfort burst inside her. Tom McGwen was here. For the strangest reason in the world, she was glad.

"So it was ye." Tom shut the door behind him. Energy stamped his guts like hundreds of thundering hooves.

Mr. Foxcroft sat in the corner of the room, nursing a pipe. He'd opened a window, and morning light burned through the blue draperies, highlighting his rings of smoke. "Least one thing turned out right. You didn't marry her."

Tom was overpowered with the desire to turn over the man's chair—or embrace him. He did neither. "I'm still trying."

"And I'll still stop you."

A grin tried to pull Tom's mouth, but he scowled it away. "I see a knife to your stomach did nothing to rid yer devilment."

Muttering, Mr. Foxcroft waved a jerky hand. "Sit. Need to talk."

Tom took the edge of the bed. The coverlets were not even wrinkled. Had the man slept?

"How'd you know?"

"I heard the explosion," said Tom. "Brought my rifle and came. I saw Meg with ye. Knew she was safe, so I took after the blackguards who set off the gunpowder."

"And?"

"They were already gone."

"You did right." Mr. Foxcroft nodded his approval, gaze steady out the window. Birds cheeped outside. "You watched after Meg. You always do."

"Ye always have too. Until now."

"Couldn't help it."

"Who's doing this?"

"Don't know." Mr. Foxcroft scratched his face. Lines marred his features that had never been there before, and heaviness purpled under his eyes. "Got this two days before the fire." He patted his pocket. A crinkling sound, like paper.

"A letter?"

He affirmed with a grunt.

"What did it say?"

"Doesn't matter. Message was clear, though. Same as the others. They want me dead and my girl along with me."

"I willnae let that happen."

"Good. Don't."

Silence.

Mr. Foxcroft crossing and uncrossing his knee.

The bed squeaking every time Tom shifted.

His heart pounding.

"Sir, I've a word to speak with ye."

"The answer is no."

"This is not about Meg."

"Still no." Mr. Foxcroft sprang from his chair too quickly. He moved to the window. Fidgeted with it. Finally yanked it shut with enough force the room seemed to rattle.

Tom stood and stared at the man's back. A man he was not certain he knew. "The notes say ye killed them." His voice scratched. "Some of yer patients. I want to hear it from ye."

Mr. Foxcroft hurled back a fire-fueled curse.

Called Tom a name that would have made Meg blanch. Then he flung his arm toward the door with a raging, "Get out."

A hole scorched Tom's chest as he bolted from the chamber. He was not certain if it was shame because he'd failed to believe in someone he should be trusting.

Or devastation because the letter was right.

The breakfast table had never been so occupied. Nor the room so quiet.

Mr. Foxcroft—or rather Uncle—had seated himself next to Lady Walpoole, and he smacked his way through a third piece of toast. Then, using his knife to stab a boiled egg, he hunched over his plate to ravish it in two bites.

Lady Walpoole sent an appalled look across the table.

Lord Cunningham mirrored the expression for a second before masking it with an unconvincing smile. "Miss Foxcroft, I trust you slept well?"

"Violet did not awaken me once."

"Violet?" Lady Walpoole perked up. "Do you mean to say you have forsaken your own chamber to sleep with a child?" She angled her chin at Lord Cunningham. "You must put an end to such nonsense, your lordship, if you require your wife to possess any semblance of decorum."

To these words, the breakfast room doors parted, and Tom entered.

Instant heat skittered beneath her cheeks.

"Mr. McGwen." Lord Cunningham ushered him in. "Do take a seat. Mary, bring another plate." When Tom had taken the seat across from Meg, Lord Cunningham pulled the napkin out from his cravat. "I have asked Mr. McGwen to partake of breakfast with us. The very least accommodation I can offer my guest."

Tension surged throughout the room.

Her appetite waned.

"Upon your next visit, Mr. McGwen, do make me aware. You must allow me the pleasure of securing you a proper guest chamber. I imagine you shall find a bed much more restful than a chair."

If Tom detected the spur of hostility, he gave no sign. He nodded his thanks to Mary when she slid a plate of food in front of him. Why had he yet to look at Meg? Had he overheard Lady Walpoole?

Meg pushed away the memory of his hands on her face. The warm swirl of heat still stirred in her, like a terrible rash after consuming something sweet and tempting. Something she should not have. Should not wish to have. What was wrong with her? Why was she thinking of him this way?

She knew enough of the past to know he'd been trouble. She'd had enough of that already.

"She cannae be left alone."

"Mr. Foxcroft and I have been discussing as much," answered Lord Cunningham.

"Not even in the house."

"These walls have yet to be compromised." Lord Cunningham scooted back his chair. "I believe if she remains here, no calamity shall befall her. I think it wise Mr. Foxcroft do the same."

"Can't." Mr. Foxcroft drained his coffee. "Going back to Juleshead. Rebuilding the shop."

"No." All eyes turned on Meg, and she regretted her outburst. "It is not safe."

"People need medicine," said Uncle.

"And I need family." Stranger or not, he was blood. Someone she belonged to. "If you return to Juleshead, I go with you."

"You stay."

"Well." Lady Walpoole offered a pinched smile to Lord Cunningham as she folded her napkin by her plate. "This is all very stimulating. Unconventional too. But hardly the sort of topic one digests at the breakfast table."

"You are right of course, my lady." Lord Cunningham raised his goblet. "We shall resume this later. Mr. Foxcroft, I do hope you shall reconsider. At the very least, I hope you will remain a guest here until some measure of compromise has been reached."

Mr. Foxcroft snorted. He grabbed the last piece of toast from the platter, speared Tom with a hard glare, and bumbled from the room.

The door banged shut behind him.

The sound rattled through her, long after the room fell silent. She had loved her uncle. That much she knew from Tom's stories.

From all accounts, he had loved her back.

Then why could he not look at her? Nor she him? She had everything to tell him and nothing to tell him. Every encounter was strained. Was she so very changed? He so very reclusive he could not speak to her?

Forks scraped on chinaware. Tom's knee must have been bouncing, because an annoying squeak repeated over and over under the table.

Lady Walpoole was the first to rise. She requested Lord Cunningham's presence, and with a grim nod, he followed her from the table. He paused before exiting. His mouth tightened as if he were reluctant to leave Meg alone.

What did he think she was going to do? Throw herself into Tom McGwen's arms?

Her stomach flipped.

Ridiculous.

"Will you please stop?" she said to Tom once they were alone.

"This place unnerves me."

"Then eat your breakfast standing up."

He came to his feet, very little of his plate touched, and threaded both hands through his hair. He paced the room. "Ye're not going to Juleshead."

"Neither is my uncle."

"He does as he likes."

"So do I."

Tom circled around to her, leaned on the table with one arm until his face was mere inches from hers. "I'll tie ye to a chair and stand guard over ye myself, lass, and dinnae think I won't."

"Oh, I am quite confident you would try." Meg refused to shrink away. Her blood rushed at his proximity—the smell of his shirt, the fire in his eyes, the wry curve of his lips. "It is high time both you and Lord Cunningham cease behaving as if I were some witless bird in need of someone to orchestrate my every step."

"Ye're not marrying him."

"Pardon?"

"I said ye're not marrying the lordy."

"Why should I not?"

"Because."

"Because why?"

"Because this." His hand moved behind her head, pulling her in. He claimed her mouth. Hard and quick and wild and earnest. Frenzy ruptured inside her. She wasn't certain if she were yanking back her head or falling into him, because the room spun, spun, spun.

No. But the sweetness sucked her deeper. He tasted like the kiss. The first one. The one that had haunted her, trudging through layers of defiance like gold refined in the heat—and her fingers slipped up to his cheek.

His beard was soft, rich, and she couldn't breathe. She didn't need to breathe.

Tom.

He looked away. Then kissed her again. Then retreated and walked backward toward the door, never taking his eyes off her. His gaze was stunned. Glassy. Irrevocably changed.

A change she was not ready for.

But, heaven help her, had no power to stop.

CHAPTER 19

The kiss followed him like a whip lashing his soul and flesh to shreds. He rode faster. Air beat at his face, watering his eyes, and the muddy countryside became a blur to him.

That was different.

She was different.

The way she poured over his lips. The surprise. The yielding. Then the vigor, as everything else wore away and she lost her fears and her mouth ceased to tremble. The taste of her clung to him. Poisoned him.

Like the muffled words he'd heard behind the closed breakfast room door. *"You must put an end to such nonsense. . .if you require your wife to possess decorum."*

He clutched the reins, leaned forward, gaining speed the same time his heart clenched again. He'd be hanged before he'd see her marry such a fool. She didn't belong at Penrose Abbey, and she didn't belong with Lord Cunningham.

She belonged with Tom.

She'd been happy.

Loved him.

He had been the one she looked at with glowing fascination, and she the one he needed to keep drawing breath. He'd been caught in the throes of destruction. He'd been lost when she found him. Out of his mind. He'd sat alone by the forge, at thirteen years old, and emptied an entire bottle of Meade's gut-biting ale.

The next morning, Meg had smelled it on his breath. *"You going to make that your salvation, are you?"*

"What do ye mean?"

"You know what I mean."

He wasn't certain he did, but he'd never touched a bottle since. He couldn't bear the way she'd looked at him. But he'd still needed a salvation, and almost unconsciously, Meg became that. He'd needed her too much. He still did.

Now he was freefalling alone, and the holes in his soul were only yawning bigger.

Against his will, he glanced up.

The sky stared down at him, the clouds gray and shifting as sunlight ringed the edges. He'd distracted his mind against every sermon the vicar read. He'd closed his heart, because it was easier to believe God did not exist than that He'd said no.

Jagged emotions ripped through him. Pebbles burst on his flesh like the sensations he'd felt back in his childhood cottage when he'd said his prayers with Mamm. She'd called it the breath of God.

Part of him wished he could get that back.

That he could believe again.

He just wasn't certain he could.

"What are you doing?"

With one final tug, Uncle yanked the white-flowered plant from the courtyard garden. He fingered the roots. "Licorice plant."

Meg edged closer to him, rubbing her arms for lack of anything to do with her hands. Her heart ticked faster. "His lordship has been very kind to us. I think it only just we leave his garden intact."

"Huh. Still there."

"What is?"

"Your spirit." Her uncle stuffed the roots into his pocket. "Add a little honey, this will make syrup. Good for coughs."

"Which none of us has."

He spared her a quick glance before jerking his head back away. He'd disappeared all morning and had missed luncheon. Only an hour ago, a servant had spotted him out here. "Peering at all the flowers," the scullery maid had said, "like they was paintings in the prince regent's Blue Velvet Room."

Meg had moseyed back and forth from her chamber to the courtyard entrance three times before she'd finally gained enough mettle to face him. The silence she'd been dreading expanded between them.

Say something. She bit the inside of her cheek. *Anything.*

He moved to the next flower bush.

She followed. "Tom calls you a goat." Instant regret flooded her, but it was the first sensible alignment of words she could form. "You do not get along well, I presume."

Uncle harrumphed. Was that all?

"You must have disliked him greatly to deem him so utterly unsuitable a match."

"Tom's a good boy."

"Then why did you—"

"He wasn't for you."

"Why not?" With intensity, her lips began to tingle. The morning's catastrophe was like venom in her veins—not deadly, only troubling enough to make her weak and startled. His aftertaste was beautiful. No. Terrible. What made him think he had the right to kiss her? More outrageous still, why had she let him?

"You're young." Uncle rubbed a hand down his coat as if brushing off dirt that wasn't there. "I know what's best for you, and I do what's best for you."

"Without any regard for what I know myself?" Why was she defending the old Meg? "Never mind. I do not wish to quarrel. In fact, I sought you out with intentions just the contrary."

"It's in your blood."

"What?"

"Being cantankerous." A whisper of pride dulled the sharp edges of his voice. When he glanced at her, a little sheepish, the first smile crooked his lips. "Thought it over today. Won't be going to Juleshead. Going to stay here. With you, Meggie girl."

"And you've no inkling who might be responsible for this?"

"No."

"Or what we might have possibly done wrong to warrant such hate?"

"We're not perfect." Her uncle reached over and with leathery hands grabbed her fingers. He gave a swinging little squeeze. "But we do what we can to make people well. All we can do."

She desperately wanted the words to be true. But someone had penned those letters, and someone was willing to kill—just to prove it wasn't.

Finding the place was not as difficult as Tom had imagined.

The house sat alone, two miles out from the east end of Juleshead on an acre of unkempt cherry orchards and splintery grape arbors. The roughcast yellow walls, hipped slate roof, and curtained sash windows lent the house a look of domestic innocence.

Tom nearly scowled.

Innocence indeed.

He scaled the stone porch steps and rapped on the door. He assumed he should knock. He'd never visited such an establishment before. Nor listened to stories of those who had.

He may not be a saint, but he knew right from wrong well enough. This was about as wrong as what happened in Meg's alley.

"Fawgive me." A plump older woman answered the door after several long minutes. "Didn't hear you knockin' there, stranger." She grabbed his arm and guided him into a floral-papered hallway, where she motioned him to sit on the bottom step of a staircase. "New here, ain't you, governaw? Don't you worry none. Mamma Lieselotte here will find you a pretty little sweet chuck."

He remained standing. "I didnae come for that."

"You shy one, you."

"I want to speak with ye about Elisabeth."

"Of course you do. You must be him wot come to take her things." Lieselotte tucked a frizzy white ringlet back beneath her lace cap, giggling.

"She always says to me she has a cousin somewhere, and I had nigh 'bout given up hope she had."

"Nay, miss, I'm nae family. I just wish to ask ye some questions." He waited until she was finished distracting herself fingering dust film off the staircase banister before he proceeded. "How did she die?"

"She was ill, poor little bird."

"Of what?"

"Something a pint of gin and merry heart might o' cured, if you asked me. Was my husband wot thought something was wrong. He figured she. . .well, far be it from me to speak unkindly of the dead." Lieselotte climbed two of the stairs. "Come up, and I'll show you the girls, love."

"Who came?"

"Pardon?"

"Ye must have sent for a doctor."

She clucked. "We take rights fine care o' our sweet wenches, we do. Sent for Mr. Foxcroft right off. He's the apothecary, you know. A fine and handsome gent."

"He was unable to help?"

"You know the sad story, don't you, governaw?" Lieselotte shook her head. "Died, she did, right with Mr. Foxcroft still in the chamber with her."

Ice rushed through Tom's veins. He gripped the banister. "'Twas unexpected."

"'Deed, it was."

"Ye must have questioned it."

"Wot's there to question?" Lieselotte crossed her jiggling bare arms across her bosom. "I don't pretend to knows the way of Him wot made us. Just try to make the best of it. You oughts to do the same." She made one more head bob up the steps. "But if you really wants to know 'bout Elisabeth, I say you talk to Bibby."

"Who is that?"

"The last person Elisabeth spoke to 'fore she died."

"Am I to pretend I am unaware of the way you look at me?"

Meg turned another page of *The Lady's Monthly Museum*—an

insufferable magazine Lady Walpoole had shoved into her hand two hours ago.

"You must express some measure of discipline in your reading," she'd scolded. "I should be very pleased if you finished this before I return."

Meg had occupied her time in the music room watching birds out the window, counting the motifs in the Persian rug, and occasionally browsing the next page in the magazine. She retained very little of the text. Who cared a fig about colored fashion plates and celebrated British ladies?

Especially when the only thing she could think about was the kiss. The one that should not have happened.

"Violet is asking for you." Lord Cunningham must have grown weary waiting for her answer, because he turned to the rosewood cellarette. He poured sherry from a crystal decanter. "It seems she can no longer be pacified with books and dolls."

"We all require friendship."

"Which you deem I have forfeited."

His wine glass stilled at his lips, and his eyes sought hers with overt distress. "I have not, Margaret. The incident can be explained."

"That is not necessary."

"I think it is."

She tossed the magazine onto a stand and stood. "It is over, my lord. I think the tragedies of that night better left unvisited."

"The same explosion that threw you from your horse and had my footman nearly trampled wreaked an equally unfortunate reaction in my own mount. He bolted."

"And did not cease running until he reached Penrose?" She released an annoyed breath. This was not her intention. She had no desire to make him defend his actions when it hardly mattered anyway. "Excuse me. Violet is waiting—"

"As have I, which seems to matter very little to you." He gulped down the sherry, then grimaced as if both the taste and the circumstances were unfavorable to him.

But what had he expected her to do? Pretend he had not deserted her?

"What will you do? Keep me forever in suspense as to your feelings? Kill me slowly with your apathy and your not-so-veiled disgust?" He frowned.

"I have enough afflicting me, Margaret, without you injuring me too."

"I have no intention of injuring you."

"Then speak to me."

"There is nothing to say."

"You think I ran."

"Didn't you?"

The beat of silence and the tick of his jaw dimmed the last hope she had for an ample excuse. His shoulders caved. "The animal was out of control. By the time I turned my mount back around, the smoke hindered me from finding you. I thought the best course of action to return to Penrose, where I might procure enough menservants to fight off such an attack. In hindsight, I realize this was not the best course of action."

Her disappointment in him mellowed into a trickle of pity. "I suppose we cannot always be expected to think clearly in moments of disaster."

"I should have been there. I should have protected you."

"Your intentions were pure, my lord, I am sure." She forced a smile, one she hoped would reassure him. "We shall forget it. All is well." The same words Tom had once spoken to her.

Somehow, it was more comforting to hear them than to say them.

Embarrassment slinked the back of Tom's neck, and he kept his eyes on the nicks and scratches of the bedchamber threshold.

"Go on then, guv. The likes o' my little flittermouse won't hurt you." Lieselotte gave him a small push into a chamber that reeked of musky carnations.

Tom steeled his heels two steps inside. He gritted his teeth when the door slammed behind him. "I've nae wish to hurt ye, lass. I'd like to speak with ye downstairs."

The girl across the sparse, cream-colored room stood from a chair. She was thin, young, with a sweat-ringed wrapper and limp red hair. Her cheeks were smeared with pink rouge. The only color of her face. "I don't go downstairs."

"Then in the hall."

She gave a small shake of her head, though she didn't explain why. What did they do, keep her locked in here?

Tom shoved his hands into his pockets and nodded. "I'd like to speak with ye about Elisabeth. About her death."

"Who are you?"

"Tom McGwen."

Her mouth gaped.

"Something wrong?"

"Most men that come here don't have names." She limped over to the bed, ropes and wood creaking as she sat. She hugged a pillow to her chest. "You her cousin?"

"No."

"I think she lied about him, anyway." Bibby blinked convulsively. "She lied about a lot. I bet you never do that, though, do you?"

Thoughts of Caleb whirred through him. All the things he'd never told Meg.

Och, aye. He lied.

"What do ye know about her sickness?" Tom stuffed his hands into his pockets, shifting. "Lieselotte says an apothecary came to look at her."

"She wasn't sick."

"What do ye mean?"

"She never told me, but I knew the signs. She didn't want to be no mother. Especially not...not now." Bibby turned her face into the pillow. "I think she asked some gent to smuggle her in Savin. Heard of other girls doing it. Least ways she'd never have to worry about the child ending up at some baby farm."

The horrors of such a thought shook Tom. "She killed the baby."

"She didn't have a choice."

"And this was her ailment?"

"I don't know. I'm not smart." Bibby rocked back and forth an inch or two, still embracing the pillow. "All I know is that she was almost happy. Things always happen that way. He was going to marry her. She was right sure."

"Who?"

"I don't know. He never had a name. She loved him. She said he loved her. She lies, though." Bibby glanced up at Tom, her eyes puffy. "She was afraid if he found out about the baby—that it wasn't his baby—it would change things. Guess she didn't think it'd plague her like that. What she done."

"Then Mr. Foxcroft came."

"She stopped eating. She'd just lie there in her bed, not moving or anything. Mamma Lieselotte'd come up here and beat on her. Said if she didn't start working again and making herself pretty that she could never leave and get married."

"Then how did she—"

"End up dead?" Bibby pulled up the wrap that slinked off her bare shoulder. "I don't know. All I know is she didn't want to keep living and she didn't."

Thoughts tore through Tom, pieces that didn't fit together. He couldn't think about Mr. Foxcroft in a room as sad as this, ending the life of a girl who was only desperate.

He pulled at another thread instead. One he hoped would unravel answers. "Can ye tell me anything about the gentleman she loved?" If the man had been as devoted to Elisabeth as she believed, perhaps his passion had driven him to vengeance.

"Not much. Just this." Bibby tossed back the pillow and hurried to a curved, tomb chest of drawers. She opened the last drawer. "Her things. The ones for her cousin. She never could stand the thought of her treasures being throwed away soon as her room was give to the next girl."

Tom crossed the room and peered inside. A smeared powder box. Disarrayed ribbons. A couple childhood relics of worn, cutout animal illustrations. "What's this?" Tom lifted a lock of coarse brown hair, tied with a string.

"That was his. The one she wanted to marry."

"May I keep this?"

Bibby nodded. "Guess Elisabeth would like that. Just so long as it don't get tossed into the hearth."

"Was there anyone else of consequence? Anyone who might have cared deeply for her?"

"No one. Well. The father maybe."

"Who was he?"

"Him I know." Bibby shut the drawer with force. "He drinks too much of Mamma's gin when he comes. He visits all of us. Owns his own business somewhere on the west side of the village."

"What's his name?"

Bibby's whisper went hoarse, "Mr. Bartholomew Creagh."

Evening time cast her under a spell. Dinner was the first meal she'd been able to eat without the remnants of fear choking her appetite, and the soft-cushioned wingback nestled her into sleepy comfort.

Lady Walpoole had retired.

Uncle remained scarce.

As the library windows darkened to a moonlit blue, and rain began a light drumming on the panes, only Lord Cunningham remained in company. He had persuaded her here with the argument that they had not finished Shakespeare's *Venus and Adonis*.

She had nearly declined the offer. The look on his face made her accept.

Somewhere between *"The tender spring upon thy tempting lip"* and *"Witness this primrose bank whereon I lie,"* her eyes fluttered shut. The world was airy, void, painless, and then—

"Do take a seat, Mr. McGwen."

"I'll stand."

Forcing past the layers of fog, she sucked in a breath and leaned up. Everything was bleary, then her eyes focused with heart-tripping clarity on the man who had entered the library.

Rain dampened the red, windblown hair across his forehead, and he wiped moisture from his face with a brown sleeve. Too bad he could not remove the scowl so easily. "I want to speak with the lass."

"The lass." Lord Cunningham smiled as he snapped shut his book and stood from the scrolled sofa. "Very charming. Though I imagine she prefers to be called by her name."

"My lord." Meg thought it wise to interject before Lord Cunningham's veiled bark turned into snarling teeth. "I will speak with him."

"I presume it is no trouble if I remain, my dear?"

The RED COTTAGE

"It is." This from Tom. He took another dripping step into the room. "I'll speak with her alone."

"I was only attempting to ensure propriety, I assure you."

"She's nae thing to fear from me."

"Yes. To be sure." Lord Cunningham swept back a look at Meg, smiled again, and lifted his book. "We shall resume tomorrow then. In the meantime, you may speak with Mr. McGwen about our discussion over dinner."

She nodded. "I will."

"Goodnight, darling."

The words came out a little weak when she answered, "Goodnight." Breaths coming faster, she smoothed her dress and waited until Lord Cunningham departed the room before she stood. "You cannot keep doing this."

"Doing what?"

"Barging in at any given hour."

"I had to speak with ye."

"So long as *speaking* is all you do." The second the words were out, she longed to pull them back. The last thing she wished to broach was the kiss.

The glower on Tom's face shifted into a softer expression. He marched closer to her, tossing his hat to the sofa, and stood inches too close.

The air charged between them.

The memory.

Had it not been for the chair, she would have moved backward and feigned interest in searching for a book or a candle or anything. But the chair—and her palpitating heart—kept her planted. "Lady Walpoole wishes me to learn the intricacies of a dinner party."

His eyes remained fixated on hers. Then lower. Her lips.

"Lord Cunningham has already seen to the invitations. He has invited Mr. Rushworth and his wife, who were both instrumental in aiding Lord Cunningham in his search of medical books. He collects them. He is brilliant, really." The words poured out fast, like water gushing through a broken dam. Why was she rambling? "Other guests shall be in attendance. I do not recall their names. You would not know them."

Tom took one more step.

She collapsed back into the chair, and while his eyes were still watching her lips, she watched his. "His lordship wants you to be in attendance too." Breathy. "He fears you misjudge him. He is not unkind."

He hovered over her, hands on the armrests.

"Only protective."

Closer.

"He is truly very much the amiable host."

"Meg."

She begged her head to turn, her eyes to look elsewhere, but the pull in his eyes was like lightning zipping back and forth across her chest. She was struck with the numbing danger. Mesmerized by the power. "Kiss me again, and I shall pummel your face," she warned.

"I'll come."

"What?"

"To yer dinner party."

"Oh." With a hard—perhaps too hard—shove to his chest, she escaped the chair and darted to the other side of the room. She brushed her hand along a row of meaningless books. "It shall be held at the close of the week. You shall set the odds to even."

"Ye know the lordy doesn't want me here."

"Of course he does."

"I dinnae know if ye do either."

Silence.

Against her will, she angled back to him, drawing down a book, clasping it to her chest. She knew what he wanted. What he *needed*.

He'd been starved and deprived so long of the one thing he'd been secure in.

Her love.

She didn't wish to see the emptiness inside him. The sadness. The part he blinked and tried to hide away with another easy smile.

"I just wanted to see ye were safe." He plucked his hat from the sofa and left.

Her wrists pulsed with rapid speed. She stood in the same place—clutching the book, entirely frozen—for much longer than made sense.

CHAPTER 20

The ride back and forth between Juleshead and home was beginning to wear on him. Saddle sores blistered his bottom, making him eager to dismount the moment he reined to a stop in front of Mrs. Musgrave's.

He guided the horse behind the shop. He was torn betwixt the driving need to seek out answers here in the village and the frantic desire to see Meg—safe and well—every single day. The three-some hour distance made that difficult.

Securing the reins to a cast-iron hitching post, Tom knocked on the back kitchen door.

It came open almost instantly, and Joanie flew into his arms. "Tom! You're back."

He laughed, dragging her into the kitchen with him. "'Tis only been a couple days, lass."

"And the best I've had in years." Mrs. Musgrave stirred into a glazed terracotta mixing bowl with a wooden spoon. The too-warm room carried a lingering aroma of cooked sausage and muffins. "She can trim more hats in one afternoon than I can do in three."

"And look." Joanie left the room and came back with a straw, flower-brimmed bonnet. She tied it on and grinned. "Do you like it?"

"Nay, I don't." He motioned her to take it off, laughing. "Ye'll be having every young dandy in the village looking to court ye. I'll darken the daylights of anyone who tries."

Joanie's cheeks tinted pink. Before she could respond, Mrs. Musgrave pulled the child close and kissed her head. "Leave my girl alone, Tommy. Enough of your jesting. Now go along, dear, and finish sewing that last hat before this rapscallion whisks you away from me."

"Rapscallion, am I?"

"Hush with you." Mrs. Musgrave muttered something cross under her breath, but her eyes gleamed with affection. When they were alone, she ushered him into a chair. "Sit down and let me fix you something. You are hungry, are you not?"

"Starved."

"Good." Within minutes, she had a hot plate of sausage, fruit, and blueberry-jam toast before him. He tried to eat slowly. He was hungry enough to ravish everything in two minutes flat. "I spoke with those who knew Elisabeth."

He'd updated Mrs. Musgrave on what he'd found in the registry the day he visited the church. She'd shaken her head, dubious that the two had any connection.

"She died like your husband. While Mr. Foxcroft was still in the room."

She perked. "Then it is true."

"We dinnae know anything for sure."

"Tommy—"

"I've known Mr. Foxcroft a long time." His hunger dwindled. "I'm not saying he did this. Only that someone thinks he did."

"But you will not consider the possibility yourself."

"He would not do this."

"He did."

"What makes ye so sure?" Tom pushed his chair away from the table, a fume of anger traveling through him. "Last time we spoke, ye had as many questions as me."

"I still do, dear. I do not mean to be unkind." She sighed and sat in the chair across him. "You remember the day you discovered me in Dr. Bagot's chamber at the inn? I was not there to give him treats as you presumed. I wanted to speak with him. I wanted to find out if what happened to Elias was accidental or deliberate."

"He was gone."

"Yes. So I wrote to him instead." She hesitated. "The letter came two days ago. Without a body to examine and more knowledge of whatever was ailing my husband, his answer was inconclusive. But he did think it strange. That it should happen there, with Mr. Foxcroft, and without warning."

The taste of blueberries soured in Tom's mouth. He came to his feet. "I need ye to keep Joanie a wee bit longer. I've someone to speak with. Someone who knew Elisabeth."

"We have so little idea who all Mr. Foxcroft might have hurt. Is it not too hopeful, my dear, to think a loved one of this unfortunate woman might be whom we seek?"

"Aye. Maybe." Tom gripped the back of the chair with frustration. He wanted to curse. "But it's all we have."

There. She'd found him.

Meg stepped through the kitchen and leaned into the adjoining stillroom doorway. The small, mustard-colored room was crowded with a brick oven, two tables, and a pottery still. Various dried flowers hung from a board attached to the ceiling, and their strong floral scents sent a flicker of familiarity through her body.

Which was impossible.

She'd never been down here in her life.

"Took a look at the medicine cabinet." Uncle did not so much as look up as he stuffed dried chamomile into a jar. "Missing some tinctures."

"That is generous of you. I am certain Lord Cunningham shall appreciate you refilling his stock."

"Get a stool."

"Pardon?"

"You need to know these things."

"Oh." She smiled, but finding no stool, cleared off a space on the table and pushed herself up. She watched with mild interest as her uncle poured alcohol into the jar, crushed the flowers, shook it, then screwed on the lid.

"Needs to sit."

"How long?"

"Couple fortnights." He lumbered across the room and slid the jar onto a shelf. She wasn't sure it belonged there among what appeared to be a stock of freshly cut soaps, but she did not argue. "Still need clove essence. Case of any toothaches."

"I can speak with Cook. I am certain she can attain whatever you need."

He nodded, went to work brushing his mess from the table. Then he turned to leave.

"Uncle?"

He glanced at her, one wiry brow jerking up.

"I did call you that. Did I not?"

A brusque nod.

"Good." *Good?* She gripped the edge of the table until her fingers cramped. Why was it so difficult for her to speak with him? "We have talked so little. I have so many questions."

He blinked. Nodded again.

"You see, I did not. . .well, I did not lose all of my memories. I have this faint image of a cottage. A man and a woman and ducks. I was hoping you might tell me more."

He shrugged.

"They are my parents, are they not?"

"Likely."

"What were they like?"

"Don't know much. Didn't talk to my brother for years. Never met your mother."

"Why?"

"We fought. I was finishing up my apprenticeship in Juleshead while he was writing for a magazine near Eastbourne. Lived in a little cottage outside town, he did, near the sea."

She could almost catch the whiff of salt on the air as it rustled through the bluebells and cornflowers. Homesickness struck her. "How did they die?"

"Measles."

"How did you find out about me?"

"Got a letter from a neighbor. By the time I got to Eastbourne, you were over the sickness and living with a widow. Brought you home. You screamed at me to take you back."

"I did not understand."

"No."

"You must have been very patient."

He turned his face away, but not before she noticed the rising red on his cheeks. The endearment such memories obviously stirred in him. "Took a week before you'd talk. Then one evening you just came and crawled onto my lap." His laugh was a little shaken. "My girl." With an awkward grumble, he went into the kitchen, leaving an aura of nostalgia in his wake.

Meg wiped her eyes. So many doubts swarmed her, like bees stinging her peace. The letters, the threats, the questions.

One thing she knew now.

She had loved her uncle. He had loved her back. If he was the monster the letters accused him of being, was that even possible?

Nerves taut, Tom rapped on the flimsy kitchen door of the coaching inn. He rubbed his hand over his jaw. His skin was smooth. Too smooth. Why had he ever allowed Joanie and Mrs. Musgrave to talk him into this?

Over supper yesterday, he'd made the mistake of telling them both about the dinner party he would attend at Penrose Abbey. Mrs. Musgrave had bustled away in search of her husband's Sunday tailcoat and pantaloons. *"With a little snipping and trimming, it shall be perfect,"* she assured him, pressing the coat to his chest for inspection.

Joanie had found the razor. *"Please, Tom. Just so we can see what you look like."*

He'd spent an hour resisting them both. In the end, he stood still like a ninny while Mrs. Musgrave stretched a paper tape across his shoulders and Joanie held the mirror in front of his face.

Each clump of red beard floating to his feet made him groan inside. Tom bristled back to the present when the kitchen door whined open.

"Well." Betsey straightened and swooped a couple loose wisps behind her ear. "Mr. McGwen, I would hardly have recognized you."

"Is your father home?"

"Need to speak with him 'bout something?" She leaned out the doorway, snickering. "I'm not rightly particular about courtin' rules. You can just ask me, if that's why you got all shined up for."

From behind, Mrs. Creagh seized the girl's arm and hauled her back. "What you want, McGwen? The likes o' us working folk don't have time for natter."

"I came to speak with Mr. Creagh."

"He's busy."

"It's important."

"Huh." Mrs. Creagh muttered a few choice words, then shouted over her shoulder at Betsey. "Get upstairs and fetch your fat-skulled father. No dawdling!" She motioned Tom into the kitchen, shooing a couple chickens back out the door before she slammed it shut.

She went back to chopping celery and carrots with hard *thwacks*. "So. What you want with the likes o' Mr. Creagh?"

"It's a private matter."

"Came for Betsey, I reckon."

"Nay, madam."

"Now there's a clever one." She raised her knife at Tom, her smile hard. "That girl hain't worth the shillings it'd take to feed her. Hain't got a sensible thought in that flighty little head."

The slight urge to defend the girl rose in him. Perhaps if the woman did less to beat Betsey down, she would have flourished with a little more grace. And sense.

Mr. Creagh entered before Tom could say so. "What's this about?"

"I'd like to speak with ye alone."

Mr. Creagh kicked shut the door. Likely so Betsey would not squeeze back in. "Anything you wants to say can be said in front of me wife."

"Sir—"

"Out with it, McGwen, 'fore I lose my patience."

Tom swallowed hard against the notion this wasn't right. He spared a pitying glance at the missus. "It concerns Elisabeth."

Mr. Creagh blanched. Speechless.

Thwack.

Thwack.

Thwack.

"Sir, if ye will step outside—"

"Oh, don't bother. Go on and talk to him, Barty. You think I don't know 'bout your little trips to the bawdyhouse?"

Color reddened from his neck to his pockmarked face. His voice bellowed. "What you mean by barging in here and—"

"There was a baby. Your baby."

"The devil there was." Mr. Creagh shook his head, eyes crazed, hands jumping in and out of his pockets. "What's she want, eh? Thinks she can use this to make me pan out bloody earnings and—"

"Elisabeth is dead."

His jaw slackened. Even the *thwacks* ceased. "She's...er..." His cheeks inflated with air. He blew it out slowly and his voice calmed. "The baby too?"

Tom nodded.

"Just as well." He spared a look at his wife, one that surged with a hint of humiliated regret. "Haven't been to that sin house in a long time. Not going back. And I'm glad to have my hands bloody clean of it."

An uncomfortable quietness heated across the room, and Tom gave a small nod of apology to them both. He left, fingering the wigged ringlet in his pocket.

Either Mr. Creagh could playact like those from Drury Lane, or he didn't know—nor care—about Elisabeth's death. If someone wanted to avenge her, it wasn't him.

Which meant there was only one clue left.

"Impossible." Lady Walpoole draped the delicate leaves-and-pearls necklace around Meg's neck. "The guests are not to arrive for another hour. Anything earlier is deliberate insolence."

"Mr. McGwen cannot be expected to keep with social standards."

"Is he so daft?"

"No." Meg wanted to squirm from the stool, tired of gazing at herself in the mirror while Tillie and Lady Walpoole twisted and yanked her hair. The reflection staring back at her was so unlike herself.

Dramatic, wispy curls draped on either side of her face, and the faintest rouge they'd dabbed on her cheeks gave her a flushed look. Silver earbobs dangled from her ears. The pale green-blue dress, embroidered with silver thread motifs, was cut low enough on her chest that she wiggled the neckline higher.

"Stop that this instant." Lady Walpoole swatted at her hand. "Leave the dress alone. And Tillie, throw away that note. Miss Foxcroft will not be meeting such a request."

"On the contrary." Meg stood, ripping off the elbow-length gloves. For heaven's sake, she was burning up. Or was it only the thought that Tom McGwen awaited her downstairs?

He had not come in days.

Once, she'd sent a servant out to the cottage to deliver the curtains she'd finally finished. The servant returned and said the place was empty. Why had that disheartened her? The knowledge Tom was no longer close?

"Miss Foxcroft, I must insist. We are not finished with your dressing, and I daresay, this is not the sort of behavior a woman betrothed would—"

"Tom would not ask for me were it not important." Meg rushed to the door, remarking over her shoulder, "And I am not engaged to anyone."

This was not what he'd planned.

Tom perched on the edge of one of Lord Cunningham's elaborate chairs, then sprang back to his feet. He paced the length of the drawing room. Sweat trickled down his spine beneath the new clothes, and he wiped his palms down the thighs of his pantaloons.

Everything charged before him.

The look on Mr. Foxcroft's face less than twenty minutes ago, when Tom had spoken the name Elisabeth. The furious batting of his eyes. The disgusted curl of his lips.

"*Ye killed her.*" Tom had not wanted to say the words, but they sprung out anyway on the cusps of a curse. "*And ye killed Mr. Musgrave.*"

Mr. Foxcroft grabbed his coat. He shrugged into it, grumbling.

"*Look at me.*"

"*No, you look at me.*" The old goat spun, shoving Tom into his bedchamber wall, rattling a framed picture. "*Always interfering. Pushing your way in where you're not wanted.*" Spittle sprayed from his lips as he jabbed a finger into Tom's chest. "*Stay away from me. Stay away from my girl.*" He turned for the door—

Tom snatched his arm. "*I need names. I need to know who else ye killed.*"

Nothing.

"Please. For Meg."

A wave of something heaved across the man's face. A stricken look. One of reluctance, fear—and grief. He railed at Tom under his breath and escaped.

Now, echoes of those same emotions shredded their way through Tom's body.

Across the drawing room, the doors finally parted. Meg entered like a stranger, like a figure he'd seen in magazines or in fancy drawn carriages. His stomach flopped.

He missed her flyaway hairs and braids.

Her bare feet.

"I received your note." She swept toward him, a strong perfume of violets tickling his nose. "Is something the matter? You are early."

"I had to speak with yer uncle."

She smiled. "You did not praise him enough. I have spent a great deal of time with him over the past days. He told me of my parents."

That was important to her.

Well, it had been.

Before.

"Something *is* wrong." Meg's brows came together and the smile wavered. "What is it?"

"I want ye to stay away from him."

"What?"

"Ye heard me." He took a step back, toward the window, into the dusty rays of sunlight. "He left."

"He is coming back. For the dinner party."

"I dinnae think so."

"What did you say to him?" Her voice pitched higher. "If this concerns the letters, you are unjust. We know too little to determine anything."

"I know enough."

"Well, I do not." She stepped closer, forehead tightening. "If you believe the allegations against him, you must also believe them against me."

"Ye are innocent."

"Which you concluded how?"

"Because I know ye."

"And I know him." Her eyes brightened with feverish indignation. "I cannot explain this to you. I realize I have not my memories. I further realize I have spent little more than a few days in the man's company."

"Meg—"

"Yes, he is peculiar. I admit I had my own reservations upon our first encounters. But he is bashful, not malicious. He did not kill anyone."

"I want it to be true more than ye know."

"Do you? Because you seem very anxious to accuse him and be done with it. Were you not friends?"

"Aye."

"I should think you would have more allegiance. I am disappointed, Mr. McGwen." Her chin quivered, but her words hurled out faster. "Not only do I refuse to stay away from him, but I am determined to prove to you the error of your suspicions."

"Then ye leave me no choice."

"What are you—"

He brushed past her, irritated, and made it to the door before she swung herself in front of him.

She grasped his arms with a resolute grip. "Tom, please. He is the only family I have. I cannot lose him. I cannot be alone."

She wasn't.

She had Tom.

But that seemed to mean less and less to her, and that reality vibrated deep inside him. "He needs to be locked up and kept as far away from ye as possible until we figure this out."

"No."

"I'm sorry. I've nae choice."

"Yes. You do." Her shoulders stiffened. "All this time, you have begged me to trust you. For once, I am asking it back."

Seconds rushed by.

Patience disappeared, and her lips formed a hard, pinched line. "I am beginning to understand why it was my uncle did not wish us to marry—"

"That's enough."

"You have no right to—"

"Meg, enough." The strain, the bands of resistance, snapped so quickly he was engulfed in flames. "Dinnae raise yer voice at me. I've done nothing but try to help ye. From the beginning. But ye've lashed me with yer ferocious tongue, and ye've kicked me away, and ye've treated me like a dog ye can whip around on a rope." He hovered over her, tearing out of her grip. "I've a mind to do what the old goat should've done years ago."

Her chin notched higher, unwavering. "And what is that?"

"Turn ye over my knee and whack some sense into ye."

"Thank you, sir, for enlightening me as to what sort of gentleman you are." Her eyes blazed. "And as for sense, I am just this moment attaining it. I trust you can see yourself out?"

"I'm staying."

"I would think you would be too busy launching your personal manhunt against my uncle than to attend anything so trifling as a dinner party."

He glowered, bit his tongue before he said something he would regret. Before he told her everything. The guilt on Mr. Foxcroft's face. Elisabeth, locked in her wretched chamber, murdered. Mrs. Musgrave alone because they'd trusted the wrong man.

"You are no longer welcome in this house." Meg marched through the doorway and glared back at him one last time. "If you were our friend before, you certainly are not now."

He was willful, terrible, and a headstrong pig.

Meg balled her gloved fists under the white satin tablecloth, a breeze slanting the steam from various dishes. Lord Cunningham had endeavored to make the dinner party memorable, and since the weather was pleasant, had persuaded Lady Walpoole it would be ingenious to set up a table in the courtyard.

All the guests had gathered first in the drawing room, where awkward introductions were made. Tom had smiled at each new acquaintance, no trace of the earlier aggravation in his movements.

Meg was not so docile.

Chin raised, mouth tight, she unfolded her napkin. Conversation buzzed around her. Mr. Rushworth spoke to Lord Cunningham about a new remedial book he'd discovered in Hatchards Bookshop, while Captain Godfrey recited a droll conundrum to his sister and Lady Walpoole.

With deliberateness, Meg spoke to everyone.

She solved the captain's challenge while finishing off her beef olives and sweetbread.

She nodded through Mrs. Rushworth's excruciating stories. She even smiled at Lord Cunningham, unblinking when he called her dear, while footmen arrived with the second course.

All without looking, even once, at Tom McGwen—or her uncle's empty chair.

This was wrong.

He was wrong.

All the stories he'd told her rushed back. The three of them wiling away winter evenings by the hearth in the apothecary kitchen. Her slipping to Uncle's lap. Tom helping them hang rosemary and laurel on Christmas Eve.

She'd clung to those memories, decorating them in her mind until they were beginning to feel real. Now he wanted to destroy that? When Uncle was finally here? When she was just beginning to understand the inexpressible comfort of having family?

The letters were wrong.

She was not asking for Tom to believe that. Only to rein back judgment until it could be proven. Did he not owe her that?

"A toast, I think." From the head of the table, Lord Cunningham stood. His eyes swiveled with amusement between Meg and Tom. Had he noted the tension? "To dismissing the past and looking with fervency and excitement to what awaits us in the future."

"Always a master with words," Mrs. Rushworth praised, the first to lift her wine.

Glasses clinked.

Meg had expected Tom to remain still, but he raised his goblet of water and *tinged* it with hers. She almost spilled her drink. A fresh onslaught of anger tampered with her chest, and she tore her eyes away from him before she felt the full effect of his new face.

She'd never seen him like this.

In the well-fitting black tailcoat with a modest but neatly tied neckcloth and finger-combed hair. The beard was gone. His skin was smooth, his jaw firm, and long dimples appeared around his mouth when he smiled.

Which he did—right now—to the captain's eligible sister, seated next to Tom.

Miss Godfrey blushed in delight.

Hah.

Of all things. Meg's pulse skipped. Not in jealousy, of course, but annoyance. Why had he bothered staying, anyway? What was this? Another scheme to annoy her?

No wonder they had fought before.

He was insufferable.

Despicably stubborn.

Even if he was handsome. To other girls. Like the captain's sister.

The third course passed in a blur of orange soufflé, lamb chops, and a grating riddle from the captain. Both he and Lord Cunningham seemed to have imbibed too many glasses of ratafia, as the former grew too amused and the latter too loud. Miss Godfrey kept Tom engaged in a steady flow of whispered conversation.

When Lord Cunningham rose for a second toast, a sliver of apprehension jumped through Meg.

"This is lovely." He swept a hand across the courtyard, the garden behind them, the cloisters to the right. "Made lovelier by the presence of so many esteemed guests. Especially you, darling." His watery eyes lingered on Meg, a little sultry. "The woman who has agreed, much against what I deserve, to be my wife."

A murmur of cheerful excitement rippled across the table. Her frustration gained speed. What was he doing?

"But do not cheer yet, my friends. All among us are not so fortunate." He angled his head toward Tom. "It is Mr. McGwen we must raise our toast to. A better man than me."

What?

"Anyone who can rise from the ashes of his past, who can rally his own inner strength enough to overcome the hatred of not only his entire family but his entire community..."

Shock winced through Meg. What was he talking about?

"There is a man we must revere. I salute you, my friend. I never had a brother, but if I had, I cannot imagine the pain involved in knowing his death was upon my hands." His words slowed. "And yet you sit here, smiling, unaffected, as one who has no stains on his conscience. I commend you."

Breath shallow, she turned to Tom.

He leaned back in his chair, no sign of discomposure, aside from the tips of his ears burning red. His eyes remained on Lord Cunningham. Unblinking.

No one raised their glasses.

Mr. Rushworth cleared his throat.

No, no. Some raw and protective fury tingled throughout her body, making her hand shake as she lowered the fork. She wanted to speak. She didn't know what to say.

Tom scooted his chair from the table and left.

CHAPTER 21

A gouge from a drunken fool meant nothing.

Tom shrugged off the insults the same time he ripped his blasted neckcloth loose. He slung it to the stable floor. He should not have come. Meg had told him not to, and he hadn't listened.

"*Ye never listen.*" Papa only said it twice after Caleb was buried. Once, three weeks after the accident, when Tom had been helping Mamm chase down the loose guinea hens. He'd forgotten to latch the pen.

He forgot everything those days, because he couldn't eat and he couldn't sleep.

Mamm had only smiled, sad, and put on her muddy boots to help him catch the animals. Papa had watched from the window.

The second time had been four months later.

Tom had thought about it for six nights in a row—what he would say to make Papa punish him or forgive him. Whatever had to be done to make things right. When he finally approached Papa's bedchamber, while Mamm was tucking the little ones into bed, his knees had been like unstable sea legs.

"*Sir?*"

Papa had been stripping off his clothes, hair mussed and pipe still smoking from the stand beside the bed. He'd looked at Tom with a void expression.

"I'm sorry." He had so much he'd wanted to say. That was the only thing that came out.

Papa draped the clothes across the chair back.

Tom lifted the back of his shirt. He turned, breathing fast, a sob bubbling up in him. *"Ye can whip me. Ye never finished whipping me."*

"Go to bed."

"I wasnae allowed to play there. I didnae listen to ye."

"Ye never listen." Papa's rough hand had landed on Tom's shoulder. He was never certain if the squeeze was a reprimand or the first—and last—unhating feeling the man had left. *"Go. Dinnae make me tell ye again."*

Tom had cried most of the night, stifling the sounds in the feather pillow lest any of the other children hear him blubbering. He never pleaded with Papa again for forgiveness.

Now he never could.

That same old sickness opened up inside him as Tom moved down the row of cribs and found his horse. He slung on the saddle.

Och, enough of this.

'Twas over.

Done.

He didn't need Papa's forgiveness, and he didn't need God, and he sure as brimstone didn't need Meg Foxcroft. Lord Cunningham had been right.

Mayhap it was time to leave the past behind him.

Meg tore open the arched stable doors, out of breath. She'd run so hard one of her jewel-studded shoes had slipped free in the abbey, and the granite floor felt gritty and shocking against her bare foot. The dress was too tight. The bodice constricting against her pulsing chest.

"Tom."

He stepped out from one of the stalls, leading his chestnut mare into the center aisle. He turned. His eyes flickered across her face, impassive, before he murmured something to the horse and started forward.

She remained braced in the brick doorway. "He was mistaken."

He came so close she thought the horse might plow her down, but Tom halted several inches from her face.

"About the marriage," she stammered. "We are no longer betrothed."

A muscle flexed in his jaw. He tilted his head as if asking her to move aside. "If ye please."

"I am not finished."

"I am."

Her pulse jumped, and she wiggled off her second shoe so she no longer stood lopsided. Or was it because she could not bear to look at him? Because she needed to fidget. Because whatever Lord Cunningham had accused him of still hung in his eyes, bare and tenuous, like something she could reach out and shatter.

He was mischief. He was outlandish grins and the playful side of a world that had turned strict and demanding.

He was not this.

Or was he?

How much about Tom McGwen did she really know? Had she *bothered* to know? A shudder of remorse curdled in her, and against all the reasoning in the world, she lifted her hand to his arm.

Stiffening, he tried to shoulder past her. "I have to go."

She blocked him. "What Lord Cunningham said—"

"It doesnae matter."

"He was wrong."

"Move."

"I cannot allow you to leave like this. You have borne my secrets. Someone should bear yours." What was she doing? "I am sorry. I did not know about your brother. I must have known before."

He looked away.

"Did I not?"

"I cannae do this with ye."

"Tom—"

"I can't."

"Because you are afraid."

"Nay." He took another step forward, closer to her unbudging body. He was so near the sweetness of his breath carried over her face, raising her skin in bumps, vaulting her stomach upside down. "Because ye wouldnae care anyway."

"If that were true, you would have told me before." She lifted her hand to his chest, hesitated, then rested her fingers against the soft wool fabric. "But you did not. Did you?"

His eyes were hollow, then frightened, then sad, then bottomless with an unspeakable wound. He blinked and the blackness was gone. "I have to go." When he pushed past her, she did not stop him.

She leaned back into the stable doorway, gnawing her lip, as the realization drained through her. He had not told anyone. All these years, he'd been alone.

She'd failed him.

Not just as Margaret Foxcroft of Penrose Abbey without her memories.

But as the Meg of before, who'd walked beside him and loved him and played with him—but still had not known him at all.

Joanie was already asleep when Tom returned to the cottage. He took creaking steps across the room, grabbed his clothes from the floor, and was just leaving when her groggy voice called out to him.

"Back to sleep with ye. It's only me."

"I want to hear about tonight."

"In the morning."

"Was it lovely?" With a yawn, the pallet rustled. "The dinner and the courses and all the guests, I mean. It must have been grand. Like the lord's carriage."

"Aye." Grand as the devil. He pulled two floral-stamped biscuits from his pocket, ignoring the tightness bludgeoning his chest. "I saved these for ye. For breakfast."

"I have something for you too." The slightest edge of emotion in her voice made him straighten. "I hope you won't be angry. I should have given it to you sooner, like Mamm said, but I just—"

"Given me what?"

Joanie sat up, cocooning the blanket around her shoulders. "I was a little frightened when I first came. Keeping it made me. . .well, it was like I was keeping a piece of them. I could hear Papa in my head." He heard a smile in her words. "It's on the table."

He already knew.

"I dinnae want that, lass."

"You're their blood."

"Ye're their family."

"You are too." Her shadow sagged. "Just because you left doesn't change that."

'Twas not leaving that changed that. 'Twas what he'd done before he left. "Sleep, lass. Goodnight." Gripping his clothes, he shut her back into the room, shredded the fancy clothes like they were on fire, and pulled on the comfort of his own worn trousers and shirtsleeves.

He avoided the table.

He moved to the windows and inspected, not for the first time, the yellow sprigged-cotton curtains. Meg had sewn them?

No, not Meg.

A stranger.

When he finally crossed the room, when he lit the tallow candle and scooted it close to him, the frayed black book faced him. He touched the cover. The faded gold designs. The taunting words: *The Holy Bible.*

He resisted the memory of all nine children cross-legged on the cottage floor, with Mamm mending shirts or socks, and Papa raising his soothing Scottish voice with scripture.

Tom had never paid much attention.

He'd whispered to Caleb or pulled one of the girls' braids or sprawled out on his back and counted the cobwebs in the rafters. The same restlessness soared through Tom now—but with poignancy and unshakable power.

He shoved the book away from him.

Then stretched across the table and pulled it back. He took a seat and riffled through the pages. He stained them wet until the candle flickered out.

Nighttime air played with the tendrils of her hair. If she were the girl who remembered the alley, perhaps this would be frightening. Perhaps it should be anyway.

Out here, alone with the blackness.

She didn't fear the dark.

She should.

Damp grass parted around her legs, and the crescent moon cast off just enough light to glow through the treetops. She had not slept. Partly because she rose every hour, slipped to her uncle's bedchamber, and peered into a still-empty room.

And partly—mostly—because Tom festered her. Like a thorn beneath her flesh, everything bothered her. The anger on his face when he'd leaned over her in the drawing room and scolded her not to raise her voice. The dinner table. What Lord Cunningham said.

The way Tom dug into himself, built bulwarks, and blocked her out. All this time, she'd wanted him to leave her alone.

To forget her.

Then why in the name of mercy should any of this matter? Why could she not bear that he was...unhappy with her? Disappointed? Angry? Hurt?

She didn't know what he was.

No more than she understood what she was doing now. But as she scaled the last hill and the cottage appeared over the rise, a rising sense of blood-heating anticipation glided through her. She waited until her breath evened.

What would she say?

He would demand to know what she was doing. How she could be so absurd.

The same questions she asked herself.

Her hand shook a little when she tapped her knuckles against the white-painted door.

Silence.

Then creaking. Thumping. The door whining open. "What are ye doing?" He leaned out with a bleary face, hair askew across his forehead, cheek dented as if he'd slept on his fist.

She said the first thing that came to her mind. "I came to sit with you."

Tom leaned his shoulder into the doorframe. Either his brain was slush from sleep or Meg was three kinds of a fool. Had he fight in him, he would scold her—but he didn't.

Not tonight.

Hesitating, she pulled the silky hood of a silver cloak from her head. "Have I fallen so deep in your despicable graces you will not ask me in?"

"Ye walked here in the dark?"

"Yes."

"Why?"

"I told you."

Something untoward nearly sailed from his lips, but he clamped his mouth shut. He backstepped inside, clasping his hands behind his head. "Joanie is abed."

"You were not, I see." She moved to the table, where the Bible was sprawled out in front of a hastily scooted-back chair and a burnt-out candle. Her brow rose.

He frowned. "This isnae mine."

"It would be no disgrace if it were."

He whipped the book shut, then lit a candle to busy his hands.

Meg stood still.

Awkward.

Seconds drifted, and the pounding inside his chest sped out of beat as the cottage warmed in the soft orange glow.

"The curtains look lovely," she said, untying her cloak.

"Aye."

"You painted the mantel."

"Needed done."

"These are new too." She roamed toward the kitchen, where he'd hung a worn copper ladle, basin, and pan. Old treasures Mrs. Musgrave had sent home with him. "Joanie will use them much, I am certain. She is a very domestic child."

Quietness again, save for the breeze whistling through the chimney and Gyb clawing at the rug with a sleepy yawn. The air smelled sweet. Like violets.

"May I sit?"

"Aye." Tom pulled out a chair. Circled the table.

"You may sit too."

"Nae need."

She stared up at him. Her hair was loose and bed ruffled, and airy wisps floated about her face just like they'd done a thousand years ago. Och, but there was a softness about her. That same look she'd given him when he'd been lying on the street at twelve years old, wiping blood from his lip as the urchins fled away.

He had not wanted her pity then.

He didn't want it now.

"Thought ye'd find me languishing, did ye?" He rubbed his neck, frustrated. "If ye came for me, ye wasted yer time."

"It is my time to waste."

"I dinnae need your help."

"I would not know how to administer it, even if you did."

His nerve ends bounced with energy, tempting him to shift back and forth. He grabbed the back of the chair instead. "What do ye want?"

"For you to sit."

"Then?"

"I thought we might talk."

"About what?"

"Whatever you wish."

The temptation to sling her back into the cloak, throw her over his shoulder, and lug her home almost won. He sank into his seat and sighed. " 'Tis the middle of the night."

"Something I imagined would be of little consequence if stories of our midnight excursions are true."

He scowled.

She smiled.

Maybe he was only tired, but her lips stretched wider, and her eyes danced with warm, alluring candlelight. Did she tease him?

Aye.

This side of her he knew.

Against his own resolve, his lips responded to her—upturning, breaking with a laugh as he shook his head in ragged amusement. "Ye've nae wits about ye, lass. Ye always think ye can be running about to do as ye wish."

"This from the man who lured me to mischief."

"Och."

"From the man who stole my stockings."

"Stockings?" He cocked his head at her in mock denial. "Who told ye about that?"

"That was terrible of you."

"That's what ye said." The laugh hurt. The memory hurt. "I gave them back."

"All of them?"

"Some."

"You must have found it great sport to exasperate me." When he did not answer, she sighed and rested her chin in her hands. "You are not the only one." She soared off into some nonsense concerning Lady Walpoole. A languid and sleepy recount of how the woman tortured Meg to death.

The stories amused him.

Lulled him.

In an old and easy way, he was drawn back into answering everything she said in hushed tones and laughing when she made faces. He didn't measure his words. He sensed she didn't either.

Sitting between them on its pewter chamberstick, the candle dripped shorter and shorter.

Gyb climbed on his lap.

Meg slumped on the table, holding her head up with her hand, yawning and smiling while Tom told her about the time he'd sunk a fishing boat three miles from shore.

"Surely I was not the only one who noticed your absence."

"When I made it to the docks, ye were the only one there."

"Meade would have realized, doubtless."

"Next morning, mayhap."

"And..."

"And what?"

"Well." Her drooping eyes fell, and a rush of pink collected on her cheeks. "You must have known the village chits cast eyes upon you. I imagine they would have all rallied to your rescue had they known you were in peril." She troubled the edge of her bottom lip. "Captain Godfrey is a very interesting, amusing man." A longer pause. "As is his sister. Do you not agree?"

"I know what ye're doing."

"What?"

Grinning, he scooted back his chair. "Trying to fight, lass, and I'll have none of it." He was too aware that the windows were fading into a purplish dawn. That the owl no longer cooed outside. That this—whatever this was—was almost over. "Time to take ye home."

She didn't say anything as she draped on her cloak and they walked on foot back through the dew-glistened fields. When the abbey came into view, sunrise reflecting off the distant stained-glass windows, she spoke without looking at him. "Tom?"

His senses whirred. "Hmm?"

"You were nice to sit with."

Then she was gone, taking a little of his hopelessness with her.

She'd seen this before, only sooner. The precious side of Tom McGwen.

Her boots made light clacking sounds as she ascended the grand Penrose staircase, cloak billowing behind her. The touch of everything was strange. The oily banister sliding against her palm, the still air, the tickle of loose hair wild about her neck.

She floated, as if in a trance.

Emotions glided through her, too many thoughts to process, like a painting with no true form. He had not done anything, she realized. Nothing that should have affected her this way.

What was it?

Pity?

Guilt?

Maybe, at first. Or maybe it wasn't that at all. Maybe 'twas only that the abbey had been dry when he left. *She'd* been dry. Like a flower starved for light, she'd shriveled—but when she sat across from him in the cottage, his sunrays had kissed her petals.

Life had mingled with her blood again. All the unease dissipated. They'd bantered a little. Then talked about nothing. He'd been weary and she half asleep, and though he never told her about his brother, somehow he didn't have to.

Just being with him calmed her.

Seemed...right.

Ridiculous, ridiculous. At the top of the stairs, some of the air blew out of her. She had stacked so many offenses against him and harbored so much anger, did any of this make sense? Was she so lonely she needed him? Someone she knew, against all doubt, truly loved her? Was that what this was about?

Rounding the corner, Meg came to an abrupt stop in front of Violet's bedchamber. The door was ajar and light glowed from the crack. Had the child risen from bed?

Opening the door, Meg stepped into the pink-softened room. Her body tightened. "Uncle."

He glanced up, one of his weathered hands on Violet's sleeping forehead. His hair was unbrushed. Clothes a little creased and smudged, as if he'd been tramping through the forest or lingering at the beach. "Shh." He placed a finger over his lips, nodding to the child.

Meg nodded her understanding. She tried to summon relief that he had returned, that whatever Tom had threatened had not frightened him away.

But something about the way he lingered over the bed, the way his body leaned over Violet, clasped her chest like an iron fist. "Where is Jenny?"

Uncle's forehead creased as if he were about to scold her for disrupting the quiet. He folded Violet's bedlinens under her neck. "Let her rest. Come."

Bumps of apprehension scurried up Meg's arms. What was Uncle doing in this room?

CHAPTER 22

"I have to leave." Tom hated the dullness that Joanie tried to smile away as she arranged light purple blooms in a clay vase. The plants in front of the cottage had just speckled with their first dots of color.

"Should I pack you something? You'll get hungry."

"Nae time for it."

"Mrs. Musgrave would make you eat."

Leaving his pipe to cool on the mantel, Tom grabbed his coat and followed the kitten's gait toward Joanie. He snatched out the flowers.

"Tom—"

"Look blithe, or I'll not give them back."

She made a small leap for them. "I am blithe."

"Ye're not."

"I am."

"Not."

"Tom, you'll crinkle them!" Flustered and giggling, she made a final groping circle around him before slumping her shoulders in defeat. She opened up her palm.

In which he placed—unharmed—the flowers. "Get yer things and come with me. Ye can stay with Mrs. Musgrave."

"No. There is too much to do here."

"Ye dinnae like to be left alone. I can tell."

The RED COTTAGE

The look she gave him was one part wistful and the other part grateful. She dropped the purple blooms back into the vase, her profile troubled.

"Lass?"

"It isn't that, Tom."

"What's bothering ye?" When she didn't answer, a low rustling of regret hummed in his ears. Then she'd noticed.

"What did you do with it?"

"Nothing."

"Tom, you didn't—"

"Nay." He had not done what he'd wanted to do. Rip the pages out. Toss them into the hearth. Forget the memories that swelled through the Bible like ripping torrents. What had he hoped to gain by drinking the words last night? They were poison to him. A battering reminder of what he'd lost. "I put it in the barn. With some of my old things."

Joanie's eyes brimmed with moisture for just a second, then she nodded, smiled. "Good."

"I cannae promise I'll read it."

Another nod.

He pulled her to his side with a quick squeeze. "I'll be back tonight. Mayhap sooner." Extracting his coat sleeve from Gyb's playful claws, he started for the door—

"Wait." Joanie swooped to the floor and grabbed something. She delivered it to Tom with a smile. "You dropped your piece of wig."

He took the coarse clump of hair. "Wig?"

"It is, isn't it?" Joanie sniffed. "Smells just like Corporal Simmon's always did, from back home. Like orris roots, almost. Why do you have it?"

"I—" His mind whirled. Faces flitted through his mind, people he knew, villagers he'd passed on the street and doffed his hat to.

A wig. One face bleeped with rapid-fire speed.

Curly brown periwig.

Strawberry jam.

Fleshy chin.

Mr. Willmott? Though surely the man could not be the only village resident who donned a brown wig. Besides, the justice of the peace had been kind to Tom. Since he'd first arrived in Juleshead, Mr. Willmott had weathered through Tom's scrapes and trouble with an annoyed but steady forbearance.

He was rule-bent, married, and upstanding.

Not the sort of gentleman who would frequent Mamma Lieselotte's brothel. Or profess love to a strumpet like Elisabeth. Or see her death recompensed with more death.

Tom closed his fist around the hair. Mr. Willmott was not the blackguard he sought.

But perhaps he could lead Tom to someone who was.

"Find anything?"

Lord Cunningham threw another red hardback to the library rug. His usual frilled cravat was missing and the skin around his eyes was puffy as he shot a hollow glance her way. He wore the same clothes as last night. "You are come to admonish me, I suppose, for our less-than-congenial dinner party."

Had she?

Contemplations rose in her. At first, she'd been angry he could be so cold, then disappointed he could inflict pain so heedlessly. Now, looking at him on his knees in front of the bookshelf, tossing medical books into a pile, some of her resentment toward him waned.

She saw a little deeper into him than she meant to.

Beyond his eloquent speeches.

His intelligent poise.

He was little—all the way through him—but she could not despise his lack of fortitude, when all it stirred within her was pity. The very reason she'd agreed to marry him in the first place.

"In answer to your question, no." He shook a book upside down as if looking for notes tucked inside, then slammed it back into the pile. "There are no answers in these books for Violet. Nor, despite what Father would have said, in long-ago fables."

"Perhaps you search for answers in the wrong place."

He gave a dry laugh. "You insinuate I should beseech higher powers, doubtless. You are good like that." He grabbed the shelf and pulled himself to his feet. "It may surprise you to know I have prayed. Perhaps most of all."

"Then you must not lose hope."

"Hope is only the benevolent name we give our pain." He swooped two glass decanters from the floor. One swished with amber liquid. The other was empty. "As I am certain you did not find me for more of our poetry readings, I must conclude you have heard."

"Heard what?"

"Lady Walpoole departed this morning. Whether she was displeased with my gentility as host or found your late-night disappearance scandalous, I suppose we shall never know. Suffice it to say, we are both to blame."

"It does not matter anyway."

"No." His bloodshot eyes bore into hers. "I did not imagine it did." After several beats of silence, he finally smiled. He lifted the decanter into the air, like the final toast old chums make before parting ways. "If this is farewell, you have chosen a deuced good time to declare it."

"I—"

"Do not say anything." He took a couple slow steps toward her, hair falling over his forehead, his mouth weak about the edges. "You are perfect. I wish to keep you that way. I wish to solidify your image as the spotless dove and immortalize you in my mind, as did the poets of old." He glanced at the decanter gripped in his white-knuckled hand and smiled with rue. "The spirits talk so beautifully inside me, do they not?"

"I think you should rest. You do not appear well."

"Perhaps you are right. Two of the servants fell ill during the night, so perhaps whatever ailment has stirred in this house is affecting me too." He smiled. "Tomorrow, perhaps, all shall be over and we shall be well. Violet shall be better too. We will all be happy."

She must have given him a sympathetic look, because he appeared all of a sudden as if he were about to cry.

"But we both know that is untrue." He wiped his nose and turned away. "Even the fables do not end happily. A lesson my father taught me in the most terrible way possible."

"It is the noses. You must remedy the noses." Mr. Willmott hovered over the artist's shoulder, already wearing a bit of blue and green paint on the hem of his sleeve. "Genevieve, come here at once so the man may look at you."

The twin daughters—fourteen years old, if Tom remembered right—looked unconcerned about their father's worries. Or the painting, for that matter.

They sulked in their stances, one holding a basket of flowers in her lap, the other draping a limp arm about her sister's shoulder. Sunlight trickled over them, and the backdrop of oak leaves, a dense tree line, and fluffy white clouds had already made its way onto the painter's canvas.

They whispered something, giggled, then pointed at Tom.

Mr. Willmott turned. "You." He grumbled, his wig slightly askew. "Thunder and turf, McGwen, do you always have to pester me just when I am taking in a bit of pleasure? I cannot speak with you. I am busy."

"This is important."

"It usually is." Mr. Willmott shouted across the lawn at his girls, "Lydia, the nose!" When the twins had angled their heads to a satisfying degree, he flung a dismissing hand at Tom. "Come back tomorrow when I'm swearing in recruits or something or other. And if this concerns Miss Foxcroft's unfortunate circumstances, I am afraid even I cannot do anything."

"It's not that."

"Whatever it is can wait."

"Nay. It can't."

"Tare and hounds." Riled, Mr. Willmott turned back to the painter. "Keep these girls in position if you have to whack the basket over their little blonde heads. This shall only be a minute. That I can promise." He motioned to Tom. "Over here, McGwen, and make it fast before I lose what little perseverance I have left."

When he'd yanked and jerked Tom toward the secluded garden next to a lion-faced fountain, he pulled at the bottom of his waistcoat and lifted his chin. Scents from nearby wisteria vines drifted across the lawn. "Very well, McGwen. What is this dilemma you shall demand I resolve and that I shall conclude, per usual, I cannot?"

"I am looking for a man."

"A ratcatcher again, perhaps?"

"Nay. A man with a wig."

"See here—"

"I mean ye nae disrespect." Tom rubbed the hair lock in his pocket, his nerves taut. "I think he may know something about Mr. Foxcroft...and the things that have happened."

Mr. Willmott straightened his wig with defiant indignation. "Anyone with a good understanding of history and aristocracy comprehends the fact that wigs are representative of such. They should not be disparaged just because modern fashion declines."

"He frequented a bawdyhouse on the east side of Juleshead."

"Who?"

"The man I'm looking for."

"Go on."

"He visited...a woman named Elisabeth."

"Why do you not ask her?"

"She is dead."

"I see." No hitch. No shift in his expression or tone. He sighed out his impatience. "Then it is my conjecture that you have bombarded me today simply because I have good taste." Mr. Willmott cleared his throat. "And as usual, there is very little I can do to assist. It is hardly in my line of powers to administer a village-wide search for anyone not wearing their own hair."

Disappointment sank like a rock in Tom's stomach. He nodded. "I see." He started to turn, but paused and tossed over the brown ringlet from his pocket.

Mr. Willmott caught it with a frown.

"In case ye find anything." He left before his mind could process the truth. That his last lead had fizzled, smoked into nothingness, and was gone.

She missed him. Strange that she would. She remembered more days without him than days with him.

Her expelled breath was the only sound in the otherwise quiet room. She perched on the edge of the bed, staring from one wall to another as the mattress squeaked in time to her dangling feet.

His laugh resonated through her.

Stop.

He was careless, unruly, wild. Nothing about Tom should endear him to her, but everything did, mayhap all at once. The way he tempted her into the unexpected. The hardness of his arm beneath worn, man-scented fabric. The light in his eyes. The darkness in his eyes too.

She understood him, and more fascinating than that, he understood her.

Not just the Meg Foxcroft of old. Whoever she had been was gone, lost in a sea of experiences and memories she could no longer touch.

But Meg *now*.

Meg who made the wrong choices and raged at him. Meg who pushed him away. Meg who promised her hand in marriage to someone else—and Meg who needed help but had never been able to give any in return.

He had loved her when she wasn't able to love him back.

Stop. A headache meandered along her forehead, and she massaged her temples in circular motions. She stood. *Dear God, help me. Guide me.*

She was uncertain what to do. Urgency bruised her, because Violet was dying, Uncle carried secrets, Lord Cunningham was losing hope, and whoever wished her dead was only a breath away.

She wanted Tom.

She missed him.

Maybe. . .just maybe, she. . .

No. Walls of denial rose, but a powerful, tremulous yearning knocked them down. In her heart of hearts, she already knew the truth.

She was in love with Tom McGwen.

"There he is." Mrs. Musgrave ushered Tom into her drooping wingback chair. She grasped his chin and rubbed her thumb up and down across his cheek. "I shall never tire of seeing my young Tommy under all that beard."

He slumped into the chair. Closed his eyes. "I cannae do it."

"Do what?"

"Save Meg. Find the man who did this."

"You will." A shuffling sound, as if she'd scooted over her feather-stuffed stool and nestled close to him. She patted his arm. "Know how I know?"

"How?"

"Remember that first time I met you? I was helping Elias assemble a hat in the main room, and I heard this creaking and thudding on my roof." She chuckled. "It was you. Climbed up there to watch little Miss Foxcroft, you did, from behind the chimney. Elias said you were trouble, but I said you had pluck. I knew right then you could do anything you wanted to."

"This isnae so easy as climbing yer lattice," he said through a smile.

"But you are just as strong, just as determined"—another pat—"and just as smart."

He laughed, shook his head. As much as he knew her praise was overly enthused, the words still bolstered him. Mrs. Musgrave believed in him.

Something Papa had ceased doing.

And Meg.

Something he could not even do for himself.

Moving from the chair, he scratched at his forehead and faced the window. The one overlooking the ash-piled remains of the apothecary shop. Someone must have set to work removing the burned debris, because many of the black-charred timbers were gone.

The space was heartbreakingly empty.

"Tommy, dear, there is something I have not told you."

Tom turned, raised a brow.

"I did not think of it before. Not until you stopped by this morning and told me of your plans to call upon Mr. Willmott." She lifted Lenox and held him tight, despite his protesting meow. "My memory is not what it used to be. I fear you know that better than anyone."

Tom nodded her on.

"All this time, I kept trying to remember who was in my shop that day. Just before I found the letter. I knew Mrs. Whalley was there because she spilled her coin purse and we never could find her last sovereign."

"Who else?"

"There was Mrs. Hardy come to loan me the ginger I asked for, then a couple of the Stanton daughters, then. . ."

Tom's back arched a little tighter. "Then who?"

"I am not saying he might have. . .that it was him who left the letter." Mrs. Musgrave cuddled Lenox into her cheek with a torn look. "It was Mr. Willmott. And I am still not quite certain why in the world he came."

The small tap at her door was too soft to be Lord Cunningham and too patient to be Uncle. Meg waited until the fourth knock before turning from her bedchamber window. "Who is it?"

"Tillie, miss."

"I do not wish to see anyone." All day long, she'd remained here. Ever since she accosted Lord Cunningham in the library. Ever since the truth about Tom—about herself—spiked like a mountain in the valley of her chest.

Somehow, locking herself in kept everything out.

The danger.

The choices.

What she would do—what she *should* do—when she left this room. Why had Tom not come for her? She'd watched the drive for hours. She'd stared at the gates, anxiousness pulsating through her body.

He never rode through.

She wasn't certain he ever would.

Emotions roiled through her, and she twisted her hands. This was madness. That she should fear now, of all times, that he would not return. Even if he did, was she obligated to regard her previous commitment to Lord Cunningham? What would his lordship do when she left? Penrose Abbey would grow bleak. He would feign indifference, move about this empty house, riffle through his books—then he would wake up one morning and Violet would be dead.

Threads of duty convoluted around her, because no one would be here to comfort him.

He needed her.

She needed—

"Miss?" Tillie again. A muffled noise, then, "S–sent this up for you, his lordship did. Says you should be eating something."

Meg pulled open the door. "Tillie."

The platter shivered in the girl's white hands. Her mouth was twisted, sour. Her frame a little hunched. "Sorry, miss. I just. . .I just. . ."

"Here." Meg grabbed the platter and scooted it away. She touched the girl's arm. "What is it? Are you ill?"

"Yes." Tillie muttered a swift apology, then ripped from Meg with a frantic, blubbering gag. She doubled over in the hall and retched. Then circled her stomach with a moan. "Something be wrong," she gasped. "With...all of us."

Tom stood for too long outside the white iron fence. The house glowed this time of evening—the whitewashed brick luminous, the open windows candlelit. Pleasant sounds vibrated from within the parlor.

One of the twins pounding a buoyant tune on the pianoforte.

Someone nattering.

Mr. Willmott shouting a hearty story that garnered a cheering laugh from all gathered round him.

Not him. Tom shook his head, gripped the cold metal of the fence. He was unsettled, a storm brewing in his chest—perhaps because the house he was about to invade exuded so much calm and normalcy.

He pushed through the gate anyway. His steps were weighted, and when he rapped on the door, his stomach fell a little as all the cheerful noises faded to stillness.

A maid answered with a confused smile. "Sir?"

"I need to speak with Mr. Willmott."

"I am afraid he is—"

"About to ring your neck." This from the man himself, who gently shoved the maid aside with a pinch-lipped look. His wig was gone, and without the cascading brown locks, he appeared a little smaller and a little softer in the face.

More fatherly.

Husbandly.

"See here, McGwen, this is outside of enough—"

"It concerns Elisabeth."

"Which I have already told you I know nothing about."

"Then ye will have no qualms in speaking with me." Tom braced his legs. He'd fight his way in if he needed to. He'd do whatever it took.

Mr. Willmott must have sensed as much. "You better have a bloody imperative reason for cutting up my peace." He mumbled a complaint to the maid for allowing pestering little pups to bang down the door at such an hour, then motioned Tom to follow him through the house.

The door of his study squeaked as he barged inside and squeaked into his chair behind a cluttered desk. The room was small. The walls were decorated with unskilled oil paintings, likely done by his twins. Every object in the room, though a little dusty and messy, seemed to hint at some sentimental attachment.

"I want to know the truth."

"Pah, you little fool, I already told you. What is this about?"

"Mrs. Musgrave says you visited her shop."

"I did."

"Why?"

"I wanted a stovepipe bonnet to set upon the wig I wear when I visit this elusive, ahem, *dead* Elisabeth." He pressed his palms flat on his desk. "What do you think I was doing?"

Tom bit the inside of his cheek. The same doubt pulled through him. *Not him.* It couldn't be. Too many things that didn't fit.

"It seems you have succeeded, yet again, in bothering me with trifling matters that are none of my concern. I am justice of the peace, McGwen. Not your guardian angel." He stood. "Though I doubt it is of little consequence what I was doing, I visited Mrs. Musgrave's shop to pick up blue velvet ribbon for Lydia. Is that satisfactory, or should you like me to fetch my daughter to attest to this purchase?"

"No." The word rushed out on a wave of guilt. He should not have come. This was preposterous. His connections linking Elisabeth to the wigged man to the letters to the apothecary shop. . .they were all weak and falling apart.

"I am sorry." Tom turned for the door. He took one last widespread glance at the room. "I will not bother ye again." He reached for the knob. . .but froze.

Something across the room.

The round side table under the window, where a stack of books and magazine pages littered the crochet doily. A paper wolf peeked out beneath the hardbacks. Part of a pussy cat. A rooster.

His mouth dried.

The remaining worn pieces of Elisabeth's cutout collection. Mr. Willmott was a liar.

CHAPTER 23

"What is it?" The attic bedchamber was small, windowless, and warm.

Too warm.

Sweat beads already formed along Uncle's hairline as he drew the patchwork coverlet up to Tillie's neck. "Water," he barked.

Meg swept to the stoneware pitcher and bowl along the wall. She poured a glass and handed it to him. "Lord Cunningham is waiting outside. Two more have fallen ill."

"Fevers?"

"No."

"Hmph." He pulled two corked vials from his bag, dumped powder into the glass of water, and stirred with a long brass spoon. *Clink, clink, clink.* "Drink this."

Tillie paled. "I can't."

"You must." Meg slipped her hand behind the girl's neck. The skin burned her fingers, charging Meg with increased disquiet. "It is only ginger and cinnamon. You are fond of both, are you not?"

"Yes."

"Then drink and rest. You shall feel better come morning." She hoped. "Uncle, may I speak with you?" She followed him from the room and into the narrow attic hallway, where dust flecks glided across sunrays from the tiny window.

The RED COTTAGE

Lord Cunningham pushed off the wall. "The entire grounds are polluted. Aside from two scullery maids and the stable boy, they are all bedridden."

Meg fisted her dress. "It cannot be serious."

Several heartbeats.

No one answered.

"Can it?"

Uncle fidgeted with his medical bag. Snapped the latch with too much care. Looked everywhere—down the hall, at their shoes, the various servant doors—before finally turning to her face. "Phosphorus."

Lord Cunningham swore.

Meg's chest hollowed.

"Poison."

Mr. Willmott's eyes traveled long and slow between Tom and the half-hidden papers. His face slackened. "Mrs. Willmott has long called sentimentality my undoing. It seems she was right."

"Ye lied."

"We all lie, McGwen, when its effect works to our advantage." His eyes dulled. "Even you."

Rage boiled through Tom, aggressive in its ascent as the room sweltered in heat. "She believed ye."

"Elisabeth?"

"Ye said ye would marry her."

"An unfortunate conclusion she reached, I fear, without any encouragement from me." Mr. Willmott rounded his desk. None of his composure slipped, save for a little shakiness of his hands as he crinkled the paper cutouts and stuffed them into his pockets. "She was unaware that circumstances made such an aspiration impossible. I was not."

"And her death?"

"Unnatural."

"So ye knew."

"Yes." He growled. "I am many things, McGwen, but I am no imbecile. I am as aware of her demise as I am the man who caused it."

A wall clock chimed in the corner.

One of the twins must have resumed playing, because harsh piano notes hammered into the silence, striking pain along Tom's temples.

The breath lodged in his throat when Mr. Willmott stepped closer.

"That man will be punished. That man will suffer." The faintest glisten of moisture formed in the corner of his eyes. "That man is me."

"Dr. Bagot shall arrive soon." Lord Cunningham paced back and forth before the drawing room window. He'd sent the stable lad for the doctor over two hours ago.

Still, the boy had yet to return.

Meg wiped a new sheen of sweat from her forehead. "You should sit."

"If Violet falls ill, it will kill her."

"She won't." So far, the poison had only affected the servants. Whoever orchestrated this plan had slipped into the abbey unseen, worked with deliberation, and injured Meg where it hurt the most.

These people, all of them, had taken her in.

They'd loved her.

How unfair, how terrible, that they should suffer now on her account. And it *was* on her account. She didn't know how. She didn't know why.

But this was nothing more than another letter.

Another message to her.

Written in agony instead of words.

Lord Cunningham smacked both hands into the sash window, and the panes rattled. His breath fogged the glass. "He should have returned by now. I should have gone myself."

"Uncle says the poison is unlikely to render fatality."

"A fact he offered in the spirit of comfort not truth."

"You misjudge my uncle. He is not so apt to conceal distresses."

"I see." Lord Cunningham turned and glanced to where she sat perched on the sofa. If he disapproved of her unkempt hair and rumpled clothes—evidence of hours assisting Uncle—it only made him sigh. "You must rest, Margaret. Neither of us knows what this assault means, but I fear we both know it warrants more trepidation for you than me."

"I am sorry"—the words fell flat, inadequate—"that I ever appeared under your elm tree. That I ever made you love me. . .and brought this suffering into your sanctuary."

"Penrose Abbey is not my sanctuary." He shook his head. "It has not been, ever since my father died."

"I increased your pain."

"Yes." He swallowed. "But you were a balm to it as well—"

The drawing room door banged open with such force Meg's heart pitched. She stood from the sofa, hand at her chest.

A boy stumbled inside. He fell to his knees on the rug, a trickle of blood at his hairline, a wooden cudgel pinning the back of his neck. "My lord, I be sorry. I—"

The cudgel whacked his head. The boy slumped into the rug. Motionless.

No. Meg scurried backward, closer to Lord Cunningham, as two ragged figures stormed the room. Recognition ignited. The same assailants who'd set off an explosion in the forest.

The young one pressed a foot onto the stable boy's back. He grinned as he swept off his turkey-feathered hat. "And sorry I be, m'lady, but nobody's going no place at all."

Nighttime possessed a strange coldness. The streets were empty, eerily still, and every scrape of his boots on the cobblestones was loud and haunting.

Tom wandered the streets he knew by heart.

He strayed to the alley, the one where young Meg had met with tragedy, and dragged his fingers along the brick. He used to curse this place. Him and Mr. Foxcroft both.

Somehow, the pains of what had happened to her were less sharp tonight. Like the Meg of then and the Tom of then were different people.

Flipping up his coat collar, he roamed back to the streets and lingered for a while before the blacksmith shop. He didn't go in. Meade wouldn't know what to say, even if he did.

I need help.

Fog formed like storm clouds, haloing street lamps, weaving in and out of his legs as he cut toward the wharves.

Heaven knew, of all places, he shouldn't come here.

Ripping off his shoes, he splashed his way to the little fishing boat. Black water rocked the vessel. Moonlight rippled on the waves in ethereal light as he dragged both hands down his face.

I dinnae know what to do.

Mr. Willmott had positioned his back toward Tom as if unable to look him in the face. He'd bothered the tassel on his curtain with quivering fingers. *"I knew it was wrong. At first she was nothing to me."* His shoulders wilted. *"And then she was everything."*

"You wrote the letters," Tom had accused.

"If Elisabeth received letters, they were not from me." Was the man truly so clueless? *"For which I am grateful now, lest another sin be added to my charge."*

"What?"

"If you spoke with anyone at all, McGwen, you would know why she's dead." His words had caught. *"She killed herself. . .because of me."*

Tom had stood for longer than he should have. He thought of everything from slamming the blackguard into the study wall, choking the truth out of him, and dragging him to the constable without his wig or his dignity.

In the end, he left the study without imparting a word to anyone.

His throat was closed.

His mind wrecked.

God.

The word clung to his consciousness as he wiped more tears on the wool of his coat sleeve. The heaviness smothered him. Not just from tonight—the terror of not knowing who to believe, the devastation of still grappling with darkness.

But the heaviness of seven years ago.

Caleb.

Papa.

God, I dinnae think I can do this. Rage seethed through him and he pummeled the air with his fist. *I cannae help Meg. I cannae stop the letters.* His weakness slipped out in a sob. More shame. *I cannae pray.*

He missed that.

He missed God.

The RED COTTAGE

"Take a look at this." The rawboned boy stabbed his antler-handled knife into an orange. The fruit bowl tipped over. Apples, pears, and grapes scattered across the drawing room tea table, then kerthumped to the rug one at a time. "Reckon this is how the other side lives, eh wot?"

"W–w–we was told not to touch nothing, Orkey." The other man cast a wary glance to the door. "Don't go m–messing everything up."

"I'm not messin' nothing." The boy ripped into the orange, tearing through the peeling with stained, chipped teeth. Juice trickled down his chin. "You locked up the servants?"

"Door to the servant entry be locked. Tuckwell's guarding it."

"All of them up there?"

"Aye."

"Any dead?"

The man scratched his stubbled face, lips flattening, eyes sinking.

"Vern! I said any dead?"

"N–no."

"Fine." Orkey walked to the settee and hoisted a muddy boot onto the cushion. He smirked at Meg and Lord Cunningham, where they sat in the center of the rug. "Right unfair it'd be for folk like them to die for folk like these."

Meg bristled against the rope binding her wrists. Hours ago, the two men had kicked back the furniture, shattered a porcelain vase, and slung Meg to the floor among the broken glass. Lord Cunningham had joined her before they could do the same to him.

His breath wheezed.

Every time his shoulder pressed into hers, the tremble surged through him, like a hare twitching and thumping in panic. "Whatever you want, take it."

"What do you think I'm doing?" The boy laughed and slung orange peeling over his shoulder. "Vern, get outside and watch the drive. Let me know when they come."

"B–but—"

"You want me to throw this knife in your gizzard?"

"No, Orkey."

"Then do as I say. And take this." He lobbed an apple across the room. "You ain't ate all day. Something that ain't never gonna happen to us again when this is over."

Whatever had troubled Vern seemed to diminish. His dark-circled eyes brightened a little, as he nodded, rubbed the apple against his rags, and left the room.

Orkey laughed. "He wouldn't last no time without someone like me to watch out for him."

"You do that very well, I see," said Meg.

"Watch now." Orkey bounded toward her. He landed one swift slap across her face. "You're not so mighty and fine now, you little lady thing."

The sting wrought heat throughout her face.

And fury.

Lord Cunningham straightened. "If it is money you require, you shall have it. No price is too grand."

"After this is over, I'll already have money."

"Then influence. Of a certain, there must be some service I may render you."

"I'm a simple man." The boy broadened his chest. "I don't need much. Something to eat. Someplace to sleep." He dropped his hand back to Meg. This time, his fingers skirted along her jaw with softness. "Someone to sleep with."

"Unhand her this moment," gasped Lord Cunningham.

"Love her that much, do you?"

"You could not possibly comprehend the intricate passions of love. They are beyond you."

"Well, seeing as I ain't never had no one to love, you might just be right." Orkey sheathed his knife behind his tattered coat. "What if I told you there was a way I'd let you go upstairs with nary a scratch on you? Safe'n sound with that little sick daughter till all this is over."

"You already know I would give anything."

"Anything, eh?"

"What do you want?"

The RED COTTAGE

"Not much." Orkey hunched down, eye level with Meg, with a smokey darkness in his eyes that made her skin crawl. "Just her."

A candle was waiting for Tom in the millinery shop window. He'd known, somehow, that it would be.

Without knocking, he slipped in the back kitchen door and padded with wet feet to the hearth. Pease pottage simmered in a cauldron over the flames, the warm scents of peas, onions, and carrots steaming into the air.

Tom hung his shoes on a chair.

Then unrolled his wet trouser pants, water dripping down his ankles, heat pinkening his skin. His eyes still stung. He never should have cried.

Too long, he'd sat in that grimy boat with his head between his hands. Once, he'd glanced up at the sky and blamed the murky heavens for his misery. He blamed God.

No.

He blamed himself.

And somewhere between wiping his eyes and smacking his fist into the mast pole, he found himself kneeling between the wooden slats. The dirty slush and nets had ground into his knees. The boat had swayed him. *God, I know Ye hear me.*

Maybe he'd known that all along.

Maybe it was never God he'd stopped believing in, but himself.

I'm sorry.

For disobeying Papa, for killing Caleb, for abandoning the things Mamm had taught him. For the bottle of ale he'd tried to drown his pain with. For going to church with Meg and cursing the Bible from a box pew.

He'd been a wretch, all these years, to make Meg his lifeline.

She'd become everything.

His salvation—when he already had one in Christ.

Ye know what's right. I know that Ye do. I'm sorry. He'd wept the words, over and over. *I want to feel Ye again. I want to love Ye again.* Some of the weight in his chest shifted. His skin prickled, and that long-ago whisper of peace parted the sea of his pain. *I want to be Yer son.*

Even as he'd prayed the words, he knew he already was.

Had been, all this time.

"There you are." A sleepy voice drew him back to the present.

Tom squinted in the firelight as Mrs. Musgrave shuffled into the kitchen with Lenox slinking behind her.

"Did I wake ye?"

"*Tut-tut.* I never sleep anyway." She wore a loose white nightgown, her hair all tucked away beneath the lace edges of her mob cap. She glanced with a frown at the hearth. "Oh dear. I went to bed and forgot to douse the fire. Are you hungry by any chance?"

"Ye know I cannae say no to ye."

She smiled with satisfaction and turned as if she were ready to find her bowls—then paused, eyes flickering back to his face. She stepped closer, studious, then bent next to him and touched his cheek. "Tommy. You have not been crying, have you?"

He turned his chin away in embarrassment and smiled. "Listen to ye. Just like a woman to be chattering her head off when a man is starved."

"And just like a man to avoid the question." She harrumphed. "Well, whether you shed a tear or not, you have a kinder look in your eye, Tom McGwen."

He wasn't certain what to say to that. He prayed instead, as Mrs. Musgrave bustled to prepare his food. Something about lifting words to heaven stilled the tension usually so rampant in his body.

He could get used to this.

Feeling lighter.

Less alone.

"Did you speak with Mr. Willmott today?"

"Aye." Tom wrung the last little bit of water from his trousers. "He doesnae think Elisabeth was murdered."

"Oh?"

"He thinks she killed herself."

"Then he did not write our letters?"

"All I know is that he lied to me." When she handed him an ironstone bowl, he dipped out a large serving of clumpy pease pottage. "I shouldnae believe anything the man says."

"But you do."

Tom hesitated. He glanced up at her face, where she stood behind the table, her wrinkles more defined in the flickering light. "Aye." The word finally left him. "Aye, I do."

A pulse of silence.

Then softly, "What will you do now, dear?"

"Tomorrow I'll speak with the constable. We'll ride to Penrose Abbey together." He pulled out a chair and sipped from the bowl's rim as he sat. "Mr. Foxcroft needs to be locked up. At least until we know more."

"Yes." Mrs. Musgrave turned away. "Yes, you are right of course." When she didn't speak or sit across from him, a weave of discomfort needled across Tom's chest.

He glanced at her silhouette, made stronger and blacker by the candlelight. "Something wrong?"

"No, dear." When she finally faced him, tears spilled from her wide, furiously blinking eyes. "Everything is finally almost right."

He started to stand—

Something collided with the back of his skull, the force knocking his face into the table. The soup spilled. Searing hot liquid seeped under his nose as a hand grabbed his shirt and ripped him from the chair.

He toppled into the floor with spotted vision. Everything spun. The rafters above him, a stranger's bearded face, then Mrs. Musgrave.

"You've burnt him," she chided, swiping something soft across Tom's skin. "I told you he mustn't be hurt. Not him."

Confusion ripped through Tom with a fresh shock of grief. *No.*

"Tie his hands and feet."

Lord, please.

"Careful."

His heart throbbed too fast, the rafters began to swim, and everything in the world faded into nothing. He drifted away on the wave of one thought. *Not ye.*

CHAPTER 24

The silence grew claws and scratched across her throat. *Say something.*

Orkey had left. "To give m'lord time," he'd said, "while I see what I can be scroungin' up in the kitchen." He'd already finished off the fruit bowl. Evidence that the boy had suffered so much lack.

She wasn't certain she blamed him for this.

She didn't know who to blame.

Herself?

Uncle?

Or was the one who penned the letters wrong about everything?

Her back cramped, and she drew her legs up to her chest, resting her face on her knees. For the thousandth time, she looked at him.

He sat stoic beside her. Dazed. The subtle scent of his cinnamon swept to her awareness—a smell that stirred back memories of the elm tree and his eloquent murmurs to keep her safe.

"My lord." The first time she'd spoken. The windows turned dark. "You realize I have no expectation of you to sacrifice yourself for me."

He did not so much as blink.

"This is not your fight."

Nothing.

"My lord—"

"Well, well." Orkey strode back into the room, his top shirt buttons undone, revealing a protruding collarbone. He belched. "Half figured you two would be try'n make a run for it. Vern was sweatin' and bouncin' out there, thinkin' he'd have to club someone again." He moved to each wall sconce, lit them with a silver candlestick.

Light sputtered across the room. Sweat chilled the back of her neck. "Well, m'lord?"

Careful not to brush the broken shards of porcelain, Lord Cunningham scooted to his feet. He looked away from Meg when he whispered, "Take me to my daughter."

Tears blurred her vision.

Orkey laughed. "Vern!" When the older man appeared in the drawing room doorway, Orkey barked an order for Lord Cunningham to be escorted to his daughter's chamber.

They left the room with footsteps that thumped in time with her heart.

Her body braced.

The door shut.

Tears coursed free—not in anger that Lord Cunningham had abandoned her, but in the strangest and coldest disappointment she'd ever felt in her life. All his words had been so empty. All his poetry in vain.

Lord Cunningham's love was as weak as the man himself.

The edges of everything were faint and flickering. His head split. *One, two, three.* He counted the fabric-covered buttons above his head, gold and faded and lamplit, and had a foggy memory of snagging one loose with his hat once.

"Did you fix the hinge, dear?"

He'd hopped out of the rusty old carriage kept in the mews outside the millinery shop, seldom used except the Sunday afternoons Mr. Musgrave had taken his wife on a drive. Tom whacked the door shut. *"Good as new for ye."*

"I suppose it is sentimental to keep this old thing still intact." She'd blushed a little, fluttering her hands. *"But it reminds this old woman of courting, and I'm just foolish enough to climb up in there every now and again, just to sit and remember."*

A swell of nausea overturned his stomach as Tom forced back the last shadows of darkness. Confused, he lifted his head—

Just as the cold barrel of a gun met his forehead.

"That is enough, Abraham."

The voice steadied Tom. At first. Then memories jarred back into place with lightning speed, and his headache throbbed with new aggression. He pushed the gun away and sat up.

Lord, no.

The carriage was dark, all the faces shadowed save for the faint stream of lamplight filtering in through the dusty windows. The air was putrid. A devastating mixture of body odor and moldy-fabric and Mrs. Musgrave's pease pottage still wet on his shirt.

He strained his wrists against the coils of rope.

Mrs. Musgrave stared at him.

The bearded man—with his brawny shoulders and heavy breathing—finally seated himself next to her and leveled the gun with both hands.

"Ye wrote the letters," Tom rasped to her.

"It may surprise you to know, dear, that I have been writing letters for a long time. It did not avail anything. The constable did not believe the truth, and Mr. Foxcroft refused to listen. He would have killed the rest of his life had I not intervened."

"Meg." Betrayal soured through him, and the nausea surged with speed up his throat. "Ye did this to her. Ye almost killed her."

"For which you will thank me when you know the truth."

"Ye're wrong."

"And you are blind, Tommy." Leaning across the carriage, she reached out and covered his bound hands with her soft, wrinkled ones. "None of this is your fault. You are as much the victim as my Elias and that poor Elisabeth and countless others they have destroyed."

Tom should have writhed from her touch, but he couldn't move. She blurred a little. He blinked harder. Disbelief fractured him as he whispered, "Ye lied, all this time, for something ye cannae even prove."

"Which is why I must do this." She squeezed him. "You sought the truth, Tommy. I am giving it to you."

The Red Cottage

Hair whipped at her face, her mind screamed as she darted around a wingback chair and stumbled for the drawing room doors. She slung herself against them, fumbling with the knobs, thrusting her body against the paneled wood.

No, no, no.

"Got you!" Orkey's sticky fingers fisted the back of her hair. He yanked. Pain flared. "No more runnin' or I'll—"

She twisted around, spit in his face, and ripped out of his grip with a cry of agony. Her scalp stung. She made it halfway across the drawing room before the full weight of his body lunged on her back.

Her forehead smacked the rug with so much force she wilted. *Tom.* She tethered herself to his name, pulled it around her like a cocoon as Orkey turned her over.

Panting, he hauled her back to her feet. He shoved her backward into the glass-paned bookshelf. "You dirty little rich thing." Face scrunching, he barged his knuckles across her chin.

The impact snapped back her head. The bookcase rattled. She whimpered, tried to hide her face, but another blow pummeled into her stomach.

Again.

Then again.

Glass fragmented behind her. *No, please.* She crumpled, but he snatched her hair and dragged her up. "Let me go."

Tossing off his hat, he threw her to the chaise lounge and slung away the cylinder pillow.

"Please. I beg of you—"

He backhanded her mouth.

She tasted blood, warm and metallic, and her lungs suffocated when his face dipped inches above her face.

His breath poured over her. Foul, hot, panting. "You beg." Spittle sprayed her. "You have no idea how many years I been begging the streets. People like you never did nothing. You never cared about the likes of filth like Vern and me—"

A crash shook the room.

The doors banging open.

Help.

Orkey's hand pressed across her mouth before she could screech the word, but just as quickly, someone barreled into his body and tackled him away from her.

She caught a flash of red hair, familiar brown trousers, one second before a gunshot reverberated throughout the room.

Rage ignited Tom, blasting heat beneath his skin as his fingers clamped tighter around the man's neck. He'd kill him. He'd rip out every cursed bone and feed it to the dogs.

"That will be enough, Tommy." Mrs. Musgrave's voice was calm, slow, easy, devastating.

Another gunshot.

A nearby chandelier wobbled, and glass sprayed in a pinging shower.

Ducking out of the downpour, Tom slung the young blackguard to the ground and whirled to Meg.

She'd risen from the chaise lounge, one hand on the armrest as if to steady herself. Her cheeks were pink. Her chin purpling. Her eyes locked on him—unblinking and wild—with a stricken look he'd only seen on her face once.

The night she told him about the alley.

Stomach hitching, he rushed for her—

A hard force rammed into Tom's shoulder, sending him stumbling. He hit a wooden stand and chess pieces scattered around him.

"Do not hurt him, Abraham." The drawing room doors thudded open again. "Vern, I wish you to stand guard over Tommy by the mantle. He is not to move and he is not to be injured, but he is to witness the proceedings."

The rat called Vern bullied Tom to the mantle with his cudgel. His face soured with a frown, one almost of remorse, before he straightened his stance like a sentinel.

Tom's heartbeat racketed out of control. He brought the ropes to his mouth. Bit at them with his teeth. "Mrs. Musgrave."

"Orkey, can you stand?"

"Yes'm."

"Then go and fetch Mr. Foxcroft."

Orkey bounced up, turned circles until he spotted his hat, and mashed it on his head as he fled the room.

"Mrs. Musgrave." Tom's voice deepened a pitch. "Ye cannae do this."

"Abraham, you must hold her still."

"No." Tom sprang forward. The cudgel brought him down with a wind-stealing blow to his spine. "I willnae let you hurt them," he wheezed. He stood again. Pain crackled along his back as he staggered to Mrs. Musgrave, and when he caught her frail elbow, no one stopped him.

Her eyes were mellow, her voice tear-laced. "I know this will be difficult for you to watch, my dear. If it were not so necessary, I would spare you as you have always tried to spare me."

"Listen." He grabbed her tighter, breathing harder. "Yer husband wouldnae have wanted this. Ye know that. Look at me."

"I am not doing this for my husband. Elias is dead. There is nothing else I can do for him." Snot dripped from her nose. Her hand trembled as she wiped it with her floral sleeve. "I am doing this for the ones who are still alive. The innocents he has not yet touched."

"Meg is an innocent."

"No, my dear. *You* are." Her eyes lifted, a faint nod, and the cudgel battered the back of his skull.

Instant blackness stole him again. The last thing he heard was Meg scream.

She wasn't certain if it was morning. They'd drawn the heavy draperies shut hours ago, and the candles were all dripping into extinction. Everything was shadows and languid movements and voices so quiet they skittered across her consciousness without making sense.

Nothing made sense.

Abraham's fingers were hard, digging into her arms, forcing her to stand—to watch.

"Do not hurt him." The plea broke from her cracked lips, but the cudgel swung in the darkness and Uncle's chair toppled over. More sounds. Their boots destroying his face.

"Up, up." Mrs. Musgrave perched on the edge of a wingback chair. The same one Meg had curled into with a book too many times, or Lord Cunningham had frequented with his afternoon tea.

Mrs. Musgrave appeared different now. Her wrinkles were deeper, like cracks gnarling through tree bark—and she looked at Meg too often. Always quietly, pensively, as she intertwined her hands over and over. "That is enough, my dears."

Vern wiped the blood off his cudgel.

Orkey massaged his fists.

Abraham breathed hot and tickling moisture onto the back of Meg's neck.

"Mr. Foxcroft, can you hear me?"

When Uncle's head drooped to his chest, Mrs. Musgrave stood and lifted his chin with a careful finger. "Your silence shall not deter me. Miss Foxcroft deserves the truth. It is unfair she should die for something she does not hold in recollection."

"Didn't kill him." Uncle spat. Blood sprayed from his lips.

"You killed Elias and so many others."

"No."

"Tell the truth."

"Am."

"I will not let you do this again." Mrs. Musgrave's face dipped closer to his, and a strain of anguish rippled in her voice. "You have lied and you have lied, and you have hurt people and you have hurt people. All these years, you have done nothing but destroy." She waved a hand behind her to where Tom lay curled limp and motionless in the corner of the room. "You do not even realize the lives you have darkened. That boy among them. He needs this. He needs to know what you've done." Her voice cracked. "*I* need to know. Why can't you give that to me?"

Emptiness churned through Meg. The hollowness of not knowing if Uncle put sugar or honey in his tea, if he took naps between grinding new powders, if he smiled at her unabashed or tried to hide his love with bashful grunts.

If he killed the people he swore to heal.

If Meg had helped him.

"Tell her." A cry throbbed in Meg's throat. She stared into Uncle's face, his eyes, and the unspoken bond between them crossed the divide of lost memory. "Tell her you never took a life."

Uncle swore. Blood dripped from his lips to his neck and stained his white shirt collar red. Then he said the words that suffocated the light inside her soul. "I can't."

CHAPTER 25

Weakness crawled through her, cold and tingling as she gave one pathetic writhe against Abraham's hold. Air stagnated in her lungs. *Uncle, no.* He lied to save her. He lied because they were about to die.

Her chest convulsed.

They would die anyway.

"You killed little Ned Thatcher nine years ago." Mrs. Musgrave dried her face. "He hobbled into your shop with a bruised rib, and they carried him out on a handbarrow."

"Bone punctured his liver."

"He was six."

"Nothing I could do."

"There was always something you could do, but you were too busy feigning you were God." Moisture weighted her white lashes, and redness lined the underside of her eyes. She returned to her wingback. "Tell Miss Foxcroft how you used her. How you would send her off with that little basket and people perished because of it."

The accusation speared through Meg, gouging her with all the things she could not remember. Not even Tom's stories or the memories she'd created for herself could stem the blood flow. She was drenched in the crimson of her own dread.

The very thing she'd feared all along.

Herself.

"It is not true." Her gaze flung to Tom, who lifted his head from the floor with hazy, squinted eyes. Then to Uncle, who bore no expression at all. "You could not have done that to me."

"I didn't."

"Oh, for mercy's sake, Mr. Foxcroft." Mrs. Musgrave scowled. "Do you truly think Elias would not tell me? Perhaps you do not remember. Fifteen years ago. Shortly after you brought little Meg home...you left her with a neighbor and visited Kingfisher's Tavern."

Uncle barred his teeth and stared up at the ceiling, face blanching.

"You were inebriated. Elias tucked your arm over his shoulder and walked you home."

"Just kill me."

"Then you do remember." Mrs. Musgrave stood again. "You were crying and blubbering about the life you had taken. How you had alleviated his suffering, but his face was everywhere. In your coffee. The reflections in your shop. Your sleep."

"Stop."

"But that was not enough. You could not cease with killing one man. You had to kill another and another and another—but it was not until Elias was gone that I realized what you had done."

Across the room, Tom elbowed himself up. His throat worked fast, as if he could not catch his breath, and his eyes stayed on Meg.

Something about their intensity, their strength, corded the parts of her that were crumbling. She breathed in time with him. She wished she were not breathing at all.

"I never wanted to become this." Mrs. Musgrave approached Meg, reached around her, and backed away with the double-barrel pistol from Abraham's pocket.

The circle was black.

All the faces, furniture, and candles blurred away. With slowing speed, she was aware of the herbal-sweet smell of chrysanthemum in a nearby vase, Abraham stepping aside, and Pippins scratching at the closed drawing room doors because there was no one about to stroke him.

He should be with Violet.

Upstairs.

Safe.

Her heartbeat whooshed in her ears, a humming rhythm, as a flash of movement tingled into her alertness.

The frantic *thump, thump* of footsteps.

Mrs. Musgrave weeping, shoulders withering, eyes closing.

Then Tom. With a shout of protest, he lunged between the gun and Meg, just as a sharp crack resounded throughout the room.

No.

His body whipped back.

Another shot, and fire pinched her shoulder, jerking her body. All her muscles wilted.

"Tommy!"

Meg didn't know who croaked his name. She didn't know anything. Except that the room flipped and no one was there to make her stand. *Tom, Tom.* Veins strained in her neck as her mouth opened and a soundless scream unleashed. Everything was flashing colors and flitting blackness, but she reached across the rug and groped for his still body—

"I did not want to do this." Mrs. Musgrave's dress swished as she edged closer to Mr. Foxcroft's chair. "But you *will* relinquish your lies. The world will know the truth."

Everything faded but Tom's face.

His eyes were dazed.

His skin already draining.

No, no.

"Confess to the murder of every single life you took." Mrs. Musgrave's voice cracked. "Or watch the only person you love, and the only person I love, bleed to death."

Move. The command quivered throughout all of his muscles as he turned on his side and faced her. He swept his fingers to her face, grabbed the back of her neck, and scooted her closer to him.

Her eyes stayed closed. For too long she had pressed into him and staunched his blood flow with the folds of her dress. Prayers had breezed from her lips. He knew, not because the words possessed sound but because they'd stirred from her so many times before.

In the apothecary shop as she leaned over the white-covered bed, draping some cool cloth across the skin of a fevered brow. Or late at night, when she prepared a poultice. Or at church, the Sunday after someone died.

He never thought she would pray this way for him.

That he'd pray the same way back.

That he'd beg again.

God, please. His eyes closed too. The room was empty. Too long ago, the old goat had gone limp in his chair and the three blackguards had scattered to guard the house. "A horse," someone had said, their voice rough and faded. "Comin' up the drive."

Mrs. Musgrave had whimpered something. Tom couldn't remember what.

Then everyone was gone, the room was silent, and a long stream of sunlight shimmered in through a crack in the drawing room draperies. Colors flitted across his vision. Every time he blinked, the weight was stronger, the pull deeper, luring him into blackness with the cool siren of numbness.

Dinnae let her die.

Meg's face nuzzled closer. Her nose against his.

"I'm sorry." Did she hear him? When she didn't answer, he drew nearer still, the rug chafing his cheek. "Ye need to run."

"No."

"The window."

"They will see me."

"Lass—"

"I have no strength."

He said nothing, because he didn't have strength either. Her pulse throbbed beneath his palm and kept him alive. "Ye're crying."

She nodded.

"Dinnae cry."

"I wanted to sew more of them."

"What?"

"Curtains. For the windows. In the cottage."

"They dinnae need curtains."

"I knew you would say that." She smiled, the frailest laugh brushing his face. "I wanted to find an armchair too. I think you would have looked nice in it...sitting in front of the hearth."

"I dinnae like to sit."

"I would have sat with you."

"Och."

"You do not believe me?"

"Nay."

"Why not?"

"Because." Heat flushed his skin, stoking embers of grief, stillness, memories, loss. He thought of the seashore and the fishing boat anchored among lichen-covered rocks. Sand under her fingernails. Her shoes washed away by the tide. "We would have never married, lass. Ye know we would have never married."

"No. Of course not."

"I made ye furious."

"You stole my stockings."

"Even before." Hot liquid pooled at the edges of his eyes. "Even before ye forgot, 'twouldnae have worked."

"No." Her lips lifted to his. At first slow, moist, her kiss there then gone, like a feather tickling his senses. "Never."

He hesitated.

She hesitated.

Then her mouth fell into his, her lips burst with vigor, and her hand raced up his cheek. She traced her fingers—her precious, blood-stained fingers—along his hairline. Her taste was sweet, her head angling with his as their lips slid back and forth in dancing motions.

All of his senses resurrected.

Like a whirlpool, he was sucked into the vortex of their love—a love he had not possessed since the night the apothecary shop went up in flames. He tried to remind himself this wasn't Meg. This wasn't the girl he'd snuck to the assembly ball with nor chased into Brownie's loft with a bucket of cold water.

But she was.

Everything about her.

She loved him. Like she used to love him. Almost—maybe. He wasn't certain because it felt old and new at the same time and he didn't understand. He didn't know if she wanted the cottage red or brown or green or yellow.

If she would have married him.

If he could have had this...this moment—her touch, her softness—for the rest of his life. He'd never wanted to hold onto life so desperately. Never longed so much, nor groped so frantically, to live.

Against his will, his hand slackened on her face. She faded. A door whined open and closed.

Mrs. Musgrave's voice echoed across the dimming valley of death. "Someone is here. We have not time."

Save Meg. Tom clutched her as the life seeped from his veins. *God, answer me. This time. Please.*

"We have to kill them both."

"I won't let you." He was dead, and the room reeked of blood. The parts of her she knew—Margaret Foxcroft of silk dresses and abbey finery—wanted to fold her arms over her head and cower.

Against everything she wanted to believe, mayhap Mrs. Musgrave spoke the truth. Maybe Meg *had* been an instrument of death, as guilty as Uncle. If not for premeditation or wicked intention, then for ignorance.

For living with him, loving him, and never suspecting.

For always seeing good in his eyes when she should have seen iniquity.

Shoulder throbbing, mind dimming, Meg stood. She couldn't look anywhere—not at the rug nor Tom's hand sprawled open nor the enormous splotches of heavy blood on her clothes. Devastation permeated her bones. "You said in your letters God would not blame you for this. That you were doing what is right."

"I am."

"I know you cannot believe that."

Like threads unraveling from a spool of yarn, Mrs. Musgrave wobbled and framed her cheeks with both hands. "Do it, Abraham."

"I won't let you—"

"I said do it!"

The brute leveled his gun on Uncle the same time Meg sprinted. Her body shielded him. Just as Tom had done for her. Just as he would have done again and again and again.

If she wanted to die with the strength of anyone, it was him.

And the girl he'd loved.

Meg of then, who had survived the alley, who had smiled anyway, who had been brave enough to take off her shoes and run. Who had trusted herself.

Tears rushed her throat, and her trembling fingers curled into fists. "Tom told me stories. The things we did together. About Lenox and that time we brought you home an injured puffin. How it was shivering, so we all sat in front of your kitchen hearth while you wrapped its wing."

"You wrapped it too, dear. You were so gentle. There was so much good in you."

"I want to do good."

"I know."

"Why won't you let me? How could you do this to us?" Her throat burned. "To Tom?"

"It may surprise you to know that Tom was not the only one I loved." Mrs. Musgrave's head angled, her voice motherly, a little cooing. Sadness moistened her words. "I loved you too, my dear."

Abraham raised the gun.

"I'm sorry, little Meg."

No.

"You were so sweet and kind in those younger years. I watched you grow. I wish your uncle would have stopped, just once, to realize he was taking your life too."

Dead silence charged the room.

With tears trekking her cheeks, Mrs. Musgrave gave the faintest nod to Abraham—but he never fired the gun, because the drawing room doors busted open.

Distant shouts poured in.

Motion.

The RED COTTAGE

A sea of unfamiliar faces, grunts, dizziness, the ceiling above her face. Then Meade, with his strong and coal-fuming clothes, lifting her head off the floor. "You're alive."

A cry nearly broke loose from within her.

Because Tom wasn't.

CHAPTER 26

"Let me go." Air moved underneath Tom, and stained-glass colors blurred across his swaying vision. He must have kicked or thrashed, because the arms supporting him clutched tighter.

"Do that again, and you'll be face down on the floor."

Meade. Some of the terror shifted. A gruff order, a door whining, then a bed creaked beneath Tom's weight. He twisted in pain. Almost cursed.

Meade spat one instead. "Lie still, or you'll be in the dead house."

"Meg."

"I said lie—"

"Where is she?" Tom reached out, snatched the man's shirt, threads tearing. Everything swam, like leaves carried in a current bobbing up and down beneath the surface. His stomach upheaved. Why did he smell burnt flesh? "Get Meg. . .I want to see Meg."

"She be with Dr. Bagot."

"I want to see her."

"You can't."

"The devil I can." Tom lifted up, fire blazing his side, but a hard shove pinned him back.

Meade growled a succession of insults. Then a voice—a softer one—coaxed him back.

"Let me sit with him. You go on." Joanie, sweet Joanie. With hair pushed behind big ears, she tucked the coverlets over Tom's torture-wracked body. Her movements were quiet, nurturing, and steady.

Somehow, that calmed him.

"Shhh." She swiped a cloth across his forehead, the linen cool and damp. "Don't try to say anything. The body can do naught of fixing if the mind's troubled too. That's what Mamm always said."

Sounded like something she would say.

Joanie was like her.

"We got the wound cauterized while you were still on the floor. Dr. Bagot wanted the bleeding stopped before we moved you." She sighed. "But that was hours ago. You were coming awake anyway."

Questions reared, but he wrestled them down. He knew he should ask. Now that the chamber was quiet, Joanie was alone with him, and he still had his consciousness.

But he couldn't.

Minutes ticked by.

Then, on the wisps of a prayer, "Meg?"

"The bullet was lodged in her shoulder. Dr. Bagot removed it."

"She willnae die?"

"No." Joanie sang the question as if he were ridiculous. "She is already awake. Lord Cunningham is with her and Violet too. I don't think she ever had a mother. Violet, I mean."

An unexplained churn of relief and disappointment worked through Tom's gut. "What happened? How did ye…did they find us?"

"You didn't come home."

"What?"

"To the cottage. You said you would, but you didn't." Joanie shrugged. "My brother always keeps his word. One thing Mamm and Papa taught us both."

"Ye went looking for me."

"The next morning, I walked to the road and got a ride with some wrecker. He gave me this." She lifted a Spanish silver cob from her pocket. "Said he found it after his last shipwreck. He was terrible nice and took me all the way to Meade."

"The constable?"

"He came too. We thought there might be trouble."

Tom nodded, rolled his head to glance at her. "And Mr. Foxcroft."

"Back upstairs in the attic chambers. He patched himself up and wouldn't even let the doctor touch him before he went to tending the servants."

Tom wasn't certain if he should ask—if he *wanted* to ask. He swallowed hard and her name came out more raspy whisper than anything else.

"The constable took her to the village lockup. He says she'll hang." Joanie's cheeks blotched red and white. A tiredness hung in her gaze, a sudden fragility. As if it were too excruciating in a world of so few friends to lose someone this close. "She was nice to me, Tom."

"I know."

"I want to go home and. . .rip apart that hat she gave me."

"Nay." He shook his head, reached across the bed, and grabbed Joanie's hand. "Ye keep the hat, lass. She gave me things too." Meals when he'd been hungry. Those soft, encouraging pats when he'd been so deprived of human touch.

A listening ear.

The truth when no one else would give it to him.

He'd found a little bit of Mamm in her smiles, a little bit of home in her kitchen, and the first real sense of responsibility with every carriage door or clock or leaking roof he'd fixed. Now the memories were changed, appalling, and bitter. Everything about her was different. He'd lost the millinery shop to horror as much as he'd lost the apothecary shop to flames.

Och, maybe Joanie should destroy the hat. Maybe Tom should extract every part of her from his being, because Mrs. Musgrave deserved to be despised.

He turned his head away, lest Joanie see his tears. *God, show mercy.*

Because despite everything, he couldn't help wondering how wrong it would be to keep a piece, just the tiniest piece, of Mrs. Musgrave still in his heart.

Pippins curled beneath one of Meg's arms and Violet snuggled against the other. Purrs filled the room. The delicate scent of fur as well as lavender soap faded away the stench of terror.

Lord Cunningham came and went too often.

With bothered, distant looks, he seated himself next to her bed or brought lemon balm tea with tentative smiles.

"I want to see Tom."

"He is improving substantially. Dr. Bagot is optimistic concerning his recovery, and as you are already aware, the man is never optimistic about anything." Lord Cunningham had given her a light and forced laugh, sat down for another ten minutes, then bounded away with an excuse she couldn't even remember.

How much easier her mind settled in his absence. Deep, sluggish breaths rose and dropped her chest, the rhythm soothing, like the man's voice from her memory. She allowed sleep to take her. Dreams of the pink pinafore, white lilacs, and waddling ducks stole her back to a simpler life.

One where her shoulder did not throb in testament to her pain.

In punishment for what she'd done.

When she awoke, Violet had braided a strand of her hair and someone had brought a tray of food. The tempting aroma of rice pudding and gingerbread stirred a grumble in her stomach.

"I already ate three."

"Hmm?"

"Three gingerbreads." Violet reached over Meg, snatched a star-shaped gingerbread from the tray, and presented it. "You slept a long time after Dr. Bagot gave you the medicine."

Medicine? Why did she not remember?

"Laudanum." For the first time, Meg noticed the figure on the opposite side of the room. Uncle occupied a wooden chair, and though evening had already fallen, the many wall sconces and candlesticks brightened his face.

One eye was swollen shut, ringed with dark purple and red. A cut slashed through his left brow, another through his lip. "Eat."

"I shall feed you." Violet seemed eager to nurse for once in her life. "Just take gentle care to sit, and I shall spoon it right into your mouth."

"Violet." Meg winced as she sat up, then pulled the girl into her arms. She nuzzled her face into the sweet, childlike curls. "You should not have stayed with me all day. You must rest."

"I am tired of resting."

"Go along to your chamber and take Pippins with you. You may return in the morning."

"I wish to stay here." Violet crossed her arms in defiance, but at Meg's wearied look, she sighed and nodded agreement. She scooped Pippins into her arms and climbed off the bed. "But I shall return on the morrow. Father and I both. You must get well again so you can marry, and you must hurry and do so before I. . ."

Gloom stifled Meg. She wasn't certain if Violet finished the sentence or Meg was only too dispirited to listen. Whatever the case, when the child left the room, Meg's eyes already stung from blinking back the tears.

"Eat," Uncle said again.

She glanced at the tray of food. Then back to his face.

"Eat, Meggy."

"You killed everyone. Just like the letters said."

A grunt, one that bounced back and forth between the walls of the room. He stood and hobbled for the door—

"Uncle, wait." She ripped back the covers, threw her legs over the edge of the bed. A sob clenched her insides but the words came out seething, "You do not dare lie to me now. I will not let you."

"Leave it be."

"I cannot."

"What's done is done." He grabbed the knob—

Meg hurried from the bed, knees buckling, and in one spiraling motion, Uncle turned and caught her.

He swept her into his arms. Instead of draping her back atop the bed, he walked back to his chair and sat with her in his lap.

Strange, how familiar he smelled. Like wool and herbs and pipe smoke. "Do not touch me," she whispered, turning away her face.

With a calloused hand, he patted her head into his chest. She should never have derived comfort in this—in him—but she did. "Why did you ever take me," she murmured against his shirt, "if you were only going to ruin me this way?"

For a long time, he didn't say anything. The chair rocked a little, squeaking into the silence, until he finally scratched the stubble on his chin. "I worked here. Years ago. Valet for the elder Lord Cunningham a few months after his son left for school."

Surprise scratched a nervous pattern inside her chest. "You never told me."

"Didn't tell you lots of things. Too busy teaching you. Keeping you out of trouble." The chair thudded still. "Alistair Cunningham was sick. Found him one night by his bedchamber window. Sitting in his wheelchair with a dagger to his chest."

Understanding galloped through Meg faster than she wanted it to. *No.*

"He begged me to do it. Said he was tired of suffering. I said no." Uncle gave a quick, hard shake of his head. "Kept on though. Weeks. Every time we were alone. One day I did." Muscles tightening, he picked Meg up and carried her back to bed. He moved through motions he knew well—checking her wrist pulse, touching her brow, readjusting the bandage.

Anything so he did not look at her face. "Told me it was right for so long I started to believe him. 'Til he was dead. Knew then it was wrong cause I couldn't get his face out of my head."

"Uncle."

"Left Penrose and took an apprenticeship in Juleshead. Thought saving lives might make up for the one I took. Should have known it wouldn't." He grumbled, itched his head, every movement jerky. "Didn't kill anyone else. Musgrave already had a stroke once. Had a bad heart too. Stopped breathing in my shop and couldn't do anything to save him."

"There were others."

"Helped the ones I could. You did too."

Something sputtered through her veins. Warm, startling—and a little like peace. All this time, she had doubted herself. She'd cast blame upon her own shoulders as swiftly as she'd cast it upon Uncle and Tom.

Had it mattered so much that she couldn't remember the inside of the apothecary shop? That she had no recollection of the nighttime excursions or sitting on Uncle's lap or walking into church with either of them on her arm?

She knew Tom.

She began to know Uncle.

More than anything, she should have known herself. Enough to trust who she'd been—that she'd made the right decisions, that she'd loved the right people, that she'd kept her hands washed in innocence—even if she couldn't remember.

With a resigned nod, Uncle turned his back on her again.

This time, she caught his sleeve and pulled him back. "Uncle." She lifted her arms, and though he hesitated, Uncle bent down and met her embrace. His rough lips pressed against her forehead. Once, then twice, then a third and lasting time.

She wasn't certain what to say to him. If she should tell Lord Cunningham the truth about his father's death or leave the past where it had stayed buried for so long.

She only knew one thing.

Meg Foxcroft—and all the people she'd loved—were not as lost on her as she had once believed.

Sometime that night, Tom left the chamber. Meade was asleep, and Joanie had left to assist the doctor in the upstairs quarters, else they would have stopped him.

He should have stopped himself.

Energy reared, then bottomed as he walked the hall with quickening breaths. Sweat tickled down his temples. The chances of finding her chamber in this cursed old abbey were sparse—especially when he had to stop every minute or so to lean against the wall and clutch his wound.

But something drove him on.

She drove him on.

Why had it always been that way? For as long as he could remember, he'd sloshed out of his fishing boat every late afternoon and run straight for the apothecary shop. His stories were never grand, his news never significant.

But he'd always wanted to tell her, and she had always wanted to listen.

"*You smell like codfish.*" The memory slinked back to him. Dull evening light, that old oak bench back of the shop, and the array of daylily leaves strewn on her lap. "*You come out here to help?*"

"*Och, nay.*" He'd plopped down next to her with his hands behind his head. At sixteen he'd been small, a little gangly, and his one consolation was the new growth of thick red beard appearing on his cheeks. Had Meg noticed?

After all, he noticed things.

Like the way tiny new hairs curled around her face. Especially now, in late August, when the days were hot and sultry. Or the fact that she wore her dress more often. The one with the faded red flowers on creamy muslin, instead of the trousers rustling on the alley clothesline.

That and how much she smiled at him.

How lively her eyes became when he talked.

"What do you think I should put in it?" She'd lifted the half-woven basket from her lap. *"My button collection or Uncle's tobacco pouches?"*

"Ye can do better than that."

"I supposed you would say something ridiculous." She'd laughed anyway, leaned her head into his shoulder for a second, then weaved another leaf into the tiny basket. *"Very well. What is better than buttons, Tom McGwen?"*

"Well."

"I didn't think you had a better idea."

He harrumphed, then dug something from his pocket. *"What about this? Found it today caught on one of the nets. Guess it's one of those things ladies hide in their boots in case men ever pester them."*

"A hatpin?" She examined the tiny, two-beaded pin with a grin. *"I do not think ladies hide them in their boots. Besides, I don't wear hats."*

"Ye dinnae need to." Impatient, struck with a wave of vigor, Tom swept away the basket and pulled her up. *"Ye can put treasures in it. Things ye find."*

"I never find anything."

"We'll go to the seashore. Look around."

"Now?"

"Aye." He'd made swelling promises, told her all the things they'd find hidden beneath the sand or tucked inside the cliffside crevices. Truth was, they'd searched hours into the night without discovering anything. The basket had sat on top of the kitchen dresser for years, filled with nothing but multi-color buttons, the old goat's velvet pouches, and one rusty hatpin.

Why she ever looked at him like she did, Tom didn't know.

The seashore had been so small. Anything he'd ever had to offer her was small.

Doesnae matter. He shook away the past, but it clung to him now like saltwater, intensifying his thirst. All he knew was that he wanted her. That he missed her.

That he had to see her, his Meg—and he had to see her now.

Around the next bend of the hall, light poked out from a barely open door, and he knew she was inside. He leaned against the door jamb, widened the crack.

His heart faltered.

First at the sight of her—sweet, whole, and sitting up in bed. Braids cascaded down her nightgown, and the same drooping curls he'd loved a hundred years ago still wisped around her face.

Then his heart took its second plummet. Lord Cunningham leaned next to her, riffling through a book, while a little blonde-curled lass rumpled the coverlet on the bed.

Och, lass.

Some rash and insane part of him itched to tear through the door, fight Lord Cunningham away, and scoop Meg into his arms. He wanted to carry her to the cottage because she belonged there. She'd sewn the curtains. She'd dreamed it into existence. They both had.

Instead, he slipped past the door before she caught sight or sound of him. All this time, he'd done everything he knew to bring Meg back. He'd always believed she'd want him to.

If she remembered.

If she knew.

Breathing heavy, he rubbed his eyes with the back of his sleeve and found his chamber. Something he'd never considered flamed inside of him, hot and melting like lava crackling through his chest. He could tell her every story, show her every place, and teach her every lesson.

But he couldn't make her love him.

Only Meg could do that.

Tom had left the house. His absence darkened the stained-glass windows and swept the lofty abbey air with a chill of gloom. Why had he run? Why now—when she had not strength to find him—would he leave her alone?

The RED COTTAGE

Hollowness enlarged within her, a lost and untethered sense that everything was over. Mayhap Tom had told the truth when he'd tangled with her lips on the floor. Maybe they never would have married. Nor been contented. Nor ceased to fight.

Even before.

What had made young Meg so certain, all those years, that Uncle was not right? Her love for Tom McGwen must have been steadfast, but they'd fueled their passion with childish rampages, the scarce coins Tom kept in his blacksmith chamber, and some faraway dream that someday they'd build something of their own. Some elusive, dreamlike cottage. Painted red, of all ridiculous colors.

Moisture stung her eyes. Mostly because. . .well, she loved red.

And she didn't even remember why.

Tossing away the coverlets, Meg awoke Tillie. "I need to dress."

"But Dr. Bagot says—"

"Please." The tears must have flashed all over again, because Tillie looked abashed for one second before she consented. "You will be finding his lordship, won't you? He said I ought to tell him if you stir."

"Yes." Dread dampened her palms. "I shall find him."

"In the garden, he be. At the folly."

Pain throbbed from dull pinpricks to plunging knife blades as Tillie maneuvered Meg's arm through a leaf-patterned dress and wheat-colored jacket. She gritted her teeth all the way through her hair being combed, braided, and coiled in a circle back of her head. With one last pat of vanilla perfume, Tillie ushered Meg out the door.

Never had she been less ready to face him.

The corridors were too short, the journey to the courtyard over too fast. For several minutes, she stood concealed in the shadows of the cloisters, watching the folly, while a garden-scented breeze rustled her dress.

Then he saw her.

He rose from the bench, lifting an ornate hardback as if somehow beckoning. When she joined him at the entrance to the folly, he tugged her to the bench. "I shall have you know I debated the last three days if I should bring my poems to your chamber. I decided against it, in the event such trifling pleasures should dissuade you from rest."

She glanced at her hands, twisted and wringing in her lap.

Silence.

The dog slept at Lord Cunningham's feet, his soft snoring lazy and soothing in the tension-charged space.

"My lord, there are things I must tell you."

"I wish to leave them unsaid."

"They concern your father."

Lord Cunningham leaned forward, elbows on his knees, hands clasped. "It is strange, is it not? Often, matters that affect us most directly have a way of finding us too late." He nodded. "You need not pain yourself with delivering the minutiae of my father's death. Shortly after I married, I found the note."

"Then you knew."

"Yes. My father was very clear in his reasonings, and I respected him enough then—and now—to leave the details undiscovered. The demise was his own choice. I am just fainthearted enough to believe it renders less pain if left in obscurity."

"That is..." A loss for words shook her. Relief stirred, as calming as his all-too-familiar scent of cinnamon and leather. "That is very brave, my lord."

His eyes lifted to hers. He eased closer, but she sensed the movement had very little to do with her and more to do with whatever tightened the lines of his face. "I wish to God that were true."

"My lord—"

"No, you cannot think well of me. You cannot be kind." His brow distressed. "Not now. Not after the proverbial den of lions I allowed you to face alone."

"I was not alone." Tom had come. She'd known he'd come. "And I think it would be right, for both of our sakes, to say goodbye with nothing grievous between us."

"Nothing grievous." He repeated the words slowly, as if they inebriated him. "An insurmountable feat, as there is nothing *but* grief between us. Margaret, I am a coward. You must know that. All this time, you thought well of me for my generosity, and you were too angelic to see that is the deepest my virtues reach."

"You are brave. If not always in action, then certainly in conviction."

"Conviction is nothing without performance."

"I disagree."

"Only because you still do not know the truth."

"What?"

Sallowness swept across his complexation. Something about his stance—the way he stood too fast, rushed his hands into his hair—caused alarm to ring through Meg's temples.

"My lord, speak to me."

"I cannot. I am a coward, even in this."

Long, terrible seconds fluttered by. Birds cried melancholy tunes, their echoes bouncing back and forth between the vine-covered courtyard walls. When Lord Cunningham finally faced her again, a bulging vein of torture cut through his forehead. "Darling, I lied. Or rather altered the truth in such a way that it would garner your sympathy."

"My sympathy?"

"Violet is not dying."

A bolt of denial crackled through Meg. "You are mistaken. The doctor—"

"Is a pessimistic man. My medical studies in company with my initial fears have set his opinion in granite." Lord Cunningham glanced down at the hardback on the stone bench. He shrugged. "I think I was so afraid that whatever plagued my father would take Violet from me too. It was easier to imagine the worst than to face the possibility she might only be cursed with debility."

"How long?" Meg stood on legs that lacked strength. "How long have you suspected her condition was not so severe?"

"Months. Her ability to recover from the fever made me certain."

"But you did not tell me."

"No."

"To what avail?"

"To the avail that if I were so unable to secure your heart…I could, in essence, secure your compassion." He reached out, and though every part of her body wanted to shrink back, she allowed his hands to grab hers.

His thumb worked slow, repentant circles against her skin. "You understand me now. You see me clearly. In my futile attempts to show you the best of me, I have only ever shown you the worst."

A fusion of too many emotions overtook her. At first, grief that he had deceived her so long, followed by joy because Violet no longer awaited death. Then it struck Meg with sad but potent force.

The same thing she'd always felt for him.

Pity.

"We are all cowards, my lord." She leaned forward, hesitated, then pressed the faintest kiss to his tear-trekked cheek. "It was never me who made Penrose Abbey bright for you. No more than it was me you loved."

"I do love—"

"No, my lord." She shook her head, ever so slightly, as her heart pulsed with new understanding. "You loved the man I saw when I looked at you. You loved that I saw someone noble, someone I could lean on, who was strong and brave."

His lips parted, trembled, with acknowledgment of the truth.

"Be that man," she said before giving one last squeeze to his hands and walking away.

Everything was different here. Warm afternoon air bent the tall grasses like waves rippling across sea-green water. All the bushes Tom watered were a vibrant green.

A little overgrown, a little reckless in their shape.

But flecked with so many flowers, so many white and graceful blooms, that it didn't matter. The painted red walls drew her closer. How strange that they should mesmerize her like this.

Without warning, a thousand vibrations marched alive inside her. They hummed as she reached the door and stepped across the white-framed threshold. "Tom?"

No one occupied the cottage room.

Like a wanderer long gone but finally come home, she stood a little hesitant and afraid, lifting her straw bonnet to a peg. Her eyes traveled the room.

The chairs Tom made himself.

She smiled.

The braided rug Mrs. Dickey had woven.

The RED COTTAGE

A clay vase on the table, where faded purple flowers drooped and lost petals that fell to an open Bible. She approached, touching things, sweeping her fingers over hanging copper pans and the dustless mantel and the curtains she'd sewn herself.

Heavens, she was ridiculous.

For stroking his overturned pipe on the arm of a chair. For finding the metal comb and the pinch of emotion that stuck in her throat. She looked at all of this—these pointless nothings—so lovingly it hurt.

Then she pressed to the window.

Outside, a small flock of birds soared across the hazy summer sky, and the crab apple tree waved its leaves in time to the breeze. Tom sat beneath the boughs. A large basket was nestled beside him, half filled with fruit, and a rickety wooden ladder leaned against the trunk.

He slept.

Linen shirt gaped open at the chest, without his shoes, probably already sunburnt for the thousandth time in his life. Someone should wake him, send him to bed. Someone should be here to wash the fruits, peel them, bake them into tarts for when he woke up.

Dropping the curtain, she slipped back from the cottage and trekked around the side. Her steps were soundless on the grass. When she settled next to him beneath the tree, he didn't even stir.

She memorized every part of him.

Her eyes drank in his hands, his arms, the knot in his throat, the motion of his chest, until looking wasn't enough and she touched him.

Her arm slinked around his. Her head fell onto his shoulder.

Tom.

The fear, the anguish of everything was gone—and she loved him. That's all she knew. He was wonderful, not for anything he'd done in the past but for what he'd done for her now.

For taking her to the water and letting Meg forget her shoes.

For making her laugh in the curiosity shop.

For brushing her hair.

Taking the bullet.

Painting the cottage red.

With a deeper breath, he stirred. A yawn stretched his arms as he took a long, confused look from the crab apple basket to her face. "What are ye doing?"

"I came to see you."

"Ye shouldnae have come."

"But I—"

"Ye walked too, didn't ye?"

"Well, I—"

"Lass, ye've no sense. Yer shoulder—"

In one heart-leaping second, she leaned up, grabbed his face, and cut off his reprimand with her lips. She pressed with wildness. Jolts intensified as his reaction wavered from surprise to hunger to whatever it was that wept in her own heart.

Longing so precious, but so long left wanting.

"Lass." Deep, shuddering.

Her kiss found his cheek, his other cheek, then his mouth in a flurry of excitement. La, but he tasted so familiar. A little tart like crab apples, a little soothing like honey. Her stomach fluttered. "Tom—"

"I just wanted to keep ye, lass." Why did the words ache? As if they were murmured in pain and wrought from too many days of starved hope.

She dragged her hands back behind his neck. His warm skin flushed her face. "I wish I would have known us...before."

"Ye would have loved the cottage."

"I love it now." She hesitated. Then breathed against his mouth, "I love *you*."

"Ye dinnae know me."

"I do."

"Och, but there's things I never told ye. About my brother...the reason he's dead."

"I had secrets too. I do not remember when I told you, or why I did, but you must have stayed close enough for me to whisper them in your ear." Her finger slid beneath one of his eyes, brushing away the trace of moisture. "I want to be that for you. I want to be so close...that should you ever wish to tell me anything, you need only turn your head and whisper it."

"Marry me, and I'll get ye that chair."

"The wingback?"

The RED COTTAGE

"Aye."

"And you shall sit in it?"

"Aye."

"Every day?"

"Och, every day."

"Fine." She burrowed deeper into him—smiling a little, crying a little too—as he swept one last kiss across her salt-stinging lips. "Return my stockings, Tom McGwen, and it's a deal."

EPILOGUE

October 1818
Juleshead Village
North Cornwall, England

A chill seeped through his thin woolen coat as Tom tossed the anchor over the edge of the boat. A loud *pluh-plunk* burped from the black sea, followed by a spray of cold water.

"Come here with ye." He dug a hand-loomed shawl from under his coat, draped it over her head, then twisted it about her neck.

She squirmed in protest. "I think myself entirely capable of packing my own attire."

"Do ye?"

"Yes. I do."

"Watch yer ferocious tongue before I throw ye overboard." When she huffed, he turned around, braced himself on the rocking boat, and muttered for her to hurry up. He grinned when she jumped on his back. "Hold on with ye." Had she ever not?

Deserting the boat, he climbed onto a craggy, water-eroded rock, jumped to the next by memory, and didn't touch the water until his boots were taller than the sloshing waves. When they reached the dry shore, Meg leapt off him.

The RED COTTAGE

Sighing, she spread out her arms and collapsed to the ground on the sand.

Tom threw himself next to her.

The night was black, moonless, and only tiny yellow stars reflected light from the heavens. A chilling breeze roared over them. The sand stirred. Distant scents of brine and salt and whatever Meg had been baking at home filled his senses with contentment.

"What's wrong, lass?"

Another sigh.

He grumbled. "Dinnae make me chase my wife about the seashore." When she did not laugh, or kiss him, he reached for her hand and entwined her sandy fingers with his. Concern niggled him, but he waited.

Finally, she leaned her head against his. "I am only surprised. I never thought Joanie would wish to leave."

"Ye dinnae think she's doing the right thing."

"No. I think she is." Meg rolled to her side, slipped her fingers between the buttons of Tom's coat. Her touch slid beneath his shirt, frigid and soft against the skin of his chest. "Violet was never more in need of a companion, and Joanie is just good enough to be sister and nurturing friend, all at once."

Nostalgia echoed in Tom, a small pang. "She's naught but a walk away, lass."

"Yes."

"And if the cottage is too empty for ye while I'm gone, then—"

"We should fill the cottage." Meg lifted on one elbow and hovered her face overtop of his. The grin he was so wont to seeing—every morning, every evening he returned home with fresh fish slapped over his back, every nighttime in bed—poured over him again. Her hair dripped past the scarf and tickled his face. "What do you think, Tom McGwen?"

"Name it, and I'll make it for ye."

Her laugh fell over him as he slipped his hands around her back. "I think you know."

"A chair."

"We have too many already."

"A loom."

"No."

"A cupboard."

Her lips brushed his, teasing, warming his blood from the inside. "I think the cottage has everything we need," she whispered. "Except children."

"Ye cannae think any young McGwens will be as quiet as Joanie."

"I did not expect they would."

"And ye best expect them to lose their shoes."

"Indeed."

"The wee devils will have yer fury—"

"And your unruly nonsense. But if they go to climbing the barn roof and hiding from behind the chimney, I shall whack them with a broom as hard as Mr. Musgrave whacked you."

"Och, ye liked it when I spied on ye."

"Never."

"Aye, but ye. . ." The sentenced faltered. His mind snapped in too many directions, whipped through memories, as a sudden knot of disbelief swelled in his throat. "I never told ye that."

"Told me what?"

"About watching ye from the millinery shop chimney."

"Of course you did."

"No, I mean I didnae tell ye *again*." He leaned up, pulling her to his lap as her arms weaved behind the back of his head. "I never told ye again."

"You must have."

"Nay."

"Tom, I could not have. . ." A laugh choked out, but her eyes—so close to his—were glassy with starlight. "I could not have remembered. Dr. Bagot said I would never remember. Uncle too."

"I didnae think God would mind to prove the old goat wrong."

Her face pressed into his, silent for too many heartbeats, before she finally framed his cheeks. "You did not answer me, Tom McGwen. I do not want more tables or cupboards or looms. I want to go home and sit in our chair, and you to smoke your pipe, and me to watch you, and us to have children everywhere in our red cottage."

Laughing, he met her mouth. "Consider it done."

Hannah Linder resides in the beautiful mountains of central West Virginia. Represented by Books & Such, she writes Regency romantic suspense novels filled with passion, secrets, and danger. She is a five-time Selah Award winner, a 2025 and 2024 Carol Award finalist, and a member of American Christian Fiction Writers (ACFW). Also, Hannah is an international and multi-award-winning graphic designer who specializes in professional book cover design. She designs for both traditional publishing houses and individual authors, including *New York Times*, *USA Today*, and international bestsellers. She is also a self-portrait photographer of historical fashion. When Hannah is not writing, she enjoys playing her instruments—piano, guitar, ukulele, and banjolele—songwriting, painting still life, walking in the rain, square dancing, and sitting on the front porch of her 1800s farmhouse. To follow her journey, visit hannahlinderbooks.com.

If you enjoyed *The Red Cottage*, don't miss these titles from Hannah Linder

Beneath His Silence

When Tomorrow Came

Garden of the Midnights

Girl from the Hidden Forest

Never Forgotten

Find These Books and More from Barbour Publishing at Your Favorite Bookstore or at www.barbourbooks.com